Giorgio Faletti

I Kill

Baldini Castoldi Dalai
Publishers since 1897

www.bcdeditions.com

Editorial team of the English language edition:
Antony Shugaar, Muriel Jorgensen, Lenore Rosenberg,
Jeremy Parzen

Original Title: Io Uccido

ISBN 978-88-6073-295-8
Library of Congress Cataloging-in-Publication
Information is available from the
Library of Congress upon request.

Printed and bound in Italy by
Grafica Veneta S.p.A. - Trebaseleghe (PD)

To Davide and Margherita

Death walks along a street,
Wreathed in faded orange blossoms,
Singing and singing
A song
To a white guitar:
Singing and singing and singing.

Federico García Lorca

FIRST CARNIVAL

The man is one and no one.

For years, he has worn his face pasted to his head and his shadow sewn to his feet, yet he still cannot tell which is heavier. Sometimes, he has the irrepressible urge to tear them both off, hang them on a nail, and sit down on the ground, like a puppet whose strings have been cut by some pitying hand.

Other times, he is wiped out by exhaustion, which makes it impossible to understand that the only path of reason is that of surrender to madness. Around him is an endless series of faces and shadows and voices, people who do not question, but passively accept lives that don't answer for the boredom and pain of the journey. They are content with sending the occasional postcard.

There is music where he is. There are moving bodies, smiling mouths, words exchanged. And he just stands among them, one more person who watches curiously as, day by day, the photograph fades away.

The man leans against a column and thinks that every one of them is useless.

In front of him, at the far side of the room, two people, a man and a woman, are sitting next to each other at a table near a large window overlooking the garden.

In the soft light, she is as delicate and tender as melancholy. She has black hair and green eyes, so luminous and large that the man leaning on the column can see them even from where he stands. Her companion is aware of nothing but her beauty, and he whispers into her ear to make himself heard over the blaring music.

They are holding hands and she is laughing at his words, throwing her head back or hiding her face against his shoulder.

Just a moment ago, she turned, perhaps struck by the fixed stare coming from the man across the room, seeking the cause of that distant, uncomfortable sensation. Their eyes met for an instant, but hers passed indifferently over his face, like they passed over the rest of the world around her. And then those incredible eyes came to rest once more on the man next to her. He returns her gaze, impervious to anything beyond her presence.

They are young, beautiful, and happy.

The man leans against the column, thinking that soon they will die.

1

Jean-Loup Verdier pressed the button on the remote, but only started his car when the garage door was halfway up, so as not to breathe too much exhaust. His headlights slid slowly from the rising metal wall and cut through the black night before him. He slipped the automatic transmission into DRIVE and, when the garage door was fully open, stepped on the accelerator and drove his Mercedes SLK slowly outside. He raised his arm to press the CLOSE button and sat there, taking in the view from his house as he waited for the door to shut.

Monte Carlo looked like a bed of concrete by the sea. From Jean-Loup's house the city seemed amorphous, enveloped in the soft haze that reflected the evening lights. Not far below him, in French territory, the lights of the country club tennis courts, where some international tennis star was probably training, gleamed next to the protruding tower of the Parc Saint-Roman, one of the city's highest skyscrapers. Lower down, below the old city fortress toward Cap d'Ail, he could make out the neighborhood of Fontvieille that had been reclaimed from the water yard by yard, piece by piece.

He lit a cigarette and at the same time switched on the car radio, already tuned to Radio Monte Carlo, as he drove up the ramp to the street, opening the gate with his remote. He turned left and slowly drove down to the city, enjoying the warm air of late May.

"Pride" by U2 was on the radio, and Jean-Loup smiled with instant recognition at the band's unmistakable guitar riffs.

Stefania Vassallo, the show's deejay, was crazy about U2's guitarist "The Edge," and she never let a show go by without playing one of their songs. Her colleagues at the station made fun of her because of the dreamy expression she wore for months after finally managing to get an interview with her idols.

As he drove along the curvy road that led from Beausoleil to the city center, he tapped his left foot in time with the music. Marking the upbeat with his right hand on the steering wheel, he followed along as Bono sang in his rusty, melancholy voice, of a man who came "in the name of love."

Summer was in the air already, and that unique smell one finds only in cities by the sea. It was an odor of brackish water, pine trees, and rosemary, and it contained the scent of promises and bets. The former broken, the latter lost.

The sea, the pine trees, the rosemary, and the summer flowers would all still be there long after he and all the others like him had hurried by.

He drove his convertible with the top down, the wind in his hair. He wasn't cold. Promise filled his heart and his bets were placed on life.

Things could be worse.

It wasn't late, but there was no one on the road.

He poised his cigarette between thumb and middle finger and flicked it straight up into the rushing air, watching the luminous curve that marked its trajectory in his rearview mirror. He noticed the impact as it hit the asphalt and scattered in a blaze of tiny sparks. The last puff of smoke disappeared in the same blast of air.

Jean-Loup reached the bottom of the hill and hesitated a moment, deciding which route he would take to the port. As he rounded the traffic circle, he decided to go through the city and turned down Boulevard d'Italie. Tourists were beginning to crowd into the Principality. In Monaco, the Formula 1 Grand Prix, which had just ended, meant the beginning of summer. From now on, the city would be bustling with actors and spectators day and night. There would be chauffeured limousines and people inside looking privileged and bored. And then there would be small cars with sweaty, adoring passengers just like those who stand in front of store windows with their eyes reflecting the lights. Some wondered when they'd find the time to come back and buy that jacket, others where they'd find the money. Things were black and white—two extremes with many shades of gray in between. So many lived only to blow smoke in people's eyes, while others kept trying to brush it away.

Jean-Loup thought that, all told, the priorities of life were simple and repetitive, and in a few places in the world, like this one, they could be counted on one hand. Money came first. Some have it and the rest want it. Simple. A cliché becomes a cliché because it has some truth. Money might not buy happiness, but that didn't seem to bother anyone.

The cell phone in his shirt pocket started ringing. He pulled it out and answered without looking at the caller's name: he knew very well who it was. The voice of Laurent Bedon, director and writer of *Voices,* the program that Jean-Loup hosted on Radio Monte Carlo every night, reached his ear in a whir of static.

"Any chance the star will grace us with his presence tonight?"

"Hey, Laurent. I'm on my way."

"Good. You know Robert's pacemaker acts up when the deejay isn't here an hour before airtime. His balls are already smoking."

"Really? Aren't his cigarettes enough?"

"Guess not."

Meanwhile, Boulevard d'Italie had turned into Boulevard des Moulins. The brightly lit shops on both sides of the street were a sea of promises, like the beckoning eyes of high-class prostitutes. In both cases, all you needed to make your dreams come true was a little cash.

Their conversation was interrupted by the buzz of Jean-Loup's cell phone interfering with the car radio. He moved the phone to his other ear and the buzzing stopped. As if on cue, Laurent changed his tone.

"Okay seriously, hurry up. I have a couple of . . ."

"Hold on a sec. Police," interrupted Jean-Loup.

He lowered his hand and tried to look innocent. Pulling up to the intersection, he stopped in the left lane and waited for the light to change. A uniformed policeman was standing at the corner to ensure that drivers respected his illustrious colleague, the traffic light. Jean-Loup hoped he'd hidden the phone in time. They were very strict in Monte Carlo about using cell phones while driving. At that moment he had no desire to waste time arguing with a stubborn Principality cop.

When the light changed, Jean-Loup turned left, passing under the nose of the suspicious officer. Jean-Loup saw him turn and stare at the SLK as it disappeared down the hill in front of the Hôtel Metropole. As soon as he was out of sight, Jean-Loup raised his hand and put the phone back to his ear.

"Out of danger. Sorry, Laurent. You were saying?"

"I was saying that I have a couple of plausible ideas I wanted to discuss with you before we air. Step on it."

"How plausible? Like a thirty-two or a twenty-seven?"

"Fuck off, cheapskate," retorted Laurent, jokingly but a little annoyed.

"Like the man said, I don't need advice. I need addresses."

"Stop talking shit and hurry up."

"Got it. I'm heading into the tunnel now," Jean-Loup lied.

They were cut off. Jean-Loup smiled. That was how Laurent always defined his new ideas: plausible. Jean-Loup had to admit that they almost always were. But unfortunately for Laurent, that was how he also defined the numbers he *felt* would turn up on the roulette wheel, and that almost never happened.

He turned left onto Avenue des Spelugues. On his right, he

glanced at the reflection of the lights in the square, with the Hôtel de Paris and the Café de Paris one in front of the other, like sentinels on either side of the casino. The barricades and bleachers set up for the Grand Prix had been taken down in record time. Nothing was allowed to obstruct the sacred cult of gambling, money, and superficiality in Monte Carlo for too long.

The square of the casino receded behind him, and he drove leisurely down the hill on which Ferraris, Williamses, and McLarens had raced with unbelievable speed just days before. After the curve of the Virage du Portier, the sea breeze and the yellow tunnel lights caressed his face. He drove through, feeling the cool air and the blend of colors in the unnatural light. On exiting the tunnel, he saw the spectacle of the illuminated port, where a hundred million euros' worth of boats was floating. On high, to the left, the fortress with the castle swathed in a soft glow seemed to guarantee that the prince and his family would sleep undisturbed.

Though he was long used to it, Jean-Loup couldn't help admiring the view. He could understand the effect that it had on tourists from Osaka, Austin, or Johannesburg: it took their breath away and left them with an amateur photographer's case of tennis elbow.

By then, he was practically there. He drove past the port, where the barricades were slowly being removed, passed the Piscine and then the Rascasse, turned left, and drove down the ramp to the underground parking lot, three stories deep, directly under the plaza in front of the radio station.

He parked his car in the first empty spot and went up the stairs and outside. The music of Stars'N'Bars reached him through its open doors. Stars'N'Bars was a mandatory stop for habitués of Monaco's nightlife, a bar where you could grab a beer or some Tex-Mex while waiting for the night to go by, before heading off to the discos and nightclubs along the coast.

The huge building in which Radio Monte Carlo was located, right in front of the Quai Antoine Premier, housed an extremely random assortment of establishments: restaurants, yacht showrooms, art galleries, and the studios of Télé Monte Carlo. Jean-Loup reached the glass door and rang the video intercom. He stood directly in front of the camera so that it shot a tight close-up of his right eyeball.

The voice of Raquel, the secretary, emerged as threatening as she could make it sound. "Who is it?"

"Good evening. This is Mr. Eye for an Eye. Open up, will you? I'm wearing contacts, so the retina print won't work."

He stepped back so that the girl could see him. There was a soft laugh from the intercom. "Come on up, Mr. Eye for an Eye," a voice said, warmly.

"Thanks. I was coming to sell you a set of encyclopedias, but I think I need some eye drops now."

There was a loud click as the door unlocked. When he reached the fourth floor, the elevator door slid aside and he was nose to nose with the chubby face of Pierrot, standing on the landing with a pile of CDs in his hands.

Pierrot was the station mascot. He was twenty-two but he had the mind of a child. He was shorter than average, with a round face and hair that stood straight up, which made him always look to Jean-Loup like a smiling pineapple. Pierrot was a very pure soul. He had the gift, which only simple people have, of making everyone like him at first glance. He himself liked only those he thought deserved it, and his instinct was rarely wrong.

Pierrot adored music. He became confused when confronted with the most basic reasoning, but he would be suddenly analytical and linear when it came to his favorite subject. He had a computer-like memory for the vast radio archives and for music in general. All you had to do was bring up a title or the tune of a song and he dashed off, soon to return with the record or CD. He so resembled the character in the movie that the people in the station called him "Rain Boy."

"Hi, Jean-Loup."

"Pierrot, what are you still doing here at this hour?"

"Mother's working late tonight. The big guys are giving a dinner. She's coming to pick me up *when it's a little more later.*"

Jean-Loup smiled to himself at the boy's mistake. Pierrot had his own special way of expressing himself, a different language that was often the object of cruel jokes. His mother, the woman who was coming to get him *when it's a little more later,* worked as a cleaning woman for an Italian family in Monte Carlo.

Jean-Loup had met Pierrot and his mother a couple of years earlier, when they had been standing in front of the station. He'd paid almost no attention to the strange couple until the woman had come up to him and spoke timidly, with the air of someone always apologizing to the world for her presence. He had realized that she was waiting for him.

"Excuse me. Are you Jean-Loup Verdier?"

"Yes, Madame. Can I help you?"

"I'm sorry to bother you, but could you give me an autograph for my son? Pierrot always listens to the radio and you're his favorite."

Jean-Loup had looked at her modest clothing and her hair that had gone gray too early. The woman was probably younger than she looked. He had smiled.

"Of course, Madame. That's the least I can do for such a faithful listener."

As he took the paper and pen that the mother held out for him, Pierrot had come up to them. "You're just the same."

Jean-Loup was puzzled. "Just the same as what?"

"*The same as in the radio.*"

Jean-Loup had turned to the woman, puzzled. She had lowered her gaze and voice. "My son, you know, is . . ."

She had stopped, as if she didn't know a word that she had really known for years. Jean-Loup had looked at Pierrot carefully and seen the difference in his face. He had felt a stab of pity for the boy and the woman.

The same as in the radio.

Jean-Loup had realized that what Pierrot meant to say, in his own way, was that he was just as he'd imagined him. Pierrot had smiled, and at that moment the place where he stood began to glow and Jean-Loup was smitten with the immediate, instinctive liking that the boy always inspired.

"All right, young man. Now that I know you listen to me, I can say that this is really a great day. The least I can do is sign an autograph. Hold this for me a minute?"

He had handed the boy the pile of papers and postcards under his arm so that his hands were free to write. As Jean-Loup signed the autograph, Pierrot had glanced at the paper on top of the pile. He had raised his head with a satisfied air. "Three Dog Night," he had said calmly.

"What?"

"Three Dog Night. The answer to the first question is Three Dog Night. And the second is Alan Allsworth and Olli Alsall," continued Pierrot with his own very unique English pronunciation of Allan Holdsworth and Ollie Halsall.

Jean-Loup had remembered that the first sheet of paper contained a list of musical questions for a contest being held on the afternoon broadcast. He'd written it a couple of hours before. The first question was, "What group from the seventies sang the song 'Celebrate'?" And the second was, "Who were the guitarists in the group Tempest?"

Pierrot had read and correctly answered the first two questions. Jean-Loup had stared at the mother in astonishment. The woman had shrugged her shoulders as if apologizing for that too. "Pierrot loves music. If I listened to him, I'd be buying records instead of food. He's . . . well . . . he is what he is. But with music, he remembers almost everything he reads and hears on the radio."

"Try answering the others too, Pierrot," Jean-Loup had said, pointing to the list of questions the boy was still holding.

One by one, without any hesitation, Pierrot had gone through the fifteen questions, answering each one correctly as soon as he read it. And they weren't easy questions by any means. Jean-Loup was astonished.

"Madame, this is much more than simply remembering things. He's an encyclopedia."

He had taken back the pile of papers and answered the boy's smile with a smile. He had gestured toward the Radio Monte Carlo building.

"Pierrot, would you like to take a tour of the station and see where we broadcast?"

He had shown the boy around the studio, where the voices and music he heard at home came from and offered him a Coke. Pierrot had looked at everything in fascination, and mother and son's eyes shone with equal brightness as she observed his joy. But when they stepped into the basement archives with its sea of CDs and LPs, Pierrot's face had lit up like that of a soul entering Paradise.

When the employees of the station heard the story (the father had bailed as soon as he learned of his son's handicap, leaving the boy and his mother alone and penniless), and especially when they realized his musical knowledge, they had asked him to join the Radio Monte Carlo staff. The mother was shocked. Pierrot had a place to stay while she worked and even received a small salary.

But most of all, *he was happy*. Promises and bets, thought Jean-Loup. Occasionally one was kept and sometimes you won. There were better things in the world, but this, at least, was something.

Pierrot went into the elevator holding the CDs and pressed the button. "I'm going into the *room* to put these back. Then I'll come back, *so can I see your program*."

The *room* was his own personal description of the archive and *seeing your program* was not just one of his linguistic inventions. It meant that today he could stand behind the large window and watch Jean-Loup, his best friend, his idol, with adoring eyes. Pierrot was usually at home when Jean-Loup was on the air and he listened to the program on the radio.

"Okay. I'll save you a front-row seat."

The door closed on Pierrot's smile, much brighter than the lights of the elevator.

Jean-Loup crossed the landing and entered the code to open the door. The long desk where Raquel worked as both receptionist and secretary was right at the entrance. The girl, a petite brunette with a thin but pleasant face who always seemed in command of the situation, greeted him with a finger pointed in his direction. "You're taking your chances. One of these days, I'm not going to let you in."

Jean-Loup went over to her and moved the finger as if it were a loaded gun. "Didn't anyone teach you not to point your finger at people? What if it was loaded and went off? Anyway, what are you still doing here? Even Pierrot's still here. Is there a party I don't know about?"

"No parties, just overtime. And it's all your fault. You're stealing all the ratings and we have to scramble to catch up." She motioned with her head to the room behind her.

"Go see the boss. There's news."

"Good? Bad? So-so? Is he finally going to ask me to marry him?"

"He wants to tell you himself. He's in the president's office," Raquel answered, vague but smiling.

Jean-Loup passed her and stepped onto the soft blue carpet patterned with small cream-colored crowns. He stopped in front of the last door on the right, knocked, and opened it without being invited in. The boss was sitting at his desk and—Jean-Loup might have guessed—was on the phone. At that time of day, the office was so clouded with cigarette smoke that it became a mystical place—a place where the essence of the actual cigarette in his hand became one with many others he had already smoked.

Radio Monte Carlo's manager was the only person Jean-Loup knew who smoked those toxic Russian cigarettes, the ones with the long cardboard filters that had to be folded in a voodoo-like ritual before they could be used.

Robert nodded at him to sit down.

Jean-Loup took a seat in one of the black leather armchairs in front of the desk. As Robert finished his conversation and closed the case of his Motorola phone, Jean-Loup fanned his hand in the smoky air. "Are you trying to make this a place for people nostalgic for fog? London or die? No, London *and* die? Does the big boss know you pollute his office when he's not here? If I wanted, I could blackmail you for the rest of your life."

Radio Monte Carlo, the Italian-language station of the Principality, had been taken over by a company that ran a pool of private stations. Its headquarters were in Italy, in Milan. Robert Bikjalo was the man in charge of running things in Monaco and the president only appeared for important meetings.

"You're a bastard, Jean-Loup. A dirty, gutless bastard."

"How can you smoke that stuff? You're approaching the fine line between smoke and nerve gas. Or maybe you already crossed it years ago and we're talking to your ghost."

"I'm not even going to bother answering your prissy comments," said Robert, sitting there expressionless, as unaffected by Jean-Loup's humor as by the smoke of his cigarettes. "I haven't been here waiting for you to sit your precious ass down in this seat so I could listen to your snide remarks about my smoking. And notice I said that your ass was precious, since obviously that's what you use to think."

This exchange of sarcasm was a little ritual they'd shared for years, but Jean-Loup knew they were still far from calling each other friends. This harsh sarcasm veiled the fact that it was nearly impossible to get to the bottom of things with Robert Bikjalo. He was intelligent perhaps, but he was definitely shrewd. An intelligent man sometimes gives the world more than he gets back; a cunning one tries to take as much as he can while giving back as little as possible. Jean-Loup was well aware of the rules of the game, in the world in general and in his milieu in particular: he was the deejay of *Voices,* a hit show on Radio Monte Carlo. People like Bikjalo listened to you only in relation to the amount of people listening to you at home.

"I just want to tell you what I think of you and your show before I throw you out on the street for good." He leaned back in his chair and finally extinguished the cigarette in an overflowing ashtray. He let a poker silence fall between them. Then, like someone with a good hand who says, "I'll see you!" he continued. "I got a phone call today about *Voices*. It was someone very close to the Palace. Don't ask me who, because I can't tell you..."

The manager's tone of voice suddenly changed. A forty-carat grin flashed across his face as he laid out a royal flush. "The Prince in person has expressed his pleasure at the show's success!"

Jean-Loup stood up from his chair with an identical smile, high-fived the hand held out to him, and sat back down. Bikjalo was still flying on the wings of his triumph.

"Monte Carlo has always had an image of being a place for the rich, a haven to escape taxes from just about everywhere else. Recently, with all the shit happening in America, and the economic crisis practically worldwide, we seem a bit dull."

He said "we" with an air of sympathy, but he was someone who didn't seem very involved in the problems of others. He pulled a new cigarette from his pack, bent the filter, and lit it with the lighter on his desk.

"A few years ago, there were two thousand people in the

casino right about now. These days, some evenings there's a really scary morning-after feeling. The jump start you gave to *Voices,* using it to confront social issues, has brought something fresh and new. Now a lot of people think of Radio Monte Carlo as a place where they can solve problems, where they can call for help. It's been great for the station too, I don't deny it. There's a whole group of new sponsors just waiting in line, and that's a measure of the program's success."

Jean-Loup raised his eyebrows instinctively and smiled. Robert was a manager, and for him success ultimately meant a sigh of relief and a sense of satisfaction when he wrote the annual report. The heroic era of Radio Monte Carlo, that of Jocelyn and Awanagana and Herbert Pagani, in other words, was over. This was the era of economics.

"I must admit we've been good. You mostly. Apart from the program's winning formula and the new direction it's taken, it's a success because you're good at deejaying in French and Italian. I just did my job."

Bikjalo waved his hand vaguely, in a gesture of modesty that didn't suit him at all. He was referring to his very astute managerial instincts. The show's strengths and the bilingual talents of its host convinced him to try a move that he had devised with the sense of a born diplomat. Encouraged by the ratings and the enthusiasm, he'd created a sort of joint venture with Europe 21, a French station with an editorial line very similar to that of Radio Monte Carlo. It broadcast from Paris. The result was that now *Voices* could be heard in most of Italy and France.

Robert Bikjalo put his feet up on the desk and blew cigarette smoke toward the ceiling. Jean-Loup thought it a very official and symbolic pose. The president probably wouldn't have agreed. With a triumphant voice, the manager continued.

"The Music Awards are at the end of June, beginning of July. I've heard rumors that they want you to emcee. And then there's the Film and Television Festival. You're going full speed, Jean-Loup. Others like you have had trouble moving up to television. You've got looks, and if you play your cards right, I'm afraid you'll be the cause of a brutal tug-of-war between TV and radio."

"I'm afraid," said Jean-Loup, standing as he smiled and looking at his watch, "that Laurent is having a tug of war with his liver. We still haven't talked and we need a schedule for tonight's show."

"Tell that has-been writer-director that he'll be thrown out in the street just like you."

Jean-Loup headed toward the door. As he was leaving, Robert stopped him. "Jean-Loup?"

He turned. Bikjalo was sitting in his chair, rocking back and forth with the expression of the cat that finally ate the canary.

"What?"

"Needless to say, if all that TV business works out, I'm your manager . . ."

Jean-Loup decided that his price would be very high.

"I've suffered through a percentage of your cigarette smoke. You'll have to suffer just as much for a percentage of my money."

When he closed the door, Robert Bikjalo looked up at the ceiling with a dreamy stare. Jean-Loup knew that the director was already counting the money he had yet to earn.

2

Jean-Loup was looking out at the city through the large control room window, observing the play of light reflected on the still water of the port. High above, cloaked in darkness, the repeater stood on the peak of Mount Agel, visible only by its series of red lights. It was this repeater that enabled the signal to reach all of Italy.

"Break over," came Laurent's voice over the intercom. "Back to work."

Without bothering to answer, the deejay moved away from the window and went back to his place. He put on his headphones and sat down at the microphone. Laurent in the control room flashed an open hand to show five seconds to the end of the commercial break.

Laurent played the brief *Voices* theme that meant the broadcast was starting again. Until then, it had been a laid-back program, light-hearted even, without the tone of despair they sometimes had to deal with.

"Back to Jean-Loup Verdier, with *Voices* from Radio Monte Carlo. We hope nobody needs our help on this lovely May evening—only our music. Oh, I've just been told there's a phone call."

The red light on the wall lit up and Laurent was pointing at him with his right hand to show there was a call waiting. Jean-Loup leaned his elbows on the table and turned to the mike in front of him.

"Hello?"

There was some static and then silence. Jean-Loup looked up and raised his eyebrows at Laurent. The director shrugged to show that the problem wasn't on their end.

"Yes, hello?"

Finally, an answer came through on the air and was thus transmitted to every listener. It had a presence in the speakers, and in the minds and lives of all who heard it. From that moment on, and for a long time to come, the darkness would be a little darker, and a great deal of noise would be needed to cover all that silence.

"*Hello, Jean-Loup.*"

There was something unnatural in the sound of the voice. It was muffled and strangely flat, devoid of expression. The words had a muted echo like the sound of an airplane taking off far away. Again Jean-Loup glanced up questioningly at Laurent, who pointed, drawing circles in the air to mean that the distortion was on the caller's line.

"Hi. Who is this?"

There was a moment of hesitation. Then came the muffled answer with its unnatural echo.

"*It doesn't matter. I'm one and no one.*"

"It's hard to hear. Bad connection. Where are you calling from?"

Silence. The vapor of a plane wafting midair in some unknown place.

The speaker continued. "*That doesn't matter either. The only thing that counts is that the time has come to speak out, even if afterward neither of us will be the same.*"

"How so?"

"*Soon I'll be a hunted man and you'll be one of the bloodhounds sniffing in the dark. And that's a shame, because right now, at this very moment, you and I are no different, we're the same.*"

"How are we the same?"

"*We're both faceless, and people listen to us with their eyes closed, imagining. There are millions of people out there who want only to get themselves a face they can show with pride, to create one that's different from all the others. That's all they worry about. Now is the time to find out what's behind the face."*

"I don't understand."

Silence again, long enough to make Jean-Loup think they had been cut off. Then the voice came back and some listeners thought they could hear a hint of a smile.

"*You'll understand, in time.*"

"I'm not sure what you mean."

There was a slight pause, as if the man on the other end of the line was weighing his words.

"*Don't worry. Sometimes it's hard for me too.*"

"Then why did you call? Why are you talking to me?"

"*Because I'm alone.*"

Jean-Loup bent his head down and gripped the table with his hand.

"You're talking like someone who's in prison."

"We're all in prison. I built mine myself, but that doesn't make it any easier to get out."

"I'm sorry to hear that. It doesn't sound like you like people very much."

"Do you?"

"Not always. Sometimes I try to understand them and when I can't, I try at least not to judge them."

"We're the same that way too. The only difference is that when you're finished talking to them, you're able to feel tired. You can go home and turn off your mind and its troubles. I can't. I can't sleep at night, because my troubles never rest."

"So what do you do at night to stop it?"

Jean-Loup was egging him on slightly. The answer was slow to come, as though it were wrapped in layers of paper being opened one by one.

"I kill . . ."

"What does that . . ."

Jean-Loup's voice was interrupted by music coming from the speakers. It was a light plaintive song with a pretty melody, but after those two words it spread through the air like a threat. It lasted about ten seconds and then, as suddenly as it had come on, it was gone.

In the heavy silence that followed, the click of the call being cut off was heard by one and all. Jean-Loup shot his head up to look at the others. The air-conditioning was on high, but suddenly everyone could feel the scorching flames of Sodom and Gomorrah.

Someone managed to drag the rest of the program out to its closing song. No more phone calls came in. That is to say, the switchboard was flooded after the strange call, but no more calls were broadcast.

Jean-Loup took off his headphones and laid them on the table next to the mike. He realized that his hair was soaked with sweat, in spite of the air-conditioning.

Neither of us will ever be the same.

He played only music for the remainder of the show. He tried to demonstrate what he considered a strange similarity between Tom Waits and the Italian musician Paolo Conte, who were very different as singers, but both major songwriters. He translated the words of two of their songs and pointed out how important they were. Luckily, he had several such expedients in case of emergency, and this moment definitely qualified. There were some reserve phone numbers to use when the show just wouldn't come together. They'd call some singers or writers they knew, begging them to join in. Then they'd use up fifteen minutes on some poetry and the humor of Francis Cabrel.

"Jean-Loup?" The door to the control room opened and Laurent's head poked in. "You okay?"

Jean-Loup glanced over without looking at him. "Yeah, fine."

He stood up and they left the studio together, exchanging puzzled, somewhat evasive glances with Barbara and Jacques, the sound technicians. The girl was wearing a blue shirt and Jean-Loup noticed that there were large patches of sweat under her arms.

"There were dozens of calls. Two people asked if it was a mystery story and a bunch of people were furious at the cheap way we're trying to increase the ratings. The boss called too and swooped down like a hawk. He fell for it and asked if we had gone nuts. Apparently, one of the sponsors had called him immediately, and I don't think it was a pat on the back."

Jean-Loup was imagining the president's room, more smoke-filled than earlier, if that were possible. And a slightly less enthusiastic speech than the one he had gotten before tonight's show. "Why didn't the switchboard filter that call?"

"I don't know what the hell happened. Raquel says the call didn't go through her. Somehow—she doesn't know why—it went right into the studio line. There must have been a short or something. As far as I'm concerned, that new electronic switchboard has a mind of its own. We'll all be fighting with machines one day, like the *Terminator*. You'll see."

They left the studio and walked side by side to Bikjalo's office without daring to look at one another. Those two words had left a small, hollow space between them.

I kill . . .

They passed the computers, puzzled. The awful sound of that voice was still hovering in the air.

"And that music at the end? It sounded familiar."

"I thought so too. It was a soundtrack, I think. *A Man and a Woman*, an old Lelouch film. From 1966 or something like that."

"And what does it mean?"

"You're asking me?"

Jean-Loup was astonished. He was facing something entirely new, something he had never experienced before on the radio. On an emotional level more than anything else. "What do you think?"

"It doesn't mean anything." Laurent pronounced these words with a careless wave of his hand, but he sounded like he was trying to convince himself more than anyone else.

"Really?"

"Sure. Aside from the switchboard problem, I think it was just some jerk's really bad idea of a joke."

They stopped in front of Bikjalo's door and Jean-Loup turned the knob. They finally looked each other in the eye.

"It's just a weird story to tell at the gym and laugh about," said Laurent, thinking out loud. But he didn't look at all sure of what he was saying.

Jean-Loup pushed open the door. As he walked into the manager's office, he wondered whether that phone call was a promise or a bet.

3

Jochen Welder pressed the remote control of the electric windlass and held it down to lower the anchor and enough chain to hold the *Forever*. When he was sure of the anchorage, he turned off the engine. The magnificent twin-engine yacht, designed by his friend Mike Farr and built especially for him by the Beneteau shipyards, started turning slowly. Pushed by a light landward breeze, it followed the current with its prow facing out to the open sea. Arianna, still standing and watching the anchor descend, turned to him and walked easily across the deck, occasionally leaning against the lifeline to compensate for the gentle rolling of the waves. Jochen watched her, his eyes half closed, and admired once again her supple, athletic, somewhat androgynous figure. He took in her firm body and the grace of her movements with a sense of muted arousal. He felt his desire well up like an ache and he gave thanks to the kind fates for making a woman who could not have been more perfect if he had designed her himself.

He still didn't dare tell her that he loved her.

She joined him at the helm, threw her arms around his neck, and placed her mouth on his cheek in a soft kiss. Jochen felt the warmth of her breath and the natural scent of her body and thought again that there was no better perfume than clean skin. It smelled of the sea and of things to discover, slowly, unhurriedly. Arianna's smile sparkled against the light of the sunset and Jochen imagined rather than saw the reflection shining in her eyes.

"I think I'll go down and shower. You can too later on, if you want. And if you decide to shave too, I'd probably accept anything you have to offer after dinner."

Jochen returned her intimate smile and ran his hand over his two-day beard. "I thought women liked a man with stubble." And imitating the voice of a 1950s movie preview, he said, "Someone who holds you around the waist with one arm and steers his ship into the sunset with the other."

"I can easily"—answered Arianna, withdrawing from his embrace as she headed belowdecks like a silent film star—"imagine myself heading off into the sunset with you, my hero, but does my face have to get all scratched up?"

She disappeared over the threshold like an actress vanishing into the wings after her best line.

"Arianna Parker, your enemies think you're a chess player, but I'm the only one who knows what you really are."

"What's that?" she asked, peeking her head back through the door, curious.

"The loveliest joker I've ever met."

"Exactly! That's why I'm so good at chess. I don't take it seriously." And she disappeared again.

Jochen saw the reflection of the light on the deck and then heard the water of the shower. He was unable to wipe the smile off his face.

He'd met Arianna a few months earlier during the Brazilian Grand Prix, at a reception organized by one of the team's sponsors, a sportswear manufacturer. He generally tried to avoid those kinds of parties, especially just before a race, but this time it was a UNICEF benefit and he couldn't refuse.

He had wandered through the rooms full of people feeling uncomfortable, elegant in a tuxedo so perfect you couldn't tell it was just rented for the occasion. He was carrying a glass of champagne that he couldn't drink, with an expression of boredom that he couldn't hide.

"Do you always have so much fun, or are you exerting yourself?"

He had turned at the sound of the voice and found himself face-to-face with Arianna's smile and green eyes. She was wearing a man's tuxedo with the shirt open and no tie. There were white sneakers on her feet. Her clothing and short dark hair made her look like an elegant version of Peter Pan. He'd seen her picture in the paper several times and immediately recognized Arianna Parker, the eccentric girl from Boston who became famous by beating the pants off the world's greatest chess players. She had spoken to him in German and Jochen answered in the same language.

"They offered to put me in front of a firing squad, but I had plans for the weekend so I chose this instead."

He had nodded toward the room full of people. The girl's smile widened and her amused look made Jochen feel like he'd just passed a test. She had held out her hand. "Arianna Parker."

"Jochen Welder."

He had wrapped his hand around hers and had known that the gesture had special meaning, that there was already something being said in the look they were exchanging. Only later would it be explained in words. They were now outside on the large terrace suspended over the quiet pulse of the Brazilian night.

"How come you speak such good German?"

"My father's second wife, who happens to be my mother, is from Berlin. Lucky for me, she stayed married to him long enough to teach me."

"Why would a girl with such a beautiful face keep it bent over a chessboard for so many hours?"

"Why," Arianna had retorted, raising an eyebrow and throwing the ball back at him, "would a man with such an interesting face keep it hidden in those soup pots you race car drivers wear on your heads?"

Léon Uriz, the UNICEF representative who organized the event, had come over just then to request Jochen's presence in the ballroom. He had left Arianna reluctantly and followed, determined to answer her last question as soon as he could. Just before entering the room, he had turned back to look at her. She was standing near the balustrade watching him, one hand in her pocket. With a complicit smile, she had raised her glass of champagne in his direction.

The next day, after the Thursday practice race, he had gone to watch her in a tournament. His arrival had excited the audience and reporters. The presence of Jochen Welder, a two-time Formula 1 world champion, at a game with Arianna Parker was no accident and unrelated to any interest he might have in chess, which nobody had ever heard of. She was seated at the tournament table, separated from the judges and the public by a wooden barrier. She had turned her head in the direction of the disturbance and when she had seen him, there was no change in her expression, as if she hadn't recognized him. She had gone back to staring at the chessboard that divided her from her opponent. Jochen admired her concentration, her head bent down to study the arrangement of the pieces. That slight female figure was strange in a milieu that usually spoke the language of men. After that, Arianna had made some inexplicable mistakes. He knew nothing about chess, but he could sense it from the remarks of the chess lovers crowded into the room. Suddenly, she had stood up and leaned her king on the chessboard as a sign that she was giving up. Without looking at anyone, her head down, she had walked to the door at the back of the room. Jochen had tried to follow her, but she was already gone.

The clocked trial races and the accompanying craziness kept him from seeking her out again. But he had spotted her in the pits, the morning of the Grand Prix, right after the drivers' briefing. He was checking the changes in the car that he'd suggested to the mechanics right after the warm-up and her voice had surprised him as it had at their first meeting.

"Well, I have to admit, your jumpsuit doesn't look as good as your tux, but it's certainly more colorful."

He had turned and there she was in front of him, her huge green eyes shining, her hair half hidden by a beret. She was wearing a lightweight T-shirt with no bra and, like almost every else around them, Bermuda shorts. A FOCA pass was hanging around her neck, along with her sunglasses. He was so surprised that Alberto Regosa, his track engineer, had started teasing him. "Hey, Jochen, if you don't close your mouth, you won't be able to get your helmet on."

"Come on, let's get out of here," he had said, and placed his hand on Arianna's shoulder, answering her and his friend at the same time. "I'd introduce you but there's no point. He'll be looking for a new job tomorrow anyway, so you won't see him again."

He had escorted the girl outside, and replied to the engineer's wisecrack with his middle finger behind his back as his friend shamelessly stared at the girl's legs in her shorts.

"Honestly, you didn't look so bad in a tux yourself, but I prefer this. There's always a little doubt when a girl's legs are hidden by pants."

They had laughed, and then Jochen had given her a brief tour of the confusion and activity of the world of race car driving, unfamiliar to Arianna. He had explained who was who and what was what, sometimes having to raise his voice above the din of the engines. When it was time to line up at the starting grid, he had asked her if she wanted to watch the race from the pits. "I'm afraid I have to put my soup pot on now, as you put it." He had said good-bye and left her in the care of Greta Ringer, the team's PR rep.

He had slid into his seat and as the mechanics fastened his seat belts, he had looked up at her. Their eyes had spoken again through the slit in his helmet and it was a language that went far beyond the emotion of the race. He had left the race almost immediately, after only about ten laps. He had started well but then, when he was in fourth place, the rear suspension, the car's weak point, had suddenly given out, sending him into a tailspin at the end of a sharp curve to the left. He had crashed into the guardrail, bouncing into the center track and half destroying his Klover Formula 109. He had informed the team by radio that everything was all right and had returned on foot. He had looked for Arianna as soon as he got back to the pits but couldn't find her. Only after describing the accident to the team manager and technicians could he look for her again. He had found her at the trailer, sitting next to Greta who discreetly moved away when he arrived. Arianna had stood up and put her arms around his neck.

"I'll accept the fact that your presence can make me lose the semifinal of an important tournament, but I think it'll be harder to lose a year of my life every time you risk yours. But you can kiss me now, if you'd like."

They had been together ever since.

Jochen lit a cigarette and stood on the deck alone in the twilight. As he smoked, he observed the lights along the coast. He'd dropped anchor not far from Cap Martin, at Roquebrune, to the right of the large blue "V" of the Vista Palace, the large hotel built on the peak of the mountain. It was three days after the Grand Prix with its crowds of people: the city had quickly returned to its normal self. Now, the lazy, orderly traffic of a sunny day in May had replaced the speeding race cars. This summer promised to be different, for him and for everyone else.

At thirty-four, Jochen Welder felt old, and he was afraid.

He knew about fear; it was a Formula 1 driver's regular companion. He'd gone to bed with it for years, every Saturday night before a race, no matter which woman was sharing his life and his bed at the time. He'd learned to recognize even the smell of it in his jumpsuits soaked with sweat, hanging up to dry in the pits. He'd faced and battled his fear for a long time, forgetting it whenever he fastened his helmet or buckled up in the car, waiting for the strong rush of adrenaline to course through his veins. But now it was different. Now he was afraid of the fear. The fear that substitutes reason for instinct, that makes you take your foot off the accelerator or feel for the brake an instant before you need to. The fear that suddenly strikes you dumb and speaks only through the chronometer, which shows how fast a second is for ordinary mortals and how slow for race car drivers.

His cell phone rang. He was sure he'd turned it off and he looked at it, tempted to do so now. Then, he took it out with a sigh and answered.

"Where the hell have you been?" came the voice.

It was the voice of Roland Shatz, his manager, bursting from the phone like that of a TV game show host, except that game show hosts weren't usually so angry with their contestants. Jochen had expected it, but was still caught unaware. "Around," he answered evasively.

"Around, like hell. Do you have any idea what kind of shit is going on?"

He didn't know, but could very well imagine. After all, a driver who loses a race he had all but won because of an error on one of the final curves was great fodder for sports pages all over the world. Roland did not wait for him to reply.

"The team did all it could to cover you with the press, but Ferguson is fucking furious. You didn't pass once—for the whole Grand Prix you were only at the top because the others were out or crashed, and then you throw away a race like that. The kindest headline was 'Jochen Welder at Monte Carlo: Loses the Race and Loses Face!' "

Jochen halfheartedly tried to protest. "I told you there was something wrong with the seat."

His manager cut him off. "Bullshit! The range finders were there and they sing better than Pavarotti. The car was perfect but

Malot was beating you as long as his engine held out, and he left the grid after you."

François Malot was the team's second driver, a fresh young talent that Ferguson, the Klover Formula 1 Racing Team manager, was developing and pampering. He didn't have the experience yet, but he was a great tester and had guts and courage to spare. It was no accident that the Circus experts had had their eyes on him from back when he was racing in F3. Ferguson had beaten everyone to the punch and signed him for two years. Even Shatz had plotted and schemed to become his agent. That was the rule of the sport, Formula 1 in particular—a small planet where the sun rose and set with cruel speed.

Over the phone, Roland's tone of voice suddenly changed and revealed a hint of the friendship, something more than a normal business relationship. Yet he was still playing good cop, bad cop. "Jochen, there are problems. There's a session of private tests in Silverstone with Williams and Jordan. If I understand correctly, they're not calling you. They'd rather have Malot and Barendson, the test driver, to check the new suspension. You know what this means?"

Of course he did. He knew the racing world too well not to. When a driver wasn't informed of a team's technical improvements, it was very likely that the boss didn't want him to be able to give another team precious information. It was practically an announcement that they weren't renewing his contract.

"What do you expect me to say, Roland?"

"Nothing. I don't expect you to say anything. I just want you to use your brain and your foot like you've always done when you race."

He paused before adding, "You're with her, aren't you?"

Jochen smiled in spite of himself.

Roland disliked Arianna and wouldn't even call her by name. Just "her." But no manager liked a woman if he thought she was the reason his driver was going soft. Jochen had had dozens of women before and Shatz had always judged them for what they were: the inevitable perks of someone constantly in the limelight, pretty objects that shone in the reflection of the champion's sun. But Shatz went on high alert when Arianna entered Jochen's life. It was time for Jochen to explain that Arianna was just a symptom, not the disease. He spoke like someone trying to convince a stubborn child to wash behind his ears.

"Roland, hasn't it occurred to you that it might be over? I'm thirty-four and most drivers my age have already retired. The ones who are still around are just caricatures of what they once were."

He carefully avoided mentioning those who were dead. The names and faces and laughter of men who suddenly became corpses in the twisted bodywork of a single-seater, a bright-colored helmet thrown aside, an ambulance that never came fast enough, a doctor who couldn't save them.

"What are you saying?" blurted Roland with a flash of rebellion at his words. "We both know what Formula 1 is like, but I have a bunch of offers from America for the CART. You still have some time left to enjoy yourself and make piles of money without any risk."

Jochen didn't have the heart to dampen Roland's managerial hopes. Money certainly wouldn't change his mind. He had enough money for generations. He had earned it by risking his hide all those years and, unlike many of his fellow drivers, he hadn't been tempted to get a personal jet or helicopter or houses all over the world. He didn't feel like telling Shatz that it was something else, that he didn't enjoy it anymore. The thread had snapped for some reason and he was just lucky it hadn't happened while he was still hanging by it.

"Okay, we'll talk about it," he said instead.

For now, Shatz realized, there was no use insisting. "Okay. Get in shape for Spain. The season's not over yet and all you need are a couple of good races and you'll be riding high. Meanwhile, enjoy yourself, man."

Roland hung up and Jochen sat there staring at the phone. He could practically see his manager's face.

"Great! You wait for me to leave and then you start with the phone calls. What am I supposed to think? Is there another woman?"

Arianna came up the steps, rubbing her hair with a towel.

"No, it was Roland."

"Ah."

Their whole situation was contained in that monosyllable. "He doesn't like me, right?

Jochen pulled her toward him, encircling her tiny waist with his arms. He leaned his cheek against her belly and spoke without looking at her.

"That's not the problem. Roland has issues, like everyone, but he's a friend and his heart is in the right place."

"Did you tell him?" asked Arianna, running her fingers through his hair.

"I didn't want to talk about it over the phone. I think I'll tell him and Ferguson in Barcelona next week. But I'll make the official announcement at the end of the season. I don't want to be followed around by journalists any more than I am now."

The international press was having a field day with their relationship. Their faces were plastered on the front pages of all the gossip magazines, and reporters were making up all kinds of stories about them.

Jochen raised his head and sought her eyes. His voice was a whisper of emotion.

"I love you, Arianna. I loved you even before I met you."

She didn't answer, but silently watched the glimmer of light from below. Jochen felt a shudder of insecurity but he had already said it, and he couldn't and wouldn't go back now.

The man's head emerges from the water not far from the prow of the Beneteau. Through his underwater mask, he spots the anchor chain and swims to it slowly. His right hand grabs hold and he observes the boat, whose fiberglass hull is reflecting the full moon. His breath, fed by his oxygen tank, is calm and relaxed.

The five-liter tank on his shoulders is not for long dives, but it is light, manageable, and gives him enough air for his needs. He is wearing a plain black wetsuit, without logos or colors, thick enough to protect him from the cold water. He cannot use a flashlight but the almost glaring light of the full moon is more than enough. Careful not to splash, he slides back underwater, following the outline of the submerged hull with its long keel extending down to the sea bottom. He reaches the stern and grabs onto the ladder still hanging down.

Good.

No acrobatics needed to get on board. He loosens the rope around his waist. After affixing a snap hook to the ladder, the first thing he does is attach it to the other end of the hermetically sealed box he is carrying. He removes the tank, the fins, and the belt of weights and leaves them hanging on the ladder, a couple of feet below the water's surface. He does not want to limit his movements, although he is taking two people by surprise in their sleep, which will certainly facilitate things.

He is about to remove his fins when he hears footsteps on the deck above. He abandons the ladder and moves to the right so that he is hidden by the wall. From his position in the shadows, he sees the girl come over and stand there, enchanted by the play of moonlight on the calm, flat sea. For an instant, her white bathrobe is yet another reflection and then, in a fluid gesture, she lets it fall to the ground and stands naked in the light.

From his position, the man sees her profile and admires her toned body, the perfect form of her small, firm breasts. His gaze follows the line of her buttocks that melts into her long, nervous legs.

With quicksilver movements, the young woman reaches the ladder and sticks out a foot to test the water.

The man smiles, a tapered smile like that of a shark. A stroke of luck!

He deeply hopes that the girl won't mind the cold and will give in to the temptation of a moonlit dip in the sea. As if she read his mind, the girl turns and starts climbing down the ladder, gently slipping down into the waves, shaking as the cold water gives her goose bumps and firms her nipples.

She swims away from the boat, out toward the open sea in the opposite direction from where he is waiting in his black wetsuit. The man's silent movement below the water has the sinister fluidity of a hunter starting to play catch with his unknown prey. The game is cruel and its stakes are life and death.

Using his hands, he empties his lungs completely through his mouthpiece to descend more easily. Then, parallel to the bottom of the sea, he starts swimming toward the girl and reaches her almost immediately. He looks up and sees her above him, a dark stain against the light on the surface of the water. He rises unhurriedly, breathing very slowly so that the air bubbles do not betray his presence. When the girl is within arm's reach, he grabs her by the ankles and pulls her brutally down.

Arianna is stunned by the violent thrust underwater. She doesn't even have time to fill her lungs with air. Almost immediately, the grasp on her ankle is loosened. She instinctively kicks to push herself upward but two hands are placed on her shoulders and their weight pushes her further down toward the bottom, far from the film of water shining above her head like a mocking promise of air and light. She feels the slimy contact of the wetsuit, two predatory arms gripping her like a belt above her breasts, and an unknown body attached to hers as her aggressor encircles her pelvis with his legs to keep her from moving.

Terror encloses reason within a wall of ice.

Wildly, she tries to free herself, whimpering, but her lungs, already lacking oxygen, instantly burn out all her reserves. As her need for air intensifies, Arianna feels her strength fade, still at the mercy of that body clutching hers, pulling her down toward the moonless night at the bottom of the sea.

She senses that she is about to die, that someone is killing her and she doesn't know why. Salty tears of regret intermingle with the millions of drops of indifferent water around her. She feels the darkness of that embrace expand and become part of her like a bottle of black ink pouring into the clean water. A cold, pitiless hand starts exploring every part of her, inside and out, trying to extinguish any tiny flame of life, until it reaches her young woman's heart and stops it forever.

The man feels the body suddenly relax at the moment that it is abandoned by life. He waits a second, then turns the girl so that her face is toward him, puts his hands under her armpits, and starts kicking with his fins to rise to the surface. As he heads upward, the young woman's face is no longer a dark blotch outside his goggles. Her delicate features, small nose, and half-opened mouth from which a few last air bubbles escape are all visible to him. Her magnificent, lifeless green eyes are immobile in the flash of death as they approach the light that they can no longer see.

The man looks at the face of the woman he has killed like a photographer observing a particularly important negative develop. When he is completely sure of the beauty of her face, he smiles.

The man's head finally emerges from the water. Still holding the body, he swims to the ladder. He takes the line that he had attached to the metal box and winds it around the woman's neck so that it holds her as he removes his tank and mouthpiece. The body slips underwater, rippling slightly, and the girl's hair remains afloat, lapping like the waves against the hull, moving softly in the moonlight like the tentacles of a jellyfish.

He removes his fins and mask and puts them down carefully so as not to make any noise. When he is free, he grabs hold of the ladder with his left hand and loosens the rope holding the body, grasping it with his right arm. Without any apparent effort, he climbs the wooden steps, carrying his victim. He observes her for a while and then leans down to pick up the bathrobe she was wearing before her night swim.

In a belated gesture of pity, he spreads the robe over the woman lying on the deck, as if he wanted to protect the cold body from the chill of a night, which, for her, would never end.

"Arianna?"

The voice is suddenly heard from below. The man turns instinctively toward it. The girl's companion might have been awakened by the sense that he was alone in the cabin. Perhaps he had stretched his leg to seek contact with her skin and didn't find it in the whitish light of the moon over the bedroom.

And since there had been no answer, he was now coming to look for her.

Covered by the black wetsuit that turns him into a shadow even darker than those thrown by the moon, he gets up and goes to hide in the shelter of the place where the mast and the boom meet.

From where he stands, he first sees the head and then the body of the man looking for the woman. He is naked. Turning his head, as he climbs on deck, he sees her and stops. She is lying at the stern, near the rudder and the ladder. Her face is turned away and she appears to be sleeping, covered haphazardly by the white bathrobe. He takes a step toward her. He feels water under his feet, lowers his eyes, and notices damp patches on the wooden deck. Maybe he thinks she went for a swim and he feels a surge of tenderness for the body that seems to be asleep in the moonlight. Maybe, in his mind's eye, he sees her swimming gracefully in silence, her wet body shining as she leaves the water and carefully dries herself. He goes over to her silently, wanting perhaps to wake her with a kiss, to bring her down to the cabin and make love to her. He kneels down and puts a hand on her bare shoulder above her robe. The man with the black wetsuit can hear every word he says.

"Darling." The woman does not show the slightest sign of having heard. Her skin is like ice. "Darling, you can't stay out here in the cold."

Still no answer. Jochen feels a strange terror carve its way into the pit of his stomach.

Cautiously, he takes her head in his hands and turns Arianna toward him. His eyes meet a lifeless stare. The movement causes a stream of water to trickle from her mouth. He knows immediately that she is dead and a silent scream possesses him. He jumps up and in that very instant, feels a damp arm around his neck. The sudden pressure makes him arch backward.

Jochen is taller than average and he has the body of an athlete, perfectly trained during long hours at the gym so that he can endure the extraordinary physical stress of the Grand Prix. Still, his aggressor is taller and just as strong. He also has the advantage of surprise and of Jochen's shock at the girl's death. The driver instinctively raises his hands and grabs the arm covered by the wetsuit, which is pressing against his throat and keeping him from breathing. Out of the corner of his eye, he sees a reflection sparkle on his right. A fraction of a second later, the aggressor's knife, sharp as a razor, cuts through the air with a hiss, drawing a swift circle downward.

The victim's body shudders and contracts in the agony of death as the blade penetrates his ribs and splits open his heart. He feels the unnatural taste of his blood in his mouth, and he dies with the moon's cold smile in his eyes.

The man continues to press with the knife until the body is completely limp in his arms. Only then does he let go of the knife, supporting the body with his own. He eases it down to the deck and stands there a moment, looking at the two corpses, breathing slowly to calm his panting. Then he grabs the man's body and starts dragging it below.

He has very little time and a great deal of work to do before the sun comes up.

The only thing lacking is a little music.

4

Roger came out on the deck of the *Baglietto* and breathed the fresh morning air. It was seven thirty and it promised to be a beautiful day. After Grand Prix week, the owners of the yacht that he commanded had gone, leaving it in his care until the summer cruise, which usually lasted a couple of months. He had at least another month and a half of peace in the port of Monte Carlo without the ship owner and his wife, a huge pain in the ass with every type of plastic surgery imaginable and so covered in jewelry that you needed dark glasses to look at her in the sun.

Donatella, the Italian waitress at the Restaurant du Port, was just setting the outdoor tables. The people who worked in the offices and stores near the port would soon be coming in for breakfast. Roger stood there watching her in silence until she noticed. She smiled and pushed her chest out just a little more.

"Life's good, huh?"

"Could be a lot better," said Roger, continuing the banter that had been going on between them for a while. He pretended to look sad.

Donatella moved the few feet that separated the tables from the stern of the boat and stopped right below him. Her open blouse revealed an intriguing furrow between her breasts and Roger plunged his gaze down like a fishing line. The girl noticed but gave no sign that it bothered her.

"You know, if you used your words as well as your eyes. . . . Hey, what's that nut job doing?"

Roger turned his head in the direction of the girl's look and saw the twin-engine Beneteau heading straight toward the line of anchored boats at full speed. There was nobody on the bridge.

"Stupid idiots."

He left Donatella and ran to the prow of the *Baglietto.* He started waving his arms frantically, shouting, "Hey, you with the twin engine! Watch out!"

There was no sign of life from the yacht. It was heading straight toward the quay without slowing down in the least. Now it was just a few yards away and a collision seemed inevitable.

"Hey!!"

Roger cried out, then grabbed the handrail and waited for the impact. With a violent crash, the Beneteau's prow rammed into the *Baglietto*'s left side, wedging itself between its hull and that of the boat anchored next to it. Luckily, the engine was not powerful enough to cause too much damage and the fenders had helped to soften the blow. Still, there was a gray line where the paint was scratched. Roger was furious. He shouted at the boat that had hit him.

"What the fuck do you think you're doing?!"

There was no answer from the other boat. Roger climbed from the bridge of the *Baglietto* right onto the prow of the Beneteau as a group of curious onlookers gathered around the pier. When he reached the stern, something felt strange. The rudder was blocked. Someone had slipped in the pole hook, tying it with a rope. A red trail started on deck and continued over to the steps leading to the cabins below. It seemed bizarre and Roger got a cold knot in his stomach. As he approached, his legs started to shake. Someone had written two words on the table in the same red liquid.

I kill . . .

The threat of the words and the ellipsis following them made him sick. Roger was twenty-eight years old and no hero but something pushed him toward the door of what was probably the bedroom. He stopped for a second, his mouth dry with dread, and then he opened the door.

He was overcome by a sweetish odor that took hold of his throat and gave him a slight sense of nausea. He didn't even have the strength to cry out. For all the years he had left to live, the scene before him would return to him every night, as a nightmare.

The policeman about to come on board and the people on the pier saw him rush out on deck, bend over the edge of the boat, and vomit into the sea, his body retching convulsively.

5

Frank Ottobre awoke feeling like he was lying under strange sheets in a strange bed, in an unknown house, in a foreign city.

Then memory seeped into his brain like sunlight through the shutters and the pain was still there, just as he'd left it the night before. If there was still a world outside and if there was a way to forget that world, his mind had rejected both. Just then, the cordless phone on the bedside table to his left began to ring. He turned over in the bed and extended his hand to the phone's flashing display.

"Hello?"

"Hey, Frank."

He closed his eyes and the face called forth by the voice in the receiver came immediately to mind. The pug nose, the sandy hair, the eyes, the smell of aftershave, the pained walk, dark glasses and gray suit that was like a uniform.

"Hey, Cooper."

"It's early for you, but I knew you'd be up."

"Yeah. What's up?"

"What's up? Total pandemonium. We're on duty 24/7. If there were twice as many of us, we'd need twice as many as that to keep up with everything. Everyone's trying to pretend that nothing's happened, but everyone's afraid. And we can't blame them: we're scared too."

There was a brief pause.

"How are you doing, by the way?"

Yeah, how am I doing?

Frank asked himself the question as if just reminded that he was alive.

"Okay, I guess. I'm here in Monte Carlo hobnobbing with the jet set. Only problem is, with all these billionaires I'm in danger of feeling like one myself. I'll leave when I no longer think that buying a mile-long yacht is a crazy idea."

He got out of bed, still holding the phone to his ear, and headed to the bathroom in the nude. In semi-darkness, he sat down on the toilet and urinated.

"If you buy one, let me know so I can come try it out."

Cooper wasn't fooled by Frank's bitter humor, but he decided to play along. Frank imagined him on the phone in his office with a strained smile and a distressed look on his face. Cooper was the same as ever. He, however, was in a tailspin and they both knew it.

There was a moment of silence and then Frank distinctly heard the sigh that Cooper used to deflate their facade. His voice was harsher now and more anxious.

"Frank, don't you think . . ."

"No, Cooper," said Frank, knowing what he was going to say and cutting him off. "Not yet. I don't feel up to coming back. It's too soon."

"Frank. Frank. *Frank!* It's been almost a year. How much time do you need to . . ."

In Frank's mind, his friend's words were lost in the huge space between where he was, America, and the void of the galaxies. All he could hear was the voice of his own thoughts.

Yeah, how much time, Cooper? A year, a hundred years, a million years? How much time does it take for a man to forget that he destroyed two lives?

"Homer said you can come back on duty whenever you like, if that helps. *You'd* be a help anyway. We need people like you right now, for Christ sake. Don't you think that being here and feeling like you're part of something, after all this . . ."

Frank interrupted and destroyed any false idea of closeness.

"There's only one thing left after all this, Cooper."

Cooper was silent, with a burning question that he was afraid even to whisper. Then he spoke, and the thousands of miles separating Monte Carlo from America were nothing compared to the distance between the two men.

"What, Frank, for the love of God?"

"God has nothing to do with it. It's me; it's between me and myself. A fight to the death, and you know it."

Frank removed the phone from his ear and watched his finger in the dark as he pressed the button and ended the call. He raised his eyes toward his naked body reflected in the large bathroom mirror. Bare feet on the cold marble floor, muscular legs, then all the way up to the dull eyes and back down to examine his chest and the red scars crisscrossing it. Almost of its own accord, his right hand rose slowly to brush over them. He sat there, freely allowing the little piece of death he constantly carried inside to wash over him.

When he had awoken, Harriet's face was the first thing he had seen. Then, Cooper's face had emerged from the mist. When he had managed to focus on the room, he had seen Homer Woods, sitting impassively on an armchair in front of the bed, his hair brushed back, his blue eyes watching without expression behind his gold-rimmed glasses.

He had turned his head to his wife and realized as if in a dream that he was in a hospital room with green light filtering through the Venetian blinds, a bouquet of flowers on the table, tubes coming out of his arm, the monotonous blip of a monitor, and everything spinning around. Harriet had approached him, bringing her face close to his. She had put a hand on his forehead. He had felt her hand but couldn't hear what she was saying because once again he'd plunged back to where he had been.

When he had finally come to and was able to talk and think, Homer Woods was standing next to Harriet. Cooper was not there.

The light in the room had changed but it was still, or once again, daytime. Frank had wondered how long it had been since he had last awoken and whether Homer had been there all that time. He was wearing the same clothes and expression. Frank had realized that he had never seen him with different clothes or different expressions. Maybe he had an entire closet full of identical ones. They called him "Husky" in the office, because his steely blue eyes looked like those of a sled dog.

"Hi, sweetheart. Welcome back," Harriet had said with her hands in his hair and a tear running down her face. Her gaze made it seem like that tear had been there since the beginning of time, like it was part of her.

She had gotten up from her seat next to the bed and placed her lips on his in a salty kiss. Frank had breathed in the scent of her breath the way a sailor breathes the air that carries the fragrance of the coast, the air of home. Homer had discreetly moved away.

"What happened? Where am I?" Frank had asked in a toneless voice that didn't sound like his. His throat was strangely sore and he remembered nothing. His last memory was of a door being kicked open and of holding his gun as he entered a room. Then came the flash and the thunder and an enormous hand pushing him upward, toward a painless darkness.

"You're in the hospital. You've been in a coma for a week. You had us worried sick." The tear was melded onto his wife's cheek as if it was a fold in her skin. It sparkled with her pain.

She was standing to one side and had glanced at Homer to let him do the rest of the explaining. He had come over to the bed and looked at Frank from behind the barrier of his glasses.

"The two Larkins spread a rumor that there was a big deal about

to happen, and that they were going to be exchanging the goods and the money with their contacts at the warehouse. Lots of goods and lots of money. They did it on purpose to get Harvey Lupe and his men jealous and convince them to break in and get their hands on everything: drugs and cash. The building was stuffed with explosives. With one show of fireworks they were planning to free themselves of all the competition. But you and Cooper came along instead of Lupe. He was still outside the southern side of the warehouse when you went in through the office. In Cooper's direction, the blast was partly absorbed by the shelves inside and all he got was a little debris in his face and a few scratches. You got hit with the full force of the explosion and it's lucky for you that the Larkins are big dealers but lousy bombers. It's a miracle you're alive. I can't even tell you off for not waiting for the team. If you had all gone in there together it would have been a massacre."

Now he knew it all but still couldn't remember anything. All he could think was that he and Cooper had worked for two years to get the Larkins and instead the Larkins had gotten them. Him, to be precise.

"What's wrong with me?" Frank had asked, noticing some strange sensations in his body. He felt a vague sense of constriction and saw his right leg in a cast, as if it belonged to someone else.

A doctor had entered the room just in time to hear the question, and he had given the answer. The doctor's hair was prematurely gray but his face and manner were those of a young man. He had smiled at Frank ceremoniously, his head to one side.

"Hello, I'm Dr. Foster, one of the reasons you're still alive. Hope you don't mind. If you like, I can tell you what's wrong. A few broken ribs, a lesion of the pleura, a leg broken in two places, wounds of various sizes everywhere, serious injuries of the thorax, and a concussion. And enough bruises to make your skin three shades darker. And there is—that is, there was—a piece of metal that stopped a quarter of an inch from your heart and made us sweat

blood to get rid of it before it got rid of you. And now, if you will all allow me," he said, picking up the chart hanging at the foot of the bed, "I think it's time to examine our efforts at damage control." He had gone to the head of the bed and pressed a button, near enough for Frank to smell his freshly laundered shirt.

Harriet and Homer Woods had started toward the door, opening it just in time to let in a nurse pushing a cart. As she was leaving, Harriet had thrown a strange glance at the monitor checking her husband's heart, as though she thought her presence was necessary for both his heart and the machine to work. Then she had turned away and closed the door behind her.

As the doctor and nurse bustled around his body covered with bandages and tubes, Frank had asked for a mirror. Without a word, the nurse had taken one hanging near the door and handed it to him. What he saw in the mirror, strangely without emotion, were the pale face and suffering eyes of Frank Ottobre, FBI Special Agent, still alive.

Mirror to mirror, eye to eye. The present overlapped with the past and Frank met his own eyes once again in the big bathroom mirror and asked himself whether it had really been worth it for all those doctors to work so hard just to keep him around.

He went back into the bedroom and turned on the light. He looked for the button, among those near the bed, to open the electric shutters. He pressed it and the shutters parted with a hum, mixing sunlight with the electric light.

Frank went over to the window, pushed aside the curtains, pulled the handle of the sliding door, and softly opened it.

He went out on the terrace.

Monte Carlo, paved with gold and indifference, lay below him. Before him, under the rising sun, down at the end of the world, the blue sea reflected the sky without any knowledge of his existence. He thought back to his conversation with Cooper. His country was at war on the other side of that sea. A war that involved him and those like him. A war that concerned everyone who wanted to live without shadows or fear in the sunlight. And he should be there, defending that world and those people.

At one time, he would have gone. At one time, he would have been on the front lines like Cooper, Homer Woods, and all the others. But that time was over. He had almost given his life for his country and his scars were the proof.

And Harriet . . .

A gust of fresh air made him shudder. He realized that he was still naked. As he went back inside, he wondered what the world could still do with Frank Ottobre, FBI Special Agent, when he didn't even know what to do with himself.

6

As he got out of the car, Police Inspector Nicolas Hulot of the Sûreté Publique of the Principality of Monaco saw the sailboat wedged in between the other two, slightly listing to one side. He walked over to the wharf. Sergeant Morelli came toward him, down the gangway of the *Baglietto* that had been rammed by the other boat. When they were face-to-face, the inspector was shocked to see that the other man was extremely upset. Morelli was an excellent policeman, who had even trained with the Mossad, the Israeli secret service. He had seen all kinds of horrors. But he was pale and avoided Hulot's gaze as they spoke, as though what was happening were his fault.

"Well, Morelli?"

"Inspector, it was a massacre. I've never seen anything like it." He sighed deeply and Hulot thought for a moment that he was about to vomit.

"Calm down, Claude, and explain. What do you mean 'massacre'? They told me there was a homicide."

"Two, Inspector. A man and a woman. What's left of them, anyway."

Inspector Hulot turned around and looked at the curious crowd forming behind the police barricades that had been set up. He had a sinking sense of foreboding. The Principality of Monaco was not a place where this kind of thing happened. The police force was one of the most efficient in the world and the low crime rate was an Interior Minister's dream. There was a policeman for every sixty inhabitants and cameras everywhere. Everything was under control. Men got rich or went bankrupt here, but nobody was killed. There were no robberies, no murders, no organized crime. In Monte Carlo, by definition, nothing ever happened.

Morelli pointed to a man of about thirty who was sitting at an outdoor café table with a policeman and the medical examiner's assistant. The place, usually swarming with people in designer clothes, was half empty. Anyone who could be useful as a witness had been detained, and anyone else was denied access. The owner was sitting on the doorstep next to a busty waitress, twisting his hands nervously.

"That guy was on the *Baglietto,* the yacht that got hit. His name's Roger something or other. He went on board to confront someone about the collision. He didn't see anyone on deck so he went down below and found them. He's in shock and they're trying to get something out of him. Agent Delmore—he's new—went onto the boat after he did. He's in the car now. Not feeling so hot."

The inspector turned back again to look at the curious crowd gathered between the police barricades and Boulevard Albert Premier, where a team of workers had just finished dismantling the stands set up for the race. He missed the confusion of the Grand Prix, the crowds and the slight inconvenience it always brought.

"Let's go see."

They walked down the unsteady gangway of the *Baglietto* and then onto the Beneteau, over another gangway that had been set up. As he climbed onto the boat, he saw the rudder blocked with the hook and the trail of dried blood that started on deck and continued below where it was lost in darkness. The sun was warm but he felt the tips of his fingers grow suddenly cold. What the hell had happened on that boat?

"If you don't mind, Inspector," said Morelli, pointing to the steps leading to the cabin below, "I'll wait here. Once was more than enough."

Going down the wooden steps, Inspector Hulot nearly bumped into Dr. Lassalle, the medical examiner, who was leaving. He had a cushy job in the Principality and extremely limited experience. Hulot had no respect for him whatsoever, as a man or as a physician. He had gotten the job because of his wife's connections and he enjoyed life while doing almost none of the work he was paid to do. Hulot had always thought of him as a luxury doctor. His presence there simply meant that he was the only person around at the time.

"Good morning, Dr. Lassalle."

"Good morning, Inspector." The doctor seemed relieved by his presence. It was clear that he was facing a situation he couldn't handle.

"Where are the bodies?"

"In there. Come and see."

Now that his eyes were accustomed to the dimness, he saw the trail of blood that continued along the floor and disappeared through an open door. To his right, there was a table where someone had written something in blood.

I kill . . .

Hulot felt his hands turn to two blocks of ice. He forced himself to breathe deeply through his nose. He was hit by the sweetish smells of blood and death, smells that bring anguish and flies.

He followed the trail of blood and went into the cabin on the left. When he was at the door and could see what was inside, the ice left his hands and spread through his entire body. Lying on the bed, one next to the other, were the bodies of a man and a woman, completely naked. The woman had no apparent wounds, while there was a large red blotch on the man's chest at his heart where the blood had stained the sheet. There was blood everywhere. It seemed impossible that those two lifeless bodies had contained so much blood. The inspector forced himself to look at the faces of the corpses. Their faces were no longer there. The murderer had completely removed the skin, hair included—the way one skins an animal. He stared, sickened by the wide-open eyes, gazing at a ceiling they could not see, the muscles of the faces red with dried blood, the teeth exposed in a macabre smile that the absence of lips made eternal.

Hulot felt as though his life would stop there, that he would be standing near the door of the cabin staring at that spectacle of horror and death forever. For an instant, he prayed that the person capable of that slaughter had at least killed his victims first, before inflicting that torture on them.

He made an effort to shake himself and turned toward the kitchen, where Lassalle was waiting. Morelli finally managed to come back down and was there too. He was standing in front of the doctor, searching the inspector's face to see his reaction.

First, Hulot turned to the physician. "What can you tell me, Doctor?"

Lassalle shrugged. "The deaths occurred a few hours ago. Rigor mortis has just set in. Hypostatic testing will confirm that. The man was apparently killed with some kind of knife; a sharp thrust right to the heart. As for the woman, apart from"—the doctor paused to swallow his saliva—"apart from the mutilation, there is nothing, at least in front. I haven't moved the bodies because we're waiting for forensics. The autopsies should tell us more."

"Do we know who they are?"

"According to the ship's papers"—it was Morelli answering this time—"the yacht is the property of a Monte Carlo company. We haven't done a thorough search yet."

"Forensics is going to be furious. With all the people coming and going on this boat, the evidence is contaminated and who knows what we've lost."

Hulot looked at the floor and the trail of blood. Here and there were footprints he hadn't noticed earlier. When he turned his gaze to the table, he was surprised to realize that he was doing so in the absurd hope that those desperate words would no longer be there.

He heard two voices from the deck above. He climbed up the steps and suddenly found himself in another world, of sunlight and life, of fresh salt air, without the smell of death he was breathing below. An agent standing on deck was trying to hold back a man of about forty-five who was shouting in French with a strong German accent. The man was trying with all his might to get past the policeman.

"Let me by, I said!"

"You can't. It's not allowed. Nobody is allowed through."

"I have to get in there, I tell you. I have to know what happened." The man struggled to get free of the policeman who was holding his arms. He was red in the face and hysterical.

"I'm sorry, Inspector," said the policeman, looking at the inspector with relief. "We couldn't stop him."

Hulot nodded to say that it was all right and the policeman let go. The man straightened his clothes with a gesture of annoyance and approached the inspector as if he were someone he could finally address as an equal. He stopped and removed his sunglasses to look him straight in the eye. "Good morning, Inspector. May I please know what is going on here on this boat?"

"And may I please find out to whom I have the pleasure of speaking?"

"My name is Roland Shatz and I assure you that it's a name that means something. I am a friend of the owner of this boat. I demand an answer."

"Mr. Shatz, my name is Hulot and it probably means much less than yours, but I'm a police inspector. Which means that, until proven otherwise, I am the person who asks the questions and demands the answers on this boat."

Hulot clearly saw the anger rise in Shatz's eyes. The man took a step closer and lowered his voice slightly.

"Inspector," he whispered just a few inches from the other man's face. There was infinite contempt in his voice. "This boat belongs to Jochen Welder, two-time Formula 1 world champion, and I'm his manager and personal friend. I am also a personal friend of His Highness, Prince Albert. So will you please tell me in detail just what has happened on this boat and to the people on it?"

Hulot left those words suspended between them for a moment. Then, his hand shot out with lightning speed and he grabbed Shatz by the knot of his tie, pulling it until he couldn't breathe. The man's face turned purple.

"You want to know? Okay, I'll make you happy. Come with me and I'll show you what happened on this boat."

He was furious. He pulled violently at the manager and practically dragged him belowdecks.

"All right, my personal friend of Prince Albert. Come and see what happened with your own eyes."

He stopped at the door of the cabin and finally let the man go. He waved his hand at the two bodies on the bed.

"Look!"

Roland Shatz regained his breath, and then lost it again. When he realized the meaning of the scene before him, his face grew deathly pale. In the dim light, there was a flash in the whites of his eyes and then he fainted.

7

As he walked toward the port, Frank saw a group of people watching police cars and uniformed men work their way among the boats moored at the dock. He heard a siren approaching behind him and he slowed his step. All those police meant that something more than a mere boating accident had occurred.

And then there were the reporters. Frank had too much experience not to recognize them at first sight. They were wandering around, sniffing out news with a frenzy only caused by something big. The siren, far away at first like a premonition, became reality.

Two police cars raced from the Rascasse, hugging the coast and pulling up in front of the barricades. A policeman hurried over to move them aside so that the cars could pass. The cars stopped behind the ambulance parked parallel to the pier, its back doors open. To Frank they looked like the open jaws of a beast ready to swallow its prey.

Several uniformed and plainclothes policemen got out of the cars. They headed toward the stern of a huge yacht anchored not far away. Frank saw Inspector Hulot standing in front of the gangway. The newcomers stopped to talk to him and then they all boarded the vessel and crossed the deck onto the boat wedged, listing, between the other two.

Frank wandered slowly through the crowd and ended up at the wall to the right of the café. He found a position from which he could watch everything comfortably. From the hold of the twin-mast several men emerged, carrying with difficulty two plastic bags closed with large zippers at the top. Frank immediately recognized them as body bags. He stood there and observed the transfer of the bodies to the ambulance with indifference. At one time, crime scenes had been his natural habitat. Now the spectacle was foreign to him, neither a challenge, as for any policeman, nor a scene of horror, as for ordinary people faced with the image of violent death.

As the ambulance doors closed behind their cargo, Inspector Hulot and the others with him walked down the *Baglietto* gangway, single file. Hulot went directly to the small crowd of reporters that two policemen were now trying to hold back. There were reporters from newspapers, radio stations, and television. Before he got there, the inspector could already hear the overlapping questions and see the microphones thrust at the policeman's mouth to force some scrap of information out of him, even a fragment that they could manipulate to arouse interest. When reporters couldn't offer the truth, they were content to stir up curiosity.

As Hulot dealt with the press, he turned his head in Frank's direction. Frank realized that Hulot had seen him. The inspector abandoned the group of reporters with the expression of an officer who repeats an interminable series of "no comment." He left, trailed by the desperate flight of questions that he would not or could not answer. He stopped at the barricade below and waved Frank over. Reluctantly, Frank detached himself from the wall, made his way through the crowd, and reached Hulot on the other side of the barricade. The two men looked at each other. The commissioner had probably only been up for a little while, but he already looked tired, as if he hadn't slept in forty-eight hours.

"Hi, Frank. Come inside."

He motioned to a policeman standing near them who moved the barricade so that he could pass through. They sat down at one of the café's outdoor tables, under an umbrella. Hulot's eyes wandered as if he couldn't explain to himself what had just happened. Frank removed his Ray-Bans and waited for his gaze.

"What's up?"

"Two dead, Frank. Murdered," he said, without looking at him. He paused. Then he finally turned and sought Frank's eyes. "And not just any two. Jochen Welder, the Formula 1 racing driver. And his girlfriend, Arianna Parker, a famous chess champion." Frank said nothing. He knew, without knowing how, that it wasn't over. "They have no faces left. The killer skinned them like animals. It was horrible. I have never in my life seen so much blood."

Meanwhile, the plaintive siren of the ambulance and the forensics van were indicators that there was nothing more to see. The curiosity seekers gradually straggled off, overcome by the heat and attracted by other activities. The reporters had gathered all they could possibly get and they too were starting to leave.

Hulot paused again. He stared at Frank and said a great deal with his silence. "Want to take a look?"

Frank wanted to say no. Everything inside him said no. He would never again look at a trace of blood or overturned furniture or touch the throat of a man lying on the ground to see if he was dead. He was no longer a policeman. He was no longer even a man. He was nothing.

"No, Nicolas. I don't feel like it."

"I'm not asking for you. I'm asking for me."

Although Frank Ottobre had known Nicolas Hulot for years, he felt as though he were seeing him for the first time. They had once collaborated on an investigation that had involved the Bureau and the Sûreté Publique—some international money-laundering story tied to drugs and terrorism. Given their nature and efficiency, the Monaco police were in constant contact with police forces all over the world, including the FBI. Frank had been sent to follow the investigation on-site because of his perfect French and Italian. He got along with Hulot and they had quickly become friends. They stayed in touch and he and Harriet had come to Europe once and were guests of Hulot and his wife. The Hulots had been planning a return visit to the States when the business with Harriet had happened.

Frank still couldn't give the events their proper name, as though not naming the night meant that darkness would never come. In his mind, what had happened was still "the business with Harriet."

When he had heard, Hulot had called almost every day for months. He had finally convinced Frank to end his isolation and come to Monte Carlo to visit him. With the discretion of a true friend, he had found him the apartment where he was staying. It belonged to André Ferrand, a manager who was spending several months in Japan.

At that moment, Hulot was looking at him like a drowning man in need of a lifeboat. Frank couldn't help but ask himself which of them was drowning and which was the lifeboat. They were two people alone against the cruelty of death.

"Let's go," said Frank, replacing his sunglasses and getting up suddenly, before he could give in to the impulse to turn and flee.

He followed his friend to the Beneteau mechanically, feeling his heart beating faster and faster. The inspector pointed to the steps on the twin-mast that led belowdecks and let Frank go first. Hulot saw that his friend noticed the blocked rudder but said nothing. When they were below, Frank looked around, moving his eyes behind his dark glasses.

"Hmm . . . Luxury boat. Everything's computerized. This is the boat of the lone sailor."

"Yeah, money was not an issue. Just think, he earned it by risking his life for years in a race car and then ended up like this."

Frank saw the traces left by the killer and the familiar marks left by forensics, who had found other less obvious details. There were the signs of fingerprints taken, measurements made, and a careful examination. The smell of death still lingered, even though all the portholes had been opened.

"They found the two of them in there, in the bedroom, lying next to each other. The footprints you see were left by rubber shoes, maybe from a wetsuit. There are no fingerprints in the hand marks. The killer wore gloves and never took them off."

Frank walked down the hallway, reaching the bedroom and stopping at the doorway. Outside was calm but inside it was hell. He had often seen scenes like this, blood splashed on the ceiling. He had witnessed real slaughter. But that was men fighting other men, ruthlessly, for human things. Power, money, women, or something like that. They were criminals fighting other criminals. Men against men, at any rate. Here, floating through the air was someone's battle against his own personal demons, the ones that devour the mind the way rust eats iron. No one could understand that better than Frank. He couldn't breathe and went back out. Hulot waited for him to join him, then resumed his story.

"At the port of Fontvieille where they were anchored, we were told that Welder and Parker set sail yesterday morning. They didn't come back, so we think they dropped anchor off the coast somewhere. Nearby presumably, since they didn't have much fuel. We still have to clarify the mechanics of the crime, but we have a plausible hypothesis. We found a bathrobe on deck. The girl might have gone out for some air. Maybe she went for a swim. The killer must have swum over from land. At any rate, he surprised her, pulled her underwater and drowned her. There were no wounds on her body. Then he got hold of Welder on deck and stabbed him. He pulled them both into the bedroom and calmly did . . . what I hope God strikes him dead for. Then he pointed the boat in the direction of the port, blocked the rudder so that it headed toward the dock, and left the way he came."

Frank didn't answer. In spite of the dim light, he was still wearing his sunglasses. With his head lowered, he seemed to be staring at the trail of blood that went between them like a track.

"So what do you think?"

"You need to be fairly cold-blooded to do something like this, if that's how it happened."

He wanted to leave, to go back home. He didn't want to have to say what he was saying. He wanted to return to the pier and resume his peaceful walk in the sun toward nothing. He wanted to breathe without realizing he that he existed. But he went on talking.

"If he came from land, then he didn't do it in a fit of rage. It was premeditated and carefully planned. He knew where they were and they were quite likely the people he wanted to strike."

The other man nodded, hearing something that he thought as well.

"That's not all, Frank. He left this as a commentary on what he did."

Hulot made a gesture that underscored what was behind him. A wooden table and delirious words that could have come from the pen of Satan.

I kill . . .

Frank removed his glasses, as if he needed to see better in order to understand the words.

"If that's the way things were, these words mean only one thing, Nicolas. It's not a commentary on what he did. It means he's planning to do it again."

THIRD CARNIVAL

The man shuts the heavy hermetic door behind him.

It closes silently, fitting perfectly into the metal frame, and becomes one with the wall. The wheel, similar to that of a submarine, turns easily in his hands. The man is strong but he knows that the mechanism needs frequent oiling and he keeps it in perfect working order. The man is meticulous about his belongings. The place is in perfect order.

He is alone, locked in his secret hiding place where men, the light of day, and the simple liquidity of reason are excluded. The furtive haste of an animal returning to its den and the lucid concentration of the predator who has selected its victim, along with images of blood and the red of sunset, screams and whispers, peace and death all crowd together in his mind, finding their rightful place.

The room is a rather spacious rectangle. The wall to the left is entirely covered by a bookcase filled with electronic equipment. There is a complete sound system consisting of two Alesis 8-track units linked to a Macintosh computer. The system also includes sound equipment piled up to the right of the wall. There are compressors, Focusrite and Pro Tools filters, and some racks of Roland and Korg effects. There is a radio scanner to hear programs on all frequencies, including the police radio. The man likes to listen to voices in the air. They fly from one spot to another in space and belong to people without faces or bodies. They are imagination and the freedom to fantasize; they are his voice on tape and his voice in his head.

The man picks up the hermetically sealed box from the floor where he put it down to close the flywheel. There is a wooden table resting on two sawhorses on the right, against the metal wall. The man sets the box on it. He sits down on a rolling desk chair that allows him to reach the wall opposite the sound equipment with a simple movement. He turns on a table lamp and the light mixes with that of the neon lights hanging from the ceiling.

The man feels the growing beat of excitement slowly reach his heart as he releases the hinges on the box one by one. The night had not been spent in vain. The man smiles. There, outside, on a day no different from any other, men were looking for him. Bloodhounds with glass eyes, immobile in the shining windows of their world. Other voices were in the air, flying at each other in a futile chase.

There, in the peace of the shadows, the house is once again a home. Truth rediscovers its essence, the footstep its echo. The unbroken mirror on the ground reflects a stone uselessly thrown. His smile broadens and his eyes shine like stars announcing an ancient prophecy come true. In the absolute silence, only his mind perceives the solemn music as he slowly opens the lid of the box.

In the small space of his secret hiding place, the odors of blood and sea spread through the air. The man feels anguish tighten his stomach. The triumphant beating of his heart suddenly becomes a death knell. He jumps up, thrusts his hands in the box, and, with delicate movements, extracts what is left of the face of Jochen Welder, dripping with blood and salt water. The hermetic seal on the box did not hold and water has seeped into the container. He inspects the damage, turning it in his hands. The skin is rough and spotted with white where it came in contact with the salt. The lifeless hair is damp and tousled.

The man drops his trophy into the box as if only then it disgusts him. He slumps into the chair and holds his head in his blood-and-salt-covered hands. Unwittingly, he runs his hands through his hair while drooping his head under the weight of defeat. No use.

The man feels the rage come from far away with the rustle of wind through tall grass, panting breath, breaking thunder amid whispers of fear. His fury explodes. He jumps up, grabs the container, raises it over his head, and hurls it against the metal wall. The walls echo like a tuning fork set to the pitch of death that the man feels inside him. The box bounces and lands in the middle of the room. It spins around and stops on its side. The lid is half off from the thrust of the throw. The sorry remains of Jochen Welder and Arianna Parker fall out onto the floor. The man looks at them with contempt, the way one looks at spilled garbage on the ground.

The moment of rage is brief. His breath slowly returns to normal. His heart calms down. His hands fall to his sides, touching the fabric of his pants. His eyes once again become those of a priest who listens in silence to voices that only he can hear. There will be another night. And many more nights to come. And a thousand faces of men whose smiles will be snuffed out like a candle inside a hollow jack-o'-lantern.

He sits down and pushes himself over to the wall with the sound equipment. He rummages through the cases on the ground that go all the way around the room, packed with records and CDs. He pulls one out and puts it in the player almost frenetically. He turns it on and the sound of strings pours from the speakers. It is melancholy music, evoking a cool autumn breeze blowing crumpled leaves in a soft, swirling dance.

The man relaxes against the back of his chair. He smiles again. His failure is already forgotten, dissolved by the sweetness of the music. There will be another night. And many more nights to come. And as alluring as the air that swirls through the room, a voice arrives with the music.

Is that you, Vibo?

8

"*Merde!*"

Nicolas Hulot threw his newspaper down on top of the others cluttering his desk. All of them, French and Italian, had the news of the double murder on the front page. In spite of his attempt to keep some of the information confidential, the whole story had leaked out. The crime itself would have been enough to excite the voracity of the press like piranhas before a side of beef. But on top of that, the victims were famous, so the headlines reached the peak of creativity. A Formula 1 champion and his girlfriend, who just happened to be a world-famous chess player. It was a gold mine where reporters would be willing to dig in their bare feet.

A couple of very skilled news hawks had managed to piece together all the information, probably thanks to a statement—probably very well-compensated—from the sailor who had found the bodies. The reporters' imagination really went wild over the writing on the table. Everyone gave a personal interpretation, leaving the readers to fill in the gaps.

I kill . . .

The inspector closed his eyes but the scene before him did not change. He was unable to forget those marks written in blood on the table. Things like that did not happen in real life. Writers only invented them to sell books. They were the plots of movies that successful screenwriters wrote in Malibu beach houses while sipping cocktails. This type of investigation belonged in America with detectives like Bruce Willis and John Travolta, big guys with taut muscles and an easy gun. Not a inspector who was closer to retirement than to glory.

He got up from his desk and went over to the window with the steps of a man worn out from the fatigue of a long journey. Everyone had called him, in the proper hierarchical order. He had given the same answers, since they had all asked the same questions. He looked at his watch. There was a meeting soon to coordinate the investigation. Along with Luc Roncaille, chief of the Sûreté Publique, there would be Alain Durand, the attorney general who, as investigating magistrate, had decided to head up the investigation in person. The Councilor for the Interior Ministry was also planning to attend. The only person missing was the Prince, supreme head of the police force by internal regulations. Although one never knew who would show up.

All Hulot had at the moment was a little information and a great deal of diplomacy, and he would use them on anyone who came by.

There was a knock at the door and he turned. "Come in."

The door opened and Frank walked in, looking like he would much prefer to be elsewhere. Hulot was surprised to see him but could not help feeling a sense of relief. He knew it was a gesture of gratitude toward him, a little support in the sea of troubles where he was floundering. And Frank Ottobre, the Frank of the past, was exactly the type of policeman who could run an investigation like this, even though he knew that his friend had no desire to be a policeman ever again.

"Hi, Frank."

"Hi, Nicolas. How's it going?"

"How's it going?" answered Hulot, knowing that the other man had only asked him that question to keep him from asking it first. "I leave it to your imagination. I got hit with a meteorite when I could barely handle a pebble. I'm a total wreck. Everyone's on to me. They're dogs who think I'm a fox." Frank said nothing and went to sit down in the armchair in front of the desk. "We're waiting for the autopsy report and the forensic test results. But they haven't found much. They pored over every inch of the boat but nothing turned up. We had a handwriting analysis done of the writing on the table and we're waiting for those results too. We're all praying that it isn't what it seems."

Hulot was glancing at his American friend's face, trying to see if there was any interest in what he was saying. He knew Frank's story and that it was no easy burden to bear. After he had lost his wife, and in those circumstances, Frank seemed to be living with the sole intention of destroying himself, as if he felt guilty for all the troubles of the world. Nicolas had seen people lose themselves to alcohol or worse. He'd even seen people take their own lives in a desperate attempt to erase their remorse. Instead, Frank remained lucid, whole, as if he wanted to keep himself from forgetting, as if he were serving out a sentence, day by day, without any extenuating circumstances.

Hulot leaned his elbows on the table. Frank sat in silence, his legs crossed, expressionless. Nicolas had to struggle to continue.

"We don't have a thing. Absolutely nothing. Our man was probably wearing a wetsuit the whole time, including shoes, gloves, and cap. In other words, no skin, no hair. The hand and footprints he left are of such a normal physical type that it could be anyone." Hulot paused. Frank's eyes were two pieces of black coal. "We've started looking into the victims. Two people like that, you can imagine everyone they met with the lives they led, all over the world . . ."

Suddenly, the inspector's attitude changed, struck by the anxiety of an idea.

"Why don't you help me, Frank? I can call your boss. I can ask him to call the right people and have you join the investigation. You're prepared and familiar with the facts. We've worked together before, after all. And one of the victims was an American citizen. You're the right man for a case like this. You speak French and Italian perfectly; you know how the European police do things and how they think. You're the right man in the right place."

"No, Nicolas," The voice reached Frank like a gust of wind before a thunderstorm, but the clouds in his eyes were from a different storm. "You and I don't have the same memories anymore. I'm not the man I used to be. I'll never be that again."

"Hasn't it ever occurred to you," said the inspector, getting up from his chair, "that what happened to Harriet might not be your fault?" He went around the desk and leaned against it, standing in front of Frank. He bent over to him slightly, for more emphasis. "Or at least not entirely?"

Frank turned his head and looked out the window. His jaw contracted as if he wanted to bite back an answer he'd already given too many times. His silence increased Hulot's anger and the inspector raised his voice slightly.

"God damn it, Frank! You know what happened. You saw it with your own eyes. There's a murderer out there who has already killed two people and will probably kill again. I don't know what exactly you've got on your mind, but don't you think that stopping this maniac could be a good way to feel better? Hasn't it occurred to you that helping others might be a way of helping yourself? Helping yourself *go home*?"

Frank brought his gaze back to his friend with the eyes of a man who could go anywhere and still feel that he did not belong.

"No." That single syllable uttered in such a calm voice was a wall between them. For a moment, it blocked them both. It was the single frame of a story whose end they could not know.

Someone knocked at the door and Claude Morelli walked in without waiting for an answer.

"Inspector . . ."

"What is it, Morelli?"

"There's someone from Radio Monte Carlo outside."

"Tell him I'm not talking to reporters now. There'll be a press conference later, whenever the chief decides."

"He's not a reporter, Inspector. He's a deejay who hosts an evening radio show. He came with the station manager. They read the papers and they say they have some information on the two crimes at the port."

Hulot did not know how to take the news. Anything useful was like manna from heaven. The thing he was afraid of was a parade of maniacs convinced that they knew everything about the homicides or even wanting to confess that they were the killers. But he could not afford to leave any stone unturned.

"Show them in."

Morelli went out and it seemed like a prearranged signal. Frank got up and went to the door. He was near it when it opened and Morelli came back, accompanied by a young man with long, black hair, about thirty, and an older man, about forty-five. Frank glanced at them and moved aside to let them in. He took advantage of the occasion to slip through the half-open door.

"Frank," the voice of Nicolas Hulot stopped him. "Sure you don't want to stay?"

Frank Ottobre left the room without a word and closed the door behind him.

9

Outside police headquarters, Frank turned left on Rue Suffren Raymond and soon found himself walking down Boulevard Albert Premier, the street that ran along the coast. A crane moved lazily against the blue sky. The crew was still at work dismantling the bleachers and piling them onto the trucks.

Everything was happening by the rules. Frank crossed the street and stopped on the promenade in front of the port to watch the boats drop anchor. There was no trace of what had happened on the wharf. The Beneteau had been towed away and was certainly being kept safe somewhere so that the police could get to it during the investigation. The *Baglietto* and the other boat it had rammed were still there, floating without memory, softly nudging each other's fenders when the waves brought them close. The police barricades had been removed. There was nothing left to see.

The port café had resumed its normal activity. What had happened was probably attracting more customers, curiosity seekers who wanted to be at the center of things. Maybe the young sailor who had discovered the bodies was there, enjoying his fifteen minutes of fame and telling what he had seen. Or maybe he was sitting silently in front of a glass, trying to forget.

Frank sat down on a stone bench. A boy was speeding past on Rollerblades, followed by a younger girl having trouble with her roller skates and whimpering for him to slow down. A man with a black Labrador was patiently waiting for his dog to finish responding to the call of nature. Then he took out a plastic bag and a little shovel from his pocket and gathered up the product of the canine offense, diligently depositing it in the trash.

Ordinary people. Like everybody else, but with a little more money and happiness or at least the illusion of them. Maybe it was all just a show and nothing more. It could be made of gold, but a cage was still a cage and every person created his own destiny. Everyone built his own life or destroyed it, according to the rules he alone invented. Or rules he refused to make. There was no escape.

A boat was sailing out of the port and from the stern, a blond woman in a blue bathing suit waved good-bye to someone on shore. For a moment, the sea lapped over the sea, reflection over reflection and memory over his gaze.

After he had left the hospital, he and Harriet had rented a cottage in an isolated spot on the Georgia coast. It was a wooden house with a sloping red-tile roof built about a hundred yards from the sea in the middle of the dunes. There was a veranda with large sliding glass doors that opened in the summer, transforming it into a patio.

At night, they listened to the wind blowing through the sparse vegetation and the sound of the waves hitting the beach. They stayed in bed and he could feel his wife hold him tightly before falling asleep, with a frantic need to assure herself of his presence, as if she could not really convince herself that he was still there with her, alive.

During the day, they lay on the beach, sunbathed, and swam. That stretch of coast was practically deserted. People who loved the sea and the life of crowded beaches went elsewhere, to the "in" places, to watch bodybuilders working out or girls with breast implants strutting by as if they were auditioning for Baywatch. *Lying there on the towel, Frank could expose his thin body to the sun without being ashamed of all the red scars or the painful mark of the heart operation where they took out the piece of metal that had nearly killed him.*

Sometimes Harriet traced the sensitive flesh of the scars with her fingers, and tears shone in her eyes. Sometimes silence fell between them, when they both thought the same thing, remembering the suffering of those last months and the toll it had taken. They did not have the courage to look at each other then. They each looked out at their own piece of ocean until one of them, still in silence, found the strength to turn and embrace the other.

From time to time, they did some shopping in Honesty, a fishing village that was the nearest town and looked more like Scotland than America. It was a peaceful little town, without the slightest ambition of becoming a tourist resort. The wooden houses all looked more or less alike and were built along a street that ran parallel to the ocean, where a cement strip on the rocks stopped the waves during winter storms.

They ate in a restaurant with large glass windows across from the pier, built on piles with a wooden floor that echoed with the waiters' steps. They drank chilled white wine that clouded their glasses, and they ate freshly caught lobster, staining their fingers and splashing their clothes when they tried to crack open the claws. Harriet and Frank laughed like children. They seemed to be thinking about nothing. They spoke about nothing until the phone call.

They were at home and Frank was slicing vegetables for the salad. There was a delicious smell of fish and potatoes baking in the oven. The wind outside swirled the sand from the peaks of the dunes and the ocean was covered with white foam. The sails of a few Windsurfers cut swiftly through the air opposite a jeep parked on the beach. Harriet was on the veranda and the whistling of the wind kept her from hearing the phone. He had stuck his head out the kitchen door with a large red pepper in his hand.

"Phone, Harriet. Can you answer? My hands are dirty."

His wife had gotten up and gone over to the old wall phone that was ringing with its old-fashioned sound. She had picked up the receiver and he stood there watching her.

"Hello?"

As soon as she heard the answer, her face had changed, the way faces do when they hear bad news. Her smile had faded and she had stood in silence for a moment. Then, she had put down the receiver and looked at Frank with an intensity that would torment him for a long time.

"It's for you. It's Homer," she had said, turning and going back to the veranda without another word. He had gone to the phone and picked up the receiver, still warm from his wife's hand.

"Yes?"

"Frank, it's Homer Woods. How're you doing?"

"Fine."

"Really fine?"

"Yes."

"We got them." Homer spoke as if their last conversation had taken place ten minutes before. If he had noticed Frank's monosyllabic way of speaking, he had not let on.

"Who?"

"The Larkins. We caught them red-handed this time. Without any bombs. There was a gunfight and Jeff Larkin got killed. There was a mountain of drugs and a bigger mountain of cash. And papers. We have promising new leads. With a little luck, there's enough material to nail them all."

"Fine." He had pronounced the same word as before in the same tone of voice, but his boss hadn't picked up on it this time either. He imagined Homer Woods in his paneled office, sitting at his desk, phone in hand, his blue eyes framed by gold-rimmed glasses, as immutable as his gray suit with the vest and blue button-down shirt.

"Frank, we got to the Larkins mostly because of your work, yours and Cooper's. Everyone here knows it and I wanted to tell you. When do you think you're coming back?"

"I don't know, quite frankly. Soon."

"Okay, I don't want to pressure you. But remember what I said."

"Okay, Homer. Thanks." He had hung up and gone out to look for Harriet. She was sitting on the veranda watching the two kids dismantle their Windsurfers and load them onto their jeep.

He had sat down in silence next to her on the wooden bench. They had watched the beach until the jeep was gone. It was as if that outside presence, though far away, had kept them from speaking.

"He wants to know when you're coming back to work, doesn't he?" Harriet had asked, breaking the silence.

"Yes." There had never been lies between them and Frank had no intention of starting now.

"Do you want to?"

"Harriet," Frank had said, "I'm a policeman." He had turned to her but Harriet had carefully avoided meeting his gaze. He too had gone back to watching the ocean and the waves chasing each other in the wind, white with foam. "I didn't choose this life because I had to. I like it. I've always wanted to do what I do and I don't know if I could adjust to doing anything else. I don't even think I'd know how. As my grandfather always said, you can't fit a square peg into a round hole." He had stood up and put a hand on his wife's shoulder, now slightly stiff. "Harriet, I don't know whether I'm square or round. But I don't want to change."

He had gone back into the house and when he had come out to look for her, she had disappeared. Her footprints on the sand in front of the house went in the direction of the dunes. He had seen her walking in the distance by the shore, a tiny figure with hair flying in the wind. He had followed her with his gaze until two other dunes had hidden her from view. He thought she wanted to be alone and that it was only right. He had gone back into the house and sat down at the table, in front of food he would never want to eat.

Suddenly, he had not felt so sure about what he had said earlier. Maybe there was another life for the two of them. Maybe someone who was born square couldn't become round, but he could try to round off the edges so that nobody would be hurt. Especially those he loved. He had decided to give himself a night to think it over. He would talk to her about it the next morning. He was sure that they could find a solution together.

There was never a next morning for the two of them.

He had waited until late afternoon for Harriet to return. As the sun set and the shadows of the dunes lengthened over the beach like dark fingers, he had seen two figures walking slowly along the shore. The reflection of the fiery sunset had made him narrow his eyes. They were still too far away for him to make them out clearly. Watching through the open window, Frank could see the footprints they left with every step, a trail that started from the dunes on the horizon. Their clothing rustled in the wind and their silhouettes shimmered. When they were near enough for him to see them clearly, Frank realized that one of them was the sheriff from Honesty.

He had felt the anxiety rise up inside him. He was finally facing that man who acted more like an accountant than a policeman and his fear had become a frightening reality. Holding his hat in his hand and trying to avoid his eyes as much as possible, the sheriff had told him what had happened.

A couple of hours earlier, some fishermen had been sailing a few hundred yards from the coast and they had seen a woman corresponding to Harriet's description. She was standing at the top of a cliff that looked like a geological accident amid the coastal dunes. She was alone and looking out at the sea. When they were just about opposite her, she had jumped. Not seeing her emerge, they had immediately turned their boat around to go to the rescue. One of them had dived into the ocean right where she had jumped but they could not find her. They had called the police right away and started searching. So far they had found nothing.

The ocean had returned Harriet's body two days later, when the current had carried it to an inlet a couple of miles south of the coast.

When he had identified her body, Frank had felt like an assassin before his victim. He had looked at the face of his wife lying on the morgue slab and, nodding, confirmed both Harriet's identity and his own life sentence. There had been no inquest thanks to the fishermen's testimony, but that did not help to free Frank of the remorse consuming him. He had been so busy taking care of himself that he had not noticed Harriet's deep depression. Nobody had noticed it, but that was no excuse. He should have noticed his wife's agitation. He was supposed to *understand. All the signals had been there, but in his own delirium of self-pity, he had ignored them. And their conversation after Homer's phone call had been the last straw. When you got right down to it, he was neither square nor round. Just blind.*

He had left town with his wife's body in a coffin without even going back to the house to pack.

"Mommy, there's a man crying."

The child's voice shook him from his trance. Next to him, the mother of the little blond girl in a blue dress hushed her and smiled at him in embarrassment. She hurried away, pulling her daughter by the hand.

Frank did not realize that he was crying, nor for how long. His tears came from far away. They were not tears of salvation, nor oblivion, but just relief. They were a small truce to let him breathe for a moment, feel the heat of the sun, see the color of the sea, and listen to his heart beating in his chest without the sound of death, just once. He was paying the price of his madness. The whole world was paying the price of his madness.

He had repeated it for hours after Harriet's death, sitting on a bench in the garden of the St. James Clinic where they had admitted him on the edge of a nervous breakdown. He had understood it definitively months later with the World Trade Center disaster, when he had watched on television as the buildings fell, the way only illusions can. Men throwing themselves in airplanes against skyscrapers in the name of God, while someone sitting comfortably in an office already knew how to exploit their derangement on the stock market. Other men earned their living by building and selling land mines, and at Christmas they bought their children presents with money earned by killing and maiming other children. Conscience was an accessory whose value was tied to fluctuations in the price of oil. And in the middle of all that, it was no surprise if, from time to time, there was someone who wrote his own destiny in blood.

I kill . . .

Remorse for Harriet's death was a cruel traveling companion that would never leave his side. It alone would be enough punishment for the rest of his days. He would never forget. He could not forget even if his life went on forever. And he would never be able to forgive himself, if he lived twice as long as eternity. He could not end the insanity in the world. He could only try to end his own, and hope that those who could would follow his example. And erase those two words or others like them. He sat there crying on the bench and ignored the curious passersby until he decided he had no tears left.

Then he got up and headed slowly over to police headquarters.

10

"*I kill* . . ."

The voice remained suspended in the car and seemed to feed off the faint drone of the engine, continuing to reverberate like an echo. Inspector Hulot pressed a button on the car radio and the cassette stopped on the voice of Jean-Loup Verdier struggling to bring the program to a close. After Hulot's conversation with the deejay and Robert Bikjalo, the manager of Radio Monte Carlo, a small, cruel wisp of hope had peeped out from behind the mountain that the investigators were trying desperately to climb.

There was a slight chance that it could have been a crank call, a bizarre accident, a coincidence caused by some one-in-a-million conjunction of the stars. But those two words, "*I kill,*" hurled like a threat at the end of the show were the same as those left on the table on the yacht, written in blood.

Hulot stopped his car at a red light. A woman pushing a baby carriage crossed the street in front of them. On their right, a man on a yellow bike in a blue sweat suit was leaning against the traffic light, his hand against the pole so he wouldn't have to take his feet off the pedals. There was color and warmth all around them. The summer with its promises was arriving amid the outdoor café tables, in the streets full of people, on the lively boardwalk along the beach where men, women, and children asked only that the promises be kept. Everything was as it should be, except for the car standing at the red light, like blood in a lightbulb. A presence hovered in that car with the power to obscure light and transform the colors of the world into opaque shades of black and white.

"Any news from forensics?" Frank asked.

The red light turned green. Hulot switched gears and drove forward. The cyclist quickly sped away. With the traffic backed up along the coastal road, he could go faster on his bike than in a car.

"We've got the pathologist's report. They did the autopsy in record time. Some big shot must have lit a fire under their asses. It's all confirmed. The girl died by drowning, but there was no seawater in her lungs. That means she died without being able to come up for air. Usually the lungs fill with water when someone drowning bobs up and down several times before finally sinking. In this case, the killer must have surprised her in the water, pulled her down, and drowned her. They went over the body with a fine-tooth comb. No sign, no trace. They examined it every way they could with all the equipment they've got.

"What about him?"

"That was different." Hulot's face darkened. "He was stabbed with a very sharp pointed instrument. The wound was made from above. The blade penetrated between the fifth and sixth rib and went straight to the heart. Death was almost instantaneous. The killer must have attacked him outside, on deck where the bloodstains were found. He was taken by surprise, but Jochen Welder was a big man. He wasn't that tall, but taller than most racing drivers. And he was in good shape. Spent a lot of time in the gym. So the attacker must have been in even better shape than he was."

"Were the bodies raped?"

"No," said Hulot shaking his head. "At least he definitely wasn't. She had just had intercourse. There were traces of semen in her vagina, but it was probably Welder's. The DNA test confirmed that at ninety percent."

"That would exclude a sexual motive. At least the usual type."

Frank's tone was dry, as if he were talking about a napkin that had survived a fire.

"As far as prints and other organic traces, they found plenty. We'll send it all for DNA testing, but I doubt it will lead anywhere."

They passed Beaulieu and the luxury hotels along the beach. The parking lots were full of shiny cars, left in the peaceful shade of the trees. There were flowering bushes everywhere; a thousand colors in the light of that beautiful day. Frank let himself be distracted by the red hibiscus blossoms in the garden of a villa. Red again. More blood.

"So we have nothing," he said, bringing his mind back to the car. He moved the air-conditioning vent so that the cold air blew on his face.

"Absolutely nothing."

"Body type measurements on the prints?"

"Nothing there either. He's probably about six feet tall, give or take an inch. Weight about one seventy. Like millions of people."

"Athletic, in other words."

"Yeah, athletic. And very good with his hands."

Frank had more questions, but his friend seemed to be reflecting and drawing his own conclusions as he described the facts and Frank did not want to interrupt him.

"The job he did on the bodies is nothing to sniff at. He's certainly skilled. It definitely wasn't his first time. Maybe someone with a medical background."

"It's worth a try. You never know." Frank didn't want to dampen his friend's hopes. "But it would be too obvious. Predictable, I'd say. Unfortunately, in some ways, human anatomy is no different from that of animals. All the guy needed to do was practice on a couple of rabbits and he could do the same thing to a person."

"Rabbits, huh? People like rabbits."

"He's smart, Nicolas. A raving lunatic, but smart and

cold-blooded. You need a guy with Freon in his veins to do what he did, send the boat ramming into the others and go back home the way he came. He's taunting us, laughing at us too."

"You mean the music?"

"Yeah. He hung up with the theme song from *A Man and a Woman*."

Hulot remembered seeing the Lelouch movie years ago, just after he had started dating his wife, Céline. He remembered the love story perfectly and had taken it as a sign of good luck for their future. Frank reminded him of a detail he had not focused on until then.

"The man in the movie was a race car driver."

"Now that you mention it . . . And so was Jochen Welder. But . . ."

"Exactly. Not only did he announce the fact that he was planning to kill on the radio, he also said *whom* he was planning to kill! And I don't think it's over. He killed and he wants to kill again. We have to stop him—I don't know how, but we have to. Whatever the cost."

The car stopped for another red light at the brief descent at the end of Boulevard Carnot. The city of Nice lay before them. Nice, faded and human, far from the glossy shine of Monte Carlo and its population of wealthy retirees. As he drove toward Place Masséna, Hulot turned to look at Frank in the seat next to him. Frank was staring straight ahead with the rapt expression of Ulysses awaiting the song of the Sirens.

11

Nicolas Hulot pulled up in his 206 at the gate of the Auvare Police Department on Rue de Roquebillière. A uniformed policeman standing next to the guardhouse came over looking annoyed, to tell them to move from the entrance reserved for police personnel. The inspector showed his badge from the window.

"Inspector Hulot, Sûreté Publique, Monaco. I have an appointment with Inspector Froben."

"Sorry, Inspector, I didn't recognize you. What can I do for you?"

"Could you let him know I'm here?"

"Right away, sir. Meanwhile, come on in."

"Thanks, Officer."

Hulot drove up a few yards and parked his car on the shady side of the street. Frank got out and looked around. The rectangular buildings were arranged in a checkerboard layout. There was an outdoor stairway at the shorter end of each building, facing out onto the street.

The inspector wondered what all this looked like to an American. Nice was a different city in a different world. It might as well be another planet, where he understood the language but not the way of thinking. Small houses, small cafés, small people. No American dream, no skyscrapers to destroy. Just small dreams, often faded by the sea air like the walls of the houses. Small dreams, but when they were crushed, they too brought deep despair.

Someone had hung a poster against globalization right in front of the Police Department. Men fighting so that everyone could be the same, while others fought to keep from losing their identity. Europe, America, China, Asia. They were only colored shapes on the map, abbreviations on the list of exchange rates, names in dictionaries in libraries. Now there was the Internet, the media, and news in real time. These were signs of a world that was expanding, or contracting, depending on your point of view. But the only thing that really erased distances was evil. It was present everywhere; it spoke only one language and it always wrote its messages in the same ink.

Frank closed the car door. He was thirty-eight years old with the eyes of an old man who had been denied life's wisdom. He had a Latin face, darkened further by the shadow of his eyes and hair and the suggestion of a beard. A strong, athletic man. A man who had killed other men, protected by a badge and the justification of being on the right side. Perhaps there was no cure, no antidote for evil. But there were men like Frank, touched by and immunized from evil itself.

The war never ended.

As Hulot locked his car, they saw Inspector Froben of Homicide, who was taking part in the investigation. He came out of the building in front of them and headed in their direction. He flashed Hulot a wide grin, showing off large, regular teeth that illuminated his face and his marked features. He had a massive body that filled the jacket of his Galeries Lafayette suit, and the broken nose of someone who'd practiced boxing. Frank saw confirmation in the tiny scars around his eyebrows.

"Hi, Nicolas," Froben said, shaking Hulot's hand. His smile grew wider and his gray eyes narrowed, the scars meshing with a web of tiny wrinkles. "How're you doing?"

"You tell me how I'm doing. In this sea of shit with a storm threatening, I need all the help I can get. This is Frank Ottobre, FBI Special Agent," said Hulot as Froben's gaze moved to Frank. "Very special. His office sent him to join the investigation."

Froben said nothing, but his eyes showed he was impressed by Frank's title. He extended a hand with large, strong fingers and the same open grin. "Claude Froben, humble inspector of Homicide."

As he returned Froben's vigorous handshake, Frank felt that the other man could have broken his fingers if he had wanted to. He liked him immediately. He embodied both strength and grace at once. Frank could imagine him with his children after work, making model ships and handling the fragile parts with surprising delicacy.

"Any news on the tape?" Hulot asked, coming straight to the point.

"I handed it over to Clavert, our best technician. A magician, actually. When I left, he was working on it with his gadgets. Come, follow me."

Froben went first and they filed in the same door he had emerged from. He led them down the short hallway flooded with diffused light from a window behind them. Hulot and Frank followed until the back of Froben's salt-and-pepper head turned back and revealed his face again. He stopped in front of a staircase that led down to the left. Froben gestured with his large, square hand.

"After you."

They went down two flights of stairs and found themselves in a huge room full of electronic equipment. It was lit by cold neon tubes that supplemented the inadequate light from the basement's street-level skylights.

A thin young man was sitting at a workbench. His head was shaved to hide early baldness. He was wearing a white coat over a pair of jeans with an untucked plaid shirt. A pair of round glasses with yellow lenses was perched on his nose. The three men stopped behind the rolling chair where he was sitting, handling a potentiometer. He turned to look at them. Hulot wondered whether he risked going blind when he went out into the sun with those glasses.

Froben did not introduce them and the man didn't seem to mind. Probably, to his way of thinking, if two strangers were there, it was because they were supposed to be.

"Well, Clavert? What have you got to tell us about the tape?"

"Not much, Inspector," the technician said, shrugging his shoulders. "No good news. I analyzed the recording with everything I've got. Nothing. The voice is artificial and there is no way to identify it."

"Which means?"

Realizing that not everyone present had his technical knowledge, Clavert backtracked.

"Every human voice travels along certain frequencies that are part of one's personal identity. Voices can be identified like fingerprints and the retina. They have a certain number of high, low, and medium tones that don't vary, even if you try to alter your voice, by talking in falsetto, for example. We can visualize these frequencies with special equipment and then reproduce them in a diagram. This is fairly common machinery. They use it in recording studios, for example. They're used to distribute frequencies and keep a song from having too many high or low tones."

Clavert went over to a Mac computer and moved the mouse. He clicked some icons and a white screen appeared, with parallel lines crossing it horizontally. There were two other jagged lines, one green and one purple, wandering between them.

"This is the voice of Jean-Loup Verdier, the Radio Monte Carlo deejay," the technician said, moving the mouse pointing to the green line. "I've analyzed it and this is the phonic pattern." He clicked again and the screen turned into a graph highlighting a yellow line that zigzagged over a dark background, caught between parallel blue lines. Clavert pointed at the screen. "The blue lines are the frequency. The yellow line is the analyzed voice. If you take Verdier's voice from different points of the recording and overlap them, they match perfectly."

"This is the other voice." Clavert returned to the previous screen, clicking the purple line. The graph appeared again, but this time the yellow line was broken and the field was much smaller. "In this case, the caller passed his voice through filters to distort and compress the sound, mixing vocal frequencies and making it unrecognizable. All you have to do is change just one of the filters slightly to get a different graph every time."

"Can we analyze the recording to find out the model of the equipment he used? Maybe we could find out who sold it," Hulot asked, interrupting.

"I don't think so," the technician said doubtfully. "You can buy these machines just about anywhere. There are several brands. Performance varies according to the cost and the brand but they can all do the same thing. And electronics change all the time so there's a big secondhand market. All this stuff generally ends up in the hands of home-recording enthusiasts, and almost always without receipts. I really don't think it's feasible."

"We'll see what we can do," Froben joined in, without seconding Clavert's pessimism. "We've got so little information that we can't overlook anything."

Hulot turned to observe Frank. He was looking around, apparently absorbed in his own thoughts, as if he already knew all this. Still, the inspector was sure that he had heard every word and was filing it all away. He turned back to Clavert.

"And what can you tell us about the fact that the phone call didn't go through the switchboard?"

"Well, I can't actually advance a theory. There are two basic possibilities. All switchboards have numbers that let you through. If you know them, you can avoid the switchboard operators. Radio Monte Carlo certainly isn't NASA as far as secrecy is concerned, so it wouldn't be hard for someone to get his hands on them. The second hypothesis is a little more complicated, but it's not science fiction. Actually, I think it sounds more likely."

"And that is?"

"I made some inquiries," Clavert said, leaning back in his chair. "The Radio Monte Carlo switchboard has a computer program and there's a function that lets you see the number calling in real time, for obvious reasons." He looked around to make sure that everyone was following him. "When the call came, no number appeared on the display, which means that the person calling had attached an electronic device to the phone that neutralized the switchboard function."

"Is that hard to do?"

"Anyone who knows electronics and telephones wouldn't have any problem. Any reasonably good hacker could do it through the Internet."

"Can we find out whether the call came from a fixed phone or a cell phone?" Hulot felt like a prisoner with walls everywhere he looked.

"No, but I'd exclude a cell phone. If he used the Web, cell phones are much slower and don't work as accurately. The person who did all that is too knowledgeable not to be aware of it."

"Any more tests you can do on the recording?"

"Not with the equipment I have. I'm going to send a copy of the DAT to the science lab in Lyon to see if they can get anything out of it."

"Good. Top priority," Hulot said, resting his hand on Clavert's shoulder. "If Lyon complains, we'll pressure them."

Clavert considered the subject closed. He unwrapped a stick of gum and put it in his mouth. There was a moment of silence. The four of them, each in his own way, thought through what had been said. Froben spoke first.

"Come on, let me get you some coffee."

He led them up the stairs and turned left at the landing. There was a coffee machine in the corner. Froben took out his card.

"Coffee, everyone?" The other two nodded. The inspector inserted his card, pressed a button, and the machine started to hum, dropping a tiny plastic cup down into the slot.

"What do you think, Frank?" Hulot asked the American, who was still silent.

"We don't have much," Frank said, deciding to voice his thoughts, "and any direction we take will lead nowhere. I told you, Nicolas, our man is smart, very smart. There are too many coincidences to think that he simply got lucky. For now, our only connection to this bastard is that phone call. If we're lucky enough, and if he's enough of a narcissist, he'll make others. And if we're *very* lucky, he'll make them to the same person. And if we're even luckier, he'll make a mistake. It's our only hope if we want to catch him and stop him before he kills again." He finished drinking his coffee and threw the plastic cup into the trash. "I think it's time to have a serious talk with Jean-Loup Verdier and the people at Radio Monte Carlo. I'm sorry to say this, but for the moment we're in their hands."

They headed toward the exit.

"I imagine there is already a certain amount of . . . agitation . . . in the Principality," Froben said to Hulot.

"Calling it 'agitation' is like calling Mike Tyson 'nervous.' Things are at the point of collapse. Monte Carlo is a postcard city, you know that. Image is everything. We spend tons of money to guarantee two things: elegance and safety. And then you get this nut who has elegantly kicked us in the ass. If this doesn't end soon, heads are going to roll." Hulot paused and sighed. "Including mine."

They reached the front door and said good-bye. Froben stood there watching them as they left. His prizefighter's face showed solidarity, but also relief that he wasn't in their place.

Hulot and Frank walked over to their car in the parking lot. When they were inside, as the engine started, the inspector turned to look at Frank. It was almost dinnertime, and he realized he was hungry.

"Café de Turin?" The Café de Turin was a bare-bones place, just benches and rickety tables in Place Garibaldi. They served excellent *coquillage,* with bottles of chilled Muscadet. He'd taken Frank and his wife when they had come to Europe, and the two of them had gone crazy over the huge counter with shellfish and the gloved staff busy opening them. They had watched with shining eyes as the waiters passed with huge trays of oysters and Venus clams and gigantic red shrimp. The tiny restaurant had become their culinary sanctum sanctorum. Hulot had hesitated at mentioning the place, afraid that the memory would upset Frank. But the American seemed changed, or he was at least trying. If he wanted to pull his head up out of the sand, that was the way to do it. Frank nodded, agreeing with both the choice and Hulot's good intentions. Whatever he was thinking, it did not show on his face.

"Café de Turin it is."

"You know," Hulot said, relaxing imperceptibly, "I'm tired of acting like a TV character. I feel like a caricature of Lieutenant Columbo. I need half an hour off. If I don't unwind a little, I'll go crazy."

It was evening and the city lights had come on. Frank looked out the window at the people coming and going in and out of houses, restaurants, and offices. Thousands of people with anonymous faces. The two men both knew that Hulot was lying. There was a killer in the midst of all these gentle summer people and until it was over, neither of them would be able to think about anything else.

12

Behind the control room window, Laurent Bedon, the director, did the countdown, turning down the fingers of his raised hand one by one. Then he pointed at Jean-Loup Verdier. The red light behind him lit up. They were on the air. The deejay pulled his chair a little closer to the mike at the end of its short stand on the table in front of him.

"Hello to all of you listening right now and to all of you who will be hearing our voices this evening. There'll be music and people sharing their lives with us, lives that don't always beat to the rhythm of the music we'd like to hear."

He stopped and pulled back slightly. The mixer broadcast the fierce notes of "Born to Be Wild" by Steppenwolf. A few seconds later, there was a fade-in to Jean-Loup's warm, inviting voice.

"We're here and we're ready, if there's anything we can do to help. For those who put their hearts into something and got a heartless answer, for those who made mistakes and bad choices, for those who won't find any peace until they figure out where the spice of life is hidden, for those who risk drowning in a flood of their own tears, we're here for you and we're live, just like you. We're waiting to hear your voice. You can expect our answer. This is Jean-Loup Verdier on Radio Monte Carlo. This is *Voices*.

Again, "Born to Be Wild." Once more, the race of discordant guitars down a rocky slope, raising dust and scattering gravel.

"Wow, he's good!" Frank Ottobre, next to Laurent in the

control room, could not keep from saying. The director turned to look at him with a smile.

"Isn't he?"

"I'm not surprised he's such a success. He's got a very direct and heartfelt style."

Barbara, the mixer sitting on his right next to the director's station, waved at Frank, pointing behind him. He turned his chair and saw Hulot motioning to him through the soundproof glass door. He got up and joined him outside the studio.

The inspector looked exhausted, like an overtired insomniac. Frank noticed the dark circles under his eyes, the gray hair in need of a trim, and the ring of grime and desolation around his collar. This was a man who had been seeing and hearing things that he gladly would have lived without. He was fifty-five and looked ten years older.

"How's it going here, Frank?"

"Nothing happening. The program's a hit. He's fantastic—a natural. I don't know how much they pay him, but it's got to be a lot. As far as we're concerned, nothing. Absolute silence."

"Want a Coke?"

"Come on, I know I'm American, but my grandparents were Sicilian. I drink coffee."

They went over to the machine at the end of the hall. Hulot rummaged for some coins in his pocket.

"The manager was really impressed by the fact that I'm with the FBI," Frank said with a broad smile, pulling out a card. "Refreshments are on the radio."

He put the card in the slot and pressed a button. When the coffee came out, he handed the cup filled with black liquid to Hulot. The inspector took a sip. It was disgusting. Or was it his mouth?

"Oh, I forgot. The handwriting analysis arrived."

"And?"

"Why bother asking if you already know the answer?"

"I don't know the details, but I can imagine what you're going to say," Frank replied, shaking his head.

"That's right, I forgot. You're with the FBI. You have quick intuition and a free coffee card. The message wasn't written by hand."

"No?"

"The bastard used a stencil. He glued the letters onto a piece of cardboard and cut them out. He had it with him and when he needed it, he leaned the stencil on the table and spilled the blood on top. How did you know?"

"I didn't." Frank shook his head. "But it seemed strange that a man so goddamn thorough would then make such an obvious blunder."

Hulot gave in and, with a grimace of revulsion, threw his half-finished coffee into the trash. He looked at his watch with a sigh.

"Let me go see if my wife is still married to me. There are two cars downstairs, two cops in each. You never know. The others are at their posts. I'll be at home if you need me."

"Okay, I'll call you if anything happens."

"I shouldn't say this, but I'm glad you're here tonight. And here in general. Good night, Frank."

"Good night, Nicolas. Say hi to Céline."

"Sure."

Frank watched his friend leave, his shoulders stooped under his jacket.

With the manager's support, they'd had the radio station under surveillance for three days, waiting for something to happen. When they had first told him of their plan, Robert Bikjalo had looked at them with half-closed eyes, as if he were avoiding the smoke from the reeking cigarette between his fingers. He had weighed Inspector Hulot's words as he brushed ashes from his Ralph Lauren shirt. The slits of his eyes made him look like a ferret.

"So, you think the guy might call again?"

"We're not sure. It's only a hopeful guess. But if he does, we'll need your help."

Hulot and Frank were sitting in front of him, in two leather armchairs. Frank noticed that the height of the chairs was carefully adjusted so that anyone sitting on the other side was looking down on them from above.

Bikjalo had turned to Jean-Loup Verdier, sitting on a comfortable couch that matched the armchairs. The deejay had run his hand through his dark, longish hair. He had stared at Frank with green, questioning eyes and rubbed his hands together nervously.

"I don't know whether I can do what you want. That is, I don't know how I'm supposed to act. A show is one thing, talking on the phone with normal people. It's different with a . . . with a . . ."

"I know it's not easy." Frank had come to his rescue, realizing that Jean-Loup was having a hard time saying the word *murderer*. "It's not easy for us to try to understand what he has in mind. But we'll be here, and we'll help you all we can and we'll be ready for whatever happens. We've even called an expert." He had turned to look at Nicolas who had been silent until then.

"We've got a psychiatrist," Hulot had said, "named Dr. Cluny. He's a police consultant and he helps out handling negotiations with criminals when there are hostages."

"Okay. If you tell me what to do, I'll do it."

Jean-Loup had looked at Bikjalo to give him the last word. The manager was staring at the filter of another Russian cigarette. He was still noncommittal.

"It's a big responsibility, of course . . ."

"Listen, I don't know if you really understand the situation," Frank had said, knowing what he was getting at. He had stood up, upsetting the chair hierarchy. Now he would dominate Bikjalo from above. "Just to clarify, let me show you something." Frank had bent down and taken several 5 x 7 photos from Hulot's briefcase on the floor near the armchairs. He had thrown them on the desk. "We're hunting a man capable of doing this."

They were pictures of the bodies of Jochen Welder and Arianna Parker and their disfigured heads. Bikjalo had looked at the photos and blanched. Hulot had smiled to himself and Frank had sat back down.

"This man is still at large and we think he's going to try it again. You're our only chance at stopping him. This isn't a strategy to raise the ratings. This is a manhunt, and people could live or die as a result."

Bikjalo was mesmerized, as if under a hypnotic spell. Frank had taken the pack of cigarettes on the table and examined it with apparent curiosity. "Besides the fact that, if this case is solved thanks to you, it'll give you and Jean-Loup a popularity you wouldn't dream of in a million years."

Bikjalo had relaxed. He had pushed the photos toward Frank, touching them with only the tips of his fingers as if they were burning. He had leaned back in his armchair looking relieved. The conversation was back to a subject he could understand.

"Okay. If we have a chance to help the law, a chance to be useful, Radio Monte Carlo certainly isn't going to back down. That's what *Voices* is all about, after all. Help for people needing help. There's only one thing I would like to ask you in return, if you will." He had paused. Frank was silent, so he had continued. "An exclusive interview with you, by Jean-Loup, as soon as it's all over. Before the others. Here on the radio."

Frank had looked at Hulot who had agreed with an imperceptible nod of his head.

"It's a deal." Frank had stood up again. "Our technicians will be coming with their equipment to tap the phones. There are a few other things, but they'll explain all that. We'll start tonight."

"Okay. I'll tell our people to do all they can to help."

The meeting was over. Everyone had stood up. Frank had

found himself facing the bewildered stare of Jean-Loup Verdier. He had grabbed his arm reassuringly.

"Thanks, Jean-Loup. You're doing a great thing. I'm sure you'll be fine. Afraid?"

The deejay had looked at him with two clear eyes, green as the sea. "I'm terrified."

13

Frank looked at the time. Jean-Loup was announcing the last commercial before the end of the program. Laurent gestured toward Barbara. The mixer turned some knobs to fade out the deejay's voice. They had a five-minute break. Frank got up and stretched.

"Tired?" asked Laurent, lighting a cigarette. The smoke rose and was absorbed by the exhaust fan.

"Not really. I'm used to waiting."

"Lucky you! I'm a nervous wreck," said Barbara as she stood up, tousling her red hair with her hands. Sergeant Morelli, sitting on a padded chair near the wall, raised his eyes from the sports page he was reading. He was suddenly more interested in the girl's body under her light summer dress than in the World Cup.

"Maybe it's none of my business," Laurent remarked, turning his swivel chair to face Frank, "but I want to ask you something."

"Ask, and I'll tell you if it's your business or not."

"What's it like to do a job like yours?"

Frank stared at him for a second as if he couldn't see him. Laurent assumed he was thinking about how to answer. He didn't know that Frank Ottobre was seeing a woman lying on a marble slab in a morgue, a woman who for better or for worse had been his wife. A woman whom no voice could ever awaken.

"What's it like?" Frank repeated, as if he needed to hear it again before he could answer. "After a while, all you want to do is forget."

Laurent turned back to the control board. He didn't really like the American with the athletic build and cold eyes, who seemed so removed from the world around him. His demeanor made any type of contact impossible. He was a man who gave nothing because he asked for nothing. But he was there, waiting, and not even he knew *what* he was waiting for.

"One more commercial," said Barbara, sitting back down at the mixer. Her voice interrupted the awkward silence. Although Morelli had returned to his sports page, he kept looking up at the girl's hair falling over the back of her chair.

Laurent gestured to Jacques, the console operator. Fade-out. They played a classic by Vangelis. A red light went on in Jean-Loup's cubicle. His voice again spread through the room and over the airwaves.

"It's eleven forty-five here at Radio Monte Carlo. The night is young. We've got the music you want to hear and the words you want to listen to. Nobody's judging but everybody's listening. This is *Voices*. Give us a call."

The music swelled again in the director's booth, slowly and rhythmically, like the waves of the sea. Behind the glass, Jean-Loup moved easily—he was on his own turf. In the control room, the phone display started to flash. Frank felt a strange tremor. Laurent gestured to Jean-Loup. The deejay nodded in response.

"Someone's on the line. Hello?"

A moment of silence, then unnatural noise. The music in the background suddenly sounded like a funeral march. Everyone recognized the voice that emerged from the amplifier: it was recorded permanently in their brains.

"Hello, Jean-Loup."

Frank straightened up in his chair as if shocked by electric current. He snapped his fingers in Morelli's direction. The sergeant roused himself immediately. He stood up and took the mike from the walkie-talkie hanging on his belt.

"Okay, guys. This is it. Contact. Keep your wits about you."

"Hi. Who is this?" asked Jean-Loup.

"You know who I am, Jean-Loup. I'm one and no one." There was a hint of a smile in the muffled voice.

"You're the one who called once before?"

Morelli rushed out of the room. He came back a moment later with Dr. Cluny, the psychiatrist who was in the hallway, waiting like everyone else. The doctor took a chair and sat down next to Frank. Laurent turned on the intercom that allowed him to speak directly into Jean-Loup's headphones without broadcasting his voice.

"Yes, my friend. I called once before and I will call again. Are the bloodhounds there?"

The electronic voice contained both fire and ice. The room felt stuffy, as though the air conditioners were sucking air in instead of blowing it out.

"What bloodhounds?"

A pause. Then the voice again.

"The ones hunting me. Are they there with you?"

Jean-Loup raised his eyes, lost. Dr. Cluny moved a little closer to the mike. "Agree with him. Tell him whatever he wants to hear, but get him talking."

"Why do you ask?" Jean-Loup resumed, with a leaden voice. "You knew they'd be here."

"I don't care about them. They don't matter. You're the one I care about."

Another pause.

"Why me? Why are you calling me?"

Another pause.

"I told you. Because you're like me, a voice without a face. But you're lucky. Of the two of us, you're the one who can get up in the morning and go out in the sun."

"And you can't?"

"No."

That sharp syllable was utter negation, a refusal that allowed no rebuttal.

"Why not?" asked Jean-Loup.

"Because someone decided it that way. There's very little I can do." The voice changed. It became suspended, softer, as if crossed by gusts of wind.

Silence. Cluny turned to Frank and whispered, surprised, "He's crying."

"There's very little I can do. But there is one way to repair the evil, and that is to fight it with the same evil."

"Why do evil when there are people all around you who can help?"

Another pause. A silence like a thought, then the voice again, and the fury of blame.

"I asked for help, but the only help I had killed me. Tell that to the bloodhounds. Tell everyone. There will be no pity because there is no pity. There will be no forgiveness because there is no forgiveness. There will be no peace because there is no peace. Just a bone for your bloodhounds . . ."

"What does that mean?"

A longer pause. The man on the phone had mastered his emotions. The voice was once again a breath of wind from nowhere.

"You like music, don't you, Jean-Loup?"

"Of course. Don't you?"

"Music doesn't let you down. Music is the end of the journey. Music is the journey."

Suddenly, just like the time before, the sound of an electric guitar, slow and seductive, was heard through the phone. A few notes, suspended and isolated, sun-lit, of a musician communicating with his instrument. Frank recognized the notes of "Samba Pa Ti," in the mastery of the fingers and imagination of whoever was playing. It was just guitar in a furious introduction, an explosion ending in thunderous applause. And as suddenly as it had come, the music was turned off.

"Here's the bone your bloodhounds wanted. I have to go now, Jean-Loup. I have things to do tonight."

"What do you have to do tonight?" the deejay asked in a shaking voice.

"You know what I'm doing tonight, my friend. You know very well."

"No, I don't. Tell me."

Silence.

"It wasn't my hand that wrote it, but now, everyone knows what I do at night . . ."

Another pause that felt like a drum roll.

"I kill . . ."

The voice clicked off the line but remained in their ears like a raven clinging to a telephone wire. His last words were like the flash of a camera: for an instant, they were all faces and bodies in a photo, as if each had lost the depth that allowed air to reach his or her lungs. Frank was the first to come to his senses.

"Morelli, call the guys and see if they found out anything. Laurent, did it all get recorded?"

The director was leaning on the table with his face in his hands. Barbara answered for him. "Yes. Can I faint now?"

Frank looked at her. Her face was white as a sheet under that mass of red hair. Her hands were shaking.

"No, Barbara. I still need you. Make a tape of that phone call right away. I need it in five minutes."

"I already have it. I had a second recorder ready on pause and I started it right after the phone call came in. All I have to do is rewind."

Morelli shot an admiring glance at the girl and made sure she noticed.

"That's great. Morelli?"

"One of the guys is coming." Morelli said. He stopped staring at Barbara and blushed, as if caught in the act. "I doubt there's any good news."

"Well?" Frank said to a swarthy young man who had just entered.

"Nothing." The technician shrugged. He looked disappointed. "We couldn't trace the call. That bastard must have some pretty good equipment."

"Cell phone or fixed?"

"We don't know. We even have a satellite unit, but we found nothing, either from a fixed phone or a cell."

"Dr. Cluny?" Frank asked, turning to the psychiatrist, still sitting in his chair. The doctor was pensive, biting the inside of his cheek.

"I don't know. I have to listen to the tape again. The only thing I can say is that I have never heard anything like this in my entire life."

Frank pulled out his cell phone and dialed Hulot's number. The inspector answered right away. He obviously was not asleep.

"Nicolas, this is it. Our friend had shown up again."

"I know. I heard the program. I'm getting dressed and I'll be right there."

"Good."

"Are you still at the station?"

"Yes. We'll wait for you." Frank hung up. "Morelli, as soon as the inspector gets here, I want a meeting. Laurent, I need your help too. I think I saw a conference room near the manager's office. Can we use it?"

"Sure. There's a DAT machine and anything else you need."

"Great. We don't have much time and we have to fly."

In the confusion, they completely forgot about Jean-Loup. His voice reached them through the intercom.

"Is it all over, now?" They saw him leaning on his chair, immobile, a butterfly pinned to a piece of velvet. Frank pressed the button to talk to him.

"No, Jean-Loup. I'm sorry to say that this is only the beginning. You were great."

In the silence that followed, they saw Jean-Loup slowly rest his arms on the table and cover his face.

14

Hulot arrived soon after, along with Bikjalo. The manager was very upset. He entered the station lagging behind the inspector, as if he didn't want to have anything to do with the whole business. He probably only now realized what it all meant. There were armed men wandering around the station, and there was a new, unfamiliar tension. There was a voice, and with that voice, an awareness of death.

Frank was waiting for them, leaning against the conference room door. Morelli was next to him, neither of them speaking. They all went into the room together where the others were sitting around the long table, waiting. The panel curtains were drawn and the windows were open. The faint noise of the Monte Carlo night traffic reached them from outside.

Hulot sat down to Frank's right, leaving him the seat at the head of the table and the tacit job of running the meeting. He was wearing the same shirt and did not seem any more rested than when he had left.

"We're all here now. Aside from Mr. Bikjalo and the inspector—who heard the program at home—we were all here this evening. Everyone heard what happened. We don't have many facts to work with. I'm sorry to say that we couldn't trace the call." Frank stopped for a moment. The young technician and his colleague shifted with embarrassment. "It's nobody's fault. The man knows what he's doing and how to avoid being traced. The technology we generally use for this was used against us today. So there's no help that way. Since it might give us some clues, I suggest we listen to the recording of the call before making any hypotheses."

Dr. Cluny nodded and everyone else seemed to agree. Frank turned to Barbara who was standing at the back of the room next to a table with a stereo.

"Barbara, start the tape, please."

The girl pressed a button and the room was again filled with a ghostly presence. Again they listened to Jean-Loup's voice from the world of the living and the voice of the man from his place of darkness. In the silence of the room, the tape played to the last words.

"I kill . . ."

"The man's out of his mind!" Bikjalo couldn't help crying out when it was over.

Dr. Cluny took the remark personally. His myopic gaze was hidden behind gold-and-tortoiseshell glasses. His pointed, aquiline nose resembled the beak of an owl. The psychiatrist addressed Bikjalo but he was speaking to everyone.

"In the strict sense of the word, he is certainly insane. Remember that this man has already killed two people by a horrifying method. That indicates an explosive inner fury but also lucidity rarely found when a crime is committed. He calls and we cannot trace his call. He kills and leaves absolutely no significant clue. He shouldn't be underestimated. That is clear from the fact that he doesn't underestimate us. He's challenging us, but not underestimating us." He removed his glasses, revealing two red marks at the bridge of his nose, and put them right back on, as if he felt naked without them. Cluny probably never wore contact lenses. "He knew very well that we would be here; he knows that the hunt has begun and he is probably better informed than most. And he knows that we are groping in the dark, because we are missing the key needed to solve any crime."

He paused. Frank noticed that Cluny was very good at getting people's attention. Bikjalo was probably thinking the same thing, because he started to look at the doctor with almost professional interest. The psychiatrist continued.

"We have absolutely no idea as to his motive. We don't know what moved him to kill and to do what he did afterward. It's clearly a ritual that has special meaning for him, though we don't know what that meaning is. His insanity alone is no clue because it isn't obvious. This man lives in our midst, like a normal person. He does the things that normal people do: he has a drink, buys the paper, goes to restaurants, and listens to music. Most of all, he listens to music. And that's why he calls here. In a program that offers help to people in trouble, he seeks help he doesn't want where there is music he likes to listen to."

"Why do you say 'help he doesn't want'?" Frank asked.

"His 'no' to the offer of help was very adamant. He has already decided that nobody can help, whatever his problem is. The trauma inside him must have conditioned him terribly until the point when it detonated the latent rage that people like him carry inside from birth. He hates the world and he probably thinks the world owes him. He must have suffered horrendous humiliations, at least from his point of view. Music seems to provide the few happy moments of his existence. The only indication we get from him is when he talks about the language of music. That's a message. He gave us another clue that we should combine with the clue from the first message. It is a challenge but also an unconscious prayer. In reality, he's begging us to stop him, if we can, because he'll never stop of his own accord."

In the room, they could feel a world of shadows, mold, and cobwebs. A place that had never seen the light of day. A kingdom of rats.

"Barbara, let's hear the part about music again."

"Okay."

The girl pushed a button. Right away, the room was filled with the notes of the guitar, lost in a version of "Samba Pa Ti." It was less meticulous than usual, less staccato, a softer interpretation. There was applause from the audience at the first notes, as in a live concert when the audience recognizes a hit song. When it was over, Frank turned to everyone.

"Remember that the piece of music in the first call was a clue about who his victims would be. The soundtrack of a movie about a race car driver and his girlfriend. *A Man and a Woman.* Like Jochen Welder and Arianna Parker. Does anyone have any idea what *this* song might mean?"

"Well, I think we all know it," said Jacques, the sound technician sitting at the end of the table. He cleared his throat as if he found it difficult to speak up in that setting.

"Don't take anything for granted," Hulot scolded politely. "Pretend that nobody in this room knows anything about music, even if that sounds ridiculous. Sometimes there are clues where you least expect them."

"I just meant to say that it's a very famous song," Jacques continued, blushing and raising his right hand as though apologizing. "It's 'Samba Pa Ti,' by Carlos Santana. It's a live performance because there's an audience. And it must have been a huge audience, like in a stadium, for that type of response—although live recordings are sometimes reinforced in the studio by adding recorded applause."

"That's it?" asked Laurent, lighting a cigarette. The smoke circled in the air and wound its way toward the open window, then disappeared into the night. The smell of sulfur from the match lingered in the air.

Jacques blushed again and sat quietly, not knowing what to add. Hulot realized that he felt awkward and smiled at him.

"Good. Thank you. That's a fine start. Does anyone have anything else to say? Does the song have any special meaning?

Was it ever associated with any strange event, or person? Is it connected to a story of any kind?"

The people in the room looked at one another, as if trying to help each other remember.

"Does anyone remember *this* version?" Frank asked, suggesting another train of thought. "If it's a live recording, does anyone have any idea where it was made? Or what album it's from? Jean-Loup?"

The deejay was sitting absentmindedly next to Laurent without saying a word, as if the conversation had nothing to do with him. He still seemed to be in shock after speaking to that unknown voice on the phone. He looked up and shook his head.

"Could it be a bootleg recording?" asked Morelli.

"I don't think so," Barbara said, shaking her head. "It sounds kind of dated to me. Artistically and technically. It's an old recording, analog, not digital. And it's on vinyl, an old LP. The quality's great. It doesn't sound like an amateur recording on low-fi equipment, given the period's technical limitations. So it must be a commercial LP, unless it's an old lacquer disc that was never produced."

"A lacquer disc?" asked Frank, looking at the girl. He could not help but share Morelli's admiration. Barbara had a great mind and a body to match. If the sergeant was interested in her, he'd better be up to par.

"A lacquer disc was a trial disc that record companies used to make, before there were CDs," Bikjalo explained for her. "Generally, there were only a few copies in circulation and they deteriorated easily. Some lacquer disks are collector's items. But since lacquer doesn't hold up, the quality of the sound gets much worse every time it's played. That's not what we're dealing with here."

There was silence again, indicating that they had said all they could. Hulot stood up, signaling the end of the meeting.

"Ladies and gentlemen, it's useless for me to remind you that even a minor detail could be of the utmost importance in this case. We have a killer at large who is mocking us. He even throws us clues about his intention, and we know what that is: to kill again. Whatever comes to mind, at any time of day or night, don't hesitate to call me, Frank Ottobre, or Sergeant Morelli. Take our phone numbers before you go."

One by one, they all got up and left the room. The two police technicians left first, to avoid any direct dealings with Hulot. The others stopped long enough to get a card with the phone numbers from Morelli. The sergeant took extra time giving his card to Barbara who did not seem to mind at all. At another time, Frank would have considered that interest a defect on her part. Just then, however, it seemed like a victory of life over the darkness of that night. He let it go and went over to Cluny who was whispering to Hulot. The two men stepped aside to let him into their conversation.

"That phone call had an important clue that'll keep us from getting confused or wasting time . . ."

"What?" asked Hulot

"It proved that the call wasn't a trick and that he really is the man who killed those two people on the boat."

"It wasn't my hand that wrote it . . ." quoted Frank, nodding.

"That's right." Cluny continued, looking at him, pleased. "Only the real killer could know that the writing was done mechanically and not by hand. I didn't mention it to the others because it's apparently one of the few things regarding the investigation that is not public knowledge."

"Exactly. Thank you, Dr. Cluny. Excellent work."

"Thank you. There are some things I have to analyze. Language, vocal stress, syntax, and so forth. I need a copy of the tape."

"It's yours. Good night."

The psychiatrist left the room.

"Now what?" asked Bikjalo.

"You've all done all you can," answered Frank. "Now it's our turn."

Jean-Loup seemed dazed. The experience had definitely taken a toll on him. Perhaps what had happened had not been as exciting as he had imagined.

Death is never exciting. Death is blood and flies, thought Frank.

"You're good, Jean-Loup. I couldn't have done any better. Radio experience had nothing to do with it. When you're dealing with a killer, it's always the first time. Go home now and try not to think about it for a while."

I kill . . .

Everyone knew that sleep would be impossible that night. Not while someone was out there searching for a pretext for his ferocity and more fuel for his madness. So that the whispers in his mind would merge with the screams of a new victim.

"Thanks. I think I'll go home." Jean-Loup said, stooping his shoulders in defeat. He said good night and left, carrying a burden that could crush a much stronger man. When you got right down to it, he was merely a deejay who broadcast music and words on the radio.

"Let's go. There's no use for us here anymore." Hulot headed to the door.

"I'll go with you. I'm leaving too. Although I don't think I'll be able to sleep tonight . . ." said Bikjalo, stepping aside for Frank.

When they reached the door, they heard someone click out the code. The door opened and Laurent appeared. He was very excited.

"Thank goodness. I was hoping I'd find you here. I have an idea. I know who can help us!"

"With what?" asked Hulot.

"With the music. I know who can help us identify it."

"Who's that?"

"Pierrot!"

Bikjalo's face lit up.

"Of course! 'Rain Boy.'"

"'Rain Boy'?" Hulot and Frank looked at each other.

"Pierrot's a kid who helps out at the radio and takes care of the archive," explained the station manager. "He's twenty-two with the mind of a child. He's Jean-Loup's discovery and the boy adores him. He would jump off a cliff if Jean-Loup asked him to. They call him 'Rain Boy' because he's like Dustin Hoffman in *Rain Man*. He's limited, but he's a human computer when it comes to music. It's the only gift he's got, but it's phenomenal."

"Where does this Pierrot live?" asked Frank, looking at his watch.

"I don't really know. His last name's Corbette and he lives with his mother just outside Menton. The father was a asshole who took off when he found out the boy was retarded."

"Does anyone have his address or phone number?"

"Our secretary's got the number," Laurent replied, going over to Raquel's computer. "Their home number and the mother's cell."

"I feel badly for Mme Corbette and her son," Inspector Hulot said, looking at the time, "but I'm afraid we're going to have to wake them in the middle of the night."

15

Everything about Pierrot's mother was the color gray, and she was wearing a dress to match.

Sitting in a chair in the conference room, she watched the men standing around her son with dazed eyes. They had woken her in the middle of the night and she had been terrified when they had said it was the police. They had made her wake Pierrot and dress quickly, and then they had pushed them into a police car that had taken off at a speed that frightened her to death.

They had left the working-class apartment complex where they lived. The woman was worried about her neighbors. Thank heaven nobody had seen them leave in a police car like common criminals. Her life was already hard enough, with all the whispering and lowered voices when she passed. She didn't need anything more.

The inspector, the old man with the nice face, had assured her that she had nothing to worry about, that they needed her son for something important. And now they were there and she was wondering how someone like her Pierrot could possibly help them, her son whom she loved as if he were a genius but whom others barely considered stupid.

She looked anxiously at Robert Bikjalo, the manager of Radio Monte Carlo, who had allowed her son to stay there in a safe place and work with what he loved most in the world, music. What did the police have to do with it? She prayed that Pierrot, simple as he was, hadn't done anything wrong. She couldn't bear the idea that they might find some pretext to take her son away from her. The idea of being without him or of him without her was terrifying. She felt the cold fingers of anxiety creep into her stomach and squeeze tightly. As long as . . .

Bikjalo flashed her a reassuring grin, a sign that everything was fine. And she turned back to watch the younger man, the one with the hard face and the unshaved beard who spoke French with a slight foreign accent. He squatted down on the floor so that he was at the level of Pierrot, who was sitting in a chair.

"I'm sorry we woke you, Pierrot, but we need your help for something important. You're the only one who knows how to do it."

The woman relaxed. The man's face might be frightening, but his voice was calm and gentle. Pierrot was not afraid of him in the least. Actually, that unexpected nocturnal adventure, the trip in the police car, and the fact that he was suddenly the center of attention filled him with pride. She felt a sharp stab of love and protectiveness for that strange son of hers who lived in a world all his own, made of music and pure thoughts.

"We're going to play some music for you, a song," the younger man continued in his soothing voice. "Listen to it. Listen carefully. See if you recognize it and if you can tell us what it is or what record it's from. Want to try?"

Pierrot was silent. Then he nodded imperceptibly.

The man stood up and pressed the button on a recorder behind him. The notes of a guitar suddenly filled the room. The woman observed her son's face, taut with concentration, engrossed in listening to the sound from the speakers. The music ended a few seconds later. The man squatted back down next to Pierrot.

"Do you want to hear it again?"

Still in silence, the boy shook his head.

"Do you recognize it?"

"It's there," Pierrot said softly, turning his eyes to Bikjalo as if he were the only person who mattered.

"You mean we have it?" The manager came closer.

Pierrot nodded again, with emphasis.

"It's there, in the room."

"What room?" asked Hulot, coming near.

"The room is the archive, downstairs in the basement. That's where Pierrot works. There are thousands of records and CDs and he knows each and every one of them."

"If you know where it is in the room, can you go get it for us?" Frank asked gently. The boy was doing them an enormous favor and he did not want to frighten him.

Pierrot looked at the manager again, as if asking permission.

"Go on, Pierrot. Bring it here, please."

Pierrot got up and crossed the room with his odd loping gait. He disappeared from view, followed by his mother's anxious, astonished gaze.

Inspector Hulot went up to the woman.

"Madame, excuse me again for the barbaric way in which we woke you and brought you here. I hope you weren't too frightened. You can't imagine how useful your son could be tonight. We are truly grateful to you for allowing him to help us."

The woman melted with pride for her son. She shrank from embarrassment at the cheap dress she had hurriedly pulled on over her nightgown.

Pierrot returned a few minutes later. He was holding a somewhat worn record cover under his arm. He went up to them and placed it on the table. He removed the vinyl record with extreme caution to avoid touching it with his fingers.

"Here it is," said Pierrot.

"Can we hear it, please?" asked the younger man with his thoughtful voice.

The boy went over to the stereo, handling it like an expert. He pressed a couple of buttons, raised the lid, and put on the record. He pushed PLAY and the turntable began to spin. Then he delicately took the arm and rested it on the LP. The notes that played were the same ones that an unknown man had sent them a little while before, daring them to put a stop to his wanderings through the night.

There was a moment of general euphoria. Everyone found a way of applauding Pierrot's small personal triumph as he turned around with an innocent smile. His mother looked at him with a dedication in her eyes that his success could only partly repay. A moment, only one moment, when the world seemed to remember her son and give him some of the satisfaction it had always denied. She started to cry. The inspector gently put a hand on her shoulder.

"Thank you, Madame. Your son was magnificent. Everything is fine now. I'll have someone take you right home in one of our cars. You work, don't you?"

The woman raised her face streaked with tears, smiling in embarrassment for that moment of weakness. "Yes, I keep house for an Italian family here in Monte Carlo."

"Leave the family's name with Sergeant Morelli, that man in the brown jacket," said the inspector, smiling back. "We'll arrange for you to have a couple of days' paid vacation for tonight's disturbance. That way you can spend some time with your son, if you like." The inspector went over to Pierrot. "As for you, young man, would you like to spend the day in a police car, talk on the radio with the switchboard, and become an honorary policeman?"

Pierrot probably didn't know what an honorary policeman was, but the idea of driving around in a police car made his eyes light up.

"Will you give me handcuffs too? And can I work the siren?"

"Of course, whenever you like. And you'll have your own pair of bright shiny handcuffs if you promise to ask our permission before you arrest anyone."

Hulot nodded to a policeman who would take Pierrot and his mother home. As they left, he could hear the boy say to his mother, "Now that I'm an *honorable policeman*, I'm going to arrest Mme Narbonne's daughter who's always laughing at me. I'll put her in prison and . . ." They never did find out what would happen to Mme Narbonne's unfortunate daughter because the three of them reached the end of the hallway and Pierrot's voice faded away.

"Carlos Santana. *Lotus,*" Frank mused, leaning against the table looking thoughtfully at the record cover that the boy had brought from the archive. "Recorded live in Japan, 1975 . . ."

"Why did that man want us to listen to a song recorded in Japan thirty years ago?" Morelli wondered, picking up the cover. "What did he want to tell us?" He looked at it carefully and turned it over.

Hulot watched out the window as the car with Pierrot and his mother drove away. He turned and raised his wrist to look at the time. Four thirty.

"I don't know, but we'd better try to find out as soon as possible." He paused before expressing everyone's thought. "Unless it's already too late."

16

Allen Yoshida signed the check and handed it to the caterer. He had brought the staff of his favorite Parisian restaurant, Le Pré Catelan in Bois de Boulogne, down for the party. It had cost him a fortune, but it was worth it. He still had the rarefied taste in his mouth of the frog and pistachio soup on that evening's menu.

"Thank you, Pierre. It was all magnificent, as usual. As you can see, I added a gratuity for you on the check."

"Thank you, Mr. Yoshida. You're very generous, as always. You don't have to see me out, I know the way. Good night."

"Good night, my friend."

Pierre gave a slight bow that Yoshida returned. The man walked out silently and disappeared behind the dark wooden door. Yoshida heard his car start. He picked up a remote control and pointed it at the panel on the wall to his left. The panel opened silently, revealing a series of screens, each connected to a closed-circuit camera located in different corners of the house. He saw Pierre's car drive out the front gate and his security guards close it after him.

He was alone.

He crossed the large room with remains of the party everywhere. The catering staff had removed what they were supposed to and left discreetly, as usual. His servants would arrive the next day to finish the job. Allen Yoshida didn't like having people in his house. His help came in the morning and left at night. He asked them to stay over only when necessary, or else he used an outside organization.

He preferred to be alone at night, without the fear that indiscreet eyes and ears might accidentally find out something he wanted to keep to himself.

He went out in the garden through the enormous French doors that opened onto the night. Outside, a skillful play of colored lights created shadows among the trees, bushes, and flower beds, the work of a landscape architect he had brought down from Finland. He loosened the bow tie of his elegant Armani tuxedo and unbuttoned his white shirt. Then he slipped off his patent leather shoes without untying them. He bent down and removed his silk socks as well, leaving them behind. He loved the feeling of bare feet on the damp grass. He walked over to the illuminated ground-level swimming pool. In daylight it seemed to end in the sea, and now it looked like an enormous aquamarine set in the dark of the night.

Yoshida lay down on a teak chaise longue by the pool and stretched his legs. He looked around. There were a few lights out at sea on that night of the waning moon. In front of him, he could make out the glare of Monte Carlo, the home of most of his guests that evening.

His house was to his left and he turned to look at it. He loved that house and felt privileged to own it. He loved its old-fashioned lines, the elegance of its construction combined with its functional severity. It was the work of a brilliant architect who had designed the house for the diva of the era, Greta Garbo. When he purchased it, the house had been closed up for years and he had it renovated by an equally brilliant contemporary architect, Frank Gehry himself, of the Guggenheim Museum Bilbao.

He had given him free rein, asking only that he retain the spirit of the house. The result was a resounding success: impeccable style married to the most advanced technology. A residence that left everyone dumbfounded, exactly as he had been the first time he had gone inside. The fee had a seemingly endless number of zeros, and he had paid it without batting an eye.

He leaned against the back of the chaise longue, moving his head to stretch his neck. He slipped his hand into the inside pocket of his jacket and took out a tiny gold bottle. Unscrewing the cap, he tapped a pinch of white powder onto the back of his hand. He brought his hand to his nose and sniffed the cocaine directly, then rubbed his nostrils with his fingers to remove the residue of powder.

Everything around him was proof of his success and power. Still, Allen Yoshida had no illusions. He remembered his father who used to break his back unloading crates of fish onto his truck from the cold store cars when they came in from the coast, and then drove around to supply the city's Japanese restaurants. He remembered when he came home from work, preceded by the stench of fish that he could never get rid of, as much as he washed his hands. He remembered their dilapidated house in the run-down neighborhood of New York and he remembered hearing his parents talk about how they needed to repair the roof and the plumbing from when he was a child. He could still hear the pipe gurgling every time they turned on a faucet, and the rush of rusty water that poured out. You had to wait a couple of minutes before the water ran clear and you could wash. He had grown up there, the son of a Japanese man and an American woman, straddling two cultures, a *gaijin* in the Japanese community's limited way of thinking and a Jap for white Americans. For everyone else—blacks, Puerto Ricans, Italians—he was just one more half-breed on the city streets.

He felt the lucid rush of the cocaine start to circulate and he ran a hand through his thick, shiny hair.

It had been a long time since he had had any illusions. Actually, he never had any. Everyone who had come to his home that evening would not have budged were he not the man he was, with those billions of dollars. None of them was really interested in knowing whether or not he was a genius. What they cared about was the fact that his genius had helped him amass a personal fortune that made him one of the world's ten richest men.

Nothing else counted very much for anyone. Once you achieved the result, it did not matter *how*. Everyone knew him as the brilliant creator of Sacrifiles, the operating system that competed with Microsoft on the world computer market. He was eighteen when he had launched it and created Zen Electronics with a loan from a bank that believed in the project after he had shown a group of astonished investors his system's simple operations.

Billy La Ruelle should have been with him to share in the success. Billy La Ruelle, his best friend, who had studied with him at the same computer school, who had come home one day with the dazzling idea for a revolutionary operating system that ran in a DOS environment. They had worked on it in absolute secrecy, he and Billy, for months, day and night, on their two computers linked in a network. Unfortunately, Billy had fallen from the roof when they had gone up to fix the TV antenna the day before the Bulls-Lakers play-off. He had slipped on the slanted roof like a sled on ice and had found himself hanging from the drainpipe. Yoshida had stood there watching, immobile, doing nothing as Billy begged him for help. His body was suspended in the air and the left side of the metal sheeting was giving way under his weight. He could see the knuckles of his hands grow white in the effort to hold on to the sharp edge of the drainpipe, and to his life.

Billy had fallen with a scream, looking at him desperately with widening eyes. He had landed with a thud on the concrete in front of the garage and laid there motionless, his neck bent in an unnatural position. The piece of drainpipe that had broken off had ironically fallen right into the basketball net attached to the wall outside the house where he and Billy played during their breaks. As Billy's mother ran out of the house screaming, Yoshida had gone into his friend's bedroom and downloaded everything on the hard drive onto floppy discs before erasing it so that nothing remained. He had slipped the discs into his back pocket and then run out into the courtyard, over to Billy's lifeless body.

Billy's mother was sitting on the ground. She had her son's head in her lap and was stroking his hair. Allen Yoshida had cried his crocodile tears. He had knelt down beside her, feeling the hard surface of the diskettes in his pocket. A neighbor had called an ambulance. It had arrived in record time, preceded by a siren that was strangely similar to the cries of Billy's mother, and stopped with a screech of tires and brakes. Men had gotten out and calmly carried off his friend's body, covered with a white sheet.

An old story. One to forget. Now, his parents lived in Florida and his father had finally managed to rub his hands clean of the stench of fish. And even if he hadn't, thanks to Allen's dollars, anyone would swear that the stench was perfume. He had paid to put Billy's mother through rehab to stop her drinking and had bought his parents a house in a nice neighborhood where they lived without any problems, thanks to the money he sent them every month. Once, when they had met, his friend's mother had kissed his hands. As often as he washed them, he had felt that kiss burning on his flesh for a long time.

Yoshida got up and went into the house. He took off his jacket, threw it over his shoulder, and carried it with one hand. He felt the dampness of the night penetrate the thin fabric of his shirt, making it stick to his skin. He picked a white gardenia from a bush and brought it to his nostrils. The cocaine numbed his nose, but he could still smell its delicate fragrance.

He went back into the living room and took the remote control out of his pocket, pushing a button. The shatterproof windows closed without a sound, sliding down on perfectly oiled hinges. He turned off the lights the same way, leaving a glimmer in a few hall lights set into the wall. He was alone, finally. It was the moment to dedicate a little time to himself and to his pleasure, his secret pleasure.

The models, the bankers, the rock stars, the actors who flocked to his parties were only splashes of color on a white wall, faces and words to be forgotten as easily as they were noticed. Allen Yoshida was a handsome man. He had inherited his Yankee proportions and height from his American mother and the tight, well-defined Asian bone structure from his father. His face was a mixture of the two races, with the arrogant charm of all accidents. His money and his looks had universal appeal. And everyone was intrigued by his solitude. Women, especially, showed off breasts and bodies full of promises so simple to fulfill in that obsessive search for contact that was life. Faces that were so open, so easy to read, that even before he got started he could already read the words "The End". To Allen Yoshida, sex was strictly the pleasure of the stupid. From the living room, he walked down a short hallway that led to the kitchen and the dining room. He stopped in front of a surface of curved briarwood. When he pushed a button on the right, the surface slid into the wall, revealing steps leading downstairs. He walked down impatiently. He had a new video to watch that had been delivered the day before. This was his first chance to do so comfortably, sitting in his projection room with his flat screen, enjoying every minute of the video with a glass of chilled champagne.

When he had let Billy La Ruelle fall off the roof, Allen Yoshida not only became one of the richest men in the world, but he had discovered something else that would change his life. Seeing his friend's widened eyes and terrified face as he fell through the air, hearing the desperation in his voice as he pleaded, *had given him pleasure*. He had only realized later, at home, when he had undressed to take a shower and discovered that his pants were soiled with semen. In the tragic moment that had caused his friend's death, Yoshida had had an orgasm.

Ever since then, since the very moment of his discovery, he had attained pleasure without hesitation, just as he had attained riches without regret. He smiled. That smile was like a luminous cobweb on an indecipherable face. Money did buy everything. Complicity, silence, crime, life and death. For money, men were willing to kill, and to give and receive suffering. He knew that well, every time he added a new video to his collection and paid an exorbitant price for it.

He had films of real torture and killings, of men, women, and sometimes children. They were taken from the street to secure places and then filmed as they were subjected to every type of torture and rape before being burned alive. A black man was literally flayed until he became a red mass of blood. Their screams of pain were music to his ears as he sipped the chilled wine and waited for the conclusion of his pleasure.

And it was all *real*.

There was a large, illuminated room at the bottom of the stairs. On the right were two Hermelin billiard tables, one traditional and one American, built especially for him and imported from Italy. The cues and everything else needed for the game were hanging from the wall. There were armchairs and couches around a bar, one of many scattered throughout the house.

He passed by and then stopped. To his right, on a wooden pedestal about four feet high, was a marble statue from the Hellenic period of Venus playing with Eros. It was lit by halogen from the ceiling. He did not stop to gaze at the delicacy of the work, or the tension between the two figures that the sculptor had artfully depicted. Instead, he put his hands on the base of the statue and pushed. The wooden lid turned on itself, revealing the hollow center of the base. On the bottom was the dial of an electronic combination lock.

Yoshida punched out the code that only he knew and the wall slid noiselessly aside, disappearing into the wall on the left. His realm was here. Pleasure awaited him, in secret, as absolute pleasure always did.

He was about to cross the threshold when he felt a violent blow between his shoulders, the flash of a sharp pain, and the immediate chill of darkness.

FOURTH CARNIVAL

When Allen Yoshida comes to, his vision is hazy and his head hurts. He tries to move his arms, but he cannot. He squints to regain his focus. Finally, he reopens his eyes and discovers that he is in an armchair in the middle of the room. His hands and legs are tied with wire. His mouth is covered by a piece of tape.

In front of him, sitting on a chair, a man is staring at him in silence. He can see nothing of him. The man is wearing what seems to be an ordinary black canvas work shirt, at least four or five sizes too large. His face is covered with a black ski mask and the upper part of his face around the eyes is protected by large dark glasses with reflective lenses. He is wearing a black hat with the brim pulled down. His hands are covered with large gloves, also black.

Yoshida's terrified gaze runs down the figure. Under the long coat, his black pants are of the same fabric as the shirt. They are much larger than the man's size. The long pants fall on canvas shoes, forming folds, hip-hop style. Yoshida notices something strange. There are protrusions at his knees and elbows that hold the material of his clothes, as if the person in front of him had extensions on his arms and legs.

They sit in silence for what seems an interminable time to Yoshida. One man who has decided not to speak and one who cannot.

How did he get in? Even though he was alone in the house, the villa was surrounded by impenetrable security, consisting of armed men, dogs, and cameras. How did he get by all that? And most of all, what did he want from him? Money? If that is the problem, he can give him all he wants. He can give him anything he wants. There is nothing that money cannot buy. Nothing. If only he could speak . . .

The man continues to look at him in silence, sitting on the chair.

Yoshida makes a faint moan, muffled by the tape on his mouth. The man's voice finally comes out of that dark blotch of his body.

"Hello, Mr. Yoshida."

The voice is warm and resonant, but strangely enough, to the man tied to the chair, it sounds harder and sharper than the wire cutting into his arms and legs.

He widens his eyes and moans again.

"Don't try to answer. I can't understand you. And in any case, I'm not remotely interested in what you have to say."

The man gets up from the chair, moving unnaturally because of the oversized clothes and the extensions on his arms and legs. He goes behind him. Yoshida tries to turn his head around to keep him in sight. He hears the voice again, coming from somewhere behind his back.

"You've got yourself a wonderful place here. A discreet place for your little private joys. Some pleasures in life are hard to share. I understand you, Mr. Yoshida. I don't think anyone can understand you better than I . . ."

As he speaks, the man returns to face him. He gestures at the room around them, rectangular and windowless. There is a ventilation system with air nozzles set in the walls just below the ceiling. In the back, there is a bed against the wall with silk sheets. There is a painting over the bed, the only lapse in the room's monklike simplicity. The two longer walls are almost entirely covered in mirrors, the optical illusion of a larger room to eliminate the sense of claustrophobia.

In front of the bed, there is a series of flat screens connected to a group of VHS and DVD players. When a movie is shown, you can feel surrounded by images and be at their center. There are also cameras that can shoot any point of the room with no corner overlooked. The cameras are also connected to the home movie system.

"Is this where you relax, Mr. Yoshida? Is this where you forget about the world when you want the world to forget about you?"

The man's warm voice transmits cold. Yoshida feels it climb up his arms and legs that are growing numb as the wire cuts his circulation. He feels the wire ripping into his flesh, just like that voice digging into his brain.

With his artificial movements, the man bends over a canvas bag on the floor next to the chair. He takes out a record, an old LP with the cover protected by a piece of plastic.

"Do you like music, Mr. Yoshida? This is heavenly, believe me. Something for a real connoisseur. Which of course is what you are." He goes over to the stereo against the wall to the left and looks at it. He turns to him and the light in the room is a brief flash reflected in his glasses. "My compliments. You've forgotten nothing. I was prepared for an alternative, in case you didn't have a record player, but I see you're well equipped."

He turns on the system and puts the record on the turntable after slipping it carefully out of its cover. He places the needle on the LP and the notes of a trumpet emerge from the speakers and spread through the room. It is sorrowful, mournful music, intended to evoke a melancholy that leaves you breathless, sharp grief demanding only to be forgotten. It is music without memory, the kind of music that memory desires so that it can cease to exist.

For a moment, the man stands motionless, listening. Yoshida imagines him with his eyes half-closed behind the dark glasses. Just for a moment, then he snaps back.

"Lovely, isn't it? Robert Fulton, one of the greats. Maybe the greatest of them all. And misunderstood, like all the great ones were." He goes and looks curiously at the controls of the video system. "I hope I can understand this. I wouldn't want your equipment to be beyond my meager abilities, Mr. Yoshida. No, it looks fairly simple."

He presses some buttons and the monitors go on, with the snowlike effect they have when there is no signal. He busies himself with the buttons and the video cameras finally go into action. The screen shows Yoshida, immobilized in the armchair in the middle of the room, sitting before an empty chair.

The man seems pleased with himself.

"Excellent. This system is excellent. But then, I wouldn't have expected anything less of you."

The man comes back in front of his prisoner, turns the chair around, and sits astride it. He leans his deformed arms on the back of the chair. The extensions on his elbows hold the canvas of his shirt.

"You're wondering what I want, aren't you?"

Yoshida gives a lengthy moan.

"I know. I know. If you think it's your money I want, don't worry. I'm not interested in money. Not yours or anyone else's. I want a trade."

Yoshida exhales through his nose. Thank god. Whoever the man is, whatever his price, there might be some way of reaching an agreement. If it isn't money he wants, it is certainly something that money can buy. There is nothing that money can't buy, he repeats to himself. Nothing.

He relaxes in the chair. The wire seems a little bit looser now that he sees a glimmer of hope, a chance to negotiate.

"I took a look at your videos while you were asleep, Mr. Yoshida. I think we have a great deal in common. Both of us, in some way, are interested in the death of people we don't know. You for your own pleasure, me, because I have to."

The man bows his head as if he is studying the shiny wood of the chair. Yoshida has the impression that he is thinking about something that for a moment is taking him far away. There is a sense of inevitability in his voice that is the very essence of death.

"And that is all we have in common. You do it through a third party. I'm forced to do it myself. You're someone who watches killing, Mr. Yoshida, while I . . ."

The man puts his faceless head next to his.

"I kill . . ."

Suddenly, Yoshida knows there is no hope. The front pages of all the newspapers flash through his mind with their headlines of the murders of Jochen Welder and Arianna Parker, the woman who was with him. For days now, the TV news has been full of the horrifying details of those two crimes, including the signature in blood that the murderer left on the table on a yacht. The same words now spoken by the man sitting in front of him. He is distraught. Nobody can come to his rescue because nobody knows of the existence of his secret room. Even if his bodyguards looked for him, they would search outside when they did not find him at home. He started to moan again, struggling, panic-stricken, in the chair.

"You have something that interests me, Mr. Yoshida. Something that interests me very much. That is why I feel obliged to propose a trade."

He gets up from the chair and goes to open the glass door of the cabinet holding the VHS cassettes. He takes out a new tape, removes its wrapping, and puts it in the VCR. He presses the RECORD button and the recording begins.

"Something for my pleasure in exchange for yours."

With a graceful gesture, he puts his hand in his shirt pocket and removes a dagger that gives out a sinister gleam. He goes up to Yoshida who thrashes violently, ignoring the wire cutting into his flesh. With the same fluid movement, the man sticks the dagger into his thigh. The prisoner's hysterical moaning becomes a scream of muffled pain from behind the tape over his mouth.

"There. This is what it feels like, Mr. Yoshida."

That last "Mr. Yoshida," said in a smothered voice, rings through the room like a funeral eulogy. He stabs the bloodstained dagger again, now in the victim's other thigh. The movement is so swift that this time Yoshida does not even feel any pain, only a cool sensation in his leg. Immediately afterward, he feels the tepid dampness of blood dripping down his calf.

"Funny, isn't it? Things change when you see them from a different point of view. But you'll see. You'll be pleased with the result anyway. You'll have your pleasure this time too."

With cold determination, the man continues stabbing his victim tied to the armchair, as his gestures are repeated on the screens by the cameras. Yoshida watches himself being stabbed over and over again. He sees the blood rush out in large red streams on his white shirt and the man who raises and lowers, in the room and on the screen, the blade of his knife, again and again. He sees his eyes widen with terror, and pain fills the indifferent space of the monitors.

Meanwhile, the music in the background has changed. The trumpet cuts through the air with high notes sustained by a rhythmic accentuation, a sound of ethnic percussion that evokes tribal rituals and human sacrifice. The man and his dagger continue their agile dance around Yoshida's body, opening wounds everywhere, with the blood rushing out in evidence, on the fabric of his clothes and on the marble floor. The music and the man stop at the same time, like a ballet rehearsed an infinite number of times.

Yoshida is still alive and conscious. He feels his blood and his life run out of the wounds opened everywhere on his body, which is now sending a lone signal of pain. A bead of sweat rolls down his forehead and drops burning into his left eye. The man wipes

Yoshida's soaked face with the sleeve of his bloodstained shirt. A reddish smudge remains on his forehead.

Blood and sweat. Blood and sweat like so many other times. And through it all, the gaze of the cameras, surprised by nothing.

The man is panting under his ski mask. He goes over to stop the VCR and rewinds the tape. When the cassette is back at the beginning, he presses PLAY.

On the screen, in front of Yoshida's half-closed eyes and slowly bleeding body, it all begins again. Again, the first stab, the one that went through his thigh like a searing iron. Then the second, with its cool breeze. And then the others . . .

The man's voice is that of fate now, soft and indifferent.

"Here's what I offer you. My pleasure for yours. Relax, Mr. Yoshida. *Relax and watch yourself die . . .*"

Yoshida hears the voice through space that seems filled with cotton. His eyes are staring at the screen. As the blood slowly abandons his body, as the cold slowly rises to occupy every cell, he cannot help but feel that same damnable pleasure.

When the light abandons his eyes, he cannot understand whether it is heaven or hell that he sees before him.

17

Margherita Vizzini drove into the parking garage at the Place du Casino. There weren't many people around at that time of morning. The residents of Monte Carlo who took part in its nightlife, the rich and the desperate, were still asleep. And it was too early for tourists. Everyone on the street now, like her, was going to work. She left the sunshine, the colorful, meticulous flower beds, and the people having breakfast at the Café de Paris for the warm, damp shadows of the garage. She pulled up her Fiat Stilo to the entrance and stuck her card in the machine. The barrier rose and she drove slowly inside.

Margherita came in every day from Ventimiglia, in Italy, where she lived. She worked at the Securities Office of ABC, Banque Internationale de Monaco, located in the Place du Casino right in front of the Chanel boutique.

She had been very lucky to find a job like that in Monaco, especially without any contacts or referrals. She'd had a number of job offers after getting her degree in business and economics with honors, like all good students. Surprisingly, one of the offers had been from ABC.

She had gone to the interview without much hope, but to her surprise she had been selected and hired. There were many advantages. First of all, her starting salary was considerably higher than anything she would have had in Italy. Then there was the fact that, working in Monte Carlo, the tax situation was very different.

Margherita smiled. She was a good-looking woman, with light

brown hair cut short to frame a face that was friendly as well as attractive. A smattering of freckles on her straight nose gave her the mischievous expression of a female elf. A car was backing up to get out and she had to stop. She took advantage of the moment to glance at her reflection in the rearview mirror. She was happy with what she saw.

Michel Lecomte was coming back that day, and she wanted to look her best.

Michel . . .

She felt pleasant warmth at the pit of her stomach at the thought of his tender gaze. What they called butterflies. A delightful game had been going on between them for some time, very delicate and therefore very intense. The time had come to step it up a notch.

The way was clear. She turned onto the ramp and started to drive down into the lot that went several levels below the plaza. She had her own spot, on the next-to-last level in an area set aside for bank employees. She drove carefully but easily down the various levels, the tires squeaking on the shiny pavement when she turned the wheel to take the curve for the next ramp. She reached her level. Her parking space was in the back, right behind the wall. She turned slightly to the right past the wall and was surprised to see her space taken by a huge limousine, a shiny black Bentley with dark windows.

Strange. One rarely saw that kind of car in the underground lot. Those cars usually had chauffeurs in dark suits holding the door open for passengers, or else they got left carelessly in front of the Hôtel de Paris for the hotel staff to park. It probably belonged to a customer of the bank. Given the make of the car, protesting would be out of the question. She decided to park in the free space next to it.

Perhaps because she was distracted by these thoughts, she misjudged the distance and hit the back of the Bentley on the left side.

She heard the sound of her car light smash as the heavy limousine absorbed the shock with a light bounce of its suspension.

Margherita backed up slowly, as if this extra caution could somehow make up for the small disaster she had just caused. Once she stopped, she looked nervously at the back of the Bentley. There was a dent on the body, not very large but visible, with a mark from her plastic fender. She banged her hands on the steering wheel in irritation. Now she would have to deal with all the annoying red tape involved in an accident, not to mention the embarrassment of confessing to a bank customer that she had damaged his car.

She got out and walked over to the limo, puzzled, stopping at the height of the back window. There appeared to be someone inside, a form she could see indistinctly through the tinted glass. She looked closer, shielding her eyes with her hands as if from a reflection. It did indeed seem that there was someone in the backseat. It was all very strange. Anyone inside would certainly have jumped out of the car after the accident.

She narrowed her eyes. Just then, the figure inside bent over and leaned to the right, his head against the window. In horror, Margherita saw the face of a man completely covered in blood, his wide-open, lifeless eyes staring at her, his teeth completely bared in the smile of a skull.

She jumped back without realizing that she had already started to scream.

18

Neither Frank Ottobre nor Inspector Hulot had been able to sleep. They had spent the night staring at a meaningless record cover, listening over and over again to a tape that told them nothing. One by one, they had constructed and demolished any possible hypothesis, and had asked anyone with the slightest expertise in music for help. Even Rochelle, a cop and music fanatic with an amazing record collection, was stumped by the agile fingers of Carlos Santana fondling the neck of his guitar.

They had surfed the Web for hours in search of any hint that might help them decipher the killer's message.

Nothing.

Before them was a locked door and the key was nowhere to be found. It had been a long night of bitterness and coffee, however many sugars they added. Time had passed, and with time, all their hopes had turned to naught.

Outside the window, beyond the rooftops, the sky was turning blue. Hulot got up from his desk and went to look through the glass at the worsening traffic. For all those people, it was a new day of work after a good night's sleep. But here, it would be another day of waiting after nothing but nightmares.

Frank was sitting on a chair, one leg swung over the arm, staring at the ceiling with apparent interest. He had been in that position for quite some time now. Hulot pinched his nostrils together with his fingers, then turned around with a sigh of fatigue and frustration.

"Claude, do me a favor."

"What is it, Inspector?"

"I know you're not a waiter, but you're the youngest so you've got to pay your dues. Could you manage to get us some coffee that's any better than the mud in that machine?"

"I was waiting for you to ask," smiled Morelli. "I wouldn't mind some decent coffee myself."

As the sergeant left the office, Hulot ran his hand through his salt-and-pepper hair, slightly parted at the nape of his neck to reveal the pink of his skin after a sleepless night.

When the call came, they knew they had failed. As Hulot lifted the receiver to his ear, it seemed to weigh two hundred pounds.

"Hulot," the inspector answered laconically. He listened to the person on the other end and paled. "Where?" Another pause. "Okay. We'll be right there." Nicolas hung up and buried his face in his hands.

Frank had gotten to his feet during the conversation. His weariness seemed to have instantly disappeared. Suddenly, he was on high alert. His jaw contracted and his red eyes narrowed to tiny slits.

"There's a body, Frank, in the underground parking garage next to the casino. Faceless, like the other two."

Hulot got up from his desk and went to the door, followed by Frank. They almost bumped into Morelli, who was holding a tray with three cups.

"Here's the coffee, Inspector."

"Put the coffee down and get us a car, Morelli. They found another one—let's get out of here."

As they left the office, Morelli addressed a policeman walking past them in the hall.

"Dupasquier, get me a car downstairs. Now."

It felt like the elevator was descending the Himalayas.

Frank and Hulot went outside where a car was waiting,

engine running, doors open. The doors had barely closed when they sped off.

"Place du Casino. Turn the siren on, Lacroix, and don't worry about the tires." The policeman at the wheel was a young man with quick reflexes. The car took off with a screech.

They drove up Saint-Dévote and reached the plaza with the siren shrieking and heads turning as they passed. In front of the entrance to the garage, the small curious crowd looked like an exact copy of the one at the port a few days before. There was a splash of color from the public garden full of flower beds and palm trees right in front of the garage. And more color in the center of the traffic circle in front of the Hôtel de Paris, where a landscaper had composed the date in flowers. Frank could not help thinking that for the new victim, today's date was written in blood.

The car got through with help from the policemen pushing the onlookers back as hundreds of eyes stared, trying to make out who was inside. They drove into the parking garage and their tires screeched again, going down to the level where two other cars were waiting with flashing lights. They made colorful designs on the walls and ceiling.

Frank and the inspector jumped out of the car as if their seats were burning, and Hulot spoke to an officer, pointing to the other cars. "Tell them to turn those lights off. It's nauseating."

They went over to the large black Bentley parked against the wall. The body of a man was leaning against the back window, the glass covered in blood. As soon as he saw him, Hulot squeezed his fist so tightly that his knuckles whitened.

"Merde! Merde! Merde!" he repeated over and over, as if that fit of rage could change the sight before his eyes. "He did it again, God damn it."

Frank felt the exhaustion of the sleepless night slide into despair. While they had been sitting in the office, desperately trying to decipher the message of a maniac, the maniac had struck again.

"Who found him?" Hulot asked, turning to the policeman behind him.

"I did, sir," replied a uniformed officer. "That is, I was the first to arrive. I was here to tow a car and I heard the girl screaming."

"What girl?"

"The girl who discovered the body. She's sitting in the car. In shock and crying like a baby. She works for the ABC Bank right over us. She hit the Bentley while parking her car, got out to check the damage, and that's when she saw . . ."

"Did anyone touch anything?" Frank interrupted.

"No, I didn't let anyone get close. We were waiting for you."

"Good."

Frank went to the police car to get a pair of latex gloves and pulled them on as he went over to the limo. He tried the handle of the front door on the driver's side. It clicked open. The car was unlocked, and he leaned in and looked at the body. The man was wearing a white shirt soaked with so much blood that Frank could barely make out its original color. His pants were black, presumably evening clothes. There were slashes from numerous stabbings all over him. Next to the body, on the leather seat, were the words written in blood.

I kill . . .

Leaning over the padded leather, Frank grabbed the body by its shoulders, pulled it upright, and leaned it against the back of the seat so that it would not slip down again. As he did so, he heard something hit the floor with a thud.

He backed out of the car and went to open the other door, next to the body. He squatted down, arms on his thighs. Hulot, standing behind him, bent over to see better, keeping his arms behind his back. He was not wearing gloves and didn't want to risk touching anything.

From his position, Frank could see what had fallen on the floor. Wedged under the front seat was a VHS videocassette. It had probably been on the corpse's lap and the movement had caused it to fall. Frank took a pen from his pocket and stuck it into one of the spindles of the tape. He lifted it and looked at it for a second. Then he took a clear plastic bag out of his pocket, slipped the cassette inside, and sealed it.

During this operation, he noticed that the dead man's feet were bare. Frank stretched out his hand and tested the flexibility of the toes. He raised the pant legs to see if there were marks on his ankles.

"This guy was bound with something stiff, probably wire. Judging from the clotting of the blood and the mobility of his limbs, he hasn't been dead long. And he didn't die here."

"From the color of his hands, I'd say he died by bleeding from the wounds."

"Exactly. So, if he died here, there'd be much more blood on the seats and the floor, not just on the clothes. And it doesn't really seem like the right place to do the job. No, this guy got killed somewhere else and was put in the car after."

"But why go to so much trouble?" Hulot stepped back so that Frank could stand up. "I mean, why take the chance of moving a body from one place to another, at night, in a car, at the risk of being discovered. Why?"

"I don't know," Frank responded, looking around him, puzzled. "That's one of the things we have to figure out."

They stood in silence a moment, looking at the body leaning against the backseat with wide-open eyes in the narrow space of its shiny, sumptuous coffin.

"Judging from his clothes and car, he must have had a shitload of money."

"Let's see whose license plate this is."

They went around the Bentley and opened the door on the

passenger side. Frank pressed a button on the dashboard and the door to the glove compartment slid open noiselessly. He took out a leather folder. The papers were inside.

"Here it is. It's a company car, Zen Electronics."

"Jesus Christ, it's Allen Yoshida." The inspector's voice was a shocked whisper. "The owner of Sacrifiles."

"Shit, Nicolas. That's what the clue meant."

"How's that?"

"The song by Santana, the one we listened to over and over. Live in Japan. Yoshida's half-American, half-Japanese. And remember the song? It's called 'Soul Sacrifice,' get it? 'Soul Sacrifice'! Sacrifiles is a play on words on sacrifice. And there's another song on *Lotus* called 'Kyoto.' I wouldn't be surprised if Yoshida had something to do with that too."

Hulot pointed at the body in the car. "Do you think it's him? Allen Yoshida?"

"I'd bet my life on it. And there's something else."

Hulot looked at the American in surprise. He could see an idea taking shape in Frank's mind.

"Nicolas, if Yoshida was killed somewhere else and then brought here to be discovered in the Place du Casino of Monte Carlo, there's a reason for it."

"What reason?"

"That bastard wants *us* to investigate."

If Frank was right, Hulot thought, then there was no end to what this man would do. He froze at the thought of what was to come, whom they were facing, and the murders they already had to solve.

The sound of screeching tires announced the arrival of an ambulance and the medical examiner. The forensic van was close behind. While Hulot briefed them, Frank stood apart from the others next to the open door. Lost in thought, his eyes fell on the car radio. There was something sticking out of the tape recorder. He pulled it out.

It was a normal audiocassette that had been recorded and rewound. Frank studied it for a moment, then stuck it in the stereo. Suddenly, everyone could hear the jeering notes of "Samba Pa Ti" floating through the still air of the garage.

19

When they returned to police headquarters, there was a crowd of reporters in front of the building.

"Fucking vultures."

"What did you expect, Nicolas? We steered clear of them at the garage, but you can't avoid them forever. They're the least of our problems. Just keep that in mind."

Hulot turned to the driver, the same one as before. "Drive around back. I can't face them now."

The car continued and stopped at the entrance. Seeing the inspector inside, the horde of reporters shifted position with a single movement, so well synchronized that it looked rehearsed. The barrier was only halfway up when the car was surrounded by people and questions. Hulot was forced to lower the window on his side. The shouting of the reporters grew louder. One man with red hair and freckles practically stuck his head in the window.

"Inspector, do you know whose body was found in the garage?"

From behind him: "Do you think it's the same man who killed Jochen Welder and Arianna Parker?" It was a reporter from *Nice Matin* that Hulot knew well, brusquely shoving his colleague aside. "Is he a serial killer?"

"What can you tell us about the phone call last night to Radio Monte Carlo?" yelled someone else behind them.

Hulot raised his hands to stop the volley of questions.

"Gentlemen, please. You're all professionals and you know very well that I can't tell you anything right now. There will be a statement from the chief of police later. That's all for now. Excuse me. Go on, Lacroix."

They drove slowly so as not to hit anyone and the car passed the barrier, which lowered behind them. When they got out of the car, Hulot rubbed his face with one hand. He had dark circles under his eyes caused by lack of sleep and the horror he had just witnessed.

He handed the videotape from the victim's car over to Morelli. Forensics had checked it for prints and returned it.

"Claude, make a back-up copy and then give it to us. And bring a monitor and VCR to my office. Then call the people in Nice and talk to Clavert. Tell him to let us know as soon as they analyze the tape from last night. I don't expect much, but you never know. We'll be in my office."

They went up the few steps at the entry and stopped in front of the glass door. Frank pushed it open and went in first. From the moment they had arrived at the radio station the evening before, he and Hulot had not been alone together. They stopped at the elevators. The inspector pressed a button and the doors swished open.

"What do you think?"

Frank shrugged.

"The problem is that I no longer know *what* to think. This guy is different. In every case I've ever been on, there's always been something left to chance, some series of clues that showed, first of all, how the serial killer could *endure* his condition. The lucidity of this guy is mind-boggling."

"Yeah. Meanwhile, three people are dead."

"One thing is really puzzling me, Nicolas."

"What's that?"

"Beyond the fact that we don't know why he removes the faces of his victims, the first case—Jochen Welder and Arianna Parker—involved a man and a woman. Here, just a man. What's the connection? In other words, if we exclude the woman for the moment, what's the connection between Jochen Welder, two-time Formula 1 world champion, and Allen Yoshida, world-famous computer tycoon?"

"Well, both are well known and around the same age, thirty-five," Hulot mused, leaning against the door of the elevator. "And, I might add, both rather handsome."

"That's fine. Then what does Arianna Parker have to do with it? Why a woman?"

The elevator stopped at their floor and opened. Hulot held out his hand to block the electric eye.

"The killer was probably interested in Jochen Welder and she just happened to be there. So he had to kill her too."

"I'll buy that. But why give her the same treatment?"

They walked down the hall and stopped in front of Hulot's office. The people walking by looked at them as if they had survived a war.

"I don't know, Frank. I don't know what to say. Three dead and no clues. We couldn't even figure out the one clue we had, so now there's one more dead man on our conscience. And all told, it was rather simple."

"I once read that all puzzles are simple once you've solve them."

They went into the office, where patterns of sunlight streaked the floor. It was almost summer outside but felt like winter in the room. Hulot went over to his desk, picked up the phone, and called Froben, the inspector in Nice. Frank went to sit down in the chair in the same position he had been in a few hours before.

"Claude? It's Nicolas. Listen, I have a problem. A new one. We just found another body in a car. Same method as the other two. The face completely flayed. The papers show that the car was owned by Zen Electronics, Allen Yoshida's company. You know, the . . ." The inspector stopped. "What?! Wait, I'm here with Frank. I'm going to put you on speaker so he can hear too. Repeat what you just said."

He pushed a button on the phone and Froben's voice filled the air, slightly distorted by the phone mike.

"I said I'm at Yoshida's house in Beaulieu. Billionaire's pad, of course. Multibillionaire. Security with armed guards and cameras everywhere. We got a call this morning about seven. The servants don't live in—they all come to work around six-thirty. Today, after they got here, they started cleaning up from a party the owner hosted last night. When they went downstairs, they found a room they didn't know about."

"What do you mean, 'didn't know about'?"

"Exactly what I just said, Nicolas. A room they knew nothing about. A secret room that opens by an electronic lock hidden in the base of a statue."

"Sorry, go on."

"They went in and found an armchair covered in blood. There was blood on the floor and the walls. A lake, as the security guard who called me put it. He wasn't exaggerating. We've been here a while and forensics is still working on it. I've started questioning but I'm not getting anywhere."

"He killed him there, Claude. He came there, killed Yoshida, did his disgusting routine, loaded him into the car, and then left the body and car at the casino garage."

"The head of security, an ex-cop named Valmeere, told me they saw Yoshida's car leave last night at four A.M."

"And they didn't see who was driving?"

"No. He said the car has tinted windows and you can't see in. And it was dark out, so it was even worse with the reflection of the light."

"Didn't he find it strange that Yoshida would go out by himself at that time of night?"

"That's exactly what I asked him. Valmeere told me that Yoshida *was* strange. He did things like that. Valmeere had pointed out to him that it wasn't safe to go around alone, but he wouldn't listen. Sure you really want to know *how* strange Yoshida was?"

"Tell me."

"We found a collection of snuff videos in the room, enough to make you sick. There's stuff here you can't even imagine. One of my boys who watched them started vomiting. Can I tell you something?" Froben continued without waiting for an answer. "If Yoshida liked this kind of stuff, he got exactly what he deserved!"

The disgust in Froben's voice was clear. That was the life of a policeman. You thought you had reached rock bottom, but something happened every time to make things worse.

"Okay, Claude. Let me know the results of your investigation: photos, prints—if there are any—and so on. And leave everything there so that we can come and take a look later, if necessary. Thanks."

"Don't mention it. Nicolas?"

"Yes?"

"The last time I thought it to myself, but this time I'll say it out loud. I wouldn't want to be in your shoes, believe me!"

"I believe you, my friend. And how."

Frank was leaning back in the chair looking at the blue patch of sky without seeing it. His voice seemed a thousand miles and a thousand years away.

"You know something, Nicolas? Whenever I think about the things that happen in the world, 9/11, this business here, wars and everything else, I start thinking about dinosaurs."

The inspector looked at him, not understanding what he was getting at.

"For a long time now, everyone's been trying to figure out why they became extinct. They wonder why these animals that dominated the earth suddenly disappeared. Maybe they died because they all went crazy. Just like us. That's what we are, you know, tiny dinosaurs. And sooner or later, this madness will be the end of us."

20

Morelli pushed the cassette into the VCR and the colored lines at the beginning of the tape filled the screen. Hulot went to lower the blinds in order to reduce the glare from the windows. Frank was sitting in his armchair, turned in the direction of the monitor. Next to him was Luc Roncaille, chief of Sûreté Publique of the Principality of Monaco. He had unexpectedly stopped by Hulot's office while Morelli and a policeman were getting the monitor and VCR ready on a small table they had wheeled in.

He was a tall, suntanned man with graying hair at his temples, a modern-day Stewart Granger. Frank looked at him with instant suspicion. The man looked more like a politician than a cop. A handsome face and a career that was more PR than fieldwork. He was the perfect poster boy to exhibit on official occasions. When Hulot introduced them, he and Frank looked each other over for a second, each sizing up the other. By the look in Roncaille's eyes, the American decided that he was not stupid. An opportunist, maybe, but not stupid. Frank could tell that if Roncaille had to throw someone overboard in order to save himself, he wouldn't hesitate for a second. And he would never get thrown overboard himself.

Roncaille had rushed over after hearing the news about Yoshida. For the moment there had been no complaints, but he was obviously there to get enough information to cover his own ass with his superiors. The Principality of Monaco was a tiny speck of land, but it was no fairy tale. There were strict rules and a first-rate government, the envy of many other countries. And the Monaco police force was considered one of the best in the world.

An image finally came on the screen. First, they saw a man tied to a chair, tape over his mouth, eyes wide with fear, looking at something to his left. There was no mistaking the face of Allen Yoshida. His photograph had been on magazine covers worldwide. Then a man in black came into the frame. Hulot held his breath. Looking at the man and his clothing, Frank thought for a moment that there was something wrong with the tape or the shot, given the bulges on his elbows and knees. Then, he saw that it was part of the disguise and realized the sophistication of the person he was watching.

"Fucking bastard," he muttered.

The others turned to look at him and Frank nodded, as if apologizing for the disturbance. Everyone turned back to the video. Their eyes filled with horror as they watched the figure in black repeatedly stab the man tied to the chair, methodically, so that none of the stab wounds would be fatal. They saw his movements, hampered by his clothes, opening wounds that would never heal. They saw the blood flow and drip slowly down Yoshida's white shirt, like a flower that had to feed on his life so that it could blossom. They saw death itself dancing around the man, tasting his pain and terror before taking him away for all eternity.

After what seemed like centuries, the man in black stood still. Yoshida's face was dripping with sweat. The man stretched out an arm and wiped Yoshida's brow with the sleeve of his shirt. On the forehead of the prisoner there remained a reddish smudge, a comma of life in that ritual of death.

There was blood everywhere. On the marble floor, on the clothes, on the walls. The man in black went over to the VCR to his left. He stretched his arm out to one of the machines. Suddenly, he stopped and leaned his head to one side, as if struck by a thought. Then he turned toward the cameras and bowed, pointing with an elegant movement of his right arm at the man dying in the chair. He turned again, pressed a button, and the freezing snow of winter covered the screen.

The silence in the room had a different meaning for each of them.

Frank was taken back in time, to the house on the shore and the images he never stopped seeing like an endless film before his eyes. The memory was once again of pain—and that pain became hate and Frank distributed it evenly between himself and the killer.

Hulot went to raise the blinds and sunlight returned to the room as a benediction.

"Jesus fucking Christ, what in hell's name is going on here?" The person who finally and thankfully spoke was Roncaille.

Frank got up from his chair. Hulot saw the light in his eyes. For a moment he felt that, if the figure in black in the video had removed his glasses, he would have seen the same light in his. Water is water, fire is fire, madness is madness. And death is death.

Hulot shuddered as if the air conditioner were blowing air from the North Pole. And Frank's voice might as well have come from the same place.

"Gentlemen, that's the devil in the flesh on that tape. The man may be completely off his rocker, but he's got superhuman clarity and shrewdness." He pointed to the monitor that was still on, covered with static." You saw how he was dressed. The bulges at the elbows and knees. I don't know if he had planned to make this tape when he went to Yoshida's house. Probably not, because he couldn't have known about the secret room and the perversion in there. He might have been improvising. Maybe he surprised Yoshida when he was opening his holy grail. He was amused at the idea that we could watch him at work, killing the guy. No, the proper term is *admire*. That's where you can see that he's crazy. Morelli, can you rewind the tape?"

The sergeant pointed the remote control and the machine started to rewind with a click and a swish. A few seconds later, Frank stopped him with a wave of his hand.

"That's enough, thanks. Can you pause it at a place where we can get a good view of our man?" Morelli pressed a button and the image on the screen froze upon the figure in black with his dagger raised. The still image showed a drop of blood falling from the knife in midair. The chief of police narrowed his eyes in disgust. He obviously didn't see that kind of thing every day. "Here." Frank went over to the screen and pointed at the elbow of the killer's raised arm.

"The man knew there'd be cameras in the house. And he knew that there are cameras all over the Principality. He knew that, by taking the car to the Parking de Boulingrin garage, he risked being taped. And most of all, he knew that anthropometric measurement is a form of identification and that you can do it by analyzing a video shot. There are average values for individuals. The size of the ears, the distance from the wrist to the elbow, from the ankle to the knee. Police all over the world have that kind of equipment. So he put protection over his elbows and knees. And we can't analyze anything. No face or body. Only his height, which tells us nothing. That's why I say that, aside from insane, he's also perfectly lucid."

"Why did that maniac have to end up here?" Roncaille was probably seeing his job as chief of police crumble away. He looked at Frank, trying to recover some semblance of levelheadedness. "What are you planning to do now?"

Frank looked at Hulot. The inspector understood that he was responding in kind to Roncaille's considerations.

"We're investigating in various directions. We don't have many clues, but we do have something. We're waiting for Lyons to send us the results of their analysis of the phone call tapes. Cluny, the psychiatrist, is preparing a report, again based on the tapes. There are results from the tests on the boat and Yoshida's car and house. We're not expecting much, but something could come out of it. The protocols of the autopsies didn't add very much to the first reports. The only real connections we have with the murderer are the phone calls he made to Radio Monte Carlo before striking. We're watching the station 24/7. But he's a clever bastard. We've seen that. And he's as well prepared as he is ferocious. All we can hope for now is that he'll slip up somehow. We've set up a special unit under Morelli here that fields calls and controls anything that might be suspicious."

"There have been lots of calls," Morelli added. He felt obliged to say something. "And now there'll be more. Sometimes the callers are raving lunatics, you know, UFOs and avenging angels. But for the rest, we're examining everything. Of course, checking all that out takes time and men, neither of which we have."

"Hmmm. I'll see what I can do. I can always ask for some support from the French police. I don't need to tell you that the Principality could have very well done without this. We've always been the picture of security, a happy island in the midst of the chaos everywhere else in the world. Now we've got this madman who has given us a shock, and we have to solve the case with a show of efficiency in keeping with our image. In other words, we have to get him. Before he kills someone else." Roncaille stood up and brushed down the folds of his linen pants. "Okay. I'll leave you to your work. I should inform you that I'll be reporting all of this to the Attorney General, which is something I'd rather not have to do. Hulot, keep us informed, at any time, day or night. Good luck, gentlemen."

He went to the door, opened it, and left the office, closing it gently behind him. By his demeanor and, most of all, his tone, the words "we have to get him" were understood by all. He meant "you have to get him," and the threat of unpleasant reprisals in the face of failure was crystal clear.

21

Frank, Hulot, and Morelli remained where they were, savoring, in silence, the bitter taste of defeat. They'd been given a clue but hadn't understood it. They'd had a chance to stop the murderer and now there was another body lying on a morgue table with its face skinned off. Roncaille had only come as a form of advance notice, to get the lay of the land before the real battle began. He wanted to warn them that from there on in, the forces above would want heads to roll. And in that case, his own head would not be the only one. Not by a long shot.

There was a knock at the door.

"Come in." Claude Froben's drawn face appeared. "Inspector, Froben reporting."

"Hi, Claude. Come on in."

"Hello, everyone. I just saw Roncaille outside. Not a good sign, huh?" Froben immediately noticed the downcast feeling in the room.

"Couldn't be any worse.

"Here, Nicolas. I brought you a present. Developed in record time, just for you. You'll have to wait a bit more for the rest of it. Sorry."

He placed a brown envelope on the table. Frank got up from his chair and went to open it. Inside were black-and-white photos. Turning them over, he saw a still version of what he'd seen in the video: an empty room that was the metaphysical image of a crime. The room where the figure in black had butchered a man with an even blacker soul. Neither of them was there now.

He flipped rapidly through the photos and handed them to Hulot. The inspector put them back on the table without even looking.

"Did you find anything?" he asked Froben with little hope.

"You can imagine the care my boys used in going over the room and the house. There are a bunch of fingerprints, but as you know, prints often mean nothing. If you let me have the prints from the body, I can compare them for a definitive ID. We found some hairs on the armchair, probably Yoshida's.

"The hair *is* Yoshida's. He's the dead man. No doubt about it," interrupted Hulot.

"How can you be so sure?"

"Before we go on, I think you should see something."

"What?"

"Sit down and brace yourself." Hulot leaned back and turned to Morelli. "Start the tape."

The sergeant pressed the remote and the screen was once again filled with the macabre dance of a man killing another man who must die. His dagger looked like a needle sewing death onto Yoshida, a bloodred costume. Froben's eyes widened. When the film ended with that strange, self-satisfied bow of the man in black, it took him a few minutes to regain his composure.

"Christ. This isn't even human anymore. I feel like crossing myself. What kind of person is this?"

"He uses all his talent to serve evil: he's cold-blooded, intelligent, and shrewd. And without an ounce of pity."

Frank's words were a condemnation of himself as well as the killer. Neither of them could stop. One would continue killing until the other nailed him to the wall. And if he wanted to succeed, he had to abandon his rational mind and put on another black costume.

"Froben, what can you tell us about the videos you found at Yoshida's place?" Frank jumped from one topic to another without changing his tone.

For an instant, the inspector seemed relieved at the change of subject. He was intimidated by the light in the American's eyes. And by his voice—he sounded like someone whispering magic words to summon ghosts. Froben pointed to the monitor with a grimace.

"Stuff like this blows your mind. We've started an investigation and we'll see where it leads. There were things in there that make me think the late Mr. Yoshida was not worth much more than the man who killed him. Things like that take away your faith in mankind. In my opinion, I'll say it again, that sadistic motherfucker got exactly what he deserved."

"There's something else I'm wondering. Why do you think the murderer decided to make this tape?" Hulot, sitting at his desk, finally spoke his thoughts.

"He didn't do it for us," said Frank, moving toward the window. He leaned on the marble windowsill and looked blindly out at the street.

"What do you mean by that?"

"There's a point toward the end of the video when he stops, just before he turns off the camera. *That's* when he thought about us. That's when he turned and bowed. No, that tape wasn't made for us."

"Then who was it for?" Froben turned around, but all he saw was the back of the American's neck and shoulders.

"He made it for Yoshida."

"For Yoshida?"

Frank turned slowly to face the room.

"Of course. Didn't you see that he made sure none of the stab wounds was fatal? He wanted Yoshida to bleed to death, slowly. Sometimes, evil has its own bizarre form of retribution. The guy who killed him made him watch a film of his own death."

FIFTH CARNIVAL

The man is back.

He carefully closes the hermetic door in the metal wall behind him. Silent and alone, as always. Now, he is once again closed off from the world, just as the world is closed off from him.

He smiles as he delicately places a black backpack on the wooden table against the wall. This time, he is certain he has made no mistakes. He sits down and turns on the light over the table with the solemn gesture of a ritual. He clicks the snaps of the bag and opens it with the same ceremonial movements, taking out a black wax-board box. Placing the box on the table, he sits for a moment looking at it, as if it is a present and he is delaying the pleasure of discovering what's inside.

The night was not spent in vain. Time gently lent itself to his needs. Another useless man has given him what he needs. The music is free now, and in his head a triumphant victory march is playing.

He opens the box and puts his hand carefully inside. The lamp illuminates Allen Yoshida's face as he gently lifts it from the wax board. A few drops of blood fall to join those at the bottom of the box. The man's smile broadens. This time he was very careful. He used the head of a plastic mannequin to support his trophy, the kind hairdressers use for wigs. Looking carefully at the funeral mask, he has more reason to smile as he thinks about how nothing has changed. From the emptiness of a human mannequin to the inert plastic of another.

He runs his hands gently over the taut skin, caressing the hair whose light has been taken by death. No cuts, no abrasions. The circle of the eyes is cut clean. The lips, the most difficult part, are full and fleshy. Only a few drops of blood dim the beauty of that face.

Excellent work. He relaxes an instant against the back of the chair and folds his hands behind his neck. He arches his back to stretch his neck. The man is weary. The night was rewarding but extremely tiring. The tension is gradually dissipating and the price has to be paid.

The man yawns but it is not yet time to sleep. First, he must finish his work. He gets up and goes to open a cabinet. He takes out a box of Kleenex and a bottle of disinfectant and sits back down at the table. He carefully cleans the spots of blood from the mask.

Now the music in his head is quiet, like a New Age piece with the delicate counterpoint of an ethereal choir. An ethnic instrument, panpipes perhaps, caresses his mind with the same delicate movement with which he caresses the man's face. Now he is finished. On the table, next to the mask, there are tissues stained a pinkish color. The man admires his masterpiece with half-closed eyes.

Since coming in, he has made almost no sound, but the voice still comes, filled with apprehension.

Is that you, Vibo?

The man raises his head and looks at the large door that is open next to the desk where he sits.

"Yes, it's me, Paso."

Why were you so late? I felt lonely, here in the dark.

The man starts nervously but it is not noticeable in his voice. He turns to the open door in the shadows to his left.

"I wasn't out having fun, Paso. I was doing it for you."

The tone is that of slight reproach, and it provokes a suddenly remissive answer.

I know, Vibo, I know. I'm sorry. It's just that time never passes when you're away.

The man feels a wave of tenderness and his slight anger fades. He is suddenly a lion remembering the infantile games of his litter. He is a wolf defending and protecting the weaker members of his pack.

"It's all right, Paso. Now I'll go to sleep here with you. And I brought you a present."

Surprise. Impatience.

What is it, Vibo?

The man smiles again. He returns the face to the box and closes the lid. He turns off the light in front of him. This time it would all be perfect. Still smiling, he takes the box and goes to the door where there is darkness and the voice.

He uses his elbow to turn on a light switch to his left.

"You'll like it, you'll see."

The man goes into the room. It is an empty room with gray metal walls, the color of lead. On the right, there is a spare metal bed with an equally simple night table and only a lamp on it. The blanket is pulled tight, without a wrinkle. The pillow and the sheet folded neatly over the blanket are perfectly clean.

Parallel to the bed, about a yard away, is a crystal case about ten feet long, held up by two sawhorses like the ones supporting the table in the other room. The back of the case has a hermetic gasket set in a hole and the rubber tube connected to it leads to a small machine on the floor between the legs of the sawhorse nearest to the door. There is a cord going from the machine to a socket in the wall.

Inside the crystal case lies a mummified body. It is the body of a man about six feet tall, completely naked. The dried-out limbs indicate that his build must have been very similar to that of the man, although the wizened skin now shows ribs and is taut over the knees and elbows that stick out like the joints of an animal.

The man goes and places a hand on the case. The warmth draws a halo on the perfectly clean glass. His smile is broader now. He raises the box and holds it up over the body, at the height of the shriveled face.

Come on, Vibo. Tell me what it is.

The man looks at the body affectionately. His gaze runs over the face and head from which someone, with surgical ability, has completely removed the skin. The man smiles mysteriously at the smile of the cadaver, seeking its lifeless eyes with his own, anxiously examining the fixed expression as if he can perceive a movement of the dried muscles, the color of gray wax.

"You'll see. You'll see. Want some music?"

Yes. No. No, afterward. First, let me see what you have there. Let me see what you brought me.

The man steps back as if playing with a baby whom he wants to restrain to protect it from its own impatience.

"No, the moment is important, Paso. We need some music. Wait here. I'll be right back."

Come on, Vibo. Afterward. Let me see.

"It'll only take a second. Wait."

The man places the box on a wooden folding chair next to the transparent case.

He disappears through the door. The body lies there alone, motionless in its tiny eternity, staring at the ceiling. Moments later, the mournful notes of Jimi Hendrix playing "Instrumental Solo" at Woodstock float through the air. The American anthem no longer sounds triumphant on that distorted guitar. There are no heroes and no flags. Only longing for those who went off to fight a stupid war and the sobbing of those who, for the same stupid war, never saw them return.

The light in the other room goes off and the man reappears in the doorway.

"You like this, Paso?"

Of course. You know I always liked it. But now, let me see what you brought.

The man goes to the box on the chair. He is still smiling. He raises the lid with a solemn gesture and puts it on the ground, next to the chair. He picks up the box and places it on top of the case over the chest of the body lying inside.

"You'll like it. You'll see. I'm sure you'll like it."

With regal gestures, he removes the face of Allen Yoshida wrapped around the mannequin's head like a plastic mask. The hair moves like it's still alive, brushed by a wind that would never reach them there, below the ground.

"Here, Paso. Look."

Oh, Vibo. It's beautiful. Is it really for me?

"Of course it's for you. I'll put it on you right now."

Holding the mask in his left hand, with his right he presses a button at the head of the case. He hears the slight whistle of air filling the transparent coffin. Now the man can open the cover by rotating it around hinges on the right.

Holding the mask with two hands, he carefully places it on the body's face, moving it delicately to match the eye openings with the dead man's glassy eyes, nose with nose and mouth with mouth. With infinite precaution, he tucks a hand behind the nape of the corpse's neck to raise it and places the mask carefully over the back of the head as well, bringing the ends together to avoid wrinkling.

The voice is impatient and fearful at the same time.

How does it look, Vibo? Let me see.

The man takes a step back and looks hesitantly at the results of his work.

"Just a minute. Just one minute. There's still something missing."

The man goes the night table, opens the drawer, and takes out a comb and a mirror. He returns to the body's side like an anxious artist putting the last brushstrokes on his masterpiece.

He combs down the hair, now opaque and dull, as if to give it a touch of life it no longer has. The man is both mother and father at this moment. He is pure dedication, without time or limit. There is infinite tenderness and affection in his gestures, as if he has life and warmth enough for them both, as if the blood in his veins and the air in his lungs were equally divided between him and the corpse lying without memory in the crystal coffin.

He raises the mirror in front of the body's face with an expression of triumph.

"There!"

A moment of stupefied silence. The strings of Hendrix's guitar unravel in the battle call of "The Star-Spangled Banner." It contains the wounds of every war and the search for meaning behind all those deaths performed in the name of empty values.

A tear rolls down the man's cheek and falls on the face of the corpse covered with the mask. On the dead man, it looks like a tear of joy.

Vibo, I'm handsome now too. I have a face like everyone else.

"Yes, now you're really handsome. More than all the others."

I don't know how to thank you, Vibo. I don't know what I would have done without you. Before . . . The voice is touched. It contains gratitude and regret. The same affection and dedication as in the man's eyes. *First, you freed me of my illness and now you've given me . . . You've given me this, a new face, a beautiful face. How can I ever thank you?*

"Don't say that, do you understand? Not ever. I did it for you, for us, because the others owe us and they have to give back what they stole. I'll do everything I can to repay you for what they did. I promise."

As if to underline the threat in that promise, the music suddenly transformed into the electric energy of "Purple Haze," with Hendrix tormenting the metal strings in his tumultuous race toward freedom and annihilation.

The man lowers the lid that slides silently along the rubber runners. He goes to the compressor on the floor and presses the button. The machine turns on with a hum and starts extracting air from inside the coffin. With the vacuum, the mask adheres even more closely to the dead man's face, making a small fold on one side, giving the body a satisfied smile.

The man goes over to the bed and removes the black shirt he is wearing. He throws it onto a stool at the foot of the iron bed. He continues removing his clothes until he is nude. He slides his athletic body between the sheets, lays his head on the pillow, and stares up at the ceiling in the same position as the body inside the shiny coffin.

The lamp goes out. The only light comes from the red and green of the electronic displays on the equipment in the next room, furtive as the eyes of a cemetery cat.

The song is over. In the tomblike silence, the living man slips into a dreamless sleep, not unlike that of the dead.

22

Frank and Hulot reached the main square of the village of Eze after passing the Fragonard perfume boutique on their left. Frank remembered with a stab in his heart that Harriet had stocked up on cologne there during their trip to Europe. He could see her body under the fabric of her light summer dress as she held out the inside of her wrist to test the perfume. He saw her rub it against her hand and wait for the liquid to evaporate before smelling the combined scent of skin and perfume. She had been wearing that perfume on the day . . .

"Are you here, or millions of miles away?"

"No, I'm here. A little tired, but here." Nicolas's voice dispersed the images running through Frank's mind. He realized that he had been completely absent.

Actually, Nicolas was the more tired of the two. He had dark circles under his reddened eyes and was in desperate need of a warm shower and a cool bed, in that order. Frank had gone up to Parc Saint-Roman and slept a few hours in the afternoon, but Nicolas had stayed at the office to do all the paperwork that comes with every police investigation. When Frank had left him like that at headquarters, it was clear to Frank that the police could probably save a lot more ordinary people and maybe even the rain forests if only they didn't have to waste half their time unraveling red tape.

Now they were going to the home of Nicolas and his wife, Céline, for dinner. They'd left the parking lot behind them, along with the restaurants and souvenir shops. They turned left on the street leading to the upper part of the town. Nicolas Hulot's house was not far from the church overlooking Eze. It was built right on the edge of the valley, and Frank often wondered what the architect had done to keep it from obeying gravity and sliding to the bottom.

They parked the Peugeot in the reserved spot and Frank waited as Nicolas opened the front door. They went inside and Frank stood and looked around. Nicolas closed the door behind them.

"Céline, we're home!"

"Hi, dear." Mme Hulot's brunette head peeked out of the kitchen door at the end of the hall. "Hi, Frank. I see you're still as handsome as I remembered. How are you?"

"Exhausted. The only thing that can revive me is your cooking. From the smell, I can tell I'll probably feel better soon."

Mme Hulot's smile lit up her suntanned face. She came out of the kitchen drying her hands on a towel. "It's almost ready. Nick, give Frank something to drink while you're waiting. I'm running a little late. It took me longer than usual to clean Stéphane's room today. I've told him to straighten up thousands of times but it's useless. His room's a mess whenever he goes out."

The woman walked back to the kitchen with her skirt swaying. Frank and Nicolas exchanged glances. There was a shadow of endless pain in the inspector's eyes.

Stéphane, Céline and Nicolas Hulot's twenty-year-old son, had died in the aftermath of a car accident a few years before, after a prolonged coma. In her mind, Céline had never accepted her son's death. She remained the woman she had always been: gentle, intelligent, and sharp-witted, losing nothing of her personality. She simply behaved as if Stéphane were still around the house instead of in a grave in the cemetery. The doctors who examined her gave up after a few sessions, suggesting that Hulot simply go along with his wife's harmless delusion. They saw it as a relatively healthy solution that was saving her psyche from worse damage.

Frank knew about Céline Hulot's problem and had adjusted to it when he had come to Europe the first time. Harriet had done the same when they had vacationed together on the Côte d'Azur. After Harriet's death, Frank and Nicolas had grown closer. Each of them knew the other's suffering and it was because of this bond that Frank had accepted the invitation to come back to the Principality of Monaco.

Hulot took off his jacket and hung it on a Thonet bentwood coatrack on the wall. The house was decorated in a modern style that blended pleasantly with the period in which it was built. He led Frank into the living room, which had double French doors that opened onto a terrace overlooking the coast.

Out on the terrace, the table was exquisitely set, with an arrangement of yellow and purple flowers in a vase placed at the center of an immaculate tablecloth. The Hulots' manner was relaxed, with carefully chosen yet simple objects and a love of the peaceful life, without ostentation. Nicolas and his wife shared an indissoluble bond: pain for what they no longer had and regret for everything that could have been.

Frank could feel it in the air. It was a state of mind he knew perfectly well, that sense of loss that inevitably comes to places that are touched by the harsh hand of suffering. Yet, strangely enough, instead of being frightened, Frank found some solace here in the lively eyes of Céline Hulot, who had the courage to survive her dead son by escaping through innocent madness.

Frank envied her and was sure that her husband felt the same. For her, the days were not numbers crossed off one after another and time was not an endless wait for someone who would never come. Céline had the happy smile of a woman in an empty house, who knows that her loved ones would soon be home.

"What can I get you to drink, Frank?"

"It feels so French here tonight. How about a French aperitif? Pastis, even."

"You got it."

Nicolas went to the bar and started taking out bottles and glasses. Frank went out on the terrace to admire the view. A long stretch of the coast was visible, with coves and inlets and cliffs that jutted into the sea like fingers pointing to the horizon. The red of the sunset was a promise that tomorrow would be another beautiful blue day, for everyone but them.

They were marked by this story forever. Frank started thinking of a Neil Young record, *Rust Never Sleeps.* All the colors of paradise were before him. Blue water, green mountains emerging from the sea, the red gold of the sky, in a sunset that could break your heart. But they were men of this earth, on the ground, who, like in a hundred other places, were at war over everything and could only agree on their desperate desire to destroy it all.

We are the rust that never sleeps.

He heard Nicolas behind him. He held two glasses full of opaque, milky liquid. The ice clinked as Nicolas handed him the aperitif.

"Here, feel French for a sip or two. Then go back to being American. For now, that's how I want you."

Frank brought the glass to his lips, tasting it and taking in the pungent flavor of anise. They drank calmly, in silence, standing beside one another, alone and resolute in the face of something that seemed endless. A day had passed since Yoshida's body had been discovered and nothing had happened. A useless day spent looking for a clue, a trace. Frenetic activity that felt like racing at breakneck speed along a road that stretched to infinity. A truce. That's what they wanted. Just a moment's truce. But even then, at that moment, when it was just the two of them and no one else, there was a presence that neither of them could exorcise.

"What do we do now, Frank?"

"I don't know, Nicolas. I really don't know. We've got nothing. Any news from Lyons?"

"They finished analyzing the first tape, but their findings are no different from Clavert's in Nice. So I don't expect anything more from the second tape. Cluny, the psychiatrist, told me I'd have his report tomorrow. I sent over a copy of the video to see if they can get anything from the measurements, but if things are the way you said, we won't find anything there either."

"Any news from Froben?"

"No. They didn't find anything in Yoshida's house. All the prints in the room where he was killed are his. The footprints on the floor are the same size as the ones on Welder's boat so we have the dubious consolation of knowing that the killer wears a size nine. The hair on the chair belonged to the victim. The blood is his too, type O negative."

"Did they find anything in the Bentley?"

"Same thing there. Lots of Yoshida's prints and other prints on the steering wheel that we're comparing with those of the bodyguard who occasionally drove the car. I ordered a handwriting test on the words on the seat. But you probably noticed it was very similar to the first writing. The same, I'd say."

"Yeah."

"The only thing we have is the hope that he keeps on calling Jean-Loup Verdier and that he'll make a mistake and lead us to him."

"Think we should put Verdier under protection?"

"I already did, just to be sure. He called me and said his house was overrun by reporters. I asked him not to talk to them and I sent a car and two officers to keep an eye out. Officially, it's to take him back and forth to the station without letting him fall into their clutches. Actually, I feel safer that way, though I decided not to say anything to him so he wouldn't be frightened. Otherwise, all we can do is keep the station under close watch. Which is exactly what we're doing."

"Good. Anything on the victims?"

"We're looking into it with the German police and your pals at the FBI. We're digging into their lives but nothing's come up so far. Three famous people, two Americans and a European. They all had intense lives but nothing aside from what we already know. They have absolutely nothing in common, except that they were all massacred by the same killer."

Frank finished his Pastis and placed the glass down on the wrought-iron balustrade. He seemed puzzled.

"What is it, Frank?"

"Nicolas, do you ever feel like you have something on the tip of your tongue, but you don't know what it is? Like when you want to remember the name of an actor you know well, but just then, hard as you try, it won't come to you?"

"Sure, quite often. At my age, it's normal."

"There's something I saw or heard, Nicolas. Something that I *should* remember but I can't think of it. And it's driving me crazy because I can feel that it's important."

"I hope you remember soon, whatever it is."

Frank turned his back on the magnificent view and crossed his arms over his chest. Fatigue and the feverish nervous energy that kept him going were visible on his face.

"Let's see. We have a killer who likes music. A connoisseur who calls the deejay of a hit show on Radio Monte Carlo to announce his intentions to murder. He leaves a musical clue that nobody recognizes and then kills two people, a man and a woman, right afterward. He leaves them for us to find, in a horrible state, as if he is laughing at us. He signs the crimes "*I kill . . .*" written in blood. He leaves absolutely no trace. He is cold-blooded, cunning, expert, and ruthless. Cluny talks about above-average intelligence. I would say *way* above average. He's so sure of himself that he gives us a second clue in the next call. Again, it's music-related and again we don't get it. And he kills again. Even more ruthlessly than the first time, and now the crime has a sense of justice about it. But he's even more contemptuous. The tape in the car, the video of the murder, the same writing as the last time. None of the victims shows signs of rape, so he's not a necrophile. But he removes all the skin of all three of the victims' faces. Why? Why does he do that to them?"

"I don't know, Frank. I hope Cluny has some ideas. I've been hitting my head against the wall, but I can't even come up with a plausible idea."

"We have to find out, Nicolas. If we manage to figure out why he does it, I'm sure we can find out who and where he is!"

"Now you two stop talking about work." Céline's voice reached them in that exchange full of shadows, darker than the night that had fallen around them. She set a plate of steaming food on the table. "Here's some bouillabaisse for you. Only one course tonight, but there's a lot of it. Frank, if you don't have at least two helpings I'll be personally offended. Nicolas, you'll take care of the wine, please?"

Frank realized that he was starving. The sandwiches he had eaten in the office without even tasting them were a distant memory. He sat down and unfolded his napkin.

"They say that food is the true culture of the people. If that's true, then your bouillabaisse is immortal poetry."

"You're a shameless flatterer, Frank." Céline laughed, illuminating her dark, lovely Mediterranean complexion. The tiny lines around her eyes only heightened her charm. "But it's nice to hear."

Hulot looked at Frank above the colorful flowers of the centerpiece. He knew what Frank was holding inside, but in spite of it all, his affection for Céline and for Hulot made him behave with a natural kindness that few people shared. Nicolas didn't know what Frank was looking for, but he hoped that he would find it soon, whatever it was, so that he could find some peace.

"You're made of gold, Frank," said Céline, raising her glass to toast him. "And your wife is a lucky woman. I'm sorry she couldn't make it tonight. But she'll come next time. And I'll take her shopping, to cut into your retirement fund."

Frank didn't move a muscle and his smile didn't change. A brief shadow passed quickly over his eyes and then disappeared in the warmth of the table. He raised his glass and responded to Céline's toast.

"Sure. I know you're not serious. You're a cop's wife, so you know that after three pairs of shoes it's grounds for divorce."

Céline laughed again and the moment passed. One by one, the lines along the coast lit up and marked the night border between land and sea. They sat there, eating the excellent food and drinking good wine on a terrace suspended over darkness, where an amber light traced the boundary that separated them from the blackness.

Two men—sentinels guarding a world at war, where people killed and got killed. For the moment, the woman held them peacefully in a gentle harbor, where nobody could ever die.

23

Frank stood at the taxi stand in the main square of Eze, but there were no cabs in sight. He looked around. There were people on the street despite the fact that it was almost midnight. Summer was coming and tourists were beginning to flock to the coast, searching for picturesque images to take home on their cameras.

He saw a large, dark limousine drive slowly through the square and head toward him. The car pulled up beside him, the door opened, and a man got out. He was at least a few inches taller than Frank, powerful but agile in his movements. He had a square face and light-colored hair in a crew cut. The man walked around the car and stopped in front of him. Frank could tell that he was carrying a gun under his well-cut jacket. He had no idea who the man was, but he already seemed dangerous.

The man looked at him with expressionless brown eyes. He seemed more or less Frank's age, maybe a few years older.

"Good evening, Mr. Ottobre," he said in English.

"Good evening. I see you already know my name." Frank showed no surprise. A flash of respect passed over the man's eyes and then they returned to neutral.

"I'm Ryan Mosse. American. Like you." Frank thought he could detect a Texas accent.

"Nice to meet you." The statement contained an implicit question.

"If you'd be so kind as to accept a ride to Monte Carlo," said

Mosse, pointing to the car, "there's someone inside who'd like to talk to you."

Without waiting for an answer, he opened the back door on his side. Frank saw someone else in the backseat, on the other side. He could see the legs of a man in dark trousers, but not his face.

Frank looked Mosse straight in the eye. He too could be dangerous and he thought he should let the other man know.

"Is there any special reason I should accept your invitation?"

"The first is that you'll avoid a long walk home since it's pretty hard to find a cab at this hour. The second is that the person who wants to talk to you is a general in the United States Army. The third is that you might find some help solving a problem that's been bothering you lately."

Without showing the slightest emotion, Frank stepped over to the door and got in the car. The man sitting inside was older but of the same type. He was more heavily built, given his age, but he emitted the same sense of strength. His hair was completely white but still thick and crew cut. In the car's dim light, Frank saw himself observed by a pair of blue eyes that were strangely youthful in the tanned, lined face. They reminded him of those of Homer Woods, his boss. He wouldn't have been surprised if the man told him he was Homer's brother. He was wearing a white shirt open at the collar with the sleeves rolled up. On the front seat, Frank noticed a jacket that matched the trousers. Outside, Mosse closed the door.

"Hello, Mr. Ottobre. Can I call you Frank?"

"Mr. Ottobre's fine for now. *Monsieur* . . .?" Frank purposefully said the word in French.

"I see the information they gave us about you is true. Drive on, Ryan."

Mosse was now in the driver's seat. The car pulled out gently and the old man turned back to Frank.

"Forgive me for stopping you so rudely. My name is General Nathan Parker, U.S. Army."

Frank shook the hand he held out. The man's grip was firm, despite his age. He probably exercised daily to keep that physique. Frank sat silently, waiting.

"And Arianna Parker's father."

The general's eyes sought an instant of surprise in Frank's but did not find it. He leaned back against the seat and crossed his legs in the narrow space of the car.

"You can probably guess what I'm doing here." He diverted his eyes as if he were looking at something out the window. Whatever it was, only he could see it. "I came to put my daughter's body in a coffin and take her back to America. The body of a woman that someone flayed like an animal."

Nathan Parker turned back to him. In the dim light of the headlights they passed, Frank saw the spark in his eyes. He wondered whether it was more from anger or from grief.

"I don't know if you've ever lost someone close to you, Mr. Ottobre . . ." Frank suddenly hated the man. The information he had about Frank certainly included the story of his wife. He realized that for him this was not a moment of shared sadness but simply an exchange of goods. Parker continued his speech in a casual tone. "I'm not here to cry over my daughter. I'm a soldier, Mr. Ottobre. A soldier doesn't cry. A soldier evens the score." The general's voice was calm, but it held a lethal fury. "No maniac bastard can do what he did and hope to get away with it."

"There's an investigation going on for exactly that reason," said Frank, gently.

Nathan Parker turned sharply.

"Frank, aside from you, none of these people would know where to stick a suppository, even if they had detailed instructions. And you know what things are like in Europe. I don't want this killer caught and put in a mental institution because he's soft in the head and then let out in a couple of years, with an apology even."

He paused and looked out the window again. The car had reached the bottom of the road out of Eze and was turning left to go down to Monte Carlo.

"Here's what I suggest. We'll organize some top guys and continue the investigation ourselves. I can have all the help I want. The FBI, Interpol, even the CIA if we need it. I can bring over a group of good, trained men, better than any cops. Quick boys who ask no questions and just obey. You'll be in charge." He nodded toward the man driving. "Captain Mosse will work with you. You'll continue the investigation until you catch him. And when you do catch him, you'll hand him over to me."

The car had reached the city in the meantime. They'd just passed the Jardin Exotique after turning down Boulevard Charles III. Continuing on Rue Princesse Caroline, they were now nearing the port.

The old soldier looked through the glass at the place where his daughter's mutilated body had been found. He squinted as if trying to see better. Frank figured that his vision had nothing to do with it. It was an instinctive reaction caused by the man's violent anger. Parker continued speaking without turning his head. He could not tear his eyes away from the port where the illuminated boats waited, afloat, for another day at sea.

"That's where they found Arianna. She was beautiful as the moon and she had a first-class mind. She was a fine girl. A rebel. Different from her sister, but a fine girl. We didn't get along so well, but we respected each other because we were equals. And they killed her like an animal." The man's voice trembled slightly. Frank sat in silence, leaving Arianna Parker's father to his thoughts.

The car drove along the port and headed toward the tunnel. Nathan Parker leaned back against the seat. The yellow lights of the tunnel colored their faces.

When they reemerged in the open air of the night, near Larvotto, and the car turned down Rue du Portier, the old man finally broke the silence.

"Well, what do you say, Frank? I'm a personal friend of Johnson Fitzpatrick, head of the FBI. And I can go even higher. I assure you, you won't regret it. Your career could take off. If it's money you're interested in, that's no problem. With what I can offer, you'll be set for life. It's an act of justice, not just revenge."

Frank remained silent, as he had been through all of General Parker's speech. He too paused to look out the window. The car was turning down Boulevard des Moulins, about to take the uphill drive to Parc Saint-Roman. The list of things they knew about him obviously included his address.

"General, nothing is as easy as it seems. You're acting as though you think all men have a price. Quite frankly, so do I. There's a price for everything. You just don't know what mine is."

"Stop playing the hero with me, Mr. Ottobre." The general's cold rage shone brighter than the lights in the lobby of Frank's building. The words *Mr. Ottobre* echoed in the small space of the car like a threat. "I know who you are. We're two of a kind."

The car pulled up smoothly in front of the glass doors of Parc Saint-Roman. Frank opened the door and got out. He stood outside the car, leaning against the door. He bent down so that his face could be seen from inside.

"That may be, General Parker. But not quite. Since you know all about me, you must know about my dead wife. Yes, I'm perfectly aware of what it's like to lose someone close. I know all about living with ghosts. We may be two of a kind, but there's one difference between us. I cried when I lost my wife. I guess I'm no soldier."

Frank gently closed the car door and walked away. The old man lowered his eyes a moment before answering. When he raised them again, Frank Ottobre was gone.

24

As soon as he woke, without even getting out of bed, Frank dialed the direct line to Cooper's office in Washington. He hoped he'd be there, in spite of the time difference. Cooper answered on the second ring.

"Cooper Danton."

"Hey, Cooper. It's Frank."

"Hey, kiddo, how's it going?" If there was surprise on the other end, Cooper didn't show it.

"Shitty."

Cooper said nothing. Frank's voice had changed. There was a new energy that hadn't been there during the last phone call. He waited in silence. "They've put me on a serial killer case here in Monaco. You wouldn't believe it!"

"I read something about it in the papers. It was on CNN too. But Homer didn't tell me you were involved. Is it that bad?"

"Worse. We're hunting shadows. This guy's made of air. No trace. No clues. And he keeps egging us on. He's making us look like complete fools. And we've got three bodies already."

"So things like that happen in good old Europe too, not just here."

"No patent on it. How're things going over there?"

"We're still on Larkin's trail. Jeff is dead and nobody misses him. Osmond's in the cooler and he's keeping his mouth shut. But we've got some good leads. One goes to Southeast Asia, a new drug racket. We'll see what happens."

"Cooper, I need a favor. I need all the information you can get on a certain General Parker and a Captain Ryan Mosse, U.S. Army."

"Parker? Nathan Parker?"

"That's the one."

"He's big time, Frank. And that's an understatement. Vietnam hero. The real mastermind behind the Gulf War and Kosovo, that kind of thing. A member of the Joint Chiefs of Staff. Very close to the White House. When he talks, everybody listens, including the President. What does Nathan Parker have to do with you?"

"His daughter was one of the victims. And now he's here with a knife between his teeth because he doesn't trust the police. I've got a feeling he's organizing a posse for his own little war."

"What's the other guy's name?"

"Mosse. Captain Ryan Mosse."

"Don't know him. I'll find out and let you know what I dig up. How can I get it to you?"

"I've got an e-mail address here in Monaco. Don't send anything to the Monaco police. I'd rather keep this out of the official investigation. We've got enough trouble. I want to handle it myself."

"Okay, I'll get to work."

"Thanks, Cooper."

"Don't mention it—anything I can do to help. Frank?"

"Yeah?"

"I'm happy for you."

Frank knew what his friend meant by that. He didn't want to disappoint him.

"I know, Cooper. Bye."

"Good luck, Frank."

He hung up and threw the cordless phone on the bed. Getting up, he walked into the bathroom naked, not looking at himself in the mirror. He opened the shower door and turned on the water.

Then Frank got in and crouched on the floor, letting the cold water run over his head and shoulders. Shivering, he waited until the water warmed up, and then he stood and started to soap himself. As the suds washed away, he tried to open his mind, leave his own body, and become someone else: that formless, faceless someone who was waiting to attack.

An idea was forming. If what he suspected was true, Arianna Parker had been one of the unluckiest women on earth. He felt the bitterness run through him. A useless death, except in the twisted mind of the assassin.

Frank turned off the faucet and the jet of water stopped. He stood there for a moment, dripping wet, watching the water gurgle down the drain.

I kill . . .

The dots of the ellipsis, three deaths. And it wasn't over. In some part of his brain, something was trying desperately to come to the light. There was a detail locked away, banging against a closed door, trying to make itself heard.

He got out of the shower and took the robe from the hook on his right, running through his conclusions one more time. Nothing was certain, but it was very plausible. And it restricted the field of investigation. He still did not understand how or when, but at least he could conjecture *who.*

That was it. That must be it.

Frank left the bathroom and crossed the dark bedroom into the living room, lit up by the French doors that opened onto the terrace. Frank went into the study, sat down at the desk, and turned on the computer. He sat and stared for an instant at the French keyboard, and then logged onto the Web. Luckily for him, Ferrand, his host, had nothing to hide, at least not on that computer, and the password entered automatically. He sent Cooper an e-mail from the address where he wanted his friend to send the information. Then he shut down the machine and went to get dressed, still mulling over his thoughts, considering them from different viewpoints to see if they would still hold water. The phone rang just as he passed the table where it sat.

He answered.

"Hello."

"Frank, it's Nicolas."

"I was just about to call you. I've got an idea. Nothing much, but it's a start."

"What?"

"I think I understand what he's after."

"And what's that?"

"It's the men he's interested in. Jochen Welder and Allen Yoshida. They were his victims."

"Then what does Arianna Parker have to do with it?"

"She was a guinea pig. It was the first time he had done it. The guy wanted someone to practice on before he did the real job, Jochen Welder's face."

"If that's true," Hulot said, after a silence on the other end, which meant that he was thinking, "then we can exclude women, and we have a smaller circle of potential victims."

"That's right, Nicolas. Men. About thirty or thirty-five, famous and good-looking. It's not much, but it's something. There aren't millions of people like that."

"It's worth considering."

"Partly because we don't have anything better. Anyway, why did you call?"

"Frank, we're in deep shit. Have you seen the papers?"

"No."

"The story's on the front page of every paper in Europe. There are TV crews here from all over. Roncaille and Durand are on the warpath. They must be facing terrible pressure, from the Interior Councilor to the Prince himself."

"I'm not surprised. Allen Yoshida wasn't just anybody."

"Exactly. All hell broke loose on that end. Roncaille told me that the U.S. Consul called him from Marseilles on behalf of your government. If we don't produce something, I'm worried my head's gonna roll. And we have another problem."

"What?"

"Jean-Loup Verdier. His nerves are shot. If you consider the position he's in, you can understand why."

"We can't risk losing him. If that maniac has no one to talk to, he might stop calling. He won't stop killing, but there will be no more clues. And if he decides to find someone else, at another radio station or something, it'll take time until we get things under control again. Which means more people killed."

"We have to talk to him, Frank. I want you to do it."

"Why me?"

"I think you have more influence on him. It's just a feeling, but the letters FBI have more of an effect than the words Sûreté Publique."

"Okay. I'll get dressed and be right there."

"I'll send a car. See you at Jean-Loup's.

"Okay."

Frank was already heading toward the bedroom. He picked out a shirt and a pair of pants, slipped into socks and shoes, and threw on a light cotton jacket. As he returned the things to his pockets that he had put on the dresser the night before, he thought about what he should say to Jean-Loup Verdier. The kid was scared stiff and that was no surprise. Frank realized that he was calling Jean-Loup a kid when he was really only a few years younger than himself. Frank felt much older. You aged faster as a cop. Or maybe some people were just born old and only discovered it when they met people who followed the normal timeline. If that was the case, Jean-Loup Verdier's timeline might have just been broken.

Frank went out in the hall and called the elevator. As he waited, he locked the apartment. The elevator doors slid open noiselessly behind him, shedding a bright light on the dark hallway.

He went in and pressed the ground floor button. They would get the killer; that was certain. Sooner or later, he would slip up and they would catch him. But how many victims with mutilated faces would there be between now and then?

The elevator stopped with a slight jolt and the doors opened onto the elegant marble lobby of Parc Saint-Roman. Frank went out and saw a police car waiting for him through the glass doors on the left. They'd gotten there fast; they had probably been nearby. The doorman saw him and nodded through the glass guard box.

"Bonjour, Monsieur Ottobre," the doorman said, addressing him in French.

"Bonjour."

"They left this for you after you got back last night." The man handed him a plain white envelope without any stamps. The only thing on it was his name written in ink.

"Thanks, Pascal."

"*Pas de quoi.* A pleasure, Monsieur."

Frank took the envelope and opened it. Inside was a sheet of paper folded in three. He opened it and read the message, written in shaky but clear handwriting.

Real men are not afraid to change their minds. Don't make me change my mind about you. You'll find me at this address and phone number.

Nathan Parker

At the bottom of the page, there was an address and two phone numbers. As he got into the car, Frank could not help thinking that now there were two bloodthirsty maniacs on the loose in Monte Carlo.

25

The police car left Monte Carlo behind and took the uphill road to Beausoleil and the A8, the highway linking Monaco to Nice and Italy beyond. Sitting in the backseat, Frank opened the window to let in some fresh air. He read the general's message a second time and slipped it into his pocket. Then he continued looking out the window. The scene outside unfolded before his eyes like one long, indistinguishable rush of color.

Parker was a complication he didn't need. Although this was a private matter, the man represented power with a capital *P*. He was not simply boasting. Not in the least. He really did have access to all the things he claimed. Which meant that, along with the police, there would be others around with cruder methods of investigation. Unofficial, true, but not required to act legally and therefore much more effective.

The fact that they were working in the Principality of Monaco, which made it a delicate situation, wouldn't deter Nathan Parker's thirst for vengeance. He was old and determined enough not to give a damn about the possible effects on his career. And if things were the way Cooper said, Parker was powerful enough to protect the men with him too. If he captured the killer, the press would turn it into the romantic account of a distraught father seeking justice, succeeding where others had failed. He would be turned into a hero and become untouchable. The United States desperately needed heroes just then. American public opinion and the U.S. government would back him all the way. Principality authorities would gag on it for a while, but then they would have to swallow their pride. *Game over*.

And then there was Jean-Loup. Another problem.

Frank had to find a way to dissuade Jean-Loup from a decision he couldn't blame him for. The fame you get from hosting a hit radio show is one thing, but having your name in all the papers because you're the only person a killer will talk to is quite another. It was enough to make anyone explode. After all, Jean-Loup was just a deejay. He had a brain and he knew how to use it. He wasn't just a dumb pretty boy like other show business people Frank had met, or at least he didn't give that impression. But he had every right to be scared.

Awful business. And time was running out, ticking away minute by minute, marked by the chronometer that the higher-up Principality officials were holding in their hands.

The car slowed down at a house on the right. It was built into the hillside and Frank could make out the roof behind a row of cypress trees on the other side of the road. It overlooked all of Monte Carlo. Must have a great view. That was the deejay's house, for sure. There were a number of cars parked outside and a couple of trucks with the call letters of TV stations. A small crowd of reporters and cameramen were laying siege to the house. There was also a police car close by. When they saw Frank arrive, the reporters quivered with excitement. The policeman in the front passenger seat picked up the mike.

"Ducross here. We're coming up."

The iron gate started to open. As the car slowed down to drive in, the reporters came up to see who was inside. Two policemen got out of the parked car to keep them from following inside the gate.

They drove slowly down a ramp paved with red nonslip tile and found themselves in the driveway, in front of the garage. Nicolas Hulot was already there, waiting. He greeted him through the open window.

"Hi, Frank. See the chaos?"

"Hi, Nicolas. I see it. Typical. I'd be surprised if they weren't here." Frank got out of the car and checked out the building. "Jean-Loup Verdier must make quite a salary to afford this."

"There's a story to this house," Hulot smiled. "Haven't you read the papers?"

"No, that's something I gladly leave to you."

"They've all written about it. Jean-Loup inherited this house."

"Nice relatives."

"It wasn't a relative. Sounds like a fairy tale, but he inherited from a rich old widow. He saved her dog."

"Her dog?"

"That's right. In the square of the casino a few years ago. This lady's dog escaped and ran into the middle of the street. Jean-Loup jumped out to save it just as it was about to get hit by a car. He almost got killed too. The woman hugged and kissed him, crying with gratitude, and that was that. A few years later, a notary called him and told him he was a homeowner."

"Not bad. I thought that kind of thing only happened in Disney movies. It's just a rough guess, but this place must be worth a couple million."

"Make it three, with the property values around here."

"Pretty nice. Okay, should we go do our duty?"

Hulot nodded. "He's over here. Come on."

They crossed the courtyard and passed some bushes with red flowers on the right of the house. There was a patio beyond the bushes and a swimming pool. It wasn't huge, but no bathtub either.

Jean-Loup and Bikjalo were sitting at a table under a bower covered with vines. The remains of breakfast were still on the table. The manager's presence was a clear indication of Jean-Loup's state. So much attentiveness meant that Bikjalo was worried about his gold mine.

"Hello, Jean-Loup. Mr. Bikjalo."

Bikjalo got up with an expression of relief. Reinforcements had arrived. Jean-Loup seemed embarrassed and couldn't look them in the eye.

"Good morning, gentlemen. I was saying to Jean-Loup . . ."

Frank interrupted brusquely. He wanted to avoid the subject at first so that Jean-Loup would not feel attacked. It was a delicate moment and Frank wanted him to feel at ease before he mentioned it.

"Is that coffee I see?"

"Yes . . ."

"Only for the household, or can we have some?"

As Hulot and Frank sat down, Jean-Loup went to get two cups from the shelf behind him. The deejay poured coffee from a thermos and Frank watched him intently. You could tell by looking at him that he hadn't slept. He was under a lot of pressure—Frank could see that. But he must not, he could not give up, and Jean-Loup would have to understand.

Hulot brought the cup to his lips.

"Mmm. Good. I wish we had coffee like this at headquarters."

Jean-Loup smiled listlessly. His gaze wandered and he avoided looking at them, Frank especially. Bikjalo sat down again, on the chair farthest away. He was showing that he wanted to keep his distance and leave the problem to them. The tension was palpable and Frank knew he had to take the bull by the horns.

"Okay, what's the problem, Jean-Loup?"

The deejay finally found the strength to look at him. Frank was surprised that there was no fright in his eyes, as he had expected. There was fatigue, concern, and perhaps the worry that he was unable to play a role that was too big for him. But he was not frightened. Jean-Loup looked away and started saying something he'd probably rehearsed many times.

"The problem is very simple. I can't take it." Frank sat in silence and waited for Jean-Loup to continue. He didn't want to make him feel he was being interrogated. "I wasn't ready for all this. Every time I hear that voice on the phone, I lose ten years of my life. And the thought that after he talks to me, that man goes . . . and . . ."

He continued as though talking about it were an enormous strain. No man likes to show weakness, and Jean-Loup was no different.

". . . does what he does. It's tearing me apart. And I keep asking myself, why me? Why does he have to make those calls to me? I have no life anymore. I'm locked indoors like a criminal. I can't even go to the window without hearing reporters scream my name. I can't go outside without being surrounded by people asking me questions. I can't take it anymore."

"But Jean-Loup," Bikjalo interrupted, putting in his two cents. "This is a once-in-a-lifetime occasion. You're incredibly popular right now. You're one of the most famous men in Europe. Every TV station wants you. All the papers are talking about you. We've even had proposals from movie producers who want to make a film."

A sharp look from Hulot brought the station manager to a halt. Frank couldn't have thought worse of him. Money-hungry prick. He would gladly have belted him one. Jean-Loup got up from his chair with an imperious gesture.

"I want to be appreciated because I talk to people, not because I talk to a killer. And I know reporters. When they're done talking about everything else, they'll start asking the same things that I do. Why him? And if they don't find an answer, they'll make one up. And they'll destroy me."

Frank knew the media well enough to agree with him. And he respected Jean-Loup too much to lie to him.

"Jean-Loup, that's exactly the way things are. You're too intelligent for me to try to convince you it's any different. I know you're not ready for all this. But who would be? I've spent half my life chasing criminals, but I'd have the same concerns and the same reaction if I were in your shoes. But you can't give up. Not now." Frank replied to a possible objection. "I know this is partly our fault. If we were better at this, it would probably all be over. But that's just not the way it is. That man is still at large and as long as he's out there, he has only one aim: to go on killing. And we have to stop him."

"I don't know if I can sit there again in front of the mike pretending nothing has happened, waiting for that voice."

Frank bowed his head. When he raised it, Hulot saw a different light in his eyes.

"There are things you look for in life. And sometimes there are things that look for you. You don't choose them and maybe you don't even want them, but they come and you're never the same again. At that point, you have two choices. You can run away, try to leave it all behind you, or you can stand and face it. Whatever you choose, you and only you are able to decide whether it's for better or for worse. There are three people dead now, killed horribly. There'll be others if you don't help. If you decide to continue, it might tear you to pieces, but afterward you'll have the time and the strength to put the pieces together again. If you run away, you'll be torn apart just the same, but the remorse will pursue you for all the time you have left. And every day, the pieces will get smaller and smaller."

Jean-Loup sat down slowly. Even the sky and the sea before them seemed to be made of silence.

"Okay, I'll do whatever you say."

"You'll go on with the show?"

"Yes."

Hulot relaxed in his chair. Bikjalo was unable to repress a slight smile of satisfaction. And Frank heard the first *tick* of a clock that had just started running again.

26

Frank walked Hulot back to his car while Jean-Loup and Bikjalo remained sitting at the table by the pool. When they were gone, the manager of Radio Monte Carlo, still anxious over what he had almost lost, put his arm around Jean-Loup. He wanted the radio host to feel his presence and he whispered advice like a boxing coach during a losing fight, convincing him to hold up for just another couple of rounds.

Frank's first impression of that man had been right after all. Through his work, Frank had gained an animal's instinct for recognizing people's true nature. He still had it. Apparently you couldn't just decide to stop being a bloodhound.

You can't fit a square peg in a round hole . . . And that was true of him, Bikjalo, and anyone else.

Hulot opened the door of the Peugeot but remained standing outside, staring at the magnificent view below. He had no desire to return to the investigation. He turned to Frank. The American could see in his eyes that he needed a long, uninterrupted, dreamless sleep. Without figures in black, without voices whispering *I kill . . .* in his ear, waking him to nightmares worse than his dreams.

"You were great with that kid . . . with him and with me."

"What do you mean?"

"I know I'm leaning on you a lot in this investigation. Don't think I don't realize it. I asked for your help and acted like I was helping *you* out, when *I* was really the one who needed the help."

In a very short time, their roles had been reversed, in one of life's many dramatic moments. Those moments kept coming, but life kept laughing at them through it all.

"That's not true, Nicolas. Not *exactly* true. Maybe this guy's psychosis is contagious and we're going crazy too. But if that's what we have to do to catch him, then we've got to keep going till it's over."

"There's just one danger in what you said." Hulot got into the car.

"What's that?"

"Once you accept madness, you can't get rid of it. You said so yourself, remember, Frank? We're little dinosaurs, nothing but dinosaurs . . ."

He closed the door, turned the key, and started the engine. The automatic gate opened, commanded by the officer in the street. Frank stood and watched the car drive up the ramp. He saw the brake lights go on as Nicolas turned into the street and then drove away. Throughout his conversation with Hulot, the agents who had accompanied him had stood off to one side, talking to each other by their car. Frank got in the backseat and the cop in the front turned to look at him inquisitively.

"Parc Saint-Roman. There's no hurry," said Frank, after thinking a moment. He needed to be alone and collect his thoughts. General Parker and his plans had not been forgotten, just put aside. He needed to know more about him and Ryan Mosse before he could decide what to do. He hoped Cooper had already sent the information he needed, though not much time had passed.

The car pulled out. Up the hill, through the gate, down the street. Left. More winding through the throngs of reporters waiting in ambush. Frank looked them over carefully as they shook themselves like dogs when another dog passes. The same guy with red hair who'd stuck his head into the inspector's car the other day was there. As Frank passed, a reporter standing next to a Mazda convertible exchanged glances with him, thoughtful.

Frank knew they'd soon be chasing him once they found out who he was and what he was doing there. There was no doubt that they would soon figure out his role in this business. They all had contacts in the Police Department—what their articles called a "reliable source." The reporters paraded in front of the car as the vanguard of a world that wanted to know the truth. And the best journalist among them was not the one who found it out. It was the one who sold the best story.

Slowly, as requested, the car turned back down the street they had climbed to get to Jean-Loup's house. As they drove along, Frank saw the woman and the boy for the first time.

They practically ran out from an unpaved road just a few hundred yards from where the reporters were stalking the house, on the left. Frank noticed them because she was holding the boy's hand and seemed frightened. She stopped at the intersection and looked around like someone who didn't know where she was or where she was going. As the car passed them, Frank felt certain that she was running away. She looked just over thirty and was wearing a pair of blue sweatpants and a shiny dark blue shirt, untucked. The color set off her magnificent blond hair that fell to her shoulders. The fabric and the hair went perfectly together and seemed to be competing for the reflection of the May sun. She was tall and fit and her movements were graceful in spite of her haste. The boy was about ten and seemed tall for his age. He was wearing baggy jeans and a T-shirt. Uncertain, he looked at the woman holding his hand with big, bewildered blue eyes.

As he turned his head and leaned against the window to continue looking at them, Frank saw Captain Ryan Mosse, U.S. Army, run up and stop the woman and the boy, stepping in front of them. He grabbed their arms and forced them to follow him back down the road they had come from. Frank turned and placed a hand on the driver's shoulder.

"Stop."

"What?"

"Stop here a second, please."

The driver stepped on the brake and the car rolled gently to the side of the road. The two agents looked at him. The one in the passenger seat shrugged. Americans . . .

Frank got out and crossed the street. He walked down the road that led to a house with a gate, set off a bit from the others. He could see their three backs. A strong man pushing a woman and a boy.

"Part of your investigation, Captain Mosse?"

The man stopped at the sound of Frank's voice, and forced the woman and the boy to stop too. He reacted without any visible effort. He turned and saw Frank, showing no surprise.

"Ah, here he is, our FBI Special Agent. What's this, Boy Scout, your good deed for the day? If you go stand at the Place du Casino and wait awhile, you might find a little old lady to help cross the street . . ."

Frank went over to the group. The woman looked at him with a mixture of hope and curiosity. He was struck by the beauty of her eyes and was astonished by his own reaction.

The boy wrenched himself free.

"You're hurting me, Ryan."

"Get in the house, Stuart. And don't move."

Mosse let go. Stuart turned to the woman who nodded at him.

"Go on, Stuart."

The boy took two steps back and went on looking at them. Then he turned and ran to the green gate.

"You too, Helena. Go in the house and stay there."

Mosse twisted the woman's arm. Frank saw his muscles

tighten under his shirt. He made the woman, who was still staring at Frank, turn to him.

"Look at me. Do you understand, Helena?"

The woman whimpered in pain and nodded. As she left, Helena shot a last, desperate glance at Frank. Then she turned and followed the boy down the road. The gate opened, then closed behind them.

Like the gates of a prison, Frank thought.

The two men faced each other. Given the way that Mosse was looking at him, Frank could tell he was of the same school of thought as Parker. You were either a friend or an enemy. Anyone who didn't follow them and love them had to accept the consequences.

There was a brief gust of wind that rustled the overgrown bushes on the side of the road. It died down immediately and the branches were still again, emphasizing the tension between them.

"You're great with women and kids. But that doesn't seem like much for someone who came here with higher goals. Am I wrong, Captain Mosse?"

Frank smiled. He got the same smile in return. A smile of contempt.

"You do pretty well yourself with women and children, don't you, Frank? Oh, I'm sorry, Frank's too familiar for you. What is it you want to be called? That's right . . . Mr. Ottobre."

As Mosse paused to admire his own words, he stepped off slightly to one side. He was shifting his weight like someone expecting to be attacked at any moment. "That's right, Mr. Ottobre. You apparently think that women are a good excuse for shirking, don't you? Nothing doing for Mr. Ottobre. Can't expect anything from him. Closed for mourning. Maybe your wife . . ."

Frank lunged at him in spite of himself, so fast that the other man didn't see him coming, even though he was expecting it. The blow hit him in the face and knocked him to the ground. Mosse was flat on his back, a trickle of blood coming from the side of his mouth. Otherwise, Frank's blow had had no effect on him. He smiled again and there was a light of triumph in his eyes.

"I'm just sorry you won't have much time to understand the mistake you just made."

He arched his back and was on his feet. Almost simultaneously, he kicked his left leg. Frank deflected the kick with his forearm and slightly lost his balance. He realized his mistake immediately. Mosse was a tough opponent and had kicked only to throw him off. The soldier slipped to the ground and with his right leg swept Frank off his feet. As he fell to the pavement, Frank managed to turn to the side, easing his fall with his shoulder. There was a time when he would not have been caught off guard.

Mosse was behind him in a flash. He immobilized Frank's legs with his own and grabbed his neck with his right arm. A military knife suddenly glimmered in his left hand and now it was pointed at Frank's throat. The two of them were tense and motionless, a sculpture fallen to the ground. They could have been carved from marble. The captain's eyes were shining, excited by the brawl. Frank realized that he *liked* it, that fighting was his reason for living. He was one of those people who believed that an *enemy* was worth his weight in gold.

"Well, Mr. Ottobre, what do you think now? Funny, they said you were good. Didn't your scout's instinct tell you not to play with kids who are bigger than you? Where's your sixth sense?"

The man holding the knife moved and Frank felt the tip enter a nostril. He was afraid Mosse might slice it. He thought of Jack Nicholson in *Chinatown* and wondered if Mosse had seen the movie. That was neither here nor there, and it made him smile. Which annoyed his adversary even more. He felt the blade push at the cartilage of his nose.

"That's enough, Ryan."

The order was barked from behind them and the tension of

the blade lessened immediately. Frank recognized the voice of General Parker. Without turning, after one last thrust of his arm against Frank's neck, Mosse let go. That last twist meant that it was not over between them. Just postponed.

A soldier never cries. A soldier never forgets. A soldier evens the score.

The captain got up, brushing the dust off his light summer pants. Frank lay there an instant, looking at the two of them standing over him, one next to the other. They were so alike physically because, in fact, they were the same. Frank remembered his Italian grandfather and his endless flow of proverbs.

Like attracts like.

It was no accident that the general and the captain stuck together. They had the same goals and probably the same means of accomplishing them. What had just happened made no difference, win or lose. It was just for show. Mosse was pissing around to define his territory. Frank was worried about what would happen later on.

"You should use a different command for your Doberman, General. They say *platz* works best."

Mosse stiffened, but Parker stopped him with a gesture. He held out his hand to Frank. Without deigning to look at him, Frank got up on his own, brushing off his clothes. He stood before the two men, breathing heavily. He looked into Parker's cold blue eyes and at the gaze of Captain Mosse, which had lost its gleam and was again a mere reflection.

A seagull circled slowly overhead. It was flying out to sea in the blue sky, its jeering cry reaching them from above.

Parker turned to Mosse.

"Ryan, could you go inside and make sure Helena doesn't do any more foolishness? Thank you."

Mosse shot one last glance at Frank. His eyes flashed for a moment.

A soldier never forgets.

The light faded instantly. Mosse turned and headed toward the house. He would probably walk the exact same way if his path were strewn with corpses. If Ryan Mosse found the words *I kill . . .* written in blood, he would probably write in the same blood underneath: *So do I . . .*

Mosse was a man without pity and Frank would not forget it.

"Please forgive Captain Mosse, Mr. Ottobre."

There was no trace of sarcasm in his voice, but Frank had no illusions. In other circumstances, if necessary, he knew very well that things would end differently. There would be no command from Parker and Ryan would not stop.

"He's . . . what can I say. Sometimes he worries too much about our family. Sometimes he goes overboard, but he's reliable and trustworthy and cares for us a great deal."

Frank had no doubt about that. He only wondered about the limits of Mosse's enthusiasm, which seemed to depend on the lines drawn by the general. And Frank was sure that the boundaries would expand.

"The woman you saw earlier is my daughter Helena. Arianna's older sister. The boy with her is Stuart, my grandson. Her son. She . . ."

Parker's tone of voice softened. There was a hint of sadness.

"To be quite frank, she's suffering from a serious nervous breakdown. Very serious. Arianna's death was the last straw. We tried to hide it from her, but it was impossible."

The general's head bent down. Nonetheless, Frank found it hard to see him in the role of a brokenhearted old father. It had not escaped him that the general defined the boy first as his grandson and then as Helena's son. Hierarchy and discipline were probably as much a part of his private life as his public one. Cynically, perhaps, Frank saw his daughter and grandson's presence in Monte Carlo as a cover for his real intentions.

"Arianna was different. She was made of steel. She was my daughter. Helena is like her mother, fragile. Very fragile. Sometimes she does things without realizing, like today. A few times, she's gotten out and wandered around for a couple of days until we find her. You can imagine her state. That's what would have happened this time too. She has to be watched so that she won't be a danger to herself and others."

"I'm sorry about your daughter, General. Helena, but especially Arianna. However, that doesn't change my opinion of you and what you're doing. Maybe I'd do the same thing in your place, I don't know. I've been put on this case and I'll do everything I can to catch this killer, you can count on that. But I will also do everything I can to keep you from whatever road you're planning to take."

Parker did not react angrily, like the night before. Frank's refusal to collaborate was probably filed away as "tactically irrelevant."

"I'll remember that. You've got character, Frank, but then so do I. So I would suggest you be very careful when you cross that road, if I'm on it, *Mr. Ottobre*."

This time, the sarcasm leaked out and Frank noticed. He smiled. *Like Ryan, like Parker.*

"I'll keep your advice in mind, General. But I hope you won't hold it against me if I continue the investigation my way. But thanks, *Mr. Parker . . .*"

Irony for irony, an eye for an eye, like the jeering cry of the seagull overhead, like a killer torn between justice and revenge.

Frank turned and walked slowly back to the main road. He could feel the general staring at his back. To his right, over the bushes, he could make out the roof of Jean-Loup's house. As he crossed the road to get to the waiting car, Frank wondered whether the fact that Parker had rented a house so close to the deejay's was coincidental or deliberate.

27

From the balcony of his Parc Saint-Roman apartment, Frank saw the car that had brought him turn right on Rue des Giroflées, then onto Boulevard d'Italie. The guys had probably parked below and received some orders from headquarters before leaving. Meanwhile, he had taken the elevator, opened the French doors, and gone out on the terrace. He tried to imagine their wisecracks about the situation, about him in particular. He was aware of the general opinion of his role in the *affaire*, as they called it. Except for Nicolas and Morelli, there was a dose of understandable chauvinism where he was concerned. Not that anyone was against him. Basically, they all had the same goal. But there were definitely some misgivings. His friendship with Hulot and his FBI qualifications were enough to earn everyone's cooperation, but not necessarily their camaraderie. The doors were only half open to their American cousin.

Too bad. He wasn't there for show, but to get a killer. It was a job, and he didn't need any pats on the back.

Frank looked at the clock. It was two thirty in the afternoon. Realizing that he was hungry, he went back inside to the tiny kitchen. He'd asked Amélie, the housekeeper who came along with the apartment, to do a little shopping. He used whatever was in the fridge to make himself a sandwich, opened a Heineken, and went back to the terrace. Sitting down on one of the two chaise longues and placing his meal on the glass tabletop, he removed his shirt and sat bare-chested in the sun. For once, he didn't worry about his scars. It was different now. He had other things to think about.

Frank looked up at the cloudless sky. The seagulls circled on high now, watching the people and catching fish. They were the only white specks in the clear blue sky. It was a fantastic day. Ever since this whole thing had started, the weather had decided not to reflect human misery and had headed toward summer all on its own. Not one cloud had covered the sun, not for an instant. Someone somewhere had decided to leave the handling of light and darkness to human beings, and to them only. Lords and masters of their own eclipse.

He let his eyes run along the coast.

Monte Carlo under the sun was a small, elegant hive with too many queen bees, and even more who just played the part. Facades, mere facades. They propped up a flimsy image of elegance, like phony buildings on a movie set. The only thing behind them was the far-away line of the horizon. And that man in a long dark coat was opening the doors one by one with a scornful bow, pointing to the void behind them with a black-gloved hand.

Frank finished his sandwich and took the sip of beer that he had saved for last, straight from the bottle. He looked at his watch again. Three o'clock. If Cooper wasn't out on another case, he would be at the office in that huge stone building that was FBI headquarters on Pennsylvania Avenue in Washington. He picked up his cordless phone and punched in the number.

"Cooper Danton," he answered at the third ring in his usual dry tone.

"Hi, Cooper. Frank again."

"Hey, man. Getting a tan on the Côte d'Azur?"

"No sun on this Côte d'Azur. Our friend has us living the nightlife. I'm white as snow."

"Yeah, right. Any progress?"

"Totally in the dark. The few lightbulbs we had are blowing

out, one by one. And if that wasn't enough, this General Parker and his sidekick are complicating things. I know I'm being a pain in the ass, but have you found anything on them?"

"Lots, if the big time doesn't scare you. I was about to send you an e-mail with a file attached. You beat me to it."

"Send it anyway but tell me a little first."

"Okay. Just a summary. General Parker, Nathan James, born in Montpelier, Vermont, in 'thirty-seven. Family not incredibly wealthy, but very well to do. When he was seventeen, he left home and forged papers to get into the army. First in his class at the Academy. Brilliant officer with a fast-track career. Involved in the Cuban missile crisis in 'sixty-one. Decorated in Vietnam. Brilliant operations in Nicaragua and Panama. Wherever they needed to flex muscles, use some fists and some brains, that's where he'd be. He was Army Chief of Staff very early on. Secret mastermind of Desert Storm and the war in Kosovo. A couple of presidents later, and he's still there. Which means that when he talks, people listen. And his opinion counts in Afghanistan now too. He's got money, power, and credibility. He can wet the bed and say he was sweating. He's tough, Frank. Real tough."

Cooper stopped to take a breath and let him process the information.

"What about the other one?"

"Who? Captain Ryan Mosse?"

Frank remembered Mosse's knife against his nostril. He scratched his nose to get rid of the memory.

"Yeah. Did you get anything on him?"

"Sure did. Captain Mosse, Ryan Wilbur. Born March 2, 1963, in Austin Texas. There's less on him. And a lot more."

"What do you mean by that?"

"At a certain point, Mosse became Parker's shadow. If you got one, you got the other. Mosse would give his life for the general."

"Is there any special reason, or is it just Parker's charm?"

"Mosse's loyalty is tied to the reason that Parker was decorated in Vietnam. One of the things he did was cross the Charlie line with a wounded soldier on his back, saving his life."

"Now you're going to give me a name."

"Right. The soldier was Willy Mosse, Ryan's father."

"Perfect."

After that, they became friends. Or rather Mosse's father became a subordinate of Nathan Parker. And Parker took care of the sergeant's son. He helped him get into military academy, had him promoted, and covered his ass when necessary."

"Meaning?"

"In short, Frank, Mosse is a bit of a psycho. He goes in for meaningless violence and gets himself in trouble. At the Academy, he once almost killed a classmate with his fists and later stabbed a soldier over a woman at an army party in Arizona. During the Gulf War, a soldier was tried for threatening him with an M-16 to stop him from going ballistic on a group of defenseless prisoners."

"Quite a guy!"

"A creep is more like it. But things were quieted down every time. Thanks to guess who."

"General Nathan Parker, I presume."

"Correct. That's why I told you to be careful, Frank. Those two are the devil squared. Mosse is Parker's henchman. And I'm sure he wouldn't think twice about using him."

"I know, Coop. Thanks. I'll be expecting your e-mail."

"It's already sent. Take care, my friend."

Frank hung up and stood in the middle of the room, his head leaning to one side. The information from Cooper only added names, dates, and facts to what he already thought about those two. They were bad enough in broad daylight. They would be vicious at night.

The intercom buzzed. He got up, turned off the radio, and went to answer.

"Hello."

"Mr. Ottobre, there's someone coming up to see you." The doorman was speaking English and sounded embarrassed. "I'm sorry I couldn't tell you earlier but . . . please understand . . . I . . ."

"Don't worry, Pascal. It's okay."

He wondered whom it was to make the doorman so upset. Someone knocked just then. He wondered why they didn't ring the bell. Frank went to open the door.

He found himself in front of a middle-aged man, about his height, undeniably American. He bore a vague resemblance to Robert Redford, with darker hair. He was tan and elegant but not pretentious. The man was wearing a blue suit and his shirt was open with no tie. He wore a Rolex but the band was leather, not one of those massive blocks of gold so common in Monaco. The man flashed him a natural grin. He was a real person, not a celebrity. No PR at any price. Frank liked him on sight.

"Frank Ottobre?"

"Yes?"

"Glad to meet you, Mr. Ottobre. I'm Dwight Durham, U.S. Consul in Marseilles."

Frank stopped a second in surprise, then shook the outstretched hand. This was an unexpected visit. His face probably reflected his thoughts, because the envoy's eyes lit up in amusement. And his grin shot up on one side, creasing his face.

"I'll leave, if that sounds offensive. But if you can get over my title and invite me in, I'd like to speak to you."

Frank collected himself. The man was certainly charming. He pointed to his bare chest. Strangely enough, he was not ashamed of showing his scars to a stranger. And in any case, Durham gave no sign of noticing them.

"Sorry. You took me by surprise, but that's okay. As you can see, I always receive my country's diplomatic corps dressed like Rambo. It's patriotic. Come on in, Mr. Durham."

The consul stepped forward. He turned to someone in the hallway behind him, a tall buff man with a gun under his jacket and letters stamped on his forehead—FBI, CIA, or DEA, but certainly not the Salvation Army.

"Could you wait for me here please, Malcolm?"

"No problem, sir."

"Thanks."

Durham closed the door. He took a few steps and stopped in the center of the room, looking around.

"Not bad. Great view."

"Yeah. I'm a guest in this apartment. I guess you already know why I'm here."

Frank made his declaration to avoid wasting time. Before arriving, Durham must have gotten all the information on him that he needed. Frank could imagine his secretary placing a folder with his name and his résumé, on the desk.

Frank Ottobre. Round man, square man.

The folder must have passed through so many hands by now that Frank no longer cared. All he wanted Durham to know was that there was no reason for embarrassment and useless verbal gymnastics between them.

The consul understood and seemed to appreciate it. In that time of his life, Frank was not a very likeable guy. Durham had the decency not to pretend, knowing that admiration and respect were a sufficient alternative.

"Please sit down, Mr. Durham."

"Dwight. Call me Dwight."

"Okay, Dwight then. Call me Frank. Do you want something to drink? Nothing fancy though. I'm not very well stocked right now," he said, going out onto the terrace to retrieve his shirt.

"Can you manage a Perrier?"

No alcohol. Good. As Frank passed him on his way to the kitchen, Durham sat down on the couch. Frank noticed that his socks were the same color as his pants. The man liked to match. Meticulous but without overdoing it.

"I think so. No frills, okay?"

Durham smiled. "No frills."

Frank came back with a bottle of Perrier and a glass and handed them to him unceremoniously. As Dwight poured the sparkling water, Frank went to sit on the other couch, at a right angle to his guest.

"You're asking yourself what I'm doing here, right, Frank?"

"No, *you're* asking. I think you came here to tell me."

Durham looked at the bubbles in his glass as if it were champagne.

"We have a problem, Frank."

"We?"

"Yes, we. You and I. I'm heads and you're tails. Or vice versa. But right now, we're two sides of the same coin. And we're in the same pocket."

He took a sip of water and placed the glass on the coffee table in front of him.

"First, I want to say that my visit is only as official as you want to make it. I consider it completely off the record, a friendly chat. I must admit that I expected a different sort of person. Not Rambo necessarily, but Elliot Ness perhaps. I'm glad I was wrong."

He picked up the glass again, as if he felt more confident holding it.

"Want me to explain the situation, Frank?"

"Might not be a bad idea. I think I need to review the subject a little."

"Well, I can tell you that Allen Yoshida's death only accelerated something that Arianna Parker's had already set off. You know that General Parker's here in the Principality, don't you?" Frank nodded. Dwight continued, showing relief and at the same time concern that he was already informed. "We're lucky you just happened to be here. It kept me from the embarrassment of insisting that one of our representatives be included in the investigation, because you already were. The United States has an image problem right now. For a country that decided to assume the leadership of modern civilization, as the one and only true superpower, we got a sound beating with 9/11. They hit us where we were strongest, where we felt invincible, at home."

He looked out the window, partially reflected in the panes of the French doors, which the first shadows of evening had turned into a mirror.

"And then this mess happens . . . Two Americans killed like that, right here in Monaco, one of the world's safest countries. Funny, no? Doesn't it feel a little like a rerun? And now we've got a brokenhearted father who has decided to take matters into his own hands. A U.S. Army general who intends to use the same terrorist tactics we're fighting elsewhere for his own ends. As you can see, we've got the makings of another big international fiasco."

"So?" Frank looked at Durham, impassive.

"So, you have to catch him, Frank. The killer. *You* have to. Before Parker does. Before the local police. In spite of the local police, if need be. Washington wants this case to be the pride and glory of America. Whether you like it or not, you have to take off your Elliot Ness shirt and turn into Rambo."

Frank thought that in different circumstances, he and Durham could have been great friends. The short time they had spent together only increased their liking of each other.

"You know I will, Dwight. I'll do it, but not for any of those reasons. Heads and tails maybe, but we're only the same coin in the same pocket by accident. I'll catch the killer, and you can give it any meaning you like. Just one thing."

"What?"

"Don't say that your meaning has to be mine too."

Dwight Durham, U.S. Consul, didn't say a word. Either he

didn't understand or he understood too well, but that was enough. He stood up and straightened his pants. The conversation was over.

"Okay, Frank. I think we've covered everything."

Frank stood up as well. They shook hands in the waning light of the late spring afternoon. The sun was setting outside and the sky was turning a paler blue. Night would fall soon, a night of voices and killers in the darkness. And everyone would try to grope his way to a hiding place.

"Don't show me out. I know the way. Bye, Frank. Good luck."

"Luck's not a lady tonight. She's going down kicking and screaming."

Durham went to the door and opened it. Malcolm could be seen standing outside as he closed the door behind him.

Frank was alone again. He decided he deserved another beer. He went into the kitchen to get it and sat down on the couch that his guest had occupied.

We're the same coin . . . Heads or tails, Dwight?

He relaxed and tried to forget Durham and their meeting. Diplomacy, wars, legal battles. He took a swig of beer and tried to do something he had not done in a long time. He called it "opening." When an investigation came to a dead end, he sat down by himself and tried to release his mind, letting all his thoughts free-associate, like a mental puzzle fitting together on its own. His only aim was to give free rein to his unconscious. Lateral thinking in images. Sometimes it brought excellent results. He closed his eyes.

Arianna Parker and Jochen Welder.

The boat, wedged into the dock, the masts listing slightly to the left.

The two of them lying on the bed, their faces skinned, their teeth uncovered in a scowl without rage.

The voice on the radio.
The writing, red as blood.
I kill . . .
Jean-Loup Verdier. His wide eyes.
Harriet's face.

No, no. Not now!

The voice on the radio again.
The music, the cover of the Santana record.
Allen Yoshida.
His head leaning against the car window.
The light-colored seat with the red writing again.
The man, the knife, the blood.
The video.
The man in black and Allen Yoshida.
The photos of the room without them.
The video. The photos. The video. The photos. The vid . . .

Suddenly, with an involuntary jump, Frank Ottobre found himself standing in front of the couch. It was such a tiny detail that his mind had recorded it and filed it away as if it was of no importance.

He had to go over to headquarters immediately and check on what he had remembered. Maybe it was just an impression, but he grasped at that scrap of hope. If he had a thousand fingers, he would have crossed them all.

28

The sun was setting as Frank reached police headquarters on Rue Notari. He had walked there from Parc Saint-Roman, slipping through the late afternoon crowds on the streets without even noticing them. He was on edge. When he was chasing a criminal, he always felt that same anxiety, that frenzy, an inner voice pushing him to run faster. Now that the investigation was at a dead end and their leads had gone nowhere, he had a small flash of inspiration. There was something shining just below the surface and Frank couldn't wait to dive down and see whether it was a real light or just a mirage.

The agent standing guard let him in without a word. As he climbed the steps to Nicolas Hulot's office, Frank wondered if they used his name when they talked about him, or just called him "the American." He walked down the hall and came to the door. He knocked a couple of times and turned the knob. The office was empty. He stood out in the hallway a moment, puzzled, then decided to go in. He was feverishly impatient to see if what he thought was true. Nicolas wouldn't mind.

The file with all the reports and papers on the case was lying on the desk. He opened it and looked for the envelope with the pictures of Allen Yoshida's house that Froben had brought over after they checked the place. He studied them carefully. He sat down at the desk, picked up the phone, and called the inspector in Nice.

"Froben?"

"Yes. Who is it?"

"Claude, it's Frank."

"Hi, Americano. How's it going?"

"Do I have to answer that?"

"I read the papers. Is it really so bad?"

"Yeah, really bad. Which means we're just relieved it's not worse."

"Great. And what can I do for you in this mess?"

"Answer a couple of questions."

"Shoot."

"As far as you know, did anyone touch anything at Allen Yoshida's place? Maybe accidentally move something before you came and took the photos?"

"I don't think so. The maid who discovered the crime didn't go in. She practically fainted at the sight of all that blood and called security right away. Valmeere, the head of Yoshida's security team, is a former cop, remember? He knows the rules. No one touched anything, for sure. The photos I gave you are exactly what we found at the house."

"Okay, Claude. Sorry, but I needed to be absolutely sure of that."

"Any leads?"

"I don't know. I hope so. I have to check one detail but I don't want to give a false alarm. Just one more thing . . ." There was silence on the other end as Froben waited.

"Do you remember if there were any vinyl LPs in Yoshida's record collection?"

"This one I can answer for sure. No, there were not. I can tell you that, because one of my men, who's into this stuff, mentioned that there was a record player in the sound system but only CDs in the collection. He commented on it."

"Great, Froben. I didn't expect anything less of you."

"Okay. I'm here if you need me."

"Thanks, Claude. You're a great help."

He hung up and was lost in thought for a moment. Now he could find out if that bastard had made one tiny mistake, the first since it had all started. Or if *he* was the one making the mistake.

He opened the desk drawer. Inside, there was the copy of the videocassette they had found in Yoshida's Bentley. Frank knew that Nicolas kept it there with the radio tapes. He took it out of the drawer and slipped it into the VCR. He turned on the equipment and pressed PLAY.

The colored bars appeared on the screen and the sequence started. If he lived a hundred years and watched those images once a day, he would still never get used to it. He saw the man in black wave the dagger in his hand. Frank felt a knot in his stomach and his throat seized up. His rage would not go away until he caught him.

Here we go. We're almost there . . . He was temped to fast-forward, but was afraid that the detail would elude him. The video finally reached the point he was waiting for. He shouted to himself.

Yes, yes, yes . . .

He paused the image. It was such a tiny detail that he couldn't have discussed it with anyone, for fear that it might be another false lead. But here it was, right in front of his eyes, and it was worth trying to see if it could mean something. Sure, it was so insignificant that it might be nothing. But it was all they had.

He looked carefully at the scene on the monitor before him. The killer was motionless, with the dagger raised over Allen Yoshida. His victim was staring at him, wide-eyed, his arms and legs bound with wire, his mouth covered with tape, a grimace of pain and fear on his face. The man would die anew, whenever someone watched that tape. And from what they knew about him, he deserved his fate each and every time.

Just then, the door opened and Morelli walked into the room. He stopped next to the door, speechless at finding him there.

Frank noticed that he was not surprised. He was *embarrassed.* He felt slightly guilty at the sergeant's discomfort.

"Hi, Claude," he said. "Sorry I burst in, but there was nobody here and I had to check something out right away."

"Not a problem. If you're looking for Inspector Hulot, he's in the conference room downstairs. The bigwigs are there too."

Frank could smell something fishy. If it was a meeting to go over the investigation and coordinate things, it was strange that they hadn't told him. He'd always been unobtrusive so as not to step on Hulot's toes. He'd stayed a step behind and only took the initiative when asked. He didn't want to lower the inspector in anyone's opinion, that of his superiors and, more important, his subordinates.

Nicolas's state of mind was another story. Frank had been struck by his outburst over Jean-Loup that morning, but it was perfectly understandable, from a personal and professional point of view. He and Hulot were really two sides of the same coin. It didn't matter who was heads and who was tails. There were no problems between them.

He compared that to the almost furtive visit from Dwight Durham. The Principality authorities probably saw things the same way Durham did, but from the opposite viewpoint. Now that the U.S. government had intervened, Frank's presence there was no longer a personal favor, a gentlemen's agreement. It was official.

Frank shrugged. He had absolutely no intention of becoming mixed up in diplomatic relations. He didn't give a damn. All he wanted to do was catch the killer, lock him in jail, and throw away the key. The credit for doing so could go to whomever they decided.

"I'm going downstairs. You coming?" Morelli recovered from the moment of awkwardness.

"Think I should?"

"I know they called you a couple of times but the line was busy."

That was possible. He had been on the phone with Cooper for quite a while and he had turned off his cell when Durham arrived. He didn't use it much anyway. It was almost always in a drawer in the Parc Saint-Roman apartment.

Frank got up from the desk, picked up the photos, and removed the videotape from the VCR. He took them with him. "Can we look at this downstairs?"

"We've got everything you need."

They left the office, walked silently down the hall, and went down the stairs. Frank's expression was hard as stone. They walked down the hallway downstairs, and when they reached the next to last door on the right, Morelli stopped and knocked.

"Come in," they heard from inside.

The sergeant pushed the door open and entered.

The large room was painted two different tones of gray en amel. There were a number of people sitting around a long, rectangular table. Nicolas Hulot, Dr. Cluny, the Sûreté chief Roncaille, and a couple of other people whom Frank did not know.

There was a moment of silence at his appearance and the fishy smell grew stronger. It was the classic pause of someone caught red-handed. Frank figured that this was their home and they had the right to have all the meetings they wanted, with or without him. But the tension confirmed his suspicions. Nicolas glanced around, embarrassed, unable to look him in the eye, like Morelli a few minutes earlier. Hulot probably had other reasons as well. In Frank's absence, he must have been soundly told off for the negative results of the investigation so far.

Roncaille collected himself first. He stood up and took a few steps in his direction.

"Hello, Frank. Come in and sit down. We were just doing a little summing up before you got here. I don't think you know Alain Durand, the attorney general, who is personally involved in the case."

He pointed to a short man with a few, sparse blond curls and tiny, deep-set eyes behind rimless glasses, sitting at the head of the table. He was wearing an elegant gray suit that did not give him the air of importance he probably thought it did. He nodded slightly.

"And Sergeant Gottet of the Computer Crime Unit . . ."

This time, the man on Durand's right nodded. He was a young man, tan with dark hair. He probably worked out in his spare time and went to the beach all summer and tanning salons in the winter. He looked more like a yuppie than a cop.

Roncaille turned to the men he had just introduced. "This is Frank Ottobre, FBI Special Agent. He has joined the Principality police for the 'No One' case."

Frank went to sit down next to Dr. Cluny on the left-hand side of the table, almost directly in front of Nicolas. He sought his gaze, but Nicolas avoided him. He continued to look somewhere under the table, as if he had lost something.

"Okay," Roncaille said, returning to his seat. "I think we can go on now. Frank, we were about to hear Dr. Cluny's report on the tapes."

Now, it was Frank who nodded silently. Cluny pushed his seat closer to the table and opened his file of notes.

"After analyzing the tapes more closely than I could during the radio show, I have reached more or less the same conclusions. The subject is extremely complex, a type that I must say I have never encountered before. There are some details in his modus operandi that are totally in keeping with most case histories of serial killers. The single territory, for example. He only operates in the Principality. The fact that he always uses knives, which allow him direct contact with the victim. Even the fact that he removes the skin can be seen as both a ritual fetish and, literally, as *overkill.* By mutilating the corpse, the killer demonstrates his total control over the person he attacks. Even the quiet period between one murder and the next is part of the general scheme. So, up to here, it all seems normal . . ."

"But?" asked Durand, with a deep voice that was disproportionate to his size.

Cluny paused for effect. He removed his glasses and rubbed the base of his nose, something Frank had noticed before. Cluny seemed to have a special ability to keep a crowd's attention. He replaced his glasses and nodded at Durand.

"That's right. Here's where the 'buts' begin. The subject has enormous verbal agility and a capacity for abstraction that is absolutely anomalous. His imagery is even poetic at times, despite the bitterness. His definition of himself as 'one and no one' is an excellent example. Aside from being highly intelligent, he must have an exceptional cultural background. University studies, the humanities, I'd say. That's different from the average serial killer, who is usually lower class with little culture or education. They almost always have a very low intelligence quotient. There's one thing in particular that puzzles me . . ."

Another pause. Frank watched the psychiatrist repeat the pantomime with his glasses and the nose rubbing. Durand cleaned his own glasses in the meantime.

A round of applause, Cluny. Great. We're all ears but go on. And get yourself some contact lenses, won't you?

"The fact that there seems to be a compulsion toward the crime, the murder, during the conversation. Common personal experiences in subjects like this—an oppressive family, a domineering parent or parents, abuse or humiliation and so on—are fairly normal. But there is an attitude that we usually find in cases of split personality, as if the subject were two people at once. Which brings us back to the 'one and no one' mentioned earlier . . ."

To Frank, this was total bullshit. An exercise in style, nothing more. In this particular case, tracing the killer's profile might be helpful but would not determine anything. The killer was not only a man who took action; he was a *thinking* man, and he thought a great deal before acting. His thinking was exceptional, and if they wanted to catch him, they had to get *beyond* his capacity for lucid thought. Frank avoided saying so, however, because he didn't want his opinion to be mistaken for admiration of the killer.

Durand interrupted, and from what he said, Frank had to admit that he was far from inexperienced. He knew how to run that kind of meeting.

"Gentlemen, there's no one here but us. This isn't a contest. Please share any doubts you have, no matter how negligible. You never know where an idea may come from. I'll start. What can we say about the killer's relationship to music?"

Cluny shrugged.

"That's another debatable topic. 'Someone and no one' again. His passion is obvious. He seems to know a lot about it and love it. It's a primary refuge for him, a sort of mental retreat. But the fact that he uses it to leave a clue, a hint as to his next victim, is a way of destroying music, using it as a weapon to challenge us. He feels superior, even though it's based on a sense of inferiority and frustration. Get it? 'Someone and no one.' "

Hulot raised his hand.

"Yes, Inspector?"

"Aside from the psychological motivation, what do you think his practical goal is in removing a particular part of the victim's anatomy? Let me make myself clear: *What does he do with their faces? What does he need them for?*"

There was silence in the room. Every one of them had asked

himself that question over and over. Now someone was saying it out loud and the silence meant that nobody had an answer.

"I can only guess, like any of us. Any guess would be valid at the moment."

"Could it be that he's unbearably ugly and is seeking revenge?" asked Morelli.

"That's possible. But keep in mind that a repulsive or even monstrous appearance is fairly conspicuous. Ugliness is something people notice immediately: ugly equals bad. If there were some kind of Frankenstein wandering around, someone would have reported it. Someone like that doesn't go unobserved."

"But it's worth a try," interrupted Durand in his low voice.

"Of course. Anything is, unfortunately."

"Thank you, Dr. Cluny."

Roncaille ended it for the moment and turned to Sergeant Gottet who had been listening in silence.

"Your turn, Sergeant."

Gottet started speaking on his subject with shining eyes, fueled by the fire of efficiency.

"We've examined all the possible causes as to why the UnSub's calls were not intercepted." Gottet looked at him. It was hard for Frank not to smile. Gottet was obsessed. The term UnSub was an abbreviation of "Unknown Subject," used during investigations in America but uncommon in Monaco. "We have a new cell phone monitoring system, the DCS1000, known as 'Carnivore.' If the phone call goes thorough that, there's no problem."

Frank had heard of it in Washington when it was still in the experimental phase. He hadn't been aware that it was now operational. But then, there were many things he was unaware of just then. Gottet continued his report.

"As far as fixed phone lines are concerned, we can enter the radio station computer, the one that manages the switchboard, directly. We can check on every access with a search for the signal, whether it comes from the phone company switchboard or directly or indirectly through the Web." He paused for effect, but without Cluny's results. "As you know, if you have the right software and some wherewithal, you can make calls from the Internet without being traced. As long as there isn't someone as good as you on the other end. That's why we've got a hacker who turned double agent. Now he's a freelance consultant helping to protect against hackers. Sometimes he works for the police in exchange for our closing an eye on his past escapades. There's some incredible technology available for this kind of search. This time, we're not going to let him get away."

Gottet's report was much shorter than Cluny's, partly because he had much less to say. The mystery of that untraced call was a stain on the department's freshly laundered shirt. Everyone would be rolling their sleeves up to their armpits to wash it clean.

"Anything else?" Durand looked around the room.

Hulot seemed to have recovered from his embarrassment of before and was cool and collected.

"We're continuing our investigation into the victims' private lives but we don't expect much from that. Meanwhile, we're keeping an eye on Radio Monte Carlo. If the subject calls again and gives us another clue, we'll be ready to intervene. We have a special plainclothes team, men and women, to check the location. There's also a sharpshooter unit equipped for night vision. We've contacted music experts who are willing to help us decipher the message, if and when it comes. Once the message is deciphered, we'll put anyone we consider a likely victim under protection. We're hoping the killer will make a mistake, since up to now he's been infallible."

Durand looked around the table. Frank finally managed to see that his eyes were hazel. He addressed nobody in particular.

"Gentlemen, it's useless for me to remind you how important it is for *us* not to make any more mistakes. This is not just a police investigation. It has become much more than that. We have to catch this man soon, before the press tears us to pieces."

And the Council of State, if not the Prince in person, thought Frank.

"Let me know anything immediately, whatever the time. Good-bye, gentlemen. I'm counting on you."

Durand got up and everyone followed. The attorney general headed to the door, followed by Roncaille who probably wanted to take advantage of his presence for a spurt of public relations. Morelli waited until the two of them were far enough away and then he left too, with a glance of support at Hulot.

Dr. Cluny was still standing by the table gathering his folders.

"If you need me at the radio, just call."

"That would be a big help, Doctor," said Hulot.

"Then I'll see you later."

Cluny left the room too, and Frank and Nicolas were alone. The inspector motioned toward the table where they had all been sitting.

"You know I had nothing to do with this."

"Of course not. Everyone's got their own problems." Frank was thinking about Parker. He felt guilty about that fact that he still had not told Nicolas about the general and Ryan Mosse.

"If you come up to my office, I have something for you."

"What?"

"A gun. A Glock Twenty. I thought you'd be familiar with it."

A gun. Frank had thought he'd never need one again.

"I don't think it's necessary."

"I wish it weren't, but at this point, we should all be ready for anything."

Frank stood there in silence. He rubbed his face where his beard was already a dark shadow. Hulot saw that he was puzzled.

"What is it, Frank?"

"Nicolas, I think I found something."

"Meaning?"

Frank went over to pick up the envelope and the cassette he had placed on the table when he came in.

"I brought this stuff, but I decided not to say anything in front of the others at the last minute because it's so insignificant. We need to check it first, before we put it out there. Remember when I told you there was something I couldn't remember? Something that I *should* have remembered but couldn't place? I finally figured out what it was. A discrepancy between the video and the pictures of Allen Yoshida's house, the ones Froben brought over."

"What?"

"Look at that cabinet," Frank began, taking a photo out of the envelope and handing it to Hulot. "The stereo cabinet behind the couch. What do you see there?"

"Nothing."

"Exactly. Now, look at this."

Frank picked up the cassette and put it in the VCR. The tape was still at the point where he had pressed PAUSE. He stopped the image again and moved his hand to a point behind the two figures.

"Here, this is the same cabinet. There's a record cover there. It's a vinyl LP. There weren't any in Yoshida's house. Froben confirmed it for me. *Not even one*. There's no trace of this record in the photos. Which means that with his mania for music, the killer couldn't resist taking home the soundtrack of his new crime. The copy was made too quickly and the picture is out of focus, but I'm sure that, if we work on the original with the right equipment, we could make out what the record is. The fact that he didn't leave it there means that it has special meaning. For him or in general. It might not be a step forward but it's the first thing we've learned about the killer, *in spite of himself*. It's tiny, but it just might be the first mistake he has made."

There was a long silence. Frank spoke first. "Can we examine the video without everybody knowing about it?" he asked Hulot.

"Not here in the Principality. Let me think . . . There's Guillaume, Mercier's son. We're old friends. He has a small production company. Makes video clips and stuff like that. He's just starting out, but I know he's good. I could get in touch with him."

"Can he be trusted?"

"He's a good boy. He was Stéphane's best friend. He'll keep his mouth shut if I ask him to."

"Good. I think it's worth checking the tape, but we need to be discreet."

"I think so too. And you said so yourself. Small as it is, it's all we've got."

They looked at each other and their gaze spoke volumes. They really *were* two sides of the same coin and they were in the same pocket. Life hadn't been kind to either of them, but each in his own way had had the courage to pick himself up and carry on. Until then, they had been at the mercy of events that were disrupting their existence. Now, thanks to an accidental discovery suspended in the air like a kite in the wind, a small, colored speck of hope floated through that gray room.

29

Laurent Bedon turned off his electric razor and looked at himself in the mirror. He'd slept late, but those extra hours had not erased the excesses of the night before. He had gotten home at dawn, dead drunk, and collapsed on the bed, already half asleep before he had hit the pillow. Now, even with the long shower and shave, he still had circles under his eyes and the pallor of someone who had not seen the sun in ages. The neon light in the bathroom mercilessly accentuated his unhealthy appearance.

Christ, I look dead.

He picked up the bottle of aftershave and splashed some over his face. He overdid it, and the sting of the alcohol burned his lips. He combed his damp hair and sprayed deodorant under his arms. And with that, he thought, he was ready for another night out.

His clothes were strewn all over the bedroom in what he considered an unavoidable mess. He used to have a housekeeper come and straighten up, putting things in precarious order, which he immediately demolished. Now, his finances no longer allowed for a housekeeper. It was a miracle he hadn't been evicted yet, since he owed four months' rent.

Things had really gotten bad over recent months. He had even lost a hefty wad of cash at the Menton Casino last night. Moreover, the money wasn't his. He'd asked Bikjalo for another advance. The station manager had complained a little, but finally decided to open his purse strings, reluctantly signing a check. As he pushed it toward him, he had told Laurent that he'd reached his limit.

It had been enough to patch up a number of critical emergencies within his dire financial situation. There was the rent, for just two crappy rooms in a building in Nice that disgusted even the cockroaches. Unbelievable. The landlord was stalking him like they were in an American B movie. Or a Laurel and Hardy comedy.

Crédit Agricole had foreclosed on his car when he had stopped making the lease payments after the third installment. Fuck them. And fuck Monsieur Plombier, the shithead bank officer who had treated him like scum when he had gone to complain. And demanded that he return his credit card and checkbook.

But that wasn't even his main problem. If only it were. He owed a roll of euros to that thug Maurice, a debt he had contracted when money was still called francs. He had scraped together enough for a few installments but the bastard wouldn't be patient forever. Everyone knew what happened to people who didn't repay their debts to that bloodsucker. The stories he had heard were far from reassuring. They were just rumors, but in this case, Laurent thought he should probably take them as the gospel truth.

He sat down on the bed and ran his hands through his hair. He looked around. Everything he saw was disgusting. He still found it impossible to believe that he was living in a dump in Ariane. Maurice had taken his wonderful apartment at the Acropolis in exchange for part of his debt, but the interest had added up so fast that he would soon be taking his balls for the rest, simply for the joy of hearing him sing soprano.

He threw on some clothes, retrieving a pair of pants and one of the cleaner shirts. He picked up yesterday's socks from under the bed. He had absolutely no idea how they had gotten there, couldn't remember getting undressed last night. There was a mirror in the wardrobe of the furnished apartment and the reflection it showed was not much better than the one in the bathroom.

Forty years old. And in that state. If he didn't make some

changes, and soon, he would end up a *clochard,* a homeless bum. There wouldn't even be enough money for razor blades. Unless of course Maurice stepped in to help . . .

But he had felt it last night: luck. Pierrot had given him the numbers and Pierrot's numbers were usually lucky. Thanks to "Rain Boy" he'd left the casino more than once with a huge smile on his face. He always squandered the money immediately, like all riches earned without effort.

He had cashed Bikjalo's check with a guy he knew who hung around the casino waiting for people like him, men with a feverish look who were used to following a ball around the wheel. He had taken a hefty commission, as that cheat called it, but Laurent had gone into the main room with the best intentions, not knowing that he was about to pave another mile of his road to hell.

A disaster. Not even one win, one big number. The croupier had mechanically swept up his bets, one after another, with the professional look of all croupiers. Just the time of a spin, the launching of a ball, and that bastard's able hands pushed the chips over with the previous win. In his case, everything had gone up in smoke.

One wisp of smoke after another. If he had burned all the money in the fireplace, it would have been more useful. Except that *now* he had no fireplace. Maurice, or someone like him, was warming himself by it, damn him.

He got up from the bed and went to turn on his computer, precariously balanced on that desklike thing in the bedroom. It was a very fast PC that he had assembled himself: Pentium IV 1600 megahertz processor, a gig of RAM, and two hard disks of thirty gigs each. At least he still had that. He would be lost without his computer. It had his notes, his program schedules, the things he wrote when he was sad. Which meant all the time, right then. And there was the Web to surf, a virtual escape from the reality where he was imprisoned.

When he turned on the computer, he saw that he had an e-mail. He opened it. It was a message from an unknown sender, in handsome Book Antiqua font:

Need money? Your rich uncle's in town.

He wondered what jerk was making such bad jokes. A friend who knew his troubles, most likely. Who? Jean-Loup? Bikjalo? Someone from the station?

And who was the "rich uncle?" For a moment, he thought of the American, the FBI agent investigating the murders. His eyes were even creepier than that voice calling in to the station. Maybe it was a way of keeping him under pressure. But he didn't seem like the type who would resort to that. He'd just throw you against a wall and beat it out of you until you vomited up your guts.

That whole business came to mind. The voice at the radio was a godsend for Jean-Loup. He was getting more popular than the Beatles. It made him miserable, but in the end, once they caught the guy, he would come out a winner. Jean-Loup would take off and he, Laurent, would stand there on the ground with his nose in the air, watching him soar. And to think that he was the one who had introduced Jean-Loup to the station after first meeting him a few years ago in front of the Café de Paris in Place du Casino. He had witnessed the episode that got that asshole his amazing house in Beausoleil. He had only found out a few years later that saving that mutt for the old broad had been a winning lottery ticket.

His fate was always the same: to observe the luck of others. He never failed to be there to see someone hit by a golden ray of sunshine, which might have hit him if its trajectory had deviated by just a foot.

He had started talking to the guy with the dark hair and green eyes after he had saved the dog. He was looking around, a little embarrassed at suddenly becoming the center of attention. One thing had led to another. Laurent had been struck by what Jean-Loup exuded, a sense of serenity and involvement at the same time. It was something that he couldn't exactly describe, but it was strong enough to make an impression on anyone who came in contact with him. Especially someone like Laurent.

Bikjalo, who was no fool, had gotten it as soon as Laurent had introduced him as a possible host for *Voices,* the program Laurent had been thinking about for some time. He had seen the old dog's eyes light up with interest. Jean-Loup had the undeniable advantage of being a good candidate and of costing little, since he knew absolutely nothing about radio.

A total beginner. Two birds with one stone. A new hit and a new host at almost zero cost. After two weeks of recorded rehearsals, with Jean-Loup proving the assumptions about him and his talent correct, *Voices* had finally gone on air. It had started well and gotten better and better. People liked the guy. They liked his way of talking and communicating: fanciful, imaginative, with bold metaphors understood by all.

Even killers, thought Laurent bitterly.

Inadvertently, the watershed episode when two boys lost at sea were saved had transformed the show into the socially conscious program it now was. The pride and joy of the radio and the Principality. And honey for the buzzing flies: its sponsors.

And the deejay became the star of a show that Laurent had conceived of, a show where he had less and less to say and which was pushing him aside, a little more each day.

"Fuck all of them. It'll change. It has to change," he muttered to himself.

He printed out his notes for that evening's show and the HP 990cxi started spitting freshly inked sheets of papers onto the tray. They would change their minds about him. All of them, one by one. Barbara especially.

He thought back to her copper hair spread on the pillow. They had had an affair. It was intense, and he had fallen for her deeply, physically and emotionally, before he had let everything go to hell. She had tried to stand by him, but it was like living with a drug addict. After a lot of back and forth, she had left him, turning her back definitively when she had realized that she would never be able to compete with the four other women in his life: spades, hearts, diamonds, and clubs.

He got up from the unsteady chair and slipped the printed sheets into a folder. He took his jacket from the armchair that he used as a coatrack and went out. The landing was no less a picture of gloom than the apartment. He pulled the door closed and sighed. The elevator wasn't working. A new notch on the building manager's belt. He walked downstairs in the dim, yellow light, brushing his hand against the beige wallpaper of the stairwell. Like him, it had seen better days.

He went into the lobby and pushed open the front door, made of glass in a rusted metal frame with chipped paint. Entirely different from the elegant buildings of Monte Carlo or Jean-Loup's lovely villa. The neighborhood outside was plunged in the shadows of evening, that intense blue that only summer sunsets leave behind like a memory of the sun. It even lent a semblance of humanity to that desolate neighborhood. Ariane was not the Promenade des Anglais or the Acropolis. The smell of the sea never reached that area or, if it did, it was overpowered by the stench of garbage.

He had to walk three blocks to reach the bus that would take him into the Principality. So much the better. A walk would do him good and clear his head, and to hell with Plombier and his shitty bank.

Vadim emerged from the shadows at the corner of the building. He was so fast that Laurent didn't see him coming. Before he even knew what was happening, he felt himself being raised off the ground and a moment later he was pushed against the wall with an arm pressing against his throat and the man's breath, stinking of garlic and gum disease, in his face.

"Well, Laurent? Why don't you remember your friends when you've got a little cash?"

"What do you mean? You know . . . that I . . ."

A thrust against his neck interrupted his protests and he gasped.

"Stop bullshitting, asshole. You laid down a whole bunch of dough last night in Menton. You forgot that the money you were playing belongs to Maurice, didn't you?"

Vadim Rohmer was his bully, his troublemaker, his tax collector. Fat and flabby as he was, Maurice could not pin people's arms behind their backs until they cried. Or push them against a wall until they felt the rough plaster rip their skin. But Vadim could, the bastard. And that other bastard who had cashed his check last night in the bar in front of the casino—he was the one who had ratted on him, piece of shit. Laurent hoped he got from Vadim exactly what he was getting now.

"I . . ."

"Shut the fuck up. There are a few things about me and Maurice you just don't get. Like how he loses patience and so do I. It's about time I refresh your memory."

The punch in his stomach left him breathless. He retched, bringing the acid taste of vomit up to his dry mouth. His legs buckled. Vadim held him up effortlessly, grabbing him by the shirt collar with an iron grip. He saw the thug's right fist and realized that his face was the target and that the blow would be so powerful that his head would smash into the wall behind him. He closed his eyes and stiffened, waiting for the fist to strike.

It never did.

He opened his eyes again as he felt the grip on his neck relax.

A tall, strong man, with light brown hair in a crew cut had come up behind Vadim and grabbed him by his sideburns, pulling violently upward.

The pain and surprise made Vadim release his grasp.

"What the hell . . ."

The man let go of Vadim's hair and the thug stepped back to face the newcomer. He looked him up and down. He was all muscle and there was absolutely no sign of fear on his face. He was much less reassuring than Laurent's harmless, sickly figure. Especially the eyes that were watching him without expression, as if he were simply asking directions.

"Great. I see help has arrived," said Vadim in a voice that sounded less secure than he would have liked.

He tried to use the fist intended for Laurent on the man standing in front of him. The reaction came in a flash. His adversary dodged the punch with a move of his head and then he stepped forward and wedged his shoulder under Vadim's. After clutching it with his arms, he pressed down with all his weight.

Laurent could clearly hear the sound of bones breaking with a crack loud enough to make him jump. Vadim screamed and bent down, holding his broken arm. The man stepped back and spun around gracefully, a pirouette to give force to the blow. His foot crashed on Vadim's face, and blood spurted from his mouth. Vadim fell to the ground without a whimper and lay there motionless.

Laurent wondered if he was dead. No, his unknown rescuer seemed much too skilled to kill by accident. He was the type who killed only when he *wanted* to. Laurent started coughing, bending over to hold his stomach as acidic saliva trickled from his mouth.

"Looks like I got here just in time, Mr. Bedon, no?" said the man who had saved him in very bad French, with a strong foreign accent. He helped him up, holding his elbow.

Laurent looked at him, thunderstruck, without understanding. He had never seen him before in his life. But the guy had saved him from Vadim's fists and knew his name. Who the hell was he?

"Do you speak English?"

Laurent nodded. The man gave a brief sigh of relief. He continued in English with an American accent.

"Thank God. I'm not very good at your language. You must have heard. You're probably wondering why I helped you with this"—he waved at Vadim's body on the ground—"this . . . I'd call it . . . embarrassing situation, if you agree."

Laurent nodded again in silence.

"Mr. Bedon, either you don't read your e-mail, or you don't trust rich uncles. I have a proposal for you."

Laurent's astonishment was written all over his face. Now he had an explanation for that strange e-mail. He would surely be getting others. This man hadn't knocked Vadim out and saved his hide simply to carve a *Z* like Zorro on the wall and disappear.

"My name's Ryan Mosse and I'm American. I have a proposal for you. Very, very advantageous, economically speaking."

Laurent looked at him for an instant without speaking. He liked that "very, very advantageous, economically speaking." Suddenly, his stomach stopped hurting. He got up, breathing deeply. He could feel the color slowly returning to his face.

The man looked around. If he was disgusted by the filth of Laurent's neighborhood, he didn't show it. He looked carefully at the building.

"My apartment's over there, but I don't think you came to buy it."

"No, but if we come to an understanding, you would be able to, if you're interested."

As he straightened his clothing, Laurent's brain raced ahead. He had absolutely no idea who this guy was and what he wanted . . . what was his name? Oh, yes, Ryan Mosse. He did not know, but Mosse would now tell him. And he would also name a figure.

A very large figure, apparently.

Laurent looked at Vadim, motionless on the ground. The pig's nose and mouth were split open and a small puddle of blood was forming on the sidewalk. At that moment in his life, if anyone saved his ass from someone like Vadim and then talked to him about money, lots of money, Laurent Bedon would listen.

SIXTH CARNIVAL

Alone, far from the world, the man listens to music.

The notes of the Minuet from Franz Schubert's Symphony No. 5 float through the air. Enclosed in his metal box, the man is absorbed in the arpeggios of the strings and imagines the musicians' arms and their concentration as they perform the symphony. Now, his imagination soars above like a sky cam floating through space and time. Suddenly, he is no longer in his secret place but in a large room with frescoed walls and ceilings, illuminated from above by hundreds of candles suspended from enormous chandeliers. He shifts his gaze to the right in a view so clear that it seems real. His hand presses that of a woman moving next to him in the sensuous rhythm of a dance made up of elegant swirls, pauses, and bows, practiced so many times that it is smooth as wine poured into a glass. The woman is unable to resist his fixed stare promising the creation and destruction of the world. From time to time she turns her eyes, veiled by long lashes, to the audience, seeking confirmation of the incredible awareness that she is the chosen one. There is admiration and envy in all those who watch them dance from the sides of the drawing room.

He knows that she will be his that night. In the soft glimmering candlelight, amid the lace and ribbons of the enormous canopy bed, he sees her emerge from the tangle of silks that cover her like rose petals. The rights of the king.

But none of that matters now. Now they are dancing and they are beautiful. And they will be even lovelier when . . .

Are you there, Vibo?

The voice arrives, gentle as always, anxious as only that voice can be. His dream, the image that he created before his closed eyes, is lost, crumbling away like burning frames of film.

It is the return, the presence of the other, duty, responsibility. It was only a moment's break that vanished like a sprinkle of snow in spring. There is no room for dreams; there never was and there will never be. They could have dreamt once, when they lived in the big house on the hill, when they managed to crawl away from the obsessive care of the man who already wanted them to be men, when they just wanted to be boys. When they wanted to run, not march. But even there, there was a voice that could break any vision their imaginations managed to create.

"Yes, I'm here, Paso."

What are you doing? I couldn't hear you.

"I was just thinking."

The man lets the music continue. The last postscript of his thin mirage. There will never be a dance with a beautiful woman for him, for them. He gets up and goes into the other room, where the lifeless body lies in its crystal coffin.

He switches on the light. There is a reflection on the corner of the transparent case. It disappears when he moves and changes position. There is another, but it is always the same. Tiny insufficient mirages. He knows what he will find. Another broken illusion, another magic mirror shattered at his feet.

He goes up to the naked body inside and runs his eyes over the dried limbs, the color of old parchment. His gaze moves slowly, from the feet to the head covered with what not long ago was the face of another man.

His heart aches.

Nothing lasts forever. The mask is showing the first signs of decomposition. The hair is dry and opaque. The skin is yellowed and shrinking. In a little while, in spite of his care, it will be no different than the skin of the face it is hiding. He looks at the body with infinite tenderness, eyes softened by the affection he cannot erase.

He darkens and clenches his jaw in defiance.

It isn't true that fate is unavoidable. It isn't true that you can only watch as time and events occur. He can change; he *must* change that eternal injustice. He can fight against the mistakes distributed by fate with open hands in the snake pit that is the life of man. Distributed haphazardly, without looking, without caring if an existence is broken off or forced into darkness forever.

Obscurity means darkness. Darkness means night. And night means that the hunt must continue.

The man smiles. Poor, stupid bloodhounds. Baying with bared teeth to hide their fear. Night-blind eyes searching in the obscurity, the darkness, the night, to discover where the prey turned hunter will come from.

He is one and no one. He is the king. The king has no questions, only answers. The king has no curiosity, only certainty. He leaves curiosity to others, to all those who ask, to all those who show it in their eyes, in their erratic gestures, in their apprehension, their anxiety of life that is sometimes so thick you can touch it.

The smell of life is in the buses in the summer, full of people with too many armpits and too many hands. It is in the smell of food and cat piss that accosts you in alleyways. It is in the sharp smell of rust and salt water that erodes metal, and in the smell of disinfectant and the rough scent of gunpowder.

Especially there, where a fade-out should be, there are two eternal questions: "When?" and "Where?"

When will that last breath come, held in with the growl of an animal, kept inside with clenched teeth, because there will never be another, never again? When, at what hour of the day or night, at what tick of an unwinding clock, will there be that last second and no other, leaving the rest of time to the world as it continues in other directions and along other routes? Where, in which bed, car seat, elevator, beach, armchair, hotel will the heart feel that sharp pain, the interminable, curious, useless expectation of another beat, after an interval that becomes longer and longer, growing infinite? Sometimes it comes so quickly that the last flash is a final calmness, but not an answer, because in that blinding light there is no time to understand it, nor even, sometimes, to feel it.

The man knows what he has to do. He has already done it and he will do it again, as long as it is necessary. There are many masks out there, worn by people who do not deserve that appearance, nor any other.

What is it, Vibo? Why are you looking at me that way? Is there something wrong?

The man is reassuring. His mouth smiles, his eyes sparkle, his voice protects.

"No, Paso, there's nothing wrong. I was looking at how handsome you are. And soon you'll be even more so."

Oh, no. Really? Don't tell me!

The man cloaks his intentions in secret tenderness.

"Stop. You mustn't speak of it. Secret of secrets. Remember?"

Oh, is it a secret of secrets? Then we can only speak of it at the full moon . . .

The man smiles at the memory of their childhood game. In the few moments when that man was not there to spoil the only game that they were allowed to play.

"That's right, Paso. And the full moon is coming soon. Very soon . . ."

The man turns and goes toward the door. The music in the other room is over. Now there is a silence that feels like the natural continuation of the music.

Where are you going, Vibo?

"I'll be right back, Paso."

He turns to look at the body lying in the crystal coffin.

"First, I have to make a phone call . . ."

30

At Radio Monte Carlo they were sitting and waiting, like every night. The story had created such a fervor that there were three times the usual number of people in the building at that hour.

Now, in addition, there was Sergeant Gottet with a couple of men who had installed a much more powerful and sophisticated computer system than that of the radio station and had hooked it up to the Internet. There was a young guy with them, about twenty-five and intelligent-looking, short brown hair with blond streaks and a ring in his right nostril. He busied himself with a pile of floppy disks and CD-ROMs, his fingers flying over the keyboard. Frank, standing behind his chair, couldn't look at his hands for very long. The kid's name was Alain Toulouse but hackers knew him as Pico. When he was introduced to Frank, he smiled and his eyes sparkled.

"FBI, huh?" he said. "I got in once. Well, actually more than once. It used to be easier, but now they've wised up. Know if they've got any hackers working for them?"

Frank couldn't answer the question, but the boy was no longer interested. He turned and sat back down at his station. He typed with lightning speed as he explained what he was doing.

"First, I'm going to set up a firewall to protect the system. If someone tries to get in, I'll know. Usually we try to stop attacks from the outside and that's it. This time it's different: we want to find out who's attacking, without their knowledge. I've installed a program that I developed. It'll let us hook on to the signal and follow it back. It might be a Trojan horse."

"What's a Trojan horse?" Frank asked.

"It's what we call a masked communication that travels covered by another one, like some viruses. So I'm also installing anti-virus protection. I only want the signal that we intercept, when we intercept it."

He stopped to unwrap a candy and stuck it in his mouth. Frank noticed that the kid had no doubt that he would intercept the call. He must have a pretty high opinion of himself. Then again, his attitude was typical of computer hackers. Their presumption and sarcasm led them to do things that might not actually be criminal but were simply aimed at showing their victims that they could avoid surveillance and get through any wall designed to keep them out. They saw themselves as modern-day Robin Hoods with a mouse and a keyboard instead of a bow and arrow.

"As I was saying," Pico continued, chewing vigorously on the caramel stuck to his teeth, "I don't want them to include a virus that gets out if they're intercepted. Otherwise, we'd lose the signal and our chance to follow it, along with our computer, obviously. A really good virus can literally melt a hard drive. If this guy can do things like that, he's really good and any virus he lets out won't smell like roses."

Until then, Bikjalo had been sitting silently at a desk behind the station. Now he asked a question. "Do you think any of your friends might play tricks on us while we're doing this?"

Frank shot him a look but the station manager didn't notice. Pico turned his chair around to look at Bikjalo directly, incredulous at his ignorance of the computer world.

"We're hackers, not hoodlums. Nobody would do anything like that. I'm here because this guy doesn't just break in where he doesn't belong and leave a smiley face behind as his signature. This guy kills—he's a murderer. No hacker worthy of the name would do anything like that."

"Okay. Get on with it," Frank said, putting a hand on his shoulder, a gesture of trust that was also an apology for Bikjalo. "I don't think there's anyone here who can teach you anything." Then he turned to Bikjalo who had gotten up and was standing next to them. "There's nothing left for us to do here. Let's go see if Jean-Loup is back yet."

What he really wanted to do was tell Bikjalo to get the hell out of the way and let them work without breathing down their necks. They had enough pressure without him. But diplomacy held Frank back. They were all working together at the station and he didn't want to ruin anything. There was already too much tension in the air.

"Okay."

The station manager shot a last puzzled look at the computer and at Pico, who had forgotten about them. Excited at this new challenge, his fingers were again flying over the keys. They left the computer station and went over to Raquel's desk as Jean-Loup and Laurent came in the door.

Frank scrutinized the deejay. Jean-Loup looked better than he had that morning, but there was an indelible shadow over his eyes. Frank knew that shadow. When this was all over, he would need a lot of sun and a lot of light to get rid of it.

"Hey, guys. All set?"

Laurent answered for both of them.

"Yeah, the outline's ready. The hard part is thinking that the show has to go on, no matter what. Aside from *those* calls, we've still got our normal callers. How're things here?"

The door opened again and Hulot came into the frame looking like a blurry image. He seemed to have aged ten years since Frank had arrived in Monte Carlo.

"Oh, here you are. Evening, everyone. Frank, can I talk to you for a sec?"

Jean-Loup, Laurent, and Bikjalo moved over to let Frank and the inspector have some privacy.

"What's up?"

They walked to the other wall, next to the two glass panels covering the switchboard, the satellite connections, and the ISDN links that were there in case there was a blackout and the repeater failed.

"Everything's ready. The Crisis Unit's on call. There are ten men standing by at the police station. They can get anywhere in a flash. There are plainclothes men all over the streets. Nothing's going on. People walking dogs, strollers, things like that. The whole city's covered. We can move people in seconds if we need to. If the victim is here, in Monte Carlo, I mean. If Mr. No One has decided to get his victim somewhere else, we've alerted the police forces all along the coast. All we can do now is try to be sharper than our friend there. Otherwise, we're in the hands of God."

"And in the hands of Pierrot, whom God has treated so badly . . ." Frank pointed to two people walking in with Morelli.

Pierrot and his mother came over to them and stopped. The woman held her son's hand as if she were clutching a lifesaver. Instead of offering protection, the woman seemed to be seeking it from her innocent son who was savoring his personal participation in that moment, something that was usually denied to him.

He, Pierrot, was the only one who knew all the music that was in the room. He liked what had happened last time, when all those big shots had watched him anxiously, waiting for him to tell them whether or not it was there and then when he had gone out to find the record. He liked being there every night at the radio station with Jean-Loup, watching him from behind the glass, waiting for the man who spoke with the devils, instead of staying home and only listening to the voice coming out of the stereo. He liked this game, even though he realized that it wasn't really a game.

Sometimes he dreamt about it at night. For the first time, he was glad he didn't have a room to himself in their tiny house but that he slept in the large bed with his mother. They woke and were both afraid and couldn't fall asleep again until the pink light of dawn filtered through the shutters.

Pierrot freed himself from his mother's hand and ran to Jean-Loup, his idol, his best friend. The deejay tousled his hair.

"Hey, handsome. How ya doing?"

"Fine, Jean-Loup. Know what? Tomorrow I might ride in a police car!"

"Great. You're a cop too, then?"

"Yeah, an *honorable* policeman."

Hearing Pierrot's new, unintentional mistake, Jean-Loup smiled and instinctively pulled him toward him. He pressed his face against his chest and tousled his hair even harder.

"Here's our *honorable* policeman, engaged in ruthless hand-to-hand combat with his bitter enemy, Dr. Tickle." As he started tickling, Pierrot burst out laughing. They headed into the control room, followed by Laurent and Bikjalo.

Frank, Hulot, and Pierrot's mother watched the spectacle in silence. The woman smiled with enchantment at seeing the friendship between Jean-Loup and her son. She pulled a handkerchief out of her purse and blew her nose. Frank noticed that it was freshly laundered and well ironed. Though inexpensive, the woman's clothes were also perfectly pressed.

"Madame, we can't thank you enough for your patience."

"Me? Patient with you? But I'm the one who should thank you for all you're doing for my son. He's completely changed. If it weren't for that horrible stuff, I would be very happy."

Hulot calmed her with a soothing voice. And Frank knew that he was anything but calm at that moment.

"Don't worry, Madame. It will all be over soon, with Pierrot's help. We'll be sure that he gets the attention he deserves. Your son has become something of a hero."

The woman started walking down the hall with slow, timid steps, her shoulders slightly bent. Frank and Hulot were alone.

Just then, the theme song of *Voices* spread down the hallway and the show started. But it had no spark that evening and Jean-Loup felt it as well as the others. There was palpable tension in the air, but it didn't lend any energy to the program. The calls came in, but they were routine phone calls that Raquel had screened beforehand with the help of the police. The callers were asked not to mention the murderer. If someone did anyway, Jean-Loup ably steered the conversation to other, easier topics. Everyone knew that millions of listeners tuned in to Radio Monte Carlo every night. Along with Italy and France, the show was broadcast in many other European countries through networks that had bought the rights. They listened to it, translated it, and talked about it. And everyone was waiting for something to happen. It meant a huge amount of money for the station. A triumph of Latin wisdom.

Mors tua, vita mea. It's a dog-eat-dog world.

Everyone died a little in experiences like this, Frank thought. No one really won. He was struck by the meaning of what he had just thought. *No one really won.*

He remembered the trick of Ulysses. The intrinsic meaning of the definition that the killer had given himself, the irony, the scornful challenge. He was even more sure that they were dealing with an exceptional man and that they had to catch him as soon as possible. At the very first opportunity. He instinctively touched the gun in its holder under his jacket. That man's death, real or metaphorical, would *really and truly* mean life for someone else.

The red light lit up on the phone. Laurent sent the call to Jean-Loup.

"Hello?"

Silence. Then a simulated voice came out of the speakers.

"Hi, Jean-Loup. My name's one and no one."

Everyone froze in unison. Behind the glass of the broadcast

booth, Jean-Loup turned, the blood drained from his face. Barbara, sitting at the mixer, moved quickly away from the machine as if it were suddenly extremely dangerous.

"Who are you?" he asked, taken aback.

"It don't matter who I am. What's important is that I'm gonna strike again. Tonight, whatever happens."

Frank jumped up as if from an electric chair.

Cluny, sitting on his left, stood up too and grabbed his arm.

"It's not him, Frank," he whispered.

"What do you mean, 'It's not him?' "

"It's wrong. This one said, 'My name's one and no one.' The other says, '*I'm* one and no one.' "

"Does it make a difference?"

"In this case, it makes a big difference. And the person on the phone is uneducated. Some bastard's playing a really sick joke."

As confirmation of the psychiatrist's words, a laugh that pretended to be satanic swept out of the loudspeakers and the line went dead.

Morelli rushed into the control room.

"We've got him!"

Frank and Cluny followed him out into the hallway. Hulot, who was in the director's booth just then, was also running toward them, followed by Bikjalo.

"You've got him?"

"Yes, Inspector. The phone call came from somewhere on the outskirts of Menton."

Frank dashed their hopes. And his own, unfortunately.

"Dr. Cluny says that it might not be him, that it might be a hoax."

"The voice could be disguised in the same way," the psychiatrist broke in, compelled to speak up. That phrase left an opening that he hurried to close. "But he doesn't use the same language as the man who made the other calls. It's not him."

"Damn him, whoever he is. Have you contacted the inspector of Menton?" the inspector asked Morelli.

"As soon as we located the call. They took off like lightning."

"Of course, they wouldn't miss the chance to get him themselves." The inspector avoided looking at Cluny as if not having him in his line of vision could exclude the psychiatrist's theory.

An endless fifteen minutes passed. They heard the music playing through the speakers at the other end of the hall and Jean-Loup's voice continuing the broadcast in spite of everything. There must have been dozens of calls coming in and the switchboard was probably flooded. The mike that Morelli was wearing around his neck buzzed. The sergeant almost snapped when the call arrived.

"Sergeant Morelli."

He listened. Disappointment swept over his face like clouds covering the sun. Even before he handed over the earpiece, Hulot knew it was all over.

"Inspector Hulot."

"Hi, Nicolas. Roberts, from Menton."

"Hi. Let's hear it."

"I'm there right now. False alarm. This fucker's high as a kite and he wanted to impress his girlfriend. Even called from his own place, the idiot. When we caught them, him and the girl, they practically pissed their pants with fright."

"Those fools should *die* of fright. Can you arrest them?"

"Of course. Interfering with the police, and we found a nice hunk of cheese." By that, he meant marijuana.

"Okay. Take them in and scare the shit out of them. And make sure the press knows about it. We have to set an example; otherwise we'll be swamped with calls like this. Thanks, Roberts."

"Don't mention it. Sorry, Nicolas."

"Yeah, so am I. Good-bye."

The inspector hung up. "You were right, Doctor. False alarm." He looked at them with suddenly hopeless eyes.

"Well . . . I . . ."

"Excellent work, Doctor," interrupted Frank. "Really great. It's not anyone's fault."

They headed slowly to the control room at the end of the hall. Gottet came up to them.

"Well?"

"Nothing. A false lead."

"I thought it was weird that it would be so easy. But in a case like this, how can you . . ."

"It's fine, Gottet. What I just told Dr. Cluny goes for you as well. Excellent work."

They went back into the control room where everyone was waiting to hear what had happened. They saw their disappointed faces and didn't even need to ask. Barbara relaxed in her chair and leaned on the mixer. Laurent ran a hand through his hair in silence. Just then, the red light started flashing. The deejay looked exhausted. He took a sip of water from the glass on the table and moved closer to the mike.

"Hello?"

At first, there was only silence. The silence they had all learned to recognize. Then the muffled sound, the unnatural echo.

And finally the voice. Everyone turned their heads slowly toward the speakers, as if that voice had stiffened the muscles in their necks.

"Hello, Jean-Loup. I have the feeling that you've been waiting for me."

Cluny bent closer to Frank.

"Hear that? Perfect grammar. Proper language. *That's* him."

Jean-Loup didn't hesitate this time. His hands gripped the table so hard that his knuckles whitened, but there was no trace of that tension in his voice.

"Yes, we were waiting for you. You know we were waiting for you."

"So here I am. The bloodhounds must be worn out from chasing shadows. But the hunt must go on. Mine and theirs."

"Why do you say 'must'? What does all this mean?"

"The moon belongs to everyone and we all have the right to howl."

"Howling at the moon means pain. But you can sing to the moon too. You can be happy in the dark sometimes when you see the moon. For heaven's sake, you can be happy in this world. Believe me."

"Poor Jean-Loup. You think that the moon is real when it's only an illusion . . . Do you know what the darkness of that sky contains, my friend?"

"No. But I think you'll tell me."

The man on the phone didn't notice Jean-Loup's bitter sarcasm. Or perhaps he did, but felt above it.

"No moon and no God, Jean-Loup. The correct term for it is 'nothing.' There is absolutely nothing. And I'm so used to living in it that I no longer notice. Everywhere, wherever I turn, there is nothing."

"You're crazy," Jean-Loup blurted out, in spite of himself.

"I too have wondered about that, often. It is quite likely true, although I read somewhere that the insane do not wonder if they are or are not. I don't know what wanting *to be crazy means, which is what sometimes happens to me."*

"Even insanity can end. It can be cured. What can we do to help you?"

The man ignored the question as if it were not a solution.

"Ask me instead what I can do to help you. Here, I'll throw you another bone. For the bloodhounds who keep chasing their tail in a desperate attempt to bite it. It's a loop. A loop that goes round and round and round . . . Like in music. When there's a loop that goes round and round and round . . ."

The voice faded out. Music poured from the speakers, like the last time. No guitars tonight, no classic rock, but some contemporary dance music. A feat of electronics and sampling. The music ended as suddenly as it had begun. The silence that followed lent Jean-Loup's question even more weight.

"What does that mean? What are you saying?"

"I asked the question. It's up to you to answer. That's what life is made of, my friend. Questions and answers. Every man drags his questions along behind him, starting with the ones he has written inside him when he's born."

"What questions?"

"I'm not fate. I'm one and no one, but I'm easy to understand. When someone who sees me realizes who I am, his eyes ask the question in a split second: he wants to know when and where. I am the answer. For him, I mean now. *For him, I mean* here.*"*

He stopped. Then the voice hissed another sentence.

"And that is why I kill . . ."

A metallic click ended the conversation, leaving an echo in the air like the snap of a guillotine. In his mind, Frank saw another head roll.

For Christ sake, no, not this time!

"Did you get him?" Frank asked Sergeant Gottet who'd turned his back and was already talking to his men.

His answer took all the breath from his lungs.

"Nothing. Absolutely nothing. No signal whatsoever. Pico says that whoever's handling the calls must be really great. He didn't see anything. If the call came from the Web, the signal's so well hidden that our equipment can't visualize it. The bastard fooled us again."

"Damn him. Did anyone recognize the music?" Silence usually means consent. But in this case, the general silence was a no. "Shit. Barbara, get me a tape with the music as soon as possible. Where's Pierrot?"

Barbara was already making a copy.

"In the conference room," said Morelli.

There was feverish anxiety in the room. They all knew they had to hurry, hurry, hurry. At this very moment, the caller might be going out to start his hunt. And someone else, somewhere else, did not know that he was living out the last minutes of his life. They went to get Rain Boy, the only one who would recognize the music right away.

Pierrot was in the conference room, sitting at a table next to his mother, his head hanging down. When they got there, he looked at them with tears in his eyes, then bowed his head again.

Like the last time, Frank went over and crouched next to the chair. Pierrot raised his face a little, as if he didn't want to be seen crying.

"What is it, Pierrot? Something wrong?" The boy nodded. "Did it frighten you? There's nothing to be scared of. We're here with you."

"No, I'm not scared," Pierrot sniffed. "I'm a policeman too, now."

"Then what is it?"

"I don't know the music," he cried mournfully. There was real pain in his voice. He looked around as if he had failed the great moment of his life. The tears rolled down his cheeks.

Frank felt his last hopes vanish, but he forced himself to smile at Pierrot.

"Hey, calm down. Don't worry. We'll let you listen to it again and you'll recognize it, you'll see. It's hard, but you can do it. I'm sure that you can."

Barbara ran into the room holding a DAT. She slipped it in the recorder and turned it on.

"Listen carefully, Pierrot."

The electronic percussion cranked into the room. The 4/4

pulse of the dance music sounded like a heartbeat. One hundred thirty-seven per minute. A heart racing with fear, a heart somewhere that could stop at any moment.

Pierrot listened in silence, his head hanging down. When the music stopped, he looked up and a timid smile broke out on his face.

"It's there," he said softly.

"Did you recognize it? Is it in the room? Go get it, please."

Pierrot nodded and got up from the chair. He took off with his loping gait. Hulot nodded to Morelli who got up to go with him. They returned after what seemed like an endless wait. Pierrot held a CD in his hands.

"Here it is. It's a *complication.*"

They slid the CD into the player and went through the tracks until they found it. The song was exactly what the killer had played a little while earlier. Pierrot was a hero. His mother went over to embrace him as if he had just won the Nobel Prize. The pride in her eyes broke Hulot's heart.

" 'Nuclear Sun,' by Roland Brant. Who's that?" Frank said, reading the title on the cover of the compilation.

Nobody had heard of him. They all ran to the computer. A quick search on the Internet took them to an Italian site. Roland Brant was the pseudonym of an Italian deejay, a certain Rolando Bragante. "Nuclear Sun" was a dance track that was popular a few years ago.

Meanwhile, Laurent and Jean-Loup had finished the show and joined them. They were beside themselves. Both looked as if they'd been caught in a thunderstorm and part of it had remained inside them.

The director filled them in about dance music, a genre all to itself in the music market.

"Sometimes the deejays take on assumed names. Sometimes it's a made-up word but most of the time it's in English. There are three or four of them in France too. They're usually musicians who specialize in club music."

"What does 'loop' mean?" asked Hulot.

"It's a way of saying that you're using sampled music on the computer. A loop is the base, the heart of the song. You take a beat and you let it turn around itself so that it's always exactly the same."

"Just like the bastard said. A dog chasing its tail."

Frank cut those thoughts short and brought them immediately back to the present. There was something much more important to figure out.

"Okay, we've got a job to do. Come on, can you think of something? Think of someone famous, about thirty, forty, fifty who has something in common with all the elements we have. Here, in Monte Carlo."

Frank sounded possessed. He walked around to each of them, repeating himself. His voice seemed to be hunting an idea like a howling pack of dogs after a fox.

"A youngish, attractive, famous man. Who hangs out around here, in the area. Who lives here or is here now. CDs, compilations, 'Nuclear Sun,' discotheques, dance music, an Italian deejay with an English name, a pseudonym. Think about the papers, society news, the jet set . . ."

Frank's voice was like the whip of a jockey pushing his horse to go faster and faster. Their minds were all racing.

"Come on. Jean-Loup?" The deejay shook his head. Jean-Loup was worn out and it was clear that they could expect nothing more from him. "Laurent?"

"I'm sorry. I can't think of anything."

Barbara started and raised her head, moving her copper hair like a wave. Frank saw her face light up. He went over to her.

"What is it, Barbara?"

"I don't know . . . Maybe . . ."

Frank swooped down on her uncertain expression like a hawk.

"Barbara, there are no maybes. Say a name if you're thinking of one. Whether it's right or wrong."

The girl turned to all those present for an instant, as if apologizing for saying something ridiculous.

"Well, I think it might be Roby Stricker."

31

René Coletti really needed to take a piss. He breathed deeply through his nose. His full bladder was causing stabs of pain in his stomach and he felt like he was in one of those science fiction movies where the spaceship starts to fail and the red danger light comes on with a robotic voice repeating "Attention, please. This ship will self-destruct in three minutes. Attention, please . . ."

It was only normal for a biological need to assert itself at the worst possible moment, in keeping with the logic of causality designed to break the balls of human beings whenever possible. He was tempted to get out of his car and go take a leak on the side of the road, regardless of the people hanging around the dock and on the other side of the road. He looked hungrily at the wall on his right.

He lit a cigarette as a distraction and blew the smoke from his unfiltered Gitane out the car window. The overflowing ashtray showed that he had already been waiting a long time. He reached out to turn off the radio, tuned to Radio Monte Carlo, since the part he had wanted to hear was over now.

He had parked his Mazda MX-5 at the port near the Piscine, pointed toward the building where the station was located. It had to be swarming with cops. He had listened to the show and the killer's phone call as he sat in his car, waiting. At his newspaper, *France Soir,* a number of colleagues had done the same thing, and now they were probably digging all over the Web or God knows where else, hunting for information. Quite a few brains were working overtime to decipher the new message broadcast over the radio by "No One," as the press had dubbed him. Everyone called him that now. The power of the media. Who knew what the police had been calling him before some reporter thought up a name that had stuck.

Investigators used logic. Journalists used imagination. But one didn't necessarily exclude the other. He was a prime example in that sense. Or so he hoped.

The cell phone on the seat next to him started to ring. The ring tone was a song by Ricky Martin that his niece had practically forced him to use after she had downloaded it. He hated it but had never learned enough about cell phones to change it. Imagination and logic, yes, but with an aversion to technology. He picked up the phone and answered.

"Hello?"

"Coletti, it's Barthélemy."

"What's up?"

"We've got a tip. A fantastic piece of luck. Giorgio Cassani, our Milan correspondent, is a friend of the guy who wrote the song that No One played on the radio. He called us from Italy a couple of minutes ago. They'll give us a few more minutes before they call the police."

A stroke of luck. Let's hope nobody gets killed by it. And let's hope I don't piss my pants.

"Well?"

"It's called 'Nuclear Sun.' The guy who wrote it is an Italian, a deejay named Rolando Bragante, a.k.a. Roland Brant. Got it?"

"Sure, I got it. I'm not stupid. Text me with the details though. You never know."

"Where are you?"

"Just outside the station. Everything's under control. Nothing's happened yet."

"Be careful. If the cops get on to you, we'll be in fucking hot water."

"I know what they're like."

"Be good," was Barthélemy's laconic farewell.

"You too. Let me know if there's any news."

He clicked off. An Italian deejay with an English pseudonym. Some disco music called 'Nuclear Sun.' What the hell did that mean?

He felt another stab in his abdomen and made a decision. Throwing the cigarette out the window, he opened the door and got out. He went down a few steps on the other side of the road and hid himself in the semidarkness, away from the silhouette of the car. He took advantage of a recess in the wall next to the closed windows of a store, and with a heavy sigh, unzipped his pants and relieved himself. He felt like he was flying. He watched the yellow stream of urine fall like a torrent on the gentle downhill slope.

Letting yourself go in a case like that was an almost sensual, graphic pleasure. The satisfaction was at once physical and something deeper, human. Like when he was a child and he and his brother used to pee in the snow, making patterns.

Wait a sec, he had a thought. The snow. What did the snow have to do with it? He could see a magazine photo, a male figure in a ski suit standing next to a ski lift, ready to go, with a pretty girl at his side. There was snow. Lots of snow. He had a sudden flash of intuition and held his breath.

Fuck. Roby Stricker. That's who it was. And if it was him, he had figured it out.

His physiological needs gave no sign of relenting. The excitement made him nervous. He interrupted the flow and almost peed on his hands. He had covered stories where the risk of getting one's hands dirty was almost certain. This wouldn't be any more disgusting. But where was Roby Stricker now?

He shook his genitals vigorously and tucked them back in his briefs. Running back to the car, he paid no attention to the fact that his pants were undone. *There's a murderer in this city, René,* he told himself. *Who gives a damn if your fly's down?*

He got in the car and picked up his cell phone, calling back Barthélemy at the paper.

"It's Coletti again. Find me an address."

"Out with it."

"Roby Stricker. That's S-t-r-i-c-k-e-r with a *c* and a *k*. Roby might be short for Robert. He lives here in Monte Carlo. And if we're really, really lucky, he might even be in the phone book. If not, get it some other way, but fast."

"Hold on a sec." The newspaper wasn't the police, but they had their methods.

That minute felt endless, even longer than when his bladder had been full. Barthélemy came back on the line.

"Bingo. He lives in a condo called Les Caravelles, Boulevard Albert Premier."

Coletti held his breath. He could not believe his luck. It was just two hundred yards from where he was parked.

"Great. I know where it is. I'll be in touch."

"René, I'm telling you again. Watch out. Not just for the cops. No One's dangerous. He's already killed three people."

"Touch wood, cross your fingers. I don't want to lose my skin, but if things end up the way I think they will, it'll be a sensation." He hung up.

For a moment, he heard the voice on the radio again.

I kill . . .

He shivered in spite of himself. But the excitement and the adrenaline were already flowing and dispelling any normal sense of caution. As a man, Coletti had limits, but as a reporter, he knew his job and was willing to risk anything to do it. He could recognize something big. A piece of news to hunt down, open like an oyster and let the world see whether there was a pearl inside or not. And this time, there was a gorgeous pearl, as big as an ostrich egg.

Everyone had a drug, and this was his.

He looked at the brightly lit windows of Radio Monte Carlo. There were several police cars parked outside the entry. The blue flashing light on one of them went on and the car pulled out. Coletti relaxed. That must be the police escort that took Jean-Loup Verdier home every night. He had followed them a number of times and knew what they would do. They drove up to the deejay's house, slipped inside the gate, and that was it. With the police standing guard, any contact was impossible.

He would have given half of Bill Gates's fortune for an interview with Verdier, but for the moment there was no way. He was sealed tight, coming in and going out. He'd stood in front of that house long enough to know that it was impossible.

Everything seemed impossible recently. He'd done all he could to get an assignment in Afghanistan to cover the war. He could feel the story in his gut. He knew he could tell it better than anyone else, like he had done in the former Yugoslavia. But they had picked Rodin, maybe because they thought he was younger and hungrier and more willing to take risks. Maybe there was some politics behind it, the right connections with someone he wasn't aware of. He'd gotten his ass beat.

Coletti opened the glove compartment and pulled out his digital camera, a Nikon 990 Coolpix. He placed it on the seat beside him and checked it carefully, like a soldier testing his weapon before battle. The batteries were charged and it had four 128 meg cards. He could shoot World War III if he needed to. He got out of his Mazda without bothering to lock it and hid the camera under his jacket so it would not be noticed. He left the car and the Piscine behind him and headed off in the opposite direction. A few dozen yards away were the stairs leading up to the promenade. As he reached the street, an unmarked police car with a flashing light on its roof left the Rascasse and sped off in front of him.

He could see two people inside and imagined who they might be. Inspector Hulot and Sergeant Morelli, no doubt. Or maybe that dark-haired cop he had seen that morning coming out of Jean-Loup Verdier's house, who had looked at him as his car passed by. He had a strange feeling when their eyes met. That man had the devil inside. He was very familiar with the devil and could recognize people who carried it with them. Maybe he should find out more about that cop.

Coletti had given up on following police cars long ago. The cops were not stupid and would have detected him immediately. He'd get stopped and could forget about the scoop. He could not risk making any mistakes.

There had been that hoax of a first call earlier in the evening, as fake as a bad check. The cops must have gotten nasty. He wouldn't want to be the guy who made that call when they got hold of him. He saw no point in getting caught in a similar trap.

If the maniac's next victim was really Roby Stricker, they would use him as bait, and the only place where that could happen was at his house. So all he had to do was find some place to wait, where he could see without being seen. If his assumptions were correct and they caught No One, he would be the only eyewitness and reporter with photos of the arrest. If he could manage it, the story was worth its weight in plutonium.

The streets were practically empty. Everyone in the city must have been listening to the radio and heard No One's new call. Not many people felt like going out for a walk, knowing there was a killer lurking around.

Coletti headed for the well-lit entrance of Les Caravelles. When he reached the glass doors of the condo, he breathed a sigh of relief. It was a normal lock that did not require a code. Coletti rummaged in his pockets like any normal tenant looking for his keys.

He pulled out a gadget given to him by an informant, a sharp-witted bastard he had once helped out of a jam. The guy loved money, whatever the source—either what Coletti passed him for his leaks or the money he found by breaking into apartments. Coletti slipped the gizmo in the lock and the door opened. He entered the lobby of the luxury building. He looked around. Mirrors, leather sofas, Persian carpets on marble floors. There was no security there now, but during the day the doorman was probably pretty strict. His heart was pounding. It wasn't fear, but pure adrenaline. It was paradise on earth. It was his job.

To his right, at the shorter end of the rectangular room, there were two wooden doors. One had a brass sign that said CONCIERGE. The other, on the opposite corner, probably led down to the basement. He had no idea what floor Roby Stricker lived on, and waking the doorman at that hour to ask was definitely not a good idea. But he could take the service elevator, ride up to the top floor, and take the stairs down until he found the right floor. Then he'd find a good observation point, even if he had to hang out a window, something he had already done in the past.

The Reeboks on his feet made no noise as he reached the basement door. He pushed against it, hoping it wasn't locked. He had his gizmo, but every second saved was a second gained. He breathed another sigh of relief. The door was unlocked. It was pitch black inside. In the reflection of the lobby lights, he could see the stairs descending into darkness. The tiny red dots of the light switches shone at regular intervals like cats' eyes.

Coletti couldn't risk turning on the light. He went down the first two steps, easing the door closed and giving mental thanks for the efficiency of the person who had oiled the hinges. Feeling along the wall with his hands, he turned and groped his way. He slowly started going down the steps, being careful not to trip. Coletti's heart was beating so loudly that he wouldn't have been surprised if everyone in the building could hear.

Feeling with his foot, he realized that he had reached the bottom of the stairs. He put a hand out, felt the rough plaster, and started advancing slowly. Searching in his pocket, he realized that, along with his cigarettes, he had also left his cheap Bic lighter in the car. It would have come in handy. Proof that haste makes waste. He continued inching his way along. He was just a few steps further in that total darkness when he felt an iron grip around his neck and his body was thrown violently against the wall.

There is a man sitting in an armchair in the dark, in the large, silent apartment. He had asked to be left alone, he who always had a horror of solitude, of empty rooms, of the dark. The others had left after asking him one last time, with a note of apprehension, if he was really sure he wanted to stay there without anyone to take care of him. He had answered yes, reassuringly. He knew that big apartment so well that he could move around freely without having anything to fear.

Their voices fade away in the sound of departing steps, a door that closes, an elevator going down. Little by little, those noises become silence. So now he is alone, he thinks.

In the calm of that late May night, he thinks of the vigor of years past. He thinks of his brief summer, which is precipitating into the autumn of years to come, to travel not on tiptoe but on the solid soles of feet planted firmly on the ground, gripping anything that might keep him from falling.

The smell of the sea enters through the open window. He outstretches his hand and turns on the light on a table next to him. Almost nothing changes before his eyes, which are now a theater of shadows. He presses the button again. The light goes off with the hiss of a sigh without hope, like a candle. The man sitting in the armchair thinks again about what awaits him. He will have to become accustomed to the smell of things, to their weight and to their voices, when they are all drowned in an identical color.

The man sitting in the armchair is practically blind.

There was once a time when it was not so. There was a time when he lived in the light and in its absence and its essence. A time when his eyes defined a point that was "there" and would propel his body forward with a leap, while music seemed to be made of light itself, a light that not even applause could dispel.

It was so brief, his dance.

From the birth of his passion to the anxious discovery of his talent, to the astonishment of the world at its confirmation—all had passed in the twinkling of an eye. Yes, there were moments so full of pleasure that they were enough for an entire lifetime, moments that others would never see, even if they lived for centuries.

But time, the lying cheat who treated men like toys and years like minutes, flew up around him and suddenly took away with one hand what it had profusely dispensed with the other. There were crowds of people who had ecstatically admired his grace, the elegant poise of his steps, the silent words of his every gesture when it seemed that his entire body was generated by music itself, so harmonious were his movements.

He still carried the memories in his extinguished eyes. They burned so brightly that they could almost replace what he was losing. La Scala in Milan, the Bolshoi in Moscow, the Théâtre Princesse Grace in Monte Carlo, the Metropolitan Opera in New York, the Royal Opera in London. An infinite number of curtains opening in silence and closing with the applause of every success. Curtains that would never reopen.

Farewell, idol of the dance.

The man runs his hand through his thick, shiny hair.

His hands are his eyes now.

He touches the armchair's rough fabric, the soft fabric of the pants on his muscular legs, the silk of the shirt over his chest, the chiseled line of his pectoral muscles. He feels his smooth cheek shaved by another, until he meets the colorless trickle of a tear that streaks his face. The man had asked, and was allowed to be left alone, he who always had a horror of solitude, of empty rooms, of the dark.

And suddenly, he feels the solitude is broken, that he is not alone in the apartment. Not a noise, not a breath, not a footstep. It is a presence he perceives with a sense he did not know he had, like the primitive instinct of a bat. One hand takes away, the other hand gives.

He can sense many more things now.

The presence turns into a light step, agile, almost noiseless. Calm, regular breathing. Someone is crossing the apartment and coming closer. Now the noiseless step has stopped behind him. He controls his instinct to turn and look. It would be useless.

He smells the perfume, that of clean skin mixed with good cologne. He recognizes the cologne, but not the person. Eau d'Hadrien, by Annick Goutal. A scent of citrus, sun, and sea breeze. You gave it to Boris, some time ago. You bought it in Paris, in the shop near the Place Vendôme, the day after your triumph at the Opéra. When you still . . .

The steps resume. The newcomer goes past his armchair, with its back to the door. He can make out the shadow of his body as he comes before him. The man sitting in the armchair is not surprised. He is not afraid. He is simply curious.

"Who are you?"

A moment of silence, and then the man standing answers the man sitting in a deep, resonant voice.

"Does it matter?"

"Yes, it matters to me, very much."

"My name would mean nothing to you. Who I am is unimportant. I want to be certain that you know *what* I am and why I'm here."

"I can imagine. I've heard of you. I was waiting for you, I believe. Perhaps, deep down, I was hoping you would come." The man sitting runs his hand through his hair. He would also like to run it through the other man's hair, over his face, and his body. Because now his hands are his eyes.

"I'm here now," the same deep voice, so rich and harmonious, answers from the dark.

"I suppose there is nothing I can say or do."

"No, nothing."

"So, it's over. I think it's better this way, in a certain sense. I would never have had the courage."

"Would you like some music?"

"Yes, I think so. No, I'm sure of it. I want some."

He hears a series of small, soft noises, the hum of the CD player opening and then closing, enhanced by the darkness and the silence. He has not turned on the light. He must have the eyes of a cat if the weak glimmer from outside and the display of the CD player are enough to guide him.

A moment later, the notes of a cornet flutter through the room. The man sitting does not recognize the music, but from the very first measures, the tones of that strange instrument remind him of Nino Rota's melancholy melody in Fellini's *La Strada*. He danced to that music at La Scala in Milan, at the beginning of his career. It was a ballet based on the movie, with a prima ballerina whose name he did not remember, only the incredible grace of her body.

The man sitting in the armchair turns to the darkness where the music comes from, the same darkness that is in the room and in his eyes.

"Who is it?"

"His name is Robert Fulton. A great musician . . ."

"I can hear that. What does he mean to you?"

"An old memory of mine. Now it will be yours as well."

A long, motionless silence. For an instant, the man in the armchair has the sensation that the other man has gone. But when he speaks, his voice comes from the darkness right beside him.

"Can I ask a favor?"

"Yes, if it's possible."

"May I touch you?"

A slight swish of fabric. The man standing bends down. The man sitting feels the warmth of his breath, a man's breath. A man who, at another time and on another occasion, he might have tried to know better.

He stretches out his hand and places it on that face, running over it with his fingertips until he touches the hair. He follows the line of the face, and explores the cheekbones and forehead with his fingertips. His hands are his eyes now, and they see for him.

The man sitting is not afraid. He was curious. Now he is only surprised.

"So, it's you," he murmurs.

"Yes," answers the other, straightening up.

"Why do you do it?"

"Because I have to."

The man sitting is content with this answer. He too did what he felt he had to, in the past. He has only one last question for the other. He is, after all, only a man. A man not frightened by the final end, but only by pain.

"Will I suffer?"

The man sitting has no way of seeing the man standing take out a gun with a silencer from a canvas bag slung around his neck. He does not see the barrel pointed at him. He does not see the menacing reflection in the burnished metal of the little bit of light coming from the window.

"No, you won't suffer."

He does not see the knuckles whiten as the finger presses the trigger. The answer of the man standing mixes with the smothered hiss of the bullet, which, in the darkness, pierces his heart.

32

"I have no intention of living like a prisoner until this is over with, and, most of all, I refuse to be used as bait!"

Roby Stricker put down his glass of Glenmorangie, got up from the couch, and went to look out the window of his apartment. Malva Reinhart, a young American actress sitting on the couch opposite, rolled her magnificent violet eyes, the cause of many a close-up shot, and looked from him to Frank. She was bewildered by the whole thing and didn't say a word. She seemed to be still playing one of her characters, although her glances were longer and her cleavage lower. The aggressive attitude she had displayed when Frank and Hulot had stopped them outside Jimmy'z, the most exclusive disco in Monte Carlo, was gone.

They had been standing in the plaza next to Sporting Club d'Été, just outside the glass doors of the club, to the left of the sign's blue lights. Malva and Roby were speaking to someone, but as Frank and Hulot had gotten out of their car and approached them, the person had left and they were alone in the glare of the headlights.

"Roby Stricker?" Nicolas had asked.

Stricker had looked at them dubiously.

"Yes," he had said in a hesitant voice.

"I'm Inspector Hulot of the Sûreté Publique and this is Frank Ottobre of the FBI. We need to speak to you. Could you come with us, please?"

Their credentials seemed to make him uncomfortable. Frank

had found out why later on, when he pretended not to notice the young man awkwardly disposing of a bag of cocaine. Stricker had pointed to the young woman next to him who was looking at them, astonished. They were speaking French and she didn't understand.

"Both of us, or just me? I mean, this is Malva Reinhart and . . ."

"You're not under arrest, if that's what you think," Frank had said in Italian.

"You'd better come with us. It's in your best interest. We have reason to believe that your life is in danger. Hers too, perhaps."

They had filled him in soon afterward, in the car. Stricker had grown deathly pale and Frank knew that if he had been standing, his legs might have collapsed. Frank had translated for Reinhart and it was her turn to pale. A sexy, young, contemporary actress suddenly swept into the world of silent black-and-white film.

They had reached Stricker's building, Les Caravelles, not far from police headquarters. They couldn't help being stunned at the madman's nerve. If he was *really* aiming for Stricker, the choice was a defiant, mocking challenge. He intended to strike at someone who lived a couple hundred yards from the center of police operations.

Frank had stayed with him and the girl while Nicolas, after inspecting the apartment, went to give instructions to Morelli and his men stationed below. There was a security net around the building that was impossible to get through. Before he left, Hulot had called Frank into the hallway, given him a walkie-talkie, and asked if he had his gun. Without a word, Frank had opened his jacket to show him the Glock hanging from his belt. He had shivered slightly as he brushed against the cold, hard weapon.

Frank stepped toward the center of the room and responded patiently to Stricker's objections.

"First of all, we're trying to guarantee your safety. You might not have noticed, but practically all the police in the Principality are stationed outside. Secondly, we have no intention of using you as bait. We simply need your cooperation to try to catch the person we're after. You're not running any risk, I assure you. You live in Monte Carlo, so you must know what's been happening, don't you?"

"Listen," Roby said, as he turned toward him without moving from the window. "It's not that I'm scared, okay? I just don't like the whole situation. It feels . . . overblown, that's all."

"I'm glad you're not afraid, but that doesn't mean you should underestimate the person we're dealing with. So please get away from that window."

Stricker tried to appear nonchalant, but he stepped back and went over to the couch with what he probably considered daredevil confidence. In actuality, he was quite visibly terrified. Frank had been with him for an hour now, and if it were up to him he would have walked out of there and left the guy to his fate. Stricker fit the stereotype of a spoiled rich boy so exactly that, in other circumstances, Frank might have thought it was just a joke.

Roberto Stricker, "Roby" in the society pages, was Italian, from Bolzano to be precise, but his last name was German and he could pass for English if he wanted. He was just over thirty and very good-looking. Tall, athletic, great hair, great face, total prick. His father was a billionaire: the owner of, among other things, a chain of discos in Italy, France, and Spain called No Nukes, whose symbol was an environmentalist sun. That was what had struck Barbara when she heard the name "Nuclear Sun," the dance track that the killer had played on the radio. The track was by Roland Brant, the English pseudonym of the very Italian deejay Rolando Bragante. Roby Stricker lived in Monte Carlo, doing whatever he wanted with his time and his father's money—that is to say, absolutely nothing. The tabloids were full of his love affairs and vacations, skiing at Saint Moritz with the hottest top models or playing tennis at Marbella with Bjorn Borg. As far as work was concerned, his father probably gave him money just to keep him out of the family business, figuring that whatever his son cost him was the lesser of two evils.

"What are you going to do?" Stricker picked up his glass but put it down again when he saw that the ice had melted.

"Actually, there's really very little we can do in cases like this. We just take the right precautions and wait."

"What does this nut job have against me, anyway? Do I know him?"

If he decided to kill you, I wouldn't be surprised if he did know you. And probably pretty well, you little shit. Frank sat down in an armchair.

"I have no idea. Quite frankly, aside from what we told you, we don't have much more information on this *murderer,* except for the criteria he uses to choose his victims and what he does after he kills them."

Frank spoke in Italian, emphasizing the harshness of the word "*assassino*" for Roby Stricker's benefit. He didn't think it was a good idea to frighten the girl sitting on the couch anymore. She was gnawing on her finger in fear. Although . . .

Like attracts like.

The two of them were together for a reason. Like Nicolas and Céline Hulot, like Nathan Parker and Ryan Mosse. And like Bikjalo and Jean-Loup Verdier. Out of love. Out of hate. Out of self-interest. As for Roby Stricker and Malva Reinhart, however, it could be just simple physical attraction between two very shallow human beings.

Frank's walkie-talkie started to buzz. Strange. They had decided to observe strict radio silence. No precautions seemed excessive with this criminal, who could tap phone lines so easily that he might very well be able to listen in on any police frequency. Frank got up from the armchair and went into the foyer before removing the handpiece from his belt. He didn't want the two of them to hear. He pressed the answer button.

"Frank Ottobre."

"Frank, it's Nicolas. We may have caught him."

Frank felt as though a cannon had just fired next to his ear.

"Where?"

"Here, downstairs, by the boiler. One of my men caught a suspicious character who was sneaking down the stairs to the basement and stopped him. They're still there. I'm on my way over."

"I'll be right there." He ran back into the room. "Stay here and don't move. Don't let anyone in but me."

He left them to be shocked and scared on their own, as he opened and closed the door with a single movement. He had no time to wait for the elevator, so he rushed to the stairs and hurried down, two steps at a time. He reached the lobby just as Hulot was entering the glass doors from the street with Morelli behind him. A uniformed cop was guarding the door to the basement.

They went downstairs, guided by the dim light of a series of bulbs set in the wall, protected by grating. All the buildings in Monte Carlo looked alike to Frank. Beautiful exteriors but shoddy on the inside, where most people couldn't see. It was hot down there and it reeked of garbage.

The agent led the way. Just around the corner, they saw a policeman beside a man sitting on the ground, leaning against the wall with his hands tied behind him. The policeman had a pair of infrared glasses for night vision on top of his head.

"Everything okay, Thierry?"

"Here he is, Inspector, I . . ."

"Christ!"

Frank's shout interrupted the policeman.

The man sitting on the ground was the redheaded reporter, the one he had seen outside police headquarters when Yoshida's body had been discovered. The same one who had been standing in front of Jean-Loup's house that morning.

"This guy's a reporter, damn it!"

The journalist took advantage of the moment to make his voice heard.

"You're damn right, I'm a reporter. René Coletti of *France Soir*. I've been telling this blockhead that for the last ten minutes. If he had let me get my press card out of my pocket, we could have avoided all this aggravation."

Hulot was fuming. He crouched down beside Coletti. Frank was afraid he would punch him in the face. If he had, Frank would have understood and defended him before any court.

"This wouldn't have happened if you'd stayed in your place, you stupid jerk. And by the way, you're in a lot of shit."

"Oh really? And what's the charge?"

"For now, obstruction of a police investigation. We'll find something else in time. We've got enough work busting our asses without you media people making things worse." Hulot stood up. He nodded to the two agents. "Get him up and take him away."

The two cops picked Coletti up off the floor. Muttering to himself about the power of the press, the reporter managed to stand. He had a scrape on his forehead, probably where he had hit the wall. The lens had fallen off the camera around his neck.

Frank grabbed Hulot's arm.

"Nicolas, I'm going back up."

"Go on. I'll deal with this idiot."

Frank went back upstairs. He felt disappointment grinding in his stomach. All their work—waiting at the radio, struggling to decipher the message, all the men stationed there—was useless because of that stupid reporter with his camera. It was his fault if their presence was revealed. If the killer really did mean to get Roby Stricker, he must have changed his mind by now. The good side was that they had avoided another murder, but they had also lost any chance of catching him.

When the elevator door slid open at the fifth floor, Frank knocked at Stricker's door.

"Who is it?"

"It's me. Frank."

The door opened and Frank walked in. Roby Stricker would have to spend many hours on the beach or at a tanning salon to get rid of his pallor. Malva Reinhart didn't look any better. She was sitting on the couch and her eyes seemed even bigger and more violet against her ashen skin.

"What happened?"

"Nothing. Nothing to worry about."

"Did you arrest anyone?"

"Yes, but not the one we're looking for."

Just then the walkie-talkie buzzed. Frank took it off his belt. After his rush down the stairs he was surprised he still even had it.

"Yeah?"

He heard Hulot's voice and did not like the sound of it at all.

"It's Nicolas. I've got some bad news."

"How bad?"

"Very bad. No One screwed us, Frank. All the way. Roby Stricker wasn't his target at all." Frank knew this would be harsh. "They just found the body of Gregor Yatzimin, the ballet dancer. Same condition as the other three."

"Shit!"

"I'll be downstairs in a minute."

"I'm on my way."

Frank gripped his walkie-talkie and for a moment he was tempted to hurl it at the wall. He felt the fury well up in him like a block of granite. Stricker approached him at the front door. He was so nervous that he didn't even notice the state Frank was in.

"What's happening?"

"I have to go."

The young man looked at him, stunned.

"Again? What about us?"

"You're not in any danger. You weren't the target."

"What? I wasn't the target?" Relief cut the strings of his tension and he slumped against the wall.

"No. There has been another victim."

The certainty that he had escaped from death helped Stricker transition from fear to indignation.

"Are you telling me that you practically gave us a heart attack by mistake? While you were hanging around here showing off how great you are, that guy was going around killing someone else? You fucking incompetent idiots. When my father hears about this he'll . . ."

Frank listened in silence to the beginning of his outburst. He was right. There was an element of truth in what Stricker was saying. No One had made fools of them all over again. But they were being duped by someone who took risks, who went out and fought his battles, evil as he was. Frank couldn't let that good-for-nothing tell him off, after all they had done to try to save his miserable existence. The ice inside Frank suddenly turned to steam and he exploded with all his might. He grabbed Stricker by the balls and squeezed hard.

"Listen, you piece of shit . . ." Stricker paled and fell back against the wall, turning his head to one side to avoid Frank's flaming eyes. "If you don't shut your fucking mouth, I'll make you see your own teeth without your having to look in the mirror." He squeezed Stricker's testicles harder and the young man grimaced in pain. Frank went on in the same hissing voice. "If I had anything to say about it, I'd be glad to hand you over to that butcher, you asshole. Fate's been too good to you. Don't flaunt it and go looking for trouble."

He let go. Stricker's face slowly returned to its normal color. Frank saw that there were tears in his eyes.

"I'm going now. I've got more important things to do. Get rid of that whore you've got in there and wait right here for me. We've got some stuff to talk about, you and I. You'll have to clear up a few things about the people you hang out with here in Monte

Carlo." Frank backed away from Stricker who slowly slid down the wall until he was sitting on the floor. He put his head in his hands and started to cry. "And if you want to call Daddy in the meantime, go right ahead."

Frank turned and opened the door. As he waited for the elevator, he regretted the fact that he hadn't been able to ask Stricker about one person in particular. He was about to do so and then Nicolas had called.

He'd be back later on. He wanted to find out who Roby and Malva had been talking to when they had stopped them in front of Jimmy'z, the man who had disappeared when he saw them drive up. Frank wanted to know why Roby Stricker had been talking to U.S. Army Captain Ryan Mosse.

33

The trip to Gregor Yatzimin's home seemed to take both seconds and hours. Frank sat in the passenger seat staring straight ahead, listening to what Hulot was telling him. His face was a mask of silent fury.

"You know who Gregor Yatzimin is, I suppose." Frank's silence showed that he did. "He lives—lived here in Monte Carlo and was the artistic director of the ballet company. He was having problems with his vision recently."

Frank suddenly exploded, interrupting as if he had not heard what Hulot had just said.

"I realized how stupid we were as soon as I heard the name. We should've imagined that the bastard would step it up. The first clue, *A Man and a Woman,* was relatively easy because it was the first one. He had to give us a method. "Samba Pa Ti" was more complicated. The third one obviously had to be harder. And he even told us."

Hulot could not follow the American's line of reasoning. "What do you mean, he told us?"

"The loop, Nicolas. The loop that goes *round and round and round*. The dog chasing its tail. He did it on purpose."

"Did what on purpose?"

"He gave us a clue with a double meaning so it could be misunderstood. He made us spin around on our asses. He *knew* we'd get Roby Stricker from the deejay's English name and the No Nukes disco. And while we had the entire police force protecting that little creep, we gave the killer complete freedom to strike his next victim."

Hulot continued.

"Gregor Yatzimin, the Russian ballet dancer who was going blind from radiation he was exposed to in Chernobyl in 1986. 'Dance' didn't mean discos, it meant ballet. And "Nuclear Sun" was the radioactivity in Ukraine."

"Right. We were completely naive. We should've realized that it couldn't be that easy. And now we have another corpse on our conscience." Frank rammed his fist against the glove compartment. "Motherfucker!"

Hulot knew what Frank was going through. He felt the same way. He too wanted to bang his fist against the wall. Or against that bastard's face, again and again until he had the same bloody mask as his victims. He and Frank were both cops with a great deal of experience, and neither was stupid. But now they felt that their adversary had them exactly where he wanted them and could move them as easily as pawns on a chessboard.

Unfortunately, no conscientious policeman, like a good doctor, ever considers the number of lives he has saved. All he can think of are those he has lost. The praise and blame of the media and superiors and society have nothing to do with it. It's a personal matter, one each cop faces every morning in the mirror.

The car came to a stop in front of an elegant building on Avenue Princesse Grace, not far from the Jardin Japonais. It was the usual scene, one they had met with far too often recently and had hoped not to see again that night. Forensics and the medical examiner were already parked in front of the building. A few uniformed cops were standing guard at the front door and several reporters were already on the scene. The others would be there shortly. Hulot and Frank got out of their car and headed over to Morelli who was waiting for them at the door. His expression was all they needed in order to complete the picture of general outrage and frustration.

"What do we have in there, Morelli?" asked Hulot as they entered the building together.

"The usual. A skinned face, the words *I kill* . . . in blood. Same as the others, pretty much." Morelli waved a hand at the elevator.

"What do you mean, pretty much?"

"This time the victim wasn't stabbed. He shot him before he . . ."

"He shot him?" Frank interrupted. "A gun makes a lot of noise in the middle of the night. Someone must have heard it."

"Nothing. Nobody heard anything."

The elevator arrived silently, as only luxury elevators can. The doors slid open without a sound.

"Top floor," Morelli said to Hulot, who was about to press the button.

"Who found the body?"

"Yatzimin's assistant. Assistant and confidante. Might also be his lover. He had been out with a group of the victim's friends, ballet dancers from London, I think. Yatzimin hadn't felt up to it and insisted that they go without him."

They reached the top floor and the well-oiled elevator opened again. The door to Gregor Yatzimin's apartment was wide open and all the lights were on in the typical commotion of a crime scene. The forensic people were at work while Hulot's men were meticulously inspecting the place.

"Over here."

Morelli led the way. They walked through the luxurious, understated, but glamorous apartment. They reached the door of what was probably the bedroom just as the medical examiner was coming out. Hulot saw with relief that it was Coudin and not Lassalle. The bosses must be very worried if they had sent the top guy. He could imagine the phone calls going on back in the trenches.

"Good morning, Inspector Hulot."

"You're right, Doctor. Good morning." Nicolas said, realizing the time. "Although I don't think it'll be a very good one, at least not for me. What've you got?"

"Nothing great. As far as the investigation is concerned, I mean. The type of homicide is completely different. If you want to take a look . . ."

They followed Frank, who had already gone in. Once again they were horrified by the scene. They had all seen the like before, with different methods and in other situations, and yet it was impossible to get used to.

Gregor Yatzimin was lying on the bed, his hands crossed over his chest in the usual position of a dead body. If it were not for his grotesquely mutilated face, he would have looked like a corpse laid out by an undertaker before the funeral. On the wall was the usual mocking message written in blood and fury.

I kill . . .

They stood in silence before the corpse. In front of *that* body. A new murder without motive or explanation, except in the sick mind of the person who had committed the crime. Their anger was a searing blade, sharp as the murderer's, turning inside a painful wound. Sergeant Morelli's voice shook them from their hypnotic trance.

"Something's different."

"What do you mean?"

"Well, it's just a feeling, but this isn't delirious like the other murders. There isn't blood everywhere, and there's no ferocity. Even the position of the body. It's almost as if there's . . .respect. . . for the victim, that's what's different.

"You mean the beast can feel pity?"

"I don't know. It's probably bullshit, but that's what I felt when I came in."

"You're right." Frank placed a hand on Morelli's shoulder. "This one is different from the others. What you're saying isn't bullshit. And even if it was, it's nothing compared to the bullshit we've said and done tonight."

They glanced at the corpse of Gregor Yatzimin, the eternal dancer, the "mute swan" as critics all over the world called him. Even in that funereal pose, horribly disfigured, he still looked graceful, as if his talent had remained intact even in death.

Coudin left the room and the other three joined him.

"Well?" asked Hulot, with little hope.

The medical examiner shrugged.

"There isn't much. Aside from the mutilation, which I think was done with a fairly sharp instrument, a scalpel most likely, there's nothing to see. We have to examine the wounds on his face in a more appropriate setting. Although at first glance I'd say it was done with a great deal of skill."

"Our friend has had some practice."

"Cause of death was a firearm, shot at close range. Again, I can only speculate for the moment, but it was large, something like a nine-caliber. A shot to the heart, almost instantaneous death. From the body temperature, I'd say it was a couple of hours ago."

"While we were wasting our breath on that asshole Stricker," Frank muttered.

Hulot looked at him in agreement.

"I'm done here," said Coudin. "You can take away the body, as far as I'm concerned. I'll let you know the results of the autopsy as soon as possible."

Hulot had not doubt about that. They had probably put a fire under Coudin's ass. And that was nothing compared to what he could expect.

"Fine, Doctor. Thank you. Good morning."

The medical examiner looked at the inspector to see if he was being sarcastic. He met only the dull gaze of a defeated man.

"You too, Inspector. Good luck." They both knew how much he needed it.

The physician left. At Hulot's nod, the two men went into the bedroom with a body bag.

"Let's talk to this assistant, Morelli."

"I'll have a look around in the meantime," said Frank, pensively.

Hulot followed Morelli to the end of the hall to the right of the bedroom. The apartment was divided into living and sleeping space. They went through rooms covered with posters and images of the apartment's unfortunate owner. Gregor Yatzimin's assistant was sitting in the kitchen with a policeman.

His eyes were red and he had obviously been crying. He was practically a boy, a delicate type with pale skin and sandy hair. A box of tissues and a glass with amber-colored liquid were on the table in front of him.

He stood up when he saw them.

"I'm Inspector Nicolas Hulot. Sit down, please, Mr. . . .?"

"Boris Devchenko. I'm Gregor's assistant. I . . ."

He spoke French with a heavy Slavic accent. Tears came to his eyes again and he sat back down. He bent his head and reached for a tissue without looking.

"I'm sorry, but what happened is so horrible.."

"There's no reason to apologize," Hulot reassured him, pulling up a chair and sitting down. "Mr. Devchenko, try to calm yourself, if you can. I need to ask you a few questions."

"It wasn't me, Inspector." Devchenko's tear-stained face suddenly shot up. "I was out with friends. Everyone saw me. I was very attached to Gregor and I could never have . . . never have done . . . something like that."

Hulot felt infinite tenderness for the boy. Morelli was right. They were almost certainly lovers. That changed nothing in his approach. Love was love, however it showed itself. He knew homosexuals who lived their relationships with a delicacy of feeling that was hard to find in more conventional couples.

"Don't worry, Boris." He smiled. "Nobody's accusing you of

anything. I just need some information to help us understand what happened here tonight. That's all."

Boris Devchenko seemed to relax at the knowledge that he was not a suspect.

"Some friends arrived from London yesterday afternoon. Roger Darling, the choreographer, was supposed to come too, but at the last minute he had to stay in England. Gregor was supposed to dance the role of the adult Billy Elliot, but then his vision got worse, suddenly." Hulot remembered seeing the movie with Céline. "I went to pick them up at the airport in Nice. We came here and had dinner at home. Then we suggested going out, but Gregor didn't feel up to it. He changed so much when his eyesight got worse."

He looked at the inspector who nodded, confirming that he knew the story of Gregor Yatzimin. Exposure to the Chernobyl radiation had caused irreversible degeneration of the optic nerve, which had led to total blindness. His career was cut short when he could no longer move across the stage without assistance.

"We went out and left him alone. If I had stayed at home he might still be alive."

"Don't blame yourself. There's nothing you could have done in a case like this." Hulot did not point out that, if he had stayed at home, there might be two bodies instead of one. "Did you notice anything unusual over the last few days? Someone you saw on the street a little too often? A strange phone call? Anything out of the ordinary? Anything at all?"

Devchenko was much too upset to hear the desperation in Hulot's voice.

"No, nothing. On the other hand, I was taking care of Gregor all the time and it took all of my energy. Caring for a blind man is extremely wearing."

"Any servants?"

"None that lived in. The cleaning woman comes every day, but she leaves in the middle of the afternoon."

Hulot looked at Morelli.

"Get her name. Although I doubt it'll get us anywhere. Mr. Devchenko . . ." The inspector's voice softened as he turned back to the boy. "We'll have to ask you to come by headquarters to sign a statement and remain available to help us. I'd appreciate it if you wouldn't leave the city."

"Of course, Inspector. Anything to make sure that whoever killed Gregor pays for what he did."

From the way he said those words, Hulot was confident that Boris Devchenko would have risked his life to save Gregor Yatzimin, had he been there at the time. And that he would have died for it. Hulot stood up and left Devchenko with Morelli. He returned to the living room where the forensic people were finishing up. The two policemen came over to him.

"Inspector . . ."

"What is it?"

"We questioned the neighbors below. Nobody heard anything."

"But there was a shot."

"It's an elderly couple directly below. They take sleeping pills at night. They told me they don't even hear the fireworks for the Grand Prix, so they wouldn't have heard a shot. There's another elderly woman who lives alone in the apartment opposite theirs, but she's away right now and her grandson from Paris is there. A young guy about twenty-two. He was out all night clubbing. He came back as we were ringing the bell. He didn't see or hear anything, obviously."

"And the apartment opposite this one?"

"Vacant. We woke the doorman and he gave us the keys. The killer probably got in through there, climbing over the balcony that's connected to this apartment. But there aren't any signs of breaking and entering. We didn't want to contaminate anything, so we didn't go in. Forensics will go over there as soon as they finish in here."

"Good," said Hulot.

Frank returned from his tour of inspection. Hulot realized that he wanted to be alone for a while to cool off. And to think. He knew that they wouldn't find any real trace of the killer in the apartment. Instead, he was analyzing by instinct, letting his unconscious flow over what the crime scene conveyed, aside from normal sensorial perception. Just then, Morelli came out of the kitchen.

"Your intuition was right, Morelli." They looked at Frank in silence, waiting for him to continue. "Aside from a few stains on the bedspread, there's no trace of blood anywhere in the house. Not a trace. But a job like this produces a lot of blood. As we have seen."

Frank was back to normal. The night's defeat seemed to have had no effect on him, although Nicolas knew that it had taken a real toll. It couldn't be otherwise. Nobody could forget so soon that he could have saved a life and didn't.

"Our man cleaned the house perfectly after doing what he did. A luminal test will show the bloodstains."

"But why? Why didn't he want to leave any blood?"

"I have no idea. Maybe for the reasons Morelli said."

"Why would an animal like that feel pity for Gregor Yatzimin? If pity was really the motive?"

"It doesn't change anything, Nicolas. It's possible, but not important. They say that Hitler loved his dog."

They fell silent, moving toward the entrance. Through the open door, they could see the assistant medical examiner on the wide landing sealing Yatzimin's body in the green canvas body bag. They were going into the elevator to avoid carrying the body down six flights of stairs.

Outside, dawn was breaking. It would be a new day, like all the others they had seen since this story had begun. There would be a sea of reporters in front of Gregor Yatzimin's building. They would step out into the volley of questions like cannon fire and answer with a flurry of "no comments." The media would go wild again. Hulot's superiors would explode once more. Roncaille would lose a little more of his tan and Durand's face would turn green. As they walked down the stairs, Frank Ottobre felt that if anyone blamed them, they deserved it.

34

Frank parked Nicolas Hulot's Peugeot in a no-parking zone in front of Roby Stricker's building. He took the POLICE ON DUTY sign out of the glove compartment and placed it on the rear window under the windshield wiper. A cop walked toward him as he was getting out of the car, but he saw the sign before he saw Frank. The cop raised a hand to show that everything was okay. Frank answered with a nod, crossed the street, and headed over to Les Caravelles.

He had left the inspector and Morelli to face the onslaught of reporters who were swarming to the new murder like flies to shit. The police barricades in front of the building could barely contain them. When they'd spotted Hulot and the sergeant through the car windows, they started pressing up against the barricades and the two policemen had difficulty holding them back. It was a repeat of the scene at the port when the bodies of Jochen Welder and Arianna Parker had been discovered and the whole nasty business had begun.

They reminded Frank of locusts. They moved in swarms and consumed everything in their path. True, they were only doing their job, but that excuse could be used by anyone. Even the killer, who kept pulling the wool over their eyes, stupid sheep that they were. He too was doing his job, and Frank hoped he would burn in hell for it.

He had stopped inside the lobby and glanced out the window at the crowd.

"Claude, is there a side entrance?"

"Of course, the service entrance."

"Where is it?"

"The service elevator is behind the stairs. Press *S* and you'll be in the courtyard next to the ramp that goes to the garage. Turn right, go up the ramp, and you're on the street."

Hulot had looked at him, confused. Frank didn't want to do too much explaining. Not then, anyway.

"I've got a couple of things to do, Nicolas, and I'd like to do it without half the reporters in Europe at my heels. Can I borrow your car?"

"Sure. Keep it for now. I won't be needing it."

Hulot had handed him the keys without another word. The inspector was so tired that he even lacked the strength for curiosity. All three were unshaven and looked as though they had been through a war, worse for the fact that they had just lost another battle.

Frank had left them there and followed Morelli's directions. He had crossed the basement that smelled of mold and oil and reached the street. He had gone over to the car that was parked on the other side of Avenue Princesse Grace, right behind the reporters who were bombarding poor Nicolas with questions. Luckily, nobody had noticed him.

He pushed the glass doors and went into the building. The doorman was not at his post. Looking at his watch, Frank saw that it was exactly seven A.M. He fought back a yawn. The lack of sleep was beginning to get to him. First the radio station, then the hunt for Roby Stricker, standing guard at his house. The hope, the disappointment, the new murder, the disfigured body of Gregor Yatzimin.

Outside, the sky and sea were tinged with the blue of a new day. How he would have liked to forget everything and relax in his comfortable Parc Saint-Roman apartment, close the shutters and his eyes, and stop thinking about blood and words on walls.

I kill . . .

He remembered the wall in Yatzimin's bedroom. If they didn't stop him, that bastard would *never* stop. There wouldn't be enough walls to write on or cemeteries for the dead.

It was not yet time to sleep, even if he could. He still had to clear up the unfinished business with Roby Stricker. He wanted to know how and why Ryan Mosse had gotten in touch with him, although he could probably guess. He had to know how far the general's investigation had gone with respect to theirs and what else they were planning.

Frank looked around. Just then, the doorman came out of what must have been his apartment, buttoning his jacket. He approached, hurriedly chewing something. Caught in the act of eating his *petit déjeuner*. He went into the guard box and looked Frank over from behind the glass.

"Can I help you?"

"Roby Stricker."

"My orders are to say that he's sleeping."

Frank pulled out his badge. As he removed it from his jacket, he made sure that the doorman saw the Glock hanging from his belt.

"This says you can wake him."

The doorman changed his tune immediately. The saliva he swallowed was harder to get down than that last mouthful of food. He picked up the intercom and dialed the number in a single nervous movement, letting it ring for a long time before pronouncing his verdict.

"No answer."

Funny. The rings should have woken Roby Stricker, even if he was asleep. Frank didn't think he had the balls to skip town. He had scared him badly enough to keep him from doing anything rash. Though if he had taken off, it would be a complication, not a tragedy. If they needed him, that asshole would be very easy to find. Even hidden behind his father's legal protection.

"Try again."

The doorman shrugged.

"It's still ringing but there's no answer."

Frank had a sudden, terrible premonition. He thrust his hand at the guard.

"Give me the master key, please."

"But I'm not authorized . . ."

"I said, give me the master key, *please*. If that's not enough, I can be less polite." Frank's tone was final. The doorman swallowed more saliva. "And afterward, go outside and tell the policeman there to come right up to Roby Stricker's apartment." The man opened a drawer and gave him a key on a BMW key chain. He shifted his weight as if he were about to get up. "Get moving!" Frank headed toward the elevator and pressed the button.

Why aren't elevators ever there when you need them? And why are they always on the top floor when you're in a hurry? Damn Murphy and his law . . .

The door finally slid open and Frank got in, hurriedly pressing the button of Stricker's floor. In the eternity of that ride, he hoped that he was wrong. He hoped that his sudden suspicion would not become a mocking reality.

When he reached the fifth floor, the elevator opened with the same soft *whoosh*. Frank saw that the door to the playboy's apartment was ajar and he reached it in one step. Taking out his Glock, he pushed the barrel against the door to avoid touching the handle.

The foyer was the only thing in order. The living room where he, Stricker, and the girl had been sitting earlier was a complete mess. The curtain of the French door was half torn from the rod and hanging down like a flag at half mast. There was a glass on the floor and the bottle of whiskey that Stricker had been drinking from before lay shattered on the pearl gray carpet. The contents had spilled onto the floor, leaving a dark stain. A painting had fallen, revealing a small wall safe. The glass had slipped off the table, strangely enough without breaking, and lay on the floor beside the crooked frame. A cushion from the couch had slid down on the floor. There was nobody in the room.

Frank crossed the living room and turned right, down the short hallway that led to the bedroom. On the left, a door opened onto the bathroom, empty. That, at least, hadn't been touched. He reached the doorway of the bedroom and had to catch his breath.

"Shit. Shit. Shit. Motherfucking shit," he uttered.

Frank stepped forward, careful where he placed his foot. Roby Stricker's body lay on the marble floor in the center of the room, in a pool of blood. The entire room seemed covered in it. He was wearing the same shirt he had on when Frank had left, except now it was soaked red and glued to his body. There were a number of stab wounds on his back. His face was all bruised and there was a deep cut on his cheek. The blood covered his mouth and his left arm was broken, bent at an unnatural angle. Frank leaned over and touched his throat. No pulse. Roby Stricker was dead. Frank jumped up and tears of rage obstructed his vision.

Another one. The same night. Another fucking murder just hours later. He silently damned the world, the day, the night, and his role in the whole thing. Damn Nicolas who had gotten him involved. Damn himself for letting him do it. He damned everything he could think of.

He removed the walkie-talkie from his belt, hoping they could pick up his signal. He pressed the button.

"Frank Ottobre for Nicolas Hulot."

A crackle, a sputter, and finally the inspector's voice.

"Nicolas here. What's up, Frank?"

"Now I'm the one who has to give you some bad news, Nick. Really bad."

"What the hell happened now?"

"Roby Stricker's dead. In his apartment. Murdered."

Hulot let loose with a string of curses that he ordinarily would seem incapable of pronouncing. Frank knew exactly how he felt. When his anger cooled down, and after a little more crackling, the inspector asked what he wanted to know most.

"No One?"

"No, just plain murdered. His face is still there and there's no writing on the wall."

"Describe it."

"I'll tell you what I see at first glance. Death probably wasn't instantaneous. He was attacked and stabbed. There are signs of a struggle everywhere and blood all over the floor. His murderer thought he was dead and left while he was still alive. It sounds strange, but that poor bastard Roby Stricker accomplished much more as he was dying than he managed to do in his whole life . . ."

"Meaning?"

"Before he died, he wrote the name of his killer on the floor."

"Do we know him?"

Frank lowered his voice slightly, as if he wanted to let Hulot digest what he was about to say.

"I do. If I were you, I would call Durand and have him issue a warrant for the arrest of Ryan Mosse, captain in the U.S. Army."

35

The door opened and Morelli entered the small, windowless room and placed a stack of black-and-white photos, still damp from printing, on the gray Formica table where Frank and Nicolas Hulot were sitting. Frank leafed through them, chose one, and turned it in the direction of the man in front of him. Leaning forward, he pushed it to the other end of the table.

"Here we are. Let's see what this tells you, Captain Mosse."

Ryan Mosse, sitting handcuffed, lowered his gaze to the photo with complete indifference. He turned his expressionless hazel eyes back to Frank.

"So what?"

Morelli, who was leaning against the door beside the one-way mirror that covered the entire wall, shifted at the sound of his voice. On the other side of the mirror were Roncaille and Durand, who had rushed to headquarters at the news of the two new murders and the arrest.

Frank was conducting the interrogation in English and they were both speaking quickly. Morelli missed a word here and there, but he understood enough to realize that this suspect had steel cables in place of nerves. Confronted with the evidence, he was about as emotional as an iceberg. Even the most hardened criminals would give in and start blubbering in a situation like that. This guy made you feel uneasy despite his being in handcuffs. Morelli imagined Roby Stricker face-to-face with this guy holding a knife. It was not pretty at all. And Morelli pictured the disfigured body of Gregor Yatzimin, whose murderer had laid him out on his bed with belated pity.

Frank leaned back in his chair.

"Well, this here on the floor looks like a dead body, right?"

"So?" repeated Mosse.

"So, doesn't it seem strange to you that your name is written next to the dead body?"

"You need a good imagination to get my name out of that scribble."

Frank leaned his elbows on the Formica table. "You'd have to be illiterate not to."

"What's wrong, *Mr. Ottobre*?" Mosse smiled. "The stress getting to you?" It was the smile of a hangman opening the trap door.

And Frank's smile was that of a condemned man hanged by a rope that had suddenly broken.

"No, *Captain Mosse.* The stress got to you last night. I saw you talking to Stricker in front of Jimmy'z when we came for him. You cleared out when you saw us, but not quite fast enough. If you like, I can guess what happened afterward. You were watching his house and then you waited a little longer after you saw us leave. You saw Stricker's girlfriend leave too and then you went upstairs. You had an argument. The poor guy must have freaked out and then so did you. There was a fight and you knifed him. You thought he was dead and you left, but he had time to write your name on the floor."

"You're hallucinating, Ottobre, and you know it. I don't know what drugs you're on, but you're taking too much. Obviously, you don't know me very well." Mosse's eyes turned to steel. "If I use a knife on someone, I make *sure* he's dead before I go."

"Maybe you're losing your touch, Mosse," Frank said with a wave of his hand.

"Okay. At this point I have the right not to answer without a lawyer present. It's the same law in Europe, isn't it?"

"Sure. If you want a lawyer, you've got a right to one."

"Okay then. Go fuck yourselves, both of you. That's all I'm saying."

Mosse closed himself off. His eyes settled on his reflection in the mirror and went blank. Frank and Hulot looked at each other. They would get nothing more out of him. Frank gathered the photos on the table and they got up and went to the door. Morelli opened it to let them through and followed them out of the room.

In the next room, Roncaille and Durand were on edge. Roncaille turned to Morelli. "Would you excuse us a minute, Sergeant?"

"Sure, I'll go get some coffee."

Morelli left the four of them alone. On the other side of the mirror, they could see Mosse, sitting in the middle of the other room like a soldier fallen into enemy hands.

Captain Ryan Mosse, U.S. Army, number . . .

Durand nodded in his direction. "A tough nut to crack," he said.

"Worse. A tough nut to crack, who knows he has all the connections he needs. But even if he's connected to the Holy Ghost, he can't get out of this one."

The attorney general took the photos from Frank's hand and examined them once more.

The image showed Stricker's body on the marble floor of his bedroom, his right arm bent at a right angle, his hand on the floor. He died writing the word that nailed Ryan Mosse.

"It's a little confusing."

"Stricker was dying and his left arm was broken." He pointed to the arm bent in the unnatural position. Frank remembered the agility Mosse had displayed during their fight. He had experienced it in person. Mosse knew how to break someone's arm very easily. "We found some pictures in the apartment of Stricker playing tennis. He was clearly left-handed. Here, he was writing with his right hand. It's obviously not his normal handwriting."

Durand kept staring at the photo, puzzled.

Frank waited. He looked at Hulot, leaning silently against the wall. He too was waiting to see what was coming. Durand made up his mind. He finally took the bull by the horns, as though the study of the picture had helped him find the right words.

"All hell will break loose because of this. The diplomats will be on to it soon and it'll sound like the start of the Grand Prix. Right now we're just holding Captain Mosse. If we actually charge him, we're going to need incontrovertible proof so we don't end up with egg on our face. The No One affair has already made us look ridiculous enough."

Durand wanted to emphasize that the prompt arrest of Roby Stricker's probable killer did not in any way make up for the murder of Gregor Yatzimin, a new slap in the face for the Principality's police force in charge of the investigation. Frank's participation was simply a collaboration between investigative bodies, and the main responsibility still fell on the Monaco police force. They were the butts of biting newspaper headlines and caustic op-ed pieces by TV commentators.

"As far as Mosse is concerned," Frank shrugged, "it's obviously your decision. In my opinion, if that matters, we have more than enough evidence to go forward. We've got proof that Ryan Mosse knew Stricker. I saw them myself last night in front of Jimmy'z. There's his name in the photo. I don't see what else we need."

"And General Parker?"

Frank had been there when they had gone to pick up the captain that morning at Beausoleil. On reaching the courtyard of the Parker family's rented house, the first thing Frank had noticed was that, except for a few small details, the house was almost identical to Jean-Loup's. He made a quick mental note of it, soon buried by other considerations. He had figured that the general would make a fuss, but he realized that he had underestimated him. Parker was too smart to create a scene. He was impeccably dressed when he greeted them, as though he had been expecting them. When they had asked, he had simply nodded and called Mosse. When the police had told him to accompany them to headquarters, Mosse was visibly tense and had thrown an inquiring glance at the old man. Waiting for *orders, sir.*

Frank suspected that, if Parker had asked him, Mosse would have exploded in fury at the men who had come to arrest him. The general had simply shaken his head ever so slightly and the tension in Mosse's body had relaxed. He had held out his wrists and accepted the indignity of handcuffs without a word.

Parker had found a way to be alone with Frank as they were taking Mosse to the car. "This is bullshit, Frank, and you know it."

"What your man did last night was bullshit, General. Serious bullshit."

"I could testify that Captain Mosse never left this house last night."

"If you do and they find out it's not true, not even the President could get you off charges of aiding and abetting. Nobody in North America would risk protecting you. Want my advice?"

"Let's hear it."

"If I were you, I'd just keep out of it, General. Captain Mosse is in deep trouble and not even you can get him out. Military tactics provide for situations like these, don't they? Sometimes you simply have to cut your losses and leave one of your men to his fate."

"No one gives me lessons in military tactics. Especially you, Frank. I've taken people who were harder than you'll ever be and torn them to pieces. You'll just be one more, mark my words."

"Everyone's got to take his chances, General. That's the rule of war."

Frank had turned his back and left. On the way out, he had seen Helena standing at the living room door, to the right of the hallway. Frank could not help thinking how beautiful she was. Being awakened suddenly seemed to have had no effect on her luminous eyes and skin. Her blond hair didn't even look slept on. Their eyes had met as he passed. Frank had noticed that, contrary to what he had first thought, her eyes were blue, not gray. And their gaze held all the sorrow of the world.

Driving downtown, Frank had leaned back in his seat, his eyes studying the plastic lining of the ceiling. He had kept trying to erase two overlapping images from his mind. Harriet and Helena. Helena and Harriet. The same eyes. The same sadness.

Frank had tried to think of something else. As they reached headquarters on Rue Notari, he had pondered the general's mocking words. *No One gives me lessons in military tactics.* The general didn't realize all the implications of what he had said. Just then, there was a killer at large who could give lessons to them all.

"What do you think General Parker will do?" repeated the attorney general.

Frank was so deep in thought that he had let Durand's question go unanswered for a little too long.

"Sorry, Dr. Durand. I think Parker will do everything in his power for Mosse, but he won't throw himself off a cliff. The consulate will surely get into this, but there's one important fact to be noted. Mosse was arrested by an American FBI agent. We wash our dirty laundry among ourselves and we save face. We're the country that came up with impeachment, after all, and we've never been afraid to use it."

Durand and Roncaille exchanged glances. He was right. There were no problems there. Durand took his time getting to the point.

"Your presence here is a guarantee that everyone has the best intentions. Unfortunately, the road to hell is paved with them. Right now, we—and I mean the Principality police—need results. The Roby Stricker case has apparently nothing to do with the killer we're after."

Frank felt Nicolas Hulot standing behind him. They both knew what Durand was driving at. There were dark clouds hanging over them. And behind those clouds, there was an ax raised, ready to strike.

"There was another victim last night. The fourth. We can't just sit here letting garbage get dumped on our heads. I repeat, your collaboration is greatly appreciated Frank."

Politely tolerated, Durand. Only politely tolerated. Why don't you use the right words, even if I did just hand you General Parker and his thug on a silver platter?

Durand went on in the same vein, dumping the garbage at Hulot's door.

"I'm sure you realize that the authorities simply cannot continue to watch a chain of homicides like this without taking steps, unpleasant as they might be."

Frank watched Nicolas. He was leaning against the wall, suddenly alone on the battlefield. He looked like a man refusing a blindfold before a firing squad. Durand had the decency to look him in the eye as he spoke.

"I'm sorry, Inspector. I know you're an excellent officer, but at this point I have no choice. You are removed from the case."

"I understand, Dr. Durand," Hulot said, nodding simply. He was probably too tired to have any more of a reaction. "There won't be any problems."

"You can take some vacation time. This case has been extremely wearing for you. The press, of course . . ."

"I said there was no problem. There's no need for you to sweeten the pill. We're all adults and we know the rules of the game. The department must do as it sees fit."

If Durand was impressed with Hulot's reply, he did not let on. He turned to Roncaille. Until then, the police chief had listened in silence.

"Good. You'll take over the investigation, Roncaille. As of today. Please keep me informed of every detail. Any time of day or night. Good-bye, gentlemen." And the ever polite attorney general Alain Durand walked away, leaving a silence behind him that he was relieved not to share.

Roncaille ran a hand through his already smooth hair.

"I'm sorry, Hulot. I would have liked to avoid this."

The police chief's words were not just a formality. The man was really sorry, but not for the reasons he wanted them to believe. Now, he was in the lion's cage, and it was up to him to tame the wild beasts.

"Get some sleep. You both need it. Then I'd like to see you in my office as soon as possible, Frank. There are some details I'd like to discuss with you." With the same apparent composure as Durand, Roncaille escaped from the room as well. Frank and Hulot were left alone.

"See? I hate to say 'I told you so,' but I can't blame them."

"Nicolas, I don't think either Roncaille or Durand could have done any better than we did. This is politics, not reason. But I'm still in it."

"You. And what do I have to do with it?"

"You're still police inspector, Nicolas. You were taken off a case, not suspended from the force. And you've got something that nobody else on the case has."

"What's that?"

"Twenty-four hours a day to work on it, without having to account to anyone, without having to waste your time writing reports."

"Through the back door, huh?"

"Right. There's still something we have to check out, and you seem the best person to do it now. Actually, I don't think it was I who noticed that record cover in the video."

"Frank, you're a son of a bitch. A real son of a bitch."

"I'm your friend. And I owe it to you."

Hulot changed his tone. He stretched his neck to relieve the tension. "I think I'll get some shut-eye. I guess I can now, right?"

"Yeah, and I must not have heard Roncaille say he wants to see me 'as soon as possible.' I'm practically asleep already."

However, as they left the room, they both thought of Gregor Yatzimin's disfigured face on the bed and his eyes, already blind before he died, staring up at the ceiling.

36

Frank woke up and looked at the blue rectangle framed by the window. When he had come home to the Parc Saint-Roman apartment, he had been too tired even to shower. He had collapsed on the bed after peeling off his clothes, and left the shutters open.

I'm not in Monte Carlo, he thought. *I'm still in that house on the beach, trying to pull myself together. Harriet is sunbathing next to me, lying on a towel, the wind in her hair and a smile on her face. Now I'm getting up and going to her, and there will be no one dressed in black. There will be no one between us.*

"No One . . ." he said aloud.

The two deaths of the night before came back to him and he got up reluctantly. Through the windows he could see a strip of sea where gusts of wind had formed whitecaps far off shore. He went over to the window and opened it. A gust of warm air swelled the curtain and swept what was left of the nightmares from the room. He had only slept a few hours and felt as though he could have slept forever.

He went into the bathroom, showered, shaved, and put on fresh clothes. As he made himself some coffee, he mused over the new developments. Now that Nicolas was out of the game, things would be a lot more complicated. Roncaille wasn't capable of handling things on his own, at least not from an investigative point of view. He might be a genius at PR and talking to the press, but field investigations were not his cup of tea. Maybe a long time ago they had been, but now he was more politician than cop. However, he had a good team working for him. The Principality's police force wasn't considered one of the best in the world for nothing . . . *blah blah blah* . . .

His own presence in Monaco was becoming a diplomatic necessity. Like everything, it had advantages and disadvantages. Frank was sure that Roncaille would try to maximize the first and minimize the second. He was well acquainted with the methods of the Monte Carlo police. Nobody ever said anything, but they knew everything.

Everything except the name of the killer . . .

He decided not to worry about the police. He had felt that way all along. This was not a joint police investigation. Even if Roncaille and Durand represented authority, it didn't matter. Neither did America nor the Principality. This was a personal matter between him, Nicolas Hulot, and a man dressed in black who collected the faces of his victims in a bloody, delirious carnival. All three of them had pressed the PAUSE button and stopped their lives, waiting to see how this no-holds-barred struggle between three dead men pretending to be alive would end.

They had to change.

He sat down at the computer and turned it on. There was an e-mail from Cooper with attachments. That was the information he had found on Nathan Parker and Ryan Mosse. It wasn't much use now that Mosse was in jail and Parker was temporarily harmless. *Temporarily,* he repeated. He had no illusions about Parker. The general was a man you couldn't rule out until there were worms in his dead body.

There was a note from Cooper in the e-mail.

Give me a call after you're done sailing the seas with your new cruiser and have a free second. At any time. I need to talk to you. Coop.

He wondered what was so urgent and looked at his watch. At this hour, he could call him at home. He wouldn't be disturbing anyone. Cooper lived alone in a loft overlooking the Potomac.

His friend's sleepy voice answered after a few rings. "Hello?"

"Coop? It's Frank."

"Oh, it's you. How's it goin'?"

"A huge oil tanker just crashed and you wouldn't believe the size of the spill."

"What happened?"

"Two more murders last night."

"Christ!"

"You said it. One was killed according to the usual ritual—he's the fourth. My friend the inspector was politely kicked off the case. The other guy's dead thanks to our dear friend, Ryan Mosse. They've got him in jail now and the general is raising hell to get him out."

"Jesus, Frank." Cooper was fully awake now. "What the fuck's going on over there? Next, you'll tell me it's nuclear war."

"Don't rule that out. What did you have to tell me that was so urgent?"

"There've been some new developments here. The Larkin case, I mean. The things we're finding out make us think they've got a good cover somewhere, a joint venture with something big. But we don't know what it is yet. And Hudson McCormack's in from New York."

"Who's he? What does he have to do with Larkin?"

"That's what we want to know. Officially, he's a lawyer, defense counsel for Osmond Larkin. That surprised us because the bastard could get himself someone better. He has in the past. This McCormack's a mediocre thirty-five-year-old attorney from the Big Apple. He's better known for being on the *Stars and Stripes* team at the Louis Vuitton Cup than for his legal success."

"Checked him out?"

"Sure. Turned him inside out. Nothing doing. Lives within his means, not a penny more. No vices, no women, no coke. All he cares about besides work is sailing. And now he comes out like a jack-in-the-box to show us what a small world it is."

"What does that mean?"

"I mean that right now Hudson McCormack is on his way to Monte Carlo."

"Great. This isn't the best time to visit."

"Apparently he's going for a pretty important regatta. But . . ."

"But?"

"Frank, doesn't it seem strange that a modest New York lawyer, unknown and unproven, gets the first important case of his career and takes off, even for a few days, to go sailing in Europe? Anyone else would have thrown himself into it 24/7."

"When you put it that way . . . But what's it got to do with me?"

"You're there and you know the story. Right now this guy is Osmond Larkin's only link to the rest of the world. Maybe he's just his lawyer, but it might be more than that. There's a lot of money and a lot of drugs at stake. We all know what goes on in Monte Carlo and the money that goes through there, but in cases of terrorism and drugs we could get a few safes opened. You're in with the police there—it wouldn't be difficult for you to have McCormack watched, discreetly and efficiently."

"I'll see what I can do."

He didn't tell Cooper that in Monte Carlo almost *everyone,* including him, was being discreetly and efficiently watched.

"I attached a photo in the e-mail so you can see what he looks like. And there's some other information on McCormack's visit to Monaco."

"Okay. Go back to sleep. Guys with low IQs need sleep so their brains can function in the morning."

"Thanks, asshole. Break a leg."

He hung up and placed the cordless next to the computer. Another lap, another race, another mess. He saved the attachment with the information on Hudson McCormack onto a floppy disk without even opening it. He found a label in the drawer and wrote "Cooper."

His brief conversation had taken him home for a moment, although *home* was an elusive concept. He felt as though his astral body were floating without emotion through the ruins of his existence like an invisible ghost who sees without being seen. He was at once in Cooper's house, in the office they had shared for years at the Bureau, in his own house that had been standing empty for months, and on the dark streets of Washington.

What's the point? Is there anyone in all human history who's ever understood? And if they've understood, why haven't they explained it to anyone?

He closed his eyes and in his mind returned to a conversation he had once had with Father Kenneth, a priest who was also a psychologist at the private clinic where Frank had been admitted after Harriet's death had pulled him down to the center of the earth. When he wasn't in therapy or analysis, he sat on a bench in the park of that luxury asylum, staring into the void and fighting the desire to follow Harriet. That time, Father Kenneth had walked silently across the grass and sat down next to him on the wrought-iron bench with dark wooden slats.

"How's it going, Frank?"

Frank looked at him carefully before answering. He had studied his long, pale face, that of an exorcist, aware of the contradiction between his role as man of science and a man of faith. He wasn't wearing his collar and could easily have passed as a relative of any of the patients.

"I'm not insane, if that's what you want to hear."

"I know you're not insane and you know that's not what I was asking. When I asked you how it was going, I *really* wanted to know how things were going."

Frank spread out his arms in a gesture that could mean many things.

"When do I get out of here?"

Father Kenneth answered his question with a question. "Are you ready?"

"If you ask me, I'll never be ready. That's why I asked you."

"Do you believe in God, Frank?"

He turned to the priest with a bitter smile. "Please Father, try to avoid clichés like 'Seek God and He will hear you.' He's been pretending not to notice."

"Stop offending my intelligence and, most of all, stop offending yours. If you insist on assigning me a role to play, maybe it's because you've decided to play one. There's a reason that I asked you if you believe in God."

Frank raised his eyes to stare at a gardener who was embedding an oak tree.

"I don't care. I don't believe in God, Father Kenneth. And that's not to my advantage, whatever you might think." He turned to look at him. "It means there's no one to forgive me for the evil that I do."

And I never thought I had done any. But it turns out, I did a great deal. Bit by bit, I took life away from the person I loved, the person whom I should have protected more than anything else.

As he slipped on his shoes, the ringing phone brought him back to the present.

"Hello."

"Frank, it's Nicolas. Are you awake?"

"Awake and ready for action."

"Good. I just phoned Guillaume Mercier, the kid I was telling you about. He's waiting for us. Want to come?"

"Sure. It might help me face another night at Radio Monte Carlo. Have you read the papers yet?"

"Yes. They went wild. You can imagine."

"*Sic transit gloria mundi.* Who gives a shit? We've got other things to do. Come pick me up."

"I'll be there in two minutes."

Frank went to put on a clean shirt and the intercom rang as he was unbuttoning the collar.

"Monsieur Ottobre? There's someone here to see you."

At first Frank thought that Nicolas was being literal when he said two minutes. "I know, Pascal. Tell him I need another minute and to come up if he doesn't want to wait downstairs."

As he slipped on the shirt, he heard the elevator stop at his floor. He went to open the door and found her outside.

Helena Parker was standing in front of him, with her gray eyes meant to reflect starlight, not pain. She was in the shadow of the hallway, looking at him. Frank was holding his shirt open over his bare chest. It was the scene with Dwight Durham, the consul, all over again, except that the woman's eyes lingered over the scars on his chest before moving up again to his face. He hurriedly pulled the shirt on over his chest.

"Hello, Mr. Ottobre."

"Hello. Sorry I'm not dressed. I thought you were someone else."

"Don't worry about it." Helena's brief smile resolved the problem. "I imagined that from the doorman's answer. May I come in?"

"Of course."

Frank stood aside to let her in. Helena entered, brushing him with one arm and a delicate perfume, soft as a memory. For an instant, the room was filled with nothing but her.

Her eyes fell on the Glock that Frank had placed on the table next to the stereo. Frank quickly hid it in a drawer.

"I'm sorry that's the first thing you had to see."

"It doesn't matter. I grew up surrounded by weapons."

Frank had a brief image of Helena as a child in the home of Nathan Parker, the inflexible soldier whom fate had dared to cross by giving him two daughters.

"I can imagine."

Frank started buttoning his shirt, happy to have something to do with his hands. The presence of that woman in his apartment was a source of questions for which Frank was unprepared. Nathan Parker and Ryan Mosse were his real concern—they were people with voices, weight, feet that left tracks and arms that could strike. Until then, Helena had been a silent presence, nothing more. A mournful beauty. Frank was not interested in the reason she was there and hoped that there was none. He interrupted the silence with a voice that sounded harsher than he had intended.

"There must be a reason you're here."

Helena Parker had eyes and hair and a face and a smell, and Frank turned his back on her as he tucked his shirt into his pants, as if turning his back on everything she represented. Her voice came from behind him as he slipped on his jacket.

"Of course. I need to talk to you. I'm afraid I need your help. That is, if anyone can help me."

When he turned around again, Frank had shielded himself with a pair of dark glasses.

"My help? You live in the house of one of the most powerful men in America and you need my help?"

"I don't live in my father's house. I'm a prisoner in my father's house." A bitter smile flitted over Helena Parker's lips.

"Is that why you're so afraid of him?"

"There are many reasons to be afraid of Nathan Parker. But I'm not afraid for myself. I'm worried about Stuart."

"Stuart is your son?"

Helena hesitated a moment. "Yes, my son. He's the problem."

"And what does that have to do with me?"

Without warning, the woman went over to him, raised her hands, and removed his Ray-Bans. She looked into his eyes with an intensity that pierced Frank harder than the sharpest knife Ryan Mosse could ever find.

"You're the first person I've ever seen who can stand up to my father. If anyone can help me, it's you."

Before Frank could say anything, the phone rang again. He picked up the cordless with the relief of someone who finally has a weapon to wield against an enemy.

"Hello?"

"It's Nicolas. I'm downstairs."

"Okay, I'm coming down."

"This probably isn't a good time," Helena sighed, handing him back his sunglasses.

"I have to do a few things right now. I'll be out late and I don't know . . ."

"You know where I live. You can come see me whenever you like, even if it's late."

"Do you think Nathan Parker would appreciate a visit from me?"

"My father's in Paris. He went to speak to the ambassador and find a lawyer for Captain Mosse." A brief pause. "He took Stuart with him as . . . as a companion. That's why I'm here alone."

For a moment, Frank thought she was going to use the word *hostage*. Maybe that's what she had meant by *companion*.

"Okay. But I have to go now. There are a number of reasons why I don't want the person downstairs to see us leaving together. Would you mind waiting a couple of minutes before going down?"

Helena nodded. The last thing he saw before he closed the door were her shining eyes and the suggestion of a smile, made possible by a scrap of hope.

As he rode down in the elevator, Frank looked at himself in the artificial light of the mirror. The reflection of his wife's face was still in his eyes. There was no room for others, for other eyes, other hair, other pain. And, most of all, he did not want to help anyone because no one could help him.

He went out into the sunlight filtered though the glass doors and crossed the marble lobby of Parc Saint-Roman. Hulot was waiting for him in his car. When Frank opened the car door, he saw a pile of newspapers on the backseat. The top headline read "My Name Is No One," with references to the bluffing game of the night before. The other headlines were probably similar. Nicolas didn't seem to have slept any better than Frank.

"Hey."

"Hey, Nick. Sorry to make you wait."

"That's okay. Did anyone call you?"

"Total silence. I don't think your department is dying to see me, even though Roncaille is officially expecting me for a briefing."

"You'll have to check in sooner or later."

"Of course. For more reasons than one. But meanwhile, we have some private business to take care of." Hulot started the car and drove down the short driveway to the plaza where he could make a U-turn. "I stopped in at the office. One of the things I took from my desk was the original videotape, which was still there. I left the copy in its place."

"Think they'll notice?"

"I can always say I made a mistake," Hulot shrugged. "I don't think it's too serious. It'll be a lot worse if they find out we have a lead and haven't told them about it."

All Frank saw when they drove back past the glass doors of Parc Saint-Roman was a reflection of the sky. He turned his head to look out the rear window. As the car turned right onto Rue des Giroflées, he had a fleeting vision of Helena Parker leaving the building.

37

Guillaume Mercier was waiting in the garden when they reached his house in Eze-sur-Mer. As soon as he saw the Peugeot drive up, he pressed the remote on the gate and it opened slowly. Behind him was a one-story white house. It had a dark roof and blue shutters with a Provençal look. Nothing fancy, but solid and functional.

The yard was quite large. On the right, past the house, there was a big pine tree surrounded by a cluster of small evergreens. Beyond the shadow of the tree were some yellow and white lantana in full bloom, surrounding a lemon tree. Laurel bushes ran around the property, over the grating set into the top of the wall, hiding the view from the road completely. There were flower beds and bushes blossoming everywhere, contrasting skillfully with the neatly mowed lawn and flagstone footpath that matched the patio where Guillaume was standing. The house had a calm, peaceful air about it, a sense of comfort without the ostentation that often seemed necessary on the Côte d'Azur.

Inside the gate, Hulot turned right and parked the car under a wooden carport next to a Fiat and a large motorcycle, a BMW Enduro.

Guillaume walked over to them with a lanky gait. He was an athletic-looking guy with a pleasant if not handsome face, and the suntan of someone who plays outdoor sports. His muscular arms were covered in sun-bleached hair under his T-shirt worn over khaki Bermuda shorts with cargo pockets. He was wearing yellow sailing shoes without socks.

"Hello, Nicolas."

"Hi, Guillaume." The boy shook the inspector's hand and Nicolas nodded toward his companion. "This strong silent type is Frank Ottobre, FBI Special Agent."

Guillaume put out his hand and pretended to whistle. "So the FBI actually exists—not just in the movies. Nice to meet you."

As he shook the kid's hand, Frank felt relieved. He looked into his eyes, dark and deep-set in a face freckled by the sun. He could tell that Guillaume was the right guy for the job. He had no idea if he was any good, but he knew he'd keep his mouth shut if they asked nicely and told him the seriousness of the situation.

"That's right, we're very important in American movies and culture. And now we've gone global, as you can see."

Guillaume smiled, but the grin barely masked his curiosity. He had probably guessed that they were there for something very important, since Nicolas Hulot had come as a policeman, not a friend of the family.

"Thanks for helping us out."

Guillaume nodded, shrugged his shoulders to say "don't mention it," and led the way.

"I don't have much work right now. I'm editing a couple of underwater documentaries. Easy stuff. Doesn't take much time. And I could never say no to this man here." He pointed his thumb at the inspector.

"You said your parents are out?"

"Out? Out of their minds is more like it. After Dad stopped working, they blew on the embers and found out there was still some life in there. They're on their tenth honeymoon, or something like that. Last time they called, it was from Rome. They should be back tomorrow."

They continued along the flagstone path across the vivid green lawn and reached the side entrance. To their right was a wooden gazebo with a blue canvas roof over a patio table. The remains of a dinner, most likely from the night before, were still on the table.

"While the cat's away the mice play, I see."

Guillaume followed Nicolas's gaze and shrugged. "Some friends came over last night and the cleaning woman didn't show up today."

"Right, friends. I'm a cop. Think I can't see the table's set for two?"

Guillaume opened his arms wide to say that anything was possible.

"Listen, old man. I don't drink, I don't smoke, and I'm not tempted by any artificial paradise. Can't I have a little fun?"

He slid open the wooden door and invited them in. He followed and closed the door behind him. Once inside, Hulot shivered in his light jacket. "Chilly in here."

Guillaume pointed to the equipment lining the wall opposite the windows overlooking the garden where two air conditioners were humming.

"This stuff is sensitive to heat, so I have to keep the air on high. If your rheumatism's acting up, I can lend you one of Dad's winter coats."

Nicolas grabbed his neck and gave him a bear hug.

"Respect your elders or what you'll hear cracking will be your neck, not my joints."

Guillaume raised his arms in the sign of surrender.

"Okay, okay. I give up."

When Hulot let go, Guillaume collapsed onto a leather armchair in front of the machines. He smoothed down his ruffled hair and waved them onto the couch against the wall between the two windows. He pointed an accusing finger at Nicolas. "Don't forget that I surrendered only out of consideration for your age."

Hulot sat down and leaned back against the padded cushions of the couch, pretending to be out of breath. "Thank goodness. Between you and me, you might be right about the rheumatism."

Guillaume spun around in his chair and faced Frank and Hulot. His expression was suddenly serious.

Good, thought Frank. *The boy knows when enough is enough.*

He was even more convinced that this was the right person. Now he just hoped that Guillaume was an expert, like Nicolas said he was. He had other hopes as well. Now that they were coming to the point, Frank realized that his heart was beating faster. He looked out the window for a moment at the sun's reflection on the surface of the swimming pool. The peace and quiet of that place made everything seem far away.

His own story, and Helena's, and that of a general who refused to lose at any cost, of a inspector who wanted only to find a reason for outliving his son, of an insatiable killer who had to be gorged in madness and ferocity in order to become what he was. To think that it would all be so easy if only.

"Have you been following the No One story?" Frank asked, returning to the present. His voice barely rose above the sound of the air conditioner.

Guillaume eased back in his chair.

"The murders in Monaco, you mean? Who hasn't? I listen to the program every night on Radio Monte Carlo or Europe 2. Their ratings must be incredible by now."

Frank turned back to the garden. A gust of wind swept through the laurel bushes against the wall. Then he realized it was the air-conditioning vent, not the wind.

"Yeah. Five people have been killed. Four of them were horribly defaced. And we haven't gotten very far, because we don't have the faintest idea of who the killer might be or how to stop him. Aside from the little information he gave us himself, that madman hasn't left the slightest clue. Except for one tiny detail."

His silence gave Nicolas the floor. The inspector sat up on the edge of the couch and handed Guillaume the videotape he pulled from his jacket pocket.

"This is really the only trace we have. There's something on this tape that we want you to look at for us. It's very important, Guillaume, and people's lives may depend on it. So we need your help and your discretion. This is confidential. Extremely confidential. Do you understand?"

Nodding, Guillaume took the cassette from Hulot and held it in his hand as if it might explode.

"What's on this?"

Frank looked at him carefully. There was no irony in the boy's voice.

"You'll see. But I have to warn you that it's not easy to watch. So you know what to expect."

Guillaume said nothing. He got up and went over to close the curtains to keep the glare off the screen. The diffused light in the room was deep gold, and he sat back down and turned on the flat screen and the computer monitor. He put the tape in and the colored bars appeared on the screen, then the first images.

As Guillaume took in the scene of Allen Yoshida's murder, Frank decided to let him watch the whole thing. He could have skipped directly to the point that interested him without any further explanation, but now that he knew him, he wanted the boy to understand who they were dealing with and how important his own role was. He wondered what Guillaume was thinking as he watched the film, whether he felt the same horror that he, Frank, had when he had seen it for the first time. He had to admit in spite of himself that the movie was a sort of diabolical work of art, for the purpose of destruction not creation, and yet it did convey emotion.

A minute later, Guillaume reached out and paused the tape. The killer and his bloodied victim were stopped in the position that fate and the camera had dictated.

"Is this real or fake?" he asked in a low voice, looking at them wide-eyed.

"Unfortunately it's very real. I told you it wasn't pretty."

"Yes, but this butchery is beyond belief. How can this be possible?"

"It's possible. It really happened, as you can see for yourself. And we're trying to stop the butchery, as you call it."

Frank could see two dark patches of sweat under the boy's arms that hadn't been there before. He was sweating despite the cold in the room, a physical reaction to what he had just seen.

Death is hot and cold, both at the same time. Death is sweat and blood. Death is unfortunately our only true reminder that life really exists. Come on, kid. Don't let us down.

As if he could hear Frank's thoughts, Guillaume turned back his chair with a little squeak. He leaned as if to move away from the images he was going to see again. He pressed the button and the figures started their dance before his eyes, up to the mocking final bow and the ending static. Guillaume stopped the tape.

"What do you want me to do?" he asked.

Frank could tell from his voice that he wished he were elsewhere; he wished he had not just seen that figure of death and his surreal bow, soliciting the applause of an audience of the damned. Frank went over and placed a hand on the boy's shoulder.

"Rewind it, but slowly so we can see."

Guillaume turned a wheel and the images started flowing swiftly in reverse. In spite of the rapid backward motion, usually an entertaining caricature of human movement, the vision lost none of its horror.

"Here, slow down. Now stop."

At Guillaume's careful touch, the image stopped a few frames too soon. "Go forward, just a little bit. Very slowly now."

Guillaume moved the handle gently and the film advanced one frame at a time like a series of overlapping photographs.

"Stop!" Frank stood next to Guillaume and pointed at the screen, touching it with his finger. "There, right there, on the cabinet. There's something leaning there that looks like a record cover. We can't see that. Can you isolate it and enlarge it so we can read what it says?"

Guillaume moved over to the computer on his desk, still looking where Frank was pointing.

"I can try. Is this the original or a copy?"

"It's the original."

"Good. VHS isn't the greatest support, unless it's the original. First I'll have to make a digital image. We'll lose a little quality, but I can work better that way."

His voice was steady and calm. Now that he was in his element, Guillaume seemed to have overcome his shock. He started clicking the mouse at the computer screen. The same image that was in front of Frank appeared on the monitor. Guillaume typed for a second and the image grew clearer.

"Okay. Now, let's see what happens if we highlight that part."

He used his mouse to draw a square with a broken line around the part of the frame that Frank had indicated. Guillaume pressed a button on his keyboard and the screen was filled with an electronic mosaic.

"You can't see anything." The words escaped Frank's lips and he immediately regretted them.

Guillaume turned to him and raised his eyebrows. "Keep calm, ye of little faith. We've just begun."

He typed for about ten seconds and an image appeared on the monitor, sharp enough to make out a dark record cover. In the center of the picture was the silhouette of a man playing a trumpet. The silhouette was bending backward in the stance of a musician reaching an impossibly high note, to his own and the audience's amazement. It was the supreme moment, when an artist forgets time and place and is possessed by music itself, as both its victim and executioner. The white letters below the picture read:

Robert Fulton —"Stolen Music".

Frank said the words on the screen aloud, as if he were the only one in the room who knew how to read. "Robert Fulton—*Stolen Music*. What does that mean?"

"I have no idea. Have you heard of it, Guillaume?"

Nicolas's voice surprised them. While Guillaume was busy at his computer, Hulot had gotten up from the couch and gone to stand behind them without their noticing.

The boy continued to stare at the picture on the monitor.

"Never seen it before. Never heard of Robert Fulton. But I would guess it's an old jazz record. It's not really the kind of music I listen to."

Nicolas went back to the couch and Frank scratched his chin. He paced back and forth with his eyes half-closed. Then he started to talk, but he was obviously thinking out loud: the monologue of a man with a heavy burden on his shoulders.

"*Stolen Music*. Robert Fulton. Why did No One need to listen to that music during the murder? Why did he take it with him? What's so special about it?"

The room was filled with the silence of unanswered questions, the silence on which the mind feeds as it devours infinite distances searching for a sign, a trace, a clue. The silence of eyes staring, seeking a point that should approach and instead keeps getting farther and farther away.

He could feel a sinister sense of déjà vu. Of their same dumbfounded expressions before an unyielding record cover, an ignorant silence that had been interrupted by a phone call announcing a new murder . . .

The sound of Guillaume's fingers running over the keyboard marked the end of that momentary pause, during which the only sound had been the hum of the air conditioners.

"There's something here, maybe."

"What?" Frank spun back toward him as if he had just been released from a hypnotic trance.

"Just a minute. Let me check."

Guillaume rewound the tape to the beginning and started watching it very slowly, stopping the images occasionally and using the zoom to make out a particular detail that interested him. It was cold in the room, but Frank could feel his temples throbbing. He didn't know what Guillaume was doing, but whatever it was, he wished he could do it faster.

The boy stopped the image at the point where the killer was bending over Allen Yoshida in a position that could be interpreted as confiding. He was probably whispering something into his ear and Frank was sorry there was no soundtrack. No One was far too smart to give them a sample of his natural voice, even through a ski mask.

Guillaume returned to the computer and transferred the picture he had cut out on the screen to the LED monitor. He used the arrow of the mouse to select a portion of the image and typed something on the keyboard. There was another blotch, as the first time, that seemed to be made of colored pieces placed haphazardly by a drunken artist.

"What you see here are the pixels. They're like the tiny mosaic tiles that make up the image, the pieces of a puzzle, basically. If you enlarge them a great deal, the picture is very confused and illegible. But I"—his fingers flew over the keyboard, alternating with the mouse—"I have a program that examines the pixels damaged by enlargement and reconstructs them. There was a reason that I paid a fortune for this junk. Come on baby, don't let me down."

He hit the RETURN key. The image cleared up a little but was still confused and indecipherable.

"Shit, no. Let's see who's smarter now, you or me!"

Guillaume leapt over to the monitor, threateningly. He ran his hand through his hair and then his fingers went back to the keyboard. He typed furiously for a few seconds and then stood up and started fiddling with the equipment on the shelves in front of him, pressing buttons and turning levers. Red and green lights started flashing.

"Here we are. I was right."

He went back to his chair and moved it in front of the screen where he had stopped the image. A couple of buttons were pressed and suddenly there were two images side by side, the picture of the record cover and the one he was examining now. He touched the first with his finger.

"Here, see this? I checked, and this is the only place where you can see the entire record cover. Not completely though, because here, the top left corner is covered by the sleeve of the man with the dagger. We didn't notice it in the enlargement because the sleeve is dark, like the cover. But there are mirrors on the opposite sides of the room and the record's reflection is bounced from one to another. I thought I saw a slight difference in color compared to the picture I got from the video." Guillaume's fingers again flew over the keyboard. "I thought that, in the image reflected in the mirror, the complete one here in the center, we might see the label on the cover."

He pressed the RETURN key with the cautious finger of someone launching a missile to destroy the world. Slowly, before their eyes, the confused blotch on the monitor blended together and took on a shape. Dark letters, slightly distorted and out of focus but legible, appeared against a gold background.

"The label of the store that sold the record, perhaps. Here we are: 'Disque à Risque,' Cours Mirabeau something or other, Aix-en-Provence. Can't read the building number. Or the phone number. Sorry, you'll have to find that out yourselves."

There was a note of triumph in Guillaume's voice. He turned to Hulot with the gesture of an acrobat acknowledging the audience after a triple somersault.

Frank and Nicolas were speechless.

"Guillaume, you're fantastic!"

The boy shrugged and smiled.

"Come on, don't overdo it. I'm just the best there is, that's all."

Frank leaned down on the chair and bent closer to the monitor. Incredulously, he read the writing on the screen. After so much nothing, they finally had something. After so much aimless sailing on the sea, they finally had, far on the horizon, a dark line that could be land, but might simply be a dark mass of clouds. They were looking at it now with the fearful eyes of someone expecting another trick.

Nicolas stood up. "Can we print these out?"

"Sure, no problem. How many copies?"

"Four should do it, I think. Just in case."

Guillaume turned back to the computer and a printer started working. He got up as the pages fell onto the tray, one by one.

Frank stood in front of the boy and sought his gaze, thinking that sometimes, with some people, words weren't really necessary.

"You have no idea how much you've helped us and so many others this afternoon. Is there anything *we* can do for you?"

Guillaume turned away without speaking. He ejected the tape from the VCR, turned, and handed it to Frank. He held it firmly, without hiding his gaze.

"Just one thing. Catch the guy who did that."

"You can count on it. And it'll be partly thanks to you."

As Nicolas removed the copies from the tray, there was a positive note in his voice for the first time in a long while.

"Okay, we've got work to do. A lot of work. You don't have to show us out if you're busy. I know the way."

"Go on. I've worked enough today. I'm closing up shop and going for a ride. After what I just saw, I have to get out of the house."

"Bye, Guillaume. And thanks again."

Outside, they were greeted by a languorous sunset in the garden that seemed enchanted after the crude images they had just seen. There was a warm, early-summer breeze, splashes of color from the flower beds, the brilliant green lawn and the darker green of the laurel bushes. Frank noted that, by coincidence, none of the flowers was bloodred. He took that as a good omen and smiled.

"Why are you smiling?" asked Nicolas.

"A silly thought. Forget it. A touch of optimism after what Guillaume just gave us."

"Great kid," Hulot said. Frank didn't answer, knowing he hadn't finished. "He was my son's best friend. They were very much alike. Every time I see Guillaume, I can't help thinking that if Stéphane had lived, he would probably be very much like him. A crazy way to continue being proud of your son."

Frank did not look at him so as not to see the tears in Nicolas's eyes, which he could hear in his voice.

They walked the short distance to the car in silence. When they were inside, Frank took the printouts that the inspector had placed on top of the glove compartment and looked at them to give Nicolas a moment to recover. When Hulot started the engine, Frank put the pages back and leaned against the seat. As they buckled their seat belts, he realized that he was excited. "Know your way around Aix-en-Provence, Nicolas?"

"Not in the least."

"Then you'd better get a map, my friend. You're about to take a little trip."

38

Hulot pulled up at the corner of Rue Princesse Florestine and Rue Suffren Raymond, just a few dozen yards from police headquarters. Ironically, there was an advertisement just ahead for the PEUGEOT 206—BAD BOY.

Nicolas nodded toward the ad with a derisive grin. "There you go, the right car for the right man."

"Okay, *bad boy*. It's in your hands now. Go for it."

"I'll let you know if I find anything."

Frank opened the door and got out. He pointed a finger at the inspector through the open window.

"Not *if* you find anything. *When*. Or did you buy that story about a vacation?"

Hulot saluted him as a sign of farewell. Frank closed the door and stood there an instant, watching the car as it drove away and disappeared in the traffic.

The lead from the video was a gust of optimism for the stagnant investigation, but as yet it was too weak to mean anything. All Frank could do now was keep his fingers crossed.

He turned down Rue Suffren Raymond and started walking toward headquarters. On their way back from Eze-sur-Mer, Roncaille had called, telling him to come to the office for "important planning." From his voice, Frank could imagine what the meeting would be like. He had no doubt that Roncaille and Durand had also paid dearly for last night's failure, the new victim, new victims that is, which had led to Nicolas's removal from the case.

Frank entered headquarters and passed the guard who let him through without a glance. He was at home—here, now. He wasn't sure how long it would last, but that was how he felt at that moment. He reached Roncaille's office and knocked. The chief's voice told him to come in.

Frank opened the door and was not surprised to see Attorney General Durand there as well. What did surprise him was the presence of Dwight Durham, the U.S. Consul. It was justified of course, but Frank thought that diplomacy would be involved on another level, much higher than that of his own title as mere adjunct investigator. Durham's presence in that office was a very strong signal from the United States government, representing both the strings that Nathan Parker had pulled through his personal connections and the concern for American citizens being murdered on Principality territory. And then there was also, as a finishing touch, the unwholesome idea of a U.S. Army captain accused of murder being held in the Monaco jail.

Roncaille stood up when he entered, something he was in the habit of doing for everyone. "Come in, Frank. Good to see you. I suppose you had trouble sleeping after last night, like all of us."

Frank shook the hand he held out. Durham's rapid, surreptitious glance in his direction was full of implied meanings, which he immediately grasped. The office was slightly larger than Hulot's and there was a couch as well as an armchair. Basically, though, it was no different from the other offices at headquarters. The only concession to his role as chief of the Sûreté were a couple of paintings on the walls. They were certainly authentic, but Frank couldn't tell if they were worth anything. Roncaille sat back down at his desk.

"I also imagine you've seen the papers and what was written after the latest episodes."

Frank shrugged. "No, actually, I didn't need to. The media has its own logic. They're usually on the side of the citizens and the publisher, and not very useful for investigators. Reading the papers isn't my job. Giving them something to write about, at any cost, isn't my job either."

Durham brought his hand to his mouth to hide his smile. Durand probably realized that Frank was referring to Hulot's being taken off the case. He wanted to clarify things.

"Frank, I know your feelings for Inspector Hulot. Believe me, I deeply dislike taking steps that I know are unpopular. I also know how much Hulot is admired by the police force, but you must understand . . ."

"Of course I understand," Frank interrupted with a slight smile. "Perfectly. And I don't want it to be a problem."

Roncaille saw that the conversation had taken a downward spin, which could end badly. He hurried to smooth things over and distribute portions of ambrosia in the doses he deemed appropriate.

"There aren't, and mustn't be, any problems between us, Frank. The request for and offer of collaboration are comprehensive, unquestioning, and complete. Mr. Durham is here to confirm that."

The consul leaned back in his chair and placed his forefinger on the tip of his nose. He was in a position of power and was doing everything he could not to show it, while at the same time letting Frank know that he was not alone. Frank had the same impression of him as a decent, likeable person as during his brief visit to Parc Saint-Roman.

"Frank, it's no use pretending. The situation is very messy. And now there's this . . . uh . . . business with Captain Mosse. But that chapter is finished and the diplomats will take care of it as they see fit. As for Mr. No One, as the press calls him . . . well . . ."

He turned to Durand, leaving him the job of completing his sentence. The attorney general looked at Frank, who could tell that he would rather take his clothes off on TV than have to say what he was saying now.

"We have all agreed to put the investigation in your hands. Nobody is better qualified. You're a first-class agent with an excellent record. Exceptional, I'd say. You've been on the case since the beginning, you know everyone involved and everyone admires and respects you. Sergeant Morelli will be working with you as representative of the police and liaison with Principality authorities. But otherwise, you've got free rein. Please keep Roncaille and myself informed on any developments, keeping in mind that your goal is the same as ours: to catch this criminal before he kills anyone else."

Durand finished his speech and stared at Frank as if he had just been forced to make an unbelievable concession, like a parent who allows a naughty child a second helping of cake. Frank was ceremonious, as Roncaille and Durand expected of him, though what he really would have liked was to tell them both to kiss his ass.

"Fine. I suppose I should be honored by this appointment, and really, I am. Unfortunately, the serial killer we're after is astoundingly intelligent. So far, he hasn't made the slightest error, in spite of the fact that he's been operating in such a tiny, well-policed area."

Roncaille took this acknowledgment of the local police as personal praise. He leaned forward with his elbows on the table.

"You can use Inspector Hulot's office. As I mentioned, Sergeant Morelli is at your disposal. You'll find all the documentation, the forensic report on the last two murders, including Roby Stricker's. The autopsy report is on its way and should be on your desk tomorrow morning. If you need it, you'll be given a car and a POLICE ON DUTY sign."

"That would help."

"Morelli will have the car waiting when you leave. One last thing: Are you armed?"

"Yes, I've got a gun."

"Good. We'll get you a badge so you can work in Principality territory. Good luck, Frank."

Frank realized that the meeting was over, at least as far as he was concerned. Perhaps they still had things to discuss that involved him, but he couldn't have cared less. He got up, shook all their hands, and left the room. As he walked down the hall to Hulot's office, he thought about the events of the afternoon.

First, the lead that Guillaume Mercier had uncovered. The clue he had found by analyzing the video was worth its weight in gold in this investigation. In the world of the blind, a one-eyed man is king. In the world of ignorance, a name and an address might mean the difference between life and death. Unlike Nicolas, Frank was anxious rather than hopeful at the thought of the new lead. Hundreds of hands were pushing him forward as hundreds of inaudible voices whispered meaningless words in his ears. Words that he should understand but couldn't as he ran ahead without being able to stop. Their only hope now lay with Nicolas Hulot, inspector on leave, who would be more likely to find out something in his spare time than while officially working on the investigation.

Secondly, there was Helena Parker. What did she want from him? Why was she so frightened of her father? What was her relationship to Captain Mosse? Given the way he had treated her the day of the fight, they were more than just a general's daughter and his subordinate, even if he was almost a member of the family. And most important, did the story of an emotionally unstable woman in her father's care have any truth to it?

Questions kept running through Frank's mind, although he was trying to consider Helena Parker irrelevant, a distraction that would only take his concentration away from No One and the investigation in which he was now directly involved.

He opened the door to Nicolas's office without knocking. Now it was his, and he could do as he pleased. Morelli was sitting at the desk and jumped up when he saw him. There was a moment of embarrassment and Frank knew they needed to stop and figure out exactly where each of them stood.

"Hey, Claude."

"Hello, Frank."

"Did you hear the news?"

"Yes. Roncaille told me everything. I'm glad you're the one running the investigation now, although . . ."

"Although?"

"I think they treated Hulot like shit." Morelli did not hesitate when he said these words.

"To be honest, Claude, so do I." Frank smiled.

If that was a test, they had both passed. The tension in the room eased considerably. When the time had come to choose, Morelli had done as Frank expected. He wondered whether he could trust him enough to let him know about the latest news and Nicolas's secret pilgrimage. Morelli was an efficient, experienced officer, but he was still part of the police force of the Principality of Monaco. Revealing too much might mean getting him in trouble if anything happened. That was something Morelli did not deserve.

The sergeant pointed to a file on the desk. "Here's the forensic report."

"Did you read it?"

"I glanced through it. There's nothing we don't already know. Gregor Yatzimin was killed just like the others, without a trace. No One's still going and there's nothing to stand in his way."

That's not so, Claude. Not exactly. There's stolen music in the air . . .

"All we can do right now is keep the radio station under control. That means maximum alert, special teams ready, and so on. Agreed?"

"Sure."

"There's one favor I'd like to ask you."

"What, Frank?"

"If you don't mind, I'll let you monitor the situation at the station by yourself tonight. I don't think anything's going to happen. Last night's killing wore down his batteries and he'll lay low until he recharges. That's what usually happens with serial killers. I'll be listening to the show and you can reach me on my cell, but I need the night off. Can you handle it?"

"Not a problem, Frank."

Frank wondered how things were going between Morelli and Barbara. The sergeant's interest in the girl seemed to be mutual, but then other things had happened. Morelli did not seem the type to neglect his work for sentimental reasons, even if the reasons were as good-looking as Barbara.

"They promised me my own car. Mind finding out if they kept their word?"

"Not at all."

The sergeant left the room and Frank was alone. He took his wallet from his jacket pocket and pulled out a card folded in half. It was a piece of the letter that General Parker had left him at the hotel after their first meeting in the main square of Eze. His phone numbers were on it. Frank stared at it for a moment, then made a decision, dialing the home number on his cell phone. Helena Parker answered after two rings.

"Hello?"

"Hello, it's Frank Ottobre."

There was a brief pause. "I'm glad you called."

"Have you eaten yet?" Frank asked, without replying.

"No, not yet."

"Is that something you've given up, or do you think you might consider it this evening?"

"Sounds like a reasonable idea."

"I could pick you up in an hour, if that's enough time."

"More than enough. I'll be waiting. Do you remember where the house is?"

"I do. See you soon."

Frank hung up and stood looking at the phone as if he could see the woman in that house. As he closed the Motorola, he couldn't help wondering what kind of trouble he was getting himself into now.

39

Frank parked by the dirt road that led to Helena Parker's house and turned off the engine of the Mégane the police had given him. The car was unmarked and the only thing noticeable about it was the radio for communication with headquarters. Morelli had shown him how to use it and had given him the police frequencies. On the drive to Beausoleil and the general's rented house, he had phoned Helena to tell her he was on his way.

Earlier, he'd taken Morelli to the radio station and they had both checked to make sure everything was all right. Before leaving, Frank had taken Pierrot aside in the tiny office next to the glass doors at the entrance.

"Pierrot, can you keep a secret?"

The boy had looked at him timidly, his eyes half closed, as if wondering whether the request was within his capacities.

"A secret means that I can't tell anyone?"

"Exactly. And now that you're a policeman, you're taking part in a police investigation and policemen don't want their secrets getting out. It's *top secret*. Do you know what that means?"

The boy had nodded vehemently, shaking his head of hair that badly needed a trim.

"It means it's so secret that we're the only ones who can know. Okay, Agent Pierrot?"

"Yes, sir."

He had brought his hand to his forehead in a sort of salute, as he had probably seen on TV. Frank had pulled out the picture of the record cover that Guillaume had enlarged from the video.

"I'm going to show you a picture of a record cover. Can you tell me if it's in the room?"

He had held the image up to Pierrot, who had squinted the way he did when he was concentrating. When the boy raised his head and looked at him, he had shown no sign of satisfaction on his face, the way he usually did when he knew the answer.

"It's not there."

Frank had masked his disappointment so that Pierrot wouldn't notice, treating him as if he'd given the right answer. "Very good, Agent Pierrot. Excellent. You can go now, but don't forget. Top secret!"

Pierrot had crossed his forefingers over his lips in a vow of silence and left the room, heading toward the director's booth. Frank had put the printout back in his pocket and left the station in Morelli's hands. On his way out he had seen Barbara in a particularly attractive black dress, speaking to Morelli.

Frank was still thinking about the sergeant and his human inclinations when the gate opened and he saw Helena Parker slowly emerge from the shadows thrown by the indirect light of the reflectors.

First, he saw her graceful figure and heard her steps on the gravel, her movements fluid despite the uneven ground. Then he saw her face under the mass of blond hair, amid shadows of copper and lighter streaks, and then her eyes, those eyes that seemed to contain the sorrow of the whole world. Frank wondered what lay behind that torn veil: what kind of suffering, how many moments of unwanted solitude or uninvited company, how much bare survival instead of real life.

He would probably find out soon enough, and he asked himself just how much he really wanted to know. He suddenly realized what Helena Parker represented for him and he had trouble admitting, even to himself, that he was afraid Helena Parker's story would make him act like a coward. If it did, then he could own thousands of weapons and arrest or kill thousands of men; he could run as far and as long as he wanted, but he would never be able to reach himself. If he did nothing, if nothing happened, that fear would have no end.

He got out of the car and walked around to the other side to open the door. Helena Parker was wearing a dark pants suit with a mandarin collar, an Asian style reinterpreted by some famous designer. Still, her clothes were not a conspicuous display of wealth but rather of good taste. Frank noticed that she wore almost no jewelry and, like the other times he had seen her, makeup so light that it was almost invisible. She walked up to him, preceded by a perfume that smelled like the night itself.

"Hello, Frank. Nice of you to open the door, but don't feel like you have to." Helena got into the car and raised her face to Frank, still standing at the open door.

"I'm not just being polite." Frank nodded toward the front of the Mégane. "This is a French car. Without a certain savoir faire, it refuses to start."

Helena seemed to appreciate his attempt at levity and laughed. "You surprise me, Mr. Ottobre. Men with a sense of humor are an endangered species." Frank thought her smile more precious than any jewel. So close to it, he suddenly felt alone and disarmed.

Those were his thoughts as he walked back around to the driver's side. As he started the engine, he wondered how long that kind of banter would last before they came to the real reason for their meeting. He also wondered which of them would have the courage to bring it up first.

He looked at Helena's profile, a blend of light and darkness in the reflection of the headlights, the same light and darkness of his thoughts. She turned and they exchanged glances. In the shadows, the attempt at cheerfulness disappeared from her eyes and the sadness returned. And Frank realized that she would be the one to press the START button.

"I know your story, Frank. My father forced it on me. I have to know everything he knows, just like I have to be everything he is. I'm sorry. I feel like an intruder in your life and it's not a pleasant feeling." Frank thought of the popular belief that men are hunters and woman their prey. With Helena Parker, the roles were reversed. Without even knowing it, she was now the hunter, possibly because she had always been the prey.

"The only thing I can give you in exchange is my own story. There is no other justification for the fact that I am with you and that I represent a series of questions for which you cannot find the answers."

Frank listened to Helena's voice and drove slowly, following the flow of traffic as they rode down from Roquebrune toward Menton. There was life all around them. Lights and normal people walking along that hot, bright stretch of coast in search of frivolous things, whose only motivation was the equally futile pleasure of the search itself.

There are no treasures, no islands, no maps. Only their illusion, as long as it lasts. And sometimes the end of the illusion is a voice that murmurs two simple words: "I kill. . . ."

Without realizing what he was doing, Frank put out his hand to turn off the radio, as though he feared an unnatural voice would call him back to reality. The light music in the background fell silent.

"The fact that you know my story doesn't bother me. What bothers me is the story itself. I hope yours is better."

"If it were better, do you think I'd be here?" Helena's voice was suddenly very gentle. It was the voice of a woman in the midst of war who sought peace and offered it in return. "What was your wife like?"

Frank was surprised at the spontaneity of her question. And by his own straightforward answer.

"I don't know what she was like. She was two people at the same time, like all of us. I could tell you how I saw her, but that's useless now."

"What was her name?"

"Harriet."

Helena absorbed it like an old friend. "Harriet. I feel like I know a great deal about her, although I never met her. You're probably wondering why I'm so presumptuous." There was a short pause, And then Helena's voice again, full of bitterness. "One fragile woman can always recognize another."

Helena looked out the window. Her words were a journey that was coming to its destination.

"My sister, Arianna, was the stronger one. She understood it all and she left—she fled our father's madness. Or maybe she just wasn't interested enough to lock herself in the same prison. I couldn't escape."

"Because of your son?"

Helena hid her head in her hands. Her voice was muffled by her fingers, covering her face in a tiny prison of grief.

"He's not my son."

"He's not your son?"

"No, he's my brother."

"Your brother? But you said . . ."

"I told you that Stuart was my son," Helena said, looking up. Nobody could bear all that pain without dying, without having died long ago. "He is. But he's also my brother."

As Frank held his breath and tried to understand, Helena burst into tears. Her voice was a whisper, but in the tiny space of the car it sounded like a scream of liberation held in for far too long.

"Damn you. Damn you to hell, Nathan Parker. May you burn for a million years!"

Frank saw a parking spot on the other side of the road next to a construction site. He signaled to the left and parked. He turned off the motor, leaving the lights on.

He turned to Helena. As if it were the most natural thing in the world, the woman slid into his embrace to find protection: the fabric of his jacket for her tear-streaked face, his hand to stroke the hair that had hidden a face full of shame for so long. They stayed that way for what seemed to Frank like an eternity.

A thousand images flew through his mind, a thousand stories of a thousand lives, mixing real with imaginary, the present with the past, the true with the plausible, colors with darkness, the perfume of flowers with the stench of rotting earth.

He saw himself in his parents' home and Nathan Parker's hand as it stretched out to his daughter. Harriet's tears with a dagger raised over a man tied to a chair. The flash of a knife in his nostril and the blue-eyed gaze of a ten-year-old boy living unknowingly among depraved beasts.

Hate became a blinding light in his mind, and that light slowly changed into a silent scream that smashed to pieces all the mirrors where human evil could be reflected, all the walls that could hide it, all the closed doors where the fists of those seeking desperately to escape their torture pounded in vain.

Helena wanted only to forget. And that was exactly what Frank needed, right there in that car parked next to the rubble, in that embrace, in the meaning of that encounter between wall and ivy that could be described in one word: finally.

Frank couldn't tell who withdrew first. When their eyes met again, they both knew with the same incredulity that something important had happened. They kissed, and in that first kiss their lips joined in trepidation, not love. The trepidation that it might not really be true, that it was only desperation disguised as love, that solitude had led their voices to these words, that nothing was as it seemed.

They had to kiss again and keep kissing before they could believe it. And the suspicion became a tiny hope, for neither of them could yet afford the luxury of certainty.

Afterward, they looked at each other, breathless. Helena recovered first, caressing his face.

"Say something silly. Something silly and alive."

"I think we lost our table reservation."

Helena embraced him again and Frank listened as her giggles of relief were lost in tiny tremors against his neck.

"I'm ashamed of myself, Frank Ottobre, but I only think well of you. Turn this car around and go back to my house. There's food and wine in the fridge. I can't share you with the rest of the world tonight."

Frank started the car and drove back along the same road. When had this happened? Maybe an hour or maybe a lifetime ago. In this situation, he had lost his sense of time. But there was one thing he was sure of. If he had seen General Nathan Parker at that moment, he would have killed him.

Hidden in his secret place, the man is lying on the bed. He has drifted off to sleep with the liquid, gratifying sensation of a boat returning out to the sea. His breath is calm and peaceful, barely audible, the sheet rising only enough to show that he is alive, that the white fabric thrown over him is a blanket and not a shroud.

Beside him, equally motionless, the wizened corpse lies in its glass coffin. He is wearing Gregor Yatzimin's diaphanous face with what seems like pride. This time, the removal was a masterpiece. Instead of a mask, it looks like the mummified skull's real face.

The man lying on the bed is asleep and dreaming. Indecipherable images agitate his sleep, although the figures that his mind attempts to disentangle never manage to disturb the perfect immobility of his body.

First, there is darkness. Now a dirt road with a construction site at its end appears in the soft light of a full moon. It is a hot summer night. Step by step, the man approaches the outline of a large house barely visible in the shadows, calling to him with the familiar scent of lavender. The man feels the crunch of gravel beneath his bare feet. He wants to move forward but at the same time he is afraid.

The man notices the muffled sound of heavy breathing; his anxiety eases and evaporates when he realizes that the breathing is his own. Now he is quiet. He is in the courtyard of the house, where a stone chimney rises up from the roof like a finger pointing at the moon. The house is wrapped in a silence that feels like an invitation.

Suddenly the house dissolves and he is inside, climbing a flight of stairs. He raises his head toward the dim light from above. A light shines from the landing at the top of the stairs, casting shadows into the stairwell. A human figure is outlined clearly against the light.

The man feels his fear return like a necktie that is too tight, but he continues his slow ascent in spite of it. As he climbs reluctantly, he wonders whom he will find at the top, and realizes that he is terrified to find out.

A step. Another. The creaking of wood beneath his feet falls between the pauses in his breathing, heavy again. His hand on the wooden banister is slowly illuminated by the light from above.

As he is about to climb the last flight, the figure turns and goes out the door where the light is coming from, leaving him alone on the stairs.

The man climbs the last steps. There is an open door before him, with bright, flickering light pouring out. He slowly comes to the threshold and crosses it, bathed in the light, which is also noise.

There is a man standing in the center of the room. His body is naked, graceful and athletic, but his face is deformed. It is as though an octopus had wrapped itself around his head, erasing his features. Two light-colored eyes bulge from the monstrous tangle of fleshy growth and observe him pleadingly, begging for his pity. The unhappy creature is crying.

"Who are you?"

A voice is asking the question. He doesn't recognize it as his own. But it cannot be that of the deformed man before him, because he has no mouth.

"Who are you?" repeats the voice, and it sounds like it is coming from all over, from the blinding light that surrounds them.

Now the man knows, but is loathe to know. He sees, but is unwilling to see.

The figure extends its arms to him and transmits real terror, although its eyes continue to seek the pity of the man facing him, as they sought the pity of the world in vain. And suddenly the light is fire, high roaring flames devouring everything in their path, fire straight from hell that has come to purify the earth.

He wakes without a start, merely opening his eyes and substituting darkness for the glare of the flames. His hand rises in the dark, reaching for the lamp on the bedside table. He turns it on and a dim light spreads through the bare room.

The voice comes at once. Since they are forever asleep, the dead never rest.

What's wrong, Vibo, can't you sleep?

"No, Paso. I've slept enough for now. These days I have a lot to do. I'll have time to rest afterward."

He did not add the rest of his thought: *when it's all over.*

The man has no illusions. He knows that the end will come, sooner or later. Every human endeavor has an end, just as it had a beginning. But for now, everything is still open and he cannot deny the corpse in the coffin the sensation of a new face, and himself the satisfaction of a promise kept.

There was a broken hourglass in the fog of his sleep, time buried in the sand that spread through his memory. Here, in real time, the hourglass continues to turn on its axis and no one will ever break it. Illusions would be shattered, as they always are, but not that unbreakable hourglass. It will go on forever, even when there is no one left to contemplate the time it marks.

The man feels that the hour has come. He gets out of bed and begins to dress.

What are you doing?

"I have to go out."

Will you be long?

"I don't know. All day, probably. And maybe tomorrow."

Don't make me worry, Vibo. You know I'm anxious when you're not here.

The man goes to the crystal cabinet and smiles affectionately at the mummy inside.

"I'll leave the light on. I brought you a surprise while you were sleeping."

He reaches for the mirror and holds it over the face in the coffin so that it can see its reflection.

"Look . . ."

Oh, it's magnificent. Is that me? Vibo, I'm gorgeous! Even more handsome than before!

"Of course you are, Paso. And it will get better and better."

There is a moment of silence, a silence of inner emotion that the corpse cannot express through tears.

"I have to go now, Paso. It's very important."

The man turns his back on the body lying there and goes to the door. As he leaves, he repeats, perhaps only to himself: "Yes, it is very important."

And the hunt begins again.

40

Nicolas Hulot took a right at the sign for the exit to Aix-en-Provence. He drove slowly down the ramp, behind a tractor trailer with Spanish plates and TRANSPORTES FERNÁNDEZ written on the side. The truck pulled over in the rest area and the inspector passed it and stopped in front of the information booth. He pulled the map of the city from the glove compartment and opened it over the steering wheel.

Hulot checked the map where he had already marked Cours Mirabeau the night before. All told, the city was not very complicated and the street he was looking for was right downtown.

He restarted the Peugeot and continued driving. There was a traffic circle a few hundred yards down and he followed the signs that said CENTRE VILLE. As he drove along the hilly road with regularly placed speed bumps, Hulot noticed that the city was clean and active. The streets were full of people, mostly young people, and he remembered that Aix-en-Provence was home to a fairly prestigious university founded in the fifteenth century and that there was also a spa. That explained why there were more than the usual summer tourists milling around.

He made a few wrong turns, passing several times in front of a row of hotels and restaurants. Finally, he found Place du Général de Gaulle, the beginning of Cours Mirabeau. He put money in the parking meter and stood there for an instant, admiring the large fountain in the center of the plaza. A sign bore its official name, FONTAINE DE LA ROTONDE. As always, since he was a child, the sound of the falling water made him want to urinate.

He walked over to Cours Mirabeau looking for a café, thinking it was funny how a full bladder could make you want a cup of coffee.

He crossed the avenue where there was construction and repaving going on. A worker in a yellow helmet was talking to what looked like the job-site manager about some missing materials, insisting that he was not responsible, that it was the fault of a certain Engineer Dufour. Under a plane tree typical of Provence, two alley cats were eyeing each other with stiffened tails, deciding whether they should start a catfight or opt for a tactical retreat to save their dignity. Hulot decided that he was the darker cat and the other one was Roncaille. Leaving the animals to their battle, he went inside and ordered a café au lait while he went to the bathroom.

The coffee was waiting for him when he got back. As he added sugar, he called the waiter over, a young man who was chatting with two girls around his age who were drinking white wine at a nearby table.

"Could you give me some information please?"

"Sure, I'll try." If the young man had been reluctant to leave the two girls, he didn't show it.

"Do you know if there is, or was, a record shop called Disque à Risque here on Cours Mirabeau?"

"I don't think I ever heard that name, but I haven't been in Aix very long," said the young man, who had short blond hair and a thin, pale, pimply face. "I'm at the university," he added. The boy obviously wanted people to know that he wasn't planning on being a waiter forever, but that sooner or later he would fulfill much loftier goals. "But there's a newsstand further up on this side of the street. Tattoo might seem a little strange, but he's been there for forty years and he can tell you anything you want to know."

Hulot thanked him with a nod and started drinking his coffee. The boy felt dismissed and went back to his interrupted conversation. Hulot paid and left the change on the marble counter. When he went out, he saw that the Hulot-cat was no longer there and the Roncaille-cat was sitting peacefully under the plane tree, watching the world go by.

He walked down the shady avenue paved with large stone slabs and lined by large plane trees on either side. There was an endless series of cafés, shops, and bookstores.

A hundred yards farther down, he found Tattoo's newsstand, the one the waiter had told him about, next to a store selling antiquated books. On the street, two men around his age were playing chess at a table, sitting on folding chairs in front of the open door of the bookstore.

Hulot went over to the newsstand and spoke to the man inside, surrounded by magazines, books, and comics. He was an old man with deep-set eyes and unkempt hair, around seventy, and looked as though he'd been dragged off the set of a John Ford western.

"Good morning. Are you Tattoo?"

"That's me. What can I do for you?"

Nicolas noticed that he had a couple of teeth missing. His voice was in keeping with his appearance. He had it all—a shame that he was stuck in a newsstand in Aix-en-Provence instead of on a Wells Fargo stagecoach heading toward Tombstone.

"I need some information. I'm looking for a record store called Disque à Risque."

"You're a few years too late. Not there anymore."

Hulot barely restrained a grimace of irritation. Tattoo lit an unfiltered Gauloise and immediately started coughing. Judging from his convulsive hack, his battle with cigarettes had been going on for quite some time. It was clear who the eventual winner would be, but for the moment the man was sticking it out. He waved toward the street.

"It was on the other side of Mirabeau, two hundred yards up, on the right. Now it's a bistro."

"Do you remember the owner's name?"

"No, but his son owns the bistro. Talk to him and he'll tell you all you need to know. Café des Arts et des Artistes."

"Thanks, Tattoo. Don't smoke too much."

He would never know if that last coughing fit was Tatoo's thanks for his advice or a phlegmy invitation to go to hell. Thank God the lead was still going somewhere. The information they had was so flimsy that it felt more like Tattoo's cigarette smoke than a real clue. At the very least, he had to avoid any more delays. Morelli could have probably traced the store owner through the Chamber of Commerce but that would have taken time, and time was the one thing they didn't have.

He thought of Frank, sitting at Radio Monte Carlo waiting for the phone to ring and that voice, wherever it came from, promising another victim.

I kill . . .

He quickened his step without even meaning to and stopped in front of a blue awning with white letters that said CAFÉ DES ARTS ET DES ARTISTES. Judging from the number of customers, business was good. Every outdoor table was taken.

Inside, it took a moment for his eyes to adjust to the light. Because of the crowd, it was very busy behind the counter. A barman and a couple of twenty-five-year-old girls were getting aperitifs and appetizers ready.

He ordered a Kir Royal from a blonde who nodded as she opened a bottle of white wine. After a little while, she handed him a glass full of rose-colored liquid.

"Could I speak to the owner?" he asked as he put the drink to his lips.

"Over there."

The girl gestured toward a man about thirty with thinning hair who was coming through a glass door that said PRIVATE at the back of the restaurant. Nicolas wondered how he should explain his presence and his questions. Once the owner of Café des Arts et des Artistes was standing in front of him, he opted for the official version.

"Excuse me . . ."

"Yes."

"I'm Inspector Hulot from the Sûreté Publique of the Principality of Monaco." Nicolas showed him his badge. "I'd like to ask you a favor, Monsieur . . ."

"Francis. Robert Francis."

"Monsieur Francis, we understand that this restaurant was once a record store called Disque à Risque and that it belonged to your father."

The man looked taken aback. His eyes were full of questions. "Well . . . yes, but the store closed several years ago."

Hulot smiled reassuringly. He changed his tone and attitude.

"Don't worry, Robert. Neither you nor your father is in any trouble. I know it sounds strange, but the store might be a key element in an investigation we're working on. All I need is to speak to your father and ask him a few questions, if possible."

Robert Francis relaxed. He turned to the blond girl behind the counter and pointed at Nicolas's glass.

"Give me one too, Lucie."

While waiting for the drink, he turned back to the inspector. "My father retired a few years ago. The record store wasn't making much money. Actually, it never really made anything, but the last couple of years were a disaster. My stubborn old man is a dealer in old records, but he sold fewer than he put into his personal collection. He's a great collector but a lousy businessman."

Hulot was relieved. Francis spoke of him in the present tense, which meant that he was still alive. He had said "if possible" earlier, in case the old man was deceased.

"So at a certain point, we did a little accounting and decided to close the store, and then I opened this." He waved his hand at the crowded restaurant.

"Looks like it was worth the change."

"A whole different story. And I assure you that the oysters we serve are fresh, not dusty like my father's records."

Lucie pushed a glass toward her boss. Francis picked it up and raised the *flûte* to the inspector. Nicolas did the same.

"To your investigation."

"To your restaurant and to old records."

They took a sip and Francis placed the frosted glass on the counter. "My father is probably at home right now. Did you take the highway from Monte Carlo?"

"Yes."

"Good. Just follow the signs back. There's a Novotel by the exit to the highway and right behind the hotel is a two-story brick house with a tiny garden and rose bushes. That's where my father lives. You can't miss it. Can I offer you anything in the meantime?"

Hulot raised his glass with a smile. "This will do just fine." He put out his hand and Francis shook it.

"Thank you, Monsieur Francis. You have no idea what a help you've been."

As Hulot left the bistro, he saw a waiter opening oysters and shellfish at the *coquillage* counter. He would have liked to stop and see if the oysters were as fresh as Francis claimed, but he didn't have time.

He went back the way he had come. He could hear the hacking from Tattoo's newsstand. The chess players were no longer there and the bookstore was closed. It was lunchtime.

As he headed to his car, he passed the café where he had gotten the cup of coffee. Under the tree, the Hulot-cat was now sitting in place of the Roncaille-cat, calmly washing his dark, furry tail as he observed the world around him through half-closed eyes. Hulot figured there was no reason why he shouldn't take that feline revenge as a sign of good luck.

41

Jean-Paul Francis screwed on the cap of the plastic spray bottle and pressed down several times to pump up the insecticide. Taking the sprayer by the handle, he went over to a rosebush next to a green, plastic-covered metal grating that served as a fence and examined the small branches. They were full of parasites that had covered the stems with white fuzz.

"This means war," he said in a solemn tone.

He pressed the lever and a jet of insecticide and water vapor came out of the nozzle. Starting at the base, he sprayed all along the trunk, evenly distributing the mixture over the entire bush. As he had imagined, the insecticide smelled awful and he congratulated himself on having remembered to put on a stiff gauze mask so as not to breathe in the product, which was labeled POISONOUS IF SWALLOWED. KEEP OUT OF THE REACH OF CHILDREN. He figured that if it was poisonous for children, at his age he could probably inject the stuff without doing himself any harm.

As he sprayed, he saw out of the corner of his eye a little Peugeot come up the driveway just outside the garden. Cars did not stop there very often, except when the hotel across the way was full and there was no place to park. He saw a tired-looking man get out of the car—he was about fifty-five with neatly cut salt-and-pepper hair. The man looked around for a minute and then headed resolutely to his gate.

Jean-Paul put the sprayer on the ground and went to open the gate without giving his visitor time to ring. The man before him smiled. "Monsieur Francis?"

"Himself."

The man showed him a badge in a leather holder. His photo was visible on the document, protected by a piece of plastic.

"Inspector Hulot of the Monaco Police."

"If you've come to arrest me, you should know that taking care of this garden is prison enough already. A jail cell would be a wonderful alternative."

The inspector started to laugh in spite of himself.

"That's what they mean by not being afraid of the law. Have you got a clear conscience or a long life of crime?"

"It's the fault of evil women who broke my heart over and over again. Won't you come inside to hear my confession? The neighbors might think you're a brush salesman."

Nicolas went into the garden and Francis père closed the gate behind him. He was wearing faded jeans, a light denim shirt, and a straw hat. The gauze mask hung at his neck so that he could talk. Thick, white hair poked out from under the hat. His blue eyes, offset by his tan, looked like those of a child. Altogether it was a friendly, attractive face.

Nicolas Hulot returned his warm, vigorous handshake.

"I didn't come to arrest you, if that makes you feel any better. And I'll only take a few minutes of your time."

Jean-Paul Francis shrugged his shoulders as he removed the hat and mask. He would make an excellent understudy for Anthony Hopkins.

"I garden out of boredom, not by choice. I'll take any excuse to stop. Please come in. It's cooler inside."

They crossed the tiny garden where a cement patio, corroded by time and weather, matched the gate and the front door. It was not a luxurious house, light-years from some of the dwellings on the Côte d'Azur, but it was neat and clean. Three steps up and they were inside. There was a stairway leading up and two symmetrically placed doors on either side leading to rooms on the left and right.

Nicolas was accustomed to judging houses in a flash and he immediately realized that the owner was not wealthy, but rich in culture, good taste and ideas. He could tell by looking at the enormous number of books, knickknacks, and paintings and posters on the walls, which might not be originals but were still related to the world of art. The most impressive sight, however, was the record collection. It spilled from every corner of the house. He glanced through the door on the right and could see a living room where a huge sound system had the place of honor, probably the only consumerist luxury in the house. The rest of the room's walls were covered with shelves holding vinyl LPs and CDs.

"You're a music lover, I gather."

"I was never able to choose my passions, so I let them choose me."

Francis led the way, going into the room on the left. Nicolas found himself in a kitchen with an open door leading to what looked like a storage room. On the other side, there was a small terrace opening directly onto the garden.

"No music here, as you can see. We're in the kitchen and one shouldn't mix two types of nourishment. Something to drink? An aperitif?"

"No, thank you. I had one with your son."

"Oh, you were at Robert's."

"He told me how to get here."

Francis looked at the sweat stains under his own arms. He had the sly smile of a child who has just invented a new game. He checked the Swatch on his wrist.

"Have you eaten?"

"No."

"Good. I have an idea. Mme Sivoire, my housekeeper"—he stopped with a puzzled look—"actually, she's my cleaning lady, but she likes 'housekeeper' better and it makes me feel more important too. Mme Sivoire, one hundred percent Italian and a fine cook, left me some lasagna al pesto all ready to slip in the oven. Mme Sivoire might not be much to look at, but her lasagna is absolutely above suspicion."

Nicolas could not help laughing again. The man was a force of nature and his warmth was irresistible. He must have led quite a life with that extraordinary approach. Or at least Nicolas hoped so.

"I didn't intend to stop for lunch, but I wouldn't want to offend Mme Sivoire."

"Terrific. I'll go shower while the lasagna is heating up. My underarms could kill a man, and how could I explain the dead body of a police inspector in my kitchen?"

Jean-Paul Francis pulled a glass baking dish out of the refrigerator and put it in the oven, regulating the temperature and the timer. From his skill at handling the appliances, one could see that this was the house of a man who either loved food or lived alone. Not that one excluded the other.

"There we go. We'll eat in ten minutes. Or fifteen."

He left the kitchen and disappeared up the stairs, whistling. A moment later, from below, Hulot could hear the splash of the shower and Jean-Paul Francis's baritone in a rendition of "The Lady Is a Tramp."

When he returned, he was dressed in the same style, but with a clean shirt and socks. His hair was still damp and combed back.

"That's better. Recognize me?"

Nicolas looked at him, puzzled. "Of course."

"Funny, I always feel like a different person after a shower. I can tell you're a real policeman."

Hulot laughed again. The man's good humor was infectious.

His host set the table on the small terrace overlooking the garden, handing him a bottle of white wine and a corkscrew. "Could you open this while I take out the lasagna?"

Nicolas was pulling out the cork just as Jean-Paul placed the steaming dish of lasagna al pesto on the place mat at the center of the table.

"Here we are. Please sit down." Jean-Paul served him a copious helping of pasta. "Go ahead and eat. In this house, etiquette is only applied to wine," he said as he served himself an equally large portion.

"Delicious," said Hulot with his mouth full.

"What did I tell you? This is proof that, whatever you want from me, I'm a man of my word."

Nicolas Hulot could now reveal the reason he was there, hotter than anything out of the oven.

"You had a record store some years back, didn't you?" he asked, cutting a piece of lasagna with his fork.

From the man's expression, he realized that he had touched a nerve.

"Yes. I closed it seven years ago. Music of quality has never done good business around here."

Hulot was careful not to mention his son's remarks on the matter. Pouring salt into the wound was useless, especially since it obviously still hurt. He decided to be frank with his host. He liked the man and knew it would be all right to tell him part of the story.

"We're looking for a murderer back in Monte Carlo, Monsieur Francis."

"Isn't it right about now that the two heroes of the movie start calling each other by their first names? Mine's Jean-Paul."

"Nicolas."

"When you say a 'murderer in Monte Carlo,' you don't mean the fellow who calls in to the radio, do you? The guy they call No One?"

"That's right."

"I admit I've been following the story, like millions of people. You get goose bumps hearing that voice. How many has he killed?"

"Four. And I'm sure you've heard about the way he does it. The worst thing is that we don't have the slightest idea of how to stop him from doing it again."

"He must be sly as a whole pack of foxes. He listens to lousy music, but he must have a great brain."

"I agree with you about the brain. I came to talk to you about the music."

Nicolas rummaged in his pocket and pulled out the printouts that Guillaume had given him. He chose one and handed it to Jean-Paul.

"Recognize this record?"

The man took the sheet of paper and looked at it. Nicolas thought he saw him pale. Jean-Paul stared at him with his blue, childlike eyes full of wonder.

"Where did you get this picture?"

"It's too long to explain. All you need to know is that we have good reason to believe the record belongs to the killer and was purchased here."

He handed Jean-Paul the other picture, the one with the label bearing the name of the store. This time, Jean-Paul definitely paled. His words stuck in his throat. "But . . ."

"Do you recognize this record? Do you know what it might mean? Who is Robert Fulton?"

Jean-Paul Francis pushed his plate away and opened his arms. "Who is Robert Fulton? Any jazz lover who goes beyond Louis Armstrong knows who he is. And any music collector would give his right hand for one of his records."

"Why?"

"Because, as far as I know, there are only ten copies that exist in the entire world."

This time, it was Nicolas's turn to grow pale. Francis poured himself a glass of wine and leaned back in his chair. Suddenly, Mme Sivoire's lasagna seemed to have lost all its flavor.

"Robert Fulton was one of the greatest trumpet players in the history of jazz. Unfortunately, as often happens, he was a musical genius but mad as a hatter. He never wanted to record because he was convinced that music couldn't and shouldn't be imprisoned. As far as he was concerned, the only way to enjoy it was live, in concert. In other words, music is a different experience every time and can't be fixed in some static, unchangeable format."

"So where does this record come from?"

"I'm getting there. In the summer of 1960, he went on a short tour of America, playing in clubs with some of the best session-men of the day. A historic series of concerts. At the Be-Bop Café in New York, some friends made arrangements with a record label and recorded the concert live without telling him. They printed five hundred records and hoped Fulton would change his mind when he heard the recording."

"And that's why it's called *Stolen Music*?"

"Right. Except that they never thought he would react the way he did. Fulton went berserk with fury and destroyed all the copies. He made them give him the masters and he destroyed those too. The story went around the world and became something of a legend. Everyone embellished it in the telling. The only thing that's certain is that only ten records were saved. To collectors, they're worth their weight in gold. I had one of the ten."

"You mean you still have the record?"

"I said I *had*, not I *have.* I went through some hard times . . ."

Francis looked at his tanned hands, spotted with age. The memories coming to his mind weren't good ones.

"My wife got cancer and died. The business was going badly. I mean, really badly. I needed money for her treatments and that record was worth a fortune. So . . ."

Francis let out a sigh, and it sounded like he had been holding his breath for a lifetime. "When I sold it, with all the regret in the world, I put the store label on the record as if that was a way of holding on to it. That record was one of the few things I really felt was mine, aside from my wife and son. Three things can add up to a real fortune, in one man's life."

Nicolas Hulot's heart was beating in his chest as if it were the piston of a very powerful engine. He pronounced each word with great care. He asked the question in the tone of someone who fears the answer. "Do you remember who bought it, Jean-Paul?"

"It's been over fifteen years, Nicolas. He was a strange character, about my age, more or less. He used to come to the store to buy records, rare stuff, collectors' stuff. Money didn't seem to be an object, so I admit that I sometimes fleeced him a little. When he found out I had a copy of *Stolen Music,* he kept after me for months to sell it to him. I always refused, but then, as I told you . . . Necessity can turn a man into a thief . . . or a salesman. Or sometimes both."

"Can you recall the name?"

"I'm not a computer. I couldn't forget that record if I lived for a thousand years. But anything else . . ." He ran his fingers through his white hair and raised his eyes to the ceiling.

Nicolas leaned closer to him.

"I don't need to tell you how important this is, Jean-Paul. Human lives depend on it."

Hulot wondered how many more times he would have to use those words, how many more times he would have to remind someone how important something was in order to save other lives before that business was over and done with.

"Maybe . . ."

"Maybe what?"

"Come with me. Let's see if you're in luck."

He followed Jean-Paul out of the kitchen and looked at his

back, so straight despite his age and his head of thick, white hair. A breeze blowing through the house carried the scent of his deodorant. In the foyer, they turned left and the man went down the stairs.

They came to an unfinished basement. There was a washing machine next to the sink on one side, a woman's bicycle hanging on the wall, and a workbench with a vise and tools for wood and metal working.

On the other side of the room was a row of metal shelves with jars of preserves and bottles of wine. There were files and cardboard boxes of different sizes and colors at the other end.

"I'm a man of memories. I'm a collector. And almost all collectors are sappy and nostalgic. Except the ones who collect money."

Jean-Paul Francis stopped in front of one of the shelves and stood looking at it, puzzled. "Hmm. Let's see . . ."

He made his choice and pulled down a fairly large blue cardboard box from one of the higher shelves. On the cover was the gold label of the store, Disque à Risque. He placed the box on the workbench next to the vise and turned on the overhead light.

"This is all that's left of my business and a large part of my life. Not much, eh?"

Sometimes, it's even too much, Nicolas thought. *There are people who don't need any boxes at the end of the journey, big or small. Sometimes even pockets are too much.*

Jean-Paul opened the box and started rummaging inside, taking out papers that looked like old commercial licenses and concert brochures and ads for record fairs. At a certain point, he pulled out a note on blue paper folded in half. He looked at what was written on it and handed it to Nicolas.

"Here. It's your lucky day. The man who bought *Stolen Music* wrote this himself. He left me his number when he found out I had a copy of the record. Now that I think of it, he came in a couple more times after I sold it to him, and then I never saw him again . . ."

Nicolas read what was written on the piece of paper. There was a name and phone number, in a determined, precise script

Legrand 04/4221545.

It was a strange moment for Hulot. After so much running, so many distorted voices, camouflaged bodies, inscrutable fingerprints, and echoless footsteps; after so many faceless shadows and faceless bodies, finally, he had something human in his hands, and it was the most ordinary thing in the world: a name and phone number.

Hulot felt drained and looked at Jean-Paul Francis, unable to find the right words. His host, who had possibly just rescued him and a number of innocent victims, smiled.

"From your expression, I'd say you're pleased. If this were a movie, as I said before, the music would start to swell."

"More than that, Jean-Paul. Much more than that . . ."

He pulled out his cell phone but his new friend stopped him. "There's no reception down here. We have to go upstairs. Come on."

They went back up. As Nicolas's mind started racing, Francis added more information from the scraps that remained in his memory.

"He was from someplace around here, Cassis, if I remember correctly. A big guy, tall but not too tall. He had a military look, if you know what I mean. It was his eyes, I think. They seemed to be looking without the possibility of being looked at in return. That's the best way I can describe it. I remember that I thought it was strange that someone like him would be interested in jazz."

"Well, for someone who's not a computer, you've remembered quite a bit."

Jean-Paul turned to him on the stairs and smiled. "Have I? I'm beginning to feel proud of myself."

"You have a lot to be proud of. This is just one thing more."

They got back to the ground floor and the sunlight. The pasta on the table was cold and the wine was warm. A triangle of light was hitting the terrace floor and climbing up the leg of the table like ivy.

Hulot looked at his cell phone and saw from the display that it was within range. He wondered whether he should risk it and shrugged his shoulders. His anxiety about wire tapping was probably just paranoia. He pressed the button for a memorized number and waited to hear the voice on the other end.

"Morelli. It's Hulot. I need two things from you. Information and silence. Can you handle it?"

"Sure." One of Morelli's best qualities was his ability to avoid pointless questions.

"I'm going to give you a name and phone number. The number might be out of service. It's probably in Provence. Let me know the address, pronto."

"Okay."

He gave the sergeant the data in his possession and ended the call. He asked Jean-Paul for confirmation, but he was really just repeating to himself.

"Cassis, you said?"

"I think so. Cassis, Auriol, Roquefort. I really don't remember, but I think that's the district."

"I'll have to take a trip out that way."

Hulot glanced around the house again, as if he wanted to remember every detail. Then he looked Francis straight in the eye. "I hope you'll forgive me if I take off. I'm in a hurry. I think you understand."

"I know how you feel. No, that's not true. I don't know—I can only imagine. I hope you find what you're looking for. I'll show you out."

"Sorry I spoiled your lunch."

"You didn't spoil anything, Nicolas. Not at all. I've haven't had much company lately. At a certain age, there's a new logic. You ask yourself why, if time seems to go by so quickly on some days, on others it never passes."

As Jean-Paul spoke, they walked out to the garden and the wrought-iron gate. Nicolas looked at his car parked in the sun. It would be hot as an oven. He stuck his fingers in his jacket pocket and pulled out a card.

"Keep this, Jean-Paul. If you ever come to Monte Carlo, there's always a place to stay and a meal waiting for you."

Jean-Paul took the card and looked at it without answering. They might never see each other again, but he would not throw it away. Hulot held out his hand and felt the man's vigorous handshake.

"By the way, there's something else I wanted to ask you. It's just out of curiosity. It has nothing to do with all this."

"What's that?"

"Why 'Disque à Risque'?"

This time it was Francis who laughed.

"Oh, that . . . When I opened the store, I had absolutely no idea if it would work out. It wasn't the customer's risk. It was mine."

Hulot left, smiling and shaking his head as Francis watched him through the open gate. When he reached the car, he put his hand in his jacket pocket, looking for his keys. His fingers touched the blue paper that Jean-Paul had given him, the one with the name and phone number. He pulled it out and looked at it for a moment, lost in thought.

Disque à Risque, the rare record shop, had had its biggest success seven years after going bankrupt.

42

Morelli called as Hulot was driving through Carnoux-en-Provence on his way to Cassis. The call caused interference with the car radio, tuned to Europe 2, and it started crackling. A moment later, the mobile phone rang. Hulot picked it up from the passenger seat.

"Hello?"

"Inspector, it's Morelli. I found the address you asked for. Sorry it took a little while—you were right, the number's out of service. I had to trace it back to France Télécom."

"And?" Hulot tried to hide his disappointment.

"It was the number of a farm, Domaine La Patience, Chemin de l'hiver, Cassis. But there's something else."

"What?"

"The phone company had to disconnect the number. It was never canceled. They just stopped making payments at a certain point and the company turned it off after sending a number of reminders. The person I spoke to didn't know anything else. We'd have to do more research and I doubt we'd find anything."

"Don't worry about it, Claude. That's great. Thanks." There was some hesitation on the other end. Hulot realized that Morelli was waiting for him to speak. "What is it?"

"Everything okay?"

"Yes, Morelli. Just fine. I'll be able to tell you more tomorrow. Talk to you then."

"Okay, Inspector. Take care."

Hulot put the phone back on the seat. He didn't need to jot down the address Morelli had given him. It was imprinted in his brain and would stay there for a very long time. As he left Carnoux, a small Provençal town, clean and modern, he let other memories drift through his mind.

He had driven down that road many years before with Céline and Stéphane. They were on vacation and they had laughed and joked like there was no tomorrow. He had never felt better. Compared to his life now, those days had been real happiness, which was to be blotted out by what came after, when all his energy was devoted to grief.

His son was around seven years old then. When they had arrived at Cassis, Stéphane was very excited, as all children are at the seaside. They had parked their car at the edge of town and walked down to the beach along a narrow path, their clothes rustling in the strong breeze.

At the port, they had been greeted by dozens of sailboats. There was a lighthouse in the distance and the open sea stretched out beyond the cement ramparts designed to protect the wharf.

They had had an ice cream, taken a boat ride to see the *calanques,* the rocky inlets in the sea, tiny fjords that seemed so French in that corner of Provence. Hulot had gotten seasick during the ride, and Céline and Stéphane had laughed hysterically at the faces he made, his rolling eyes and exaggerated attempts to vomit. He had forgotten for a moment that he was a police officer and had let himself be just a husband, a father, and a clown.

Stop it, Papa. My stomach hurts from laughing.

Life seemed like cinema to Hulot. Whoever wrote the scripts had a macabre sense of humor. While he was wandering through the city streets many years before with his wife and son, happy and lighthearted—at that very moment perhaps, someone was receiving a phone call from a music store owner agreeing to sell him a rare record. Maybe they'd even crossed paths with him as they were walking. Or maybe, as they were leaving Cassis, they'd even followed his car for a while as he drove to Aix to pick up the record.

When Hulot reached the outskirts of the town, he parked his car and his memories of the happy past along with it. He looked at the view from the top floor of the parking garage—PARKING DE LA VIGUERIE, 310 SPOTS—where he left the Peugeot 206.

Cassis hadn't changed much. The cement ramparts at the port had been reinforced and a few houses rebuilt. Others were dilapidated, but there was enough limestone and paint on them to help tourists forget the passing of time. That's what vacations were for, after all: forgetting.

He thought about what to do. The simplest thing would be to ask the local police for information, but he was investigating privately and wanted to avoid attracting attention. On the other hand, anyone wandering around asking questions, even in a seaside resort full of tourists, would not remain inconspicuous for long. This was a small town where everybody knew everybody else, and he was about to dig up their flower bed.

The street leading to the port was the same one he had walked down with his family years earlier. An elderly man carrying a straw basket full of sea urchins was heading uphill in the opposite direction. Hulot stopped him. Contrary to what he had expected, the old man was not the least bit out of breath.

"Monsieur?"

"Whaddya want?" the old man barked.

"Could you give me some information please?"

The man put the basket of sea urchins on the ground and looked at them as if he were afraid they might go bad. He reluctantly raised his eyes, buried beneath thick, black eyebrows.

"What?"

"Do you know of a farm called La Patience?"

"Yes."

Hulot wondered briefly whether his respect for the elderly

would outweigh the anger he always felt toward rude people, young or old. With a sigh, he decided to let it go.

"Could you please tell me where it is?"

"Outside the city." The old man waved to a vague point somewhere beyond the houses.

"Yes, I thought it would be."

Hulot had to restrain himself from grabbing the man by the neck. He waited patiently, but the expression on his face must have warned the man not to overdo it.

"You driving?"

"Yes, I've got a car."

"Then take the road that leads out of town. Turn right at the light toward Roquefort. When you get to the traffic circle, you'll see a sign, LES JANOTS. After that, your first left will be a dirt road that crosses a stone bridge over the train tracks. Take it and bear right at the fork. The road ends at La Patience."

"Thank you."

Wordlessly, the old man picked up his basket of sea urchins and continued on his way.

Hulot finally felt the excitement that came from a good lead. He walked hurriedly up the road and was breathing hard by the time he got to the car. He followed the directions, which, though given grudgingly, were perfect, and turned onto the dirt road that went up to the rocky hills overlooking Cassis. The Mediterranean vegetation and the larches and olive trees almost completely hid the canyon where the train tracks were. As he crossed the stone bridge mentioned by the old man, a dog, some kind of Labrador, started chasing the Peugeot, barking. When Hulot reached the fork in the road, the dog obviously considered his job done. He stopped running and howling and went away, trotting toward a farmhouse on the left.

The road continued to climb. It was lined with trees whose large trunks obstructed the view of the sea. The colored patches of flowers had disappeared as he left the town, substituted by the green of pine trees and bushes and the sharp scent of undergrowth mixed with the smell of the sea. He drove a couple of miles, beginning to suspect that the old man had given him the wrong directions, simply for the satisfaction of letting him drive around in circles. He was probably at home now with some guys named Jean or René, eating his sea urchins and laughing at the stupid tourist whom he had sent round and round the mountain.

Just as that image flashed through his mind, there was a curve in the road and, after he passed it, he saw La Patience. He gave inner thanks to Jean-Paul Francis and his magic box. If he ever managed to get his hands on that Robert Fulton record, it would only be fair to return it to him. His heart was beating hard as he drove toward the farmhouse, which stood out from the mountain as if it were leaning against it.

He drove under a brick archway covered with vines and turned onto the driveway leading to the barn of the large two-story house. As he drove up, disappointment slowly overtook the feeling of triumph that the view of the house had first elicited. The gravel path was overgrown with weeds and all that was left were two tracks made by car wheels. As he drove up, the sound of his car scraping against the gravel was strangely sinister.

Now that his perspective had changed, he could see that the back of the house was in ruins. The roof had almost completely collapsed and only the front was still standing. Blackened beams rose toward the sky from what was left of the frame of the house, and the shingles had fallen to the ground. The crumbling walls were encrusted with soot, signs of a devastating fire that had practically finished off the house, but had left the facade still standing like scenery in a theater.

It must have happened some time ago if the weeds and vines had been able to regain possession of what had been theirs to begin with. It was as if nature had slowly and patiently stitched a delicate bandage to cover the wounds inflicted by man.

Hulot left his car in the courtyard, got out, and looked around. The view was magnificent. He could see the entire valley, dotted with isolated houses and vineyards alternating with vegetation that grew sparser as it reached the town. Cassis, beautiful and white, leaned over the coast like a woman on a balcony watching the sea on the horizon. There were the ragged remains of a garden, with rusty wrought-iron railings that spoke of former splendor. The garden must have been spectacular when it was in bloom. Now it was overgrown with neglected lavender bushes.

The closed shutters, the peeling walls and the weeds that reached into every crevice like a pickpocket into a woman's purse, gave off a depressing sense of desolation and abandonment.

He saw a car drive up from the road and turn into the driveway. Hulot stood in the middle of the courtyard and waited. A yellow Renault Kangoo pulled up next to his Peugeot and two men got out, both in work clothes. The older man was about sixty and the younger one in his thirties, a thickset type with a hard face and a long, dark beard. The younger man didn't even bother looking at him. He went around to open the back of the vehicle and started taking out gardening tools.

The other man gave him instructions. "Get started, Bertot. I'll be right there."

After making it clear that he was in charge, the man approached Hulot. Up close, his snub-nosed face did not exactly sparkle with intelligence. He looked like a leaner, more seasoned version of the other man.

"Hello."

"Hello."

Hulot tried to offset any trouble by acting humble right away. He smiled and tried to look innocent.

"I hope I haven't done anything wrong, and I'm sorry if I have.

I think I got lost, a ways back there. I kept going, looking for a place to make a U-turn, and ended up here. Then I saw the ruined house and curiosity got the better of me, so I came over to take a look. I'll leave right away."

"No problem. No trouble. There's nothing left here worth stealing, aside from the dirt and the weeds. You a tourist?"

"Yes."

"That's what I guessed."

You guessed, my ass, Gaston-le-beau! You just saw my Monte Carlo plates. Any halfwit could figure that out.

"Every once in a while someone comes up here." The man shrugged modestly. "By accident, like you, but mostly out of curiosity. People from Cassis don't like coming up here. I'm not thrilled about it either, to tell you the truth. After what happened . . . But a job's a job after all and you can't be too picky these days. Anyway, as you can see, we always come in pairs. So many years have passed, but I still get the chills."

"Why? What happened here?"

"You don't know the story of La Patience?"

He looked at Hulot as though it were impossible for anyone on the planet not to know the story of La Patience. The man would probably have expected him to know about it even if he had descended from a flying saucer.

Nicolas gave him an opening. "No, I don't think I've ever heard about it."

"Well, there was a crime here, actually, a series of crimes. You really never heard about it?"

"No, never." Hulot felt his pulse racing.

The man pulled out a packet of tobacco and skillfully rolled a cigarette with papers fished from his vest pocket. As always happens with people who realize they are in possession of an interesting story, he savored every moment of his narration.

"I don't know every last detail because I wasn't living in

Cassis at the time. But apparently the guy who lived here killed his son and the housekeeper before burning the house down and shooting himself in the head."

"Good heavens!"

"You said it. But in town they say he was half crazy anyway and that in the twenty years he lived here they had only seen him and his son maybe twenty or so times. The housekeeper went down to buy groceries but she didn't talk to anyone. Hello and good-bye and that was it. He didn't even farm the land anymore, and he had quite a bit of it. Gave it over to the real estate people to run and they rented it out to local winemakers. He lived alone like a hermit on top of this mountain. In the long run, I think he blew a fuse and that's what made him do what he did."

"Three people dead, you say?"

"Yeah. Two of them, the man and the woman, were completely burned up. But the boy's body was still intact when they put out the fire. Good thing they stopped the fire in time, because it could have burned away half the mountain."

He pointed to the younger man with him. "Bertot's father was with the fire department. He told me that when they reached the house, after they doused the flames, they found the boy's body in an awful state. So bad that he would have been better off burned to a crisp, like the other two. The father's body was so badly burned that the bullet he used to blow his brains out had fused with his skull."

"What do you mean, 'in an awful state'?"

"Well, Bertot's father told me he had no face left, if you know what I mean. It was as if they had scraped the face off. So tell me the old guy wasn't crazy."

Hulot felt his guts crawl inside his stomach, like the ivy on those crumbing walls. *Dear God, the boy had no face left as if they had scraped it away.* Like a slideshow from hell, a series of skinned faces passed before his eyes. Jochen Welder and Arianna Parker.

Allen Yoshida. Gregor Yatzimin. He saw their lidless eyes staring into nothingness like an endless damnation of the man who had killed them and of those who had been unable to stop him. He thought he could hear a distorted voice whispering into both his ears in a sickening stereo effect.

I kill . . .

Despite the warm summer air, he shivered in his unlined cotton jacket. A trickle of sweat ran down from his right armpit to his belt.

"Then what happened?" he asked in a suddenly different tone.

The man didn't notice, or else he must have thought it was the normal reaction of a squeamish tourist who paled at the sight of blood.

"Well, it was pretty obvious what had happened, so after excluding any other possible options, it went down as a double murder–suicide. Not good publicity for La Patience."

"Any heirs?"

"I was getting to that. No heirs, so the farm went to the town. It was put up for sale, but who'd want to buy it after what happened? I wouldn't take it if they paid me. The city council handed it over to the same real estate agency and they rent out the land. They get maintenance costs out of it and so forth. I come up once in a while to keep the weeds from taking over what's left of the house."

"Where are the victims buried?"

Hulot tried to make his questions sound like those of a normal, curious person, but he needn't have bothered. The man was so wound up that he probably would have finished the story even if Hulot had walked off in mid-sentence.

"In the cemetery down in town, I think. The one near the city gates on the hill. You must've seen it if you've been down around there."

Hulot vaguely recalled a cemetery near the parking lot where he had stopped earlier.

"And what was their name, the people who lived here, I mean?"

"I don't remember exactly. Something with Le . . . Legrand or Le Normand, something like that."

Hulot made a point of looking at his watch.

"Goodness, it's late. Time sure does fly when you're hearing a good story. My friends will be wondering what happened to me. Thanks for telling me about it."

"You're welcome. A pleasure. Have a good vacation."

The man turned around and went to let Bertot benefit from his expertise. As he was getting into the car, Hulot heard him call out, "Hey, listen, if you want to eat some really good fish, take your friends to La Coquille d'Or down at the wharf. If you get ripped off somewhere else, don't blame me. Remember, La Coquille d'Or. It's my brother-in-law's place. Tell him Gaston sent you. He'll take good care of you."

My, my Gaston. Gaston-le-Beau. How about that—I guessed right. Today's my lucky day.

As he drove excitedly back to Cassis to visit the local cemetery, Nicolas Hulot knew that he would need a great deal more luck if he really wanted to settle the score.

43

Nicolas Hulot pulled the ticket out of the machine at the parking lot entrance and put his car back in the same spot where he had parked it before. From there he could see, a little farther up from the Parking de la Viguerie, a tiny cemetery surrounded by cypress trees. He left his car, walked out of the garage, and started up the road that seemed to be a continuation of the one he had walked down earlier. Just before the cemetery, he saw a cement playground with a tennis and basketball court. A group of boys were dribbling a ball, intent on a half-court game.

Strange, he thought, that there would be a basketball court right next to a cemetery. Strange in a good way. It wasn't a lack of respect, but rather the simple, natural juxtaposition of life and death, without fear or false modesty. If he believed in ghosts, he would say it was a way for the living to share a little life with those who no longer had any.

He reached the cemetery. A blue street sign hanging from a lamp told him that he was on Allée du Souvenir Français. Another sign with a blue and red border on a wall built into the hillside said the same thing. He walked a few hundred feet to a dirt road leading to a gate under an archway. Next to the gate, another sign hanging from a weather-beaten bulletin board said that the caretaker was there from eight A.M. to five P.M. in the winter months.

Hulot walked beneath the archway and into the cemetery, hearing the gravel beneath his shoes. He noticed the silence right away. It made no difference that a group of boys was playing ball not far away, that the town was full of tourists in the heat of summer, that cars could be heard coming and going on the road. The fence seemed to have some special sound-absorbing property that did not remove the noise, but altered it so that it became part of the silence that reigned inside.

He walked slowly along the path among the graves.

The excitement from his meager progress had worn off somewhat during the short drive from La Patience. Now was the time for rational thought. Now he had to remind *himself* that someone's life depended on him and what he might find out.

The cemetery was very small, a series of pathways forming a checkerboard pattern. There was a cement stairway on the right, built to make better use of the little available space. It led up to a series of terraces with other graves, dug into the hillside that continued beyond the fence. An enormous cypress rose into the clear sky at the center of the cemetery. To the right and left were two small brick buildings with red tile roofs. Judging from the cross on top, the one on the right was a chapel. The other was probably a toolshed. As he stood looking at it, the wooden door opened and a man came out.

Hulot walked toward him, wondering how he should introduce himself. As actors and policemen—both masters of deception—often do, he decided to go with the moment and improvise. He approached the man, who had now seen him as well.

"Good morning."

"Good afternoon."

Hulot looked at the sun moving toward a triumphant sunset and realized that he hadn't even noticed how much time had passed.

"You're right, I'm sorry. Good afternoon." He stood there for a moment and then decided to play the curious tourist. He tried again to act innocent. "Are you the caretaker?"

"Yes."

"Listen, someone in town just told me a horrible story, something that happened here a while ago, at . . ."

"You mean La Patience?" the caretaker interrupted.

"That's right. I was wondering, just out of curiosity, if I could see the graves."

"You a cop?"

Nicolas stared at him, speechless. From his expression, the other man could tell that he was right and he smiled.

"Don't worry. It's not written all over your face. Just that I used to be a degenerate sort of kid and got in a lot of trouble with the police, so I can always recognize them." Hulot neither confirmed nor denied it. "You want to see the Legrand graves, right? Come with me."

Hulot asked no questions. If the man had a troubled past and had come to live in a small town where some people want to know everything and some prefer to know nothing, it was pretty clear which side he was on.

Hulot followed him to the stairs leading to the terraces. They climbed a few steps and the caretaker turned left at the first landing. He stopped in front of a few graves grouped together. Hulot let his gaze run over the headstones on the ground, inclined slightly upward. Each had a very simple epitaph, a name and date chiseled in the stone.

Laura de Dominicis	1943-1971
Daniel Legrand	1970-1992
Marcel Legrand	1992
Françoise Mautisse	1992

There were no photographs on the headstones. He noticed them on many of the other graves. Given the situation, he could understand why there weren't any, although he would have liked to have some faces to use for reference. The caretaker seemed to have read his mind.

"There aren't any photos on the graves because they were all destroyed during the fire."

"Why are the birthdates missing on two of them?"

"The two that have the birthdates are the mother and child. I think we didn't get the other two birthdates in time. And then later . . ." He waved his hand to indicate that afterward nobody had cared about adding them.

"How did it happen?" asked the inspector, without raising his eyes from the marble slabs.

"Ugly business, and not just the story itself. Legrand was a strange character, a loner. He came here after buying La Patience with his pregnant wife and another woman who must have been some kind of housekeeper. He moved in and it was clear right off the bat that he didn't want anything to do with anyone. His wife gave birth at home, alone. He and the housekeeper probably helped.

He gestured toward the gravestone.

"The woman died a few months after having the baby. It might not have happened if she had delivered in the hospital. At least that's what the doctor who wrote the death certificate said. But that's the way the man was. He seemed to hate people. No one ever saw the son. He wasn't baptized, didn't go to school. Probably had private tutors, maybe his father, because he took all the exams at the end of the school year."

"Did you ever see him?"

The caretaker nodded. "Once in a while, very rarely, he came with his father and put flowers on his mother's grave. Otherwise the housekeeper did it. One time something happened."

"What?"

"Nothing big, but it really showed what things were like between father and son. I was inside." He pointed to the small toolshed. "When I came out, I saw him, the father I mean, standing at the grave. His back was to me. The boy was standing over there, near the railing, watching the children playing soccer down below. When he heard me come out, he turned his head in my direction. He was a normal child, rather good-looking I'd say, but he had strange eyes. I guess *sad* would be the best description. The saddest eyes I've ever seen. His father was distracted for a moment and he had snuck over there, attracted by voices of the other kids. I went to speak to him, but the father ran up to us, furious. He called the boy by name. And can I tell you something?" The caretaker stopped, probably to wipe the last bit of dust off that memory. He stared, not at Hulot but as if he were reliving the moment. "When he said 'Daniel,' it was like a man saying 'fire' to a firing squad. The boy turned to his father and started shaking like a leaf. Legrand said nothing. He just looked at his son with those big crazy eyes. I don't know what normally went on in that house, but I can tell you that right then *the boy had pissed himself.*" The caretaker looked down at the ground. "So when I heard what happened years later, it didn't surprise me that Legrand had done all that. Know what I mean?"

"I heard he committed suicide after killing the housekeeper and the boy and setting fire to the house."

"That's right. Or at least, that's what the inquest said. There was no reason to suspect anything else and the man's behavior justified the hypothesis. But those eyes"—he looked off into the distance again, shaking his head—"I'll never forget those eyes, the eyes of a madman."

"Is there anything else you can tell me? Any other details?"

"Oh, yes. There were other strange things. Lots, I'd say."

"Such as?"

"Oh, the theft of the body, for example. Then the business with the flowers."

"What body?" For a moment, Hulot thought he had misunderstood.

"His."

The man nodded toward the grave of Daniel Legrand. "One

night, after about a year, the grave was vandalized. When I got here in the morning, I found the gate open, the headstone moved aside, and the coffin open. There was no trace of the boy's corpse. The police thought it might have been some crazy necrophiliac."

"You mentioned something about flowers," interrupted Nicolas.

"Yeah, there was that too. A couple of months after the funeral, the cemetery received a typewritten letter. They gave it to me because it was addressed to the caretaker of the Cassis cemetery. There was money inside. Not a check, mind you, but bills, wrapped in a letter."

"What did it say?"

"That the money was to take care of the graves of Daniel Legrand and his mother. Not one word about the father or the housekeeper. Whoever had written the letter asked me to keep the graves clean and make sure there were always fresh flowers. The money continued to arrive even after the body was stolen."

"Even now?"

"I got one last month. If there isn't any change, I should be getting the next one sometime soon."

"Did you keep the letter? Any of the envelopes?"

The caretaker shrugged and shook his head. "I don't think so. I got the letter several years ago. I could look at home, but I don't think I kept it. I don't know about the envelopes. Maybe I still have a couple. In any case, I can give you the next one if I get it."

"I'd appreciate that. And I'd also appreciate your not mentioning our conversation to anyone."

"Sure." The caretaker shrugged as if that went without saying.

While they were talking, a woman dressed in black with a scarf on her head climbed the stairs holding a bouquet of flowers. With tiny steps, she walked to a grave in the same row as the Legrands, bent down and lovingly brushed off a marble gravestone. She spoke to the grave in a soft voice. "Sorry I'm late, but I had problems with the house today. I'll go get some water and then I'll explain."

She lay the flowers on the headstone and took the dried flowers from the vase. As she went to fill it with water, the caretaker followed Nicolas's gaze and guessed his thoughts. There was pity on his face.

"Poor woman. That was a really hard time for Cassis. Just before the business at La Patience, she had a tragedy as well, an accident. It wasn't anything unusual, if you can say that about a death. A diving accident. Her son used to go fishing for sea urchins, which he sold to tourists at a stall at the port. One day, he never came back. They found his boat just outside one of the *calanques,* abandoned, with his clothes piled in it. When the body floated in with the sea, the autopsy found that he had drowned; something had probably gone wrong while he was diving. After the boy's death . . ."

The caretaker stopped and circled a forefinger at his temple. "Her brain went with him."

Hulot stood watching the woman throw the old flowers she had removed from the grave into the trash. He thought about his wife, Céline. The same thing had happened to her after the death of Stéphane. The caretaker had said it perfectly. *Her brain went with him.*

He wondered with a stab in his heart if people made the same gesture when they spoke of Céline. But the caretaker's voice brought him back to the small-town cemetery of Cassis, where he stood before the graves of a ruined family.

"If that's all you need . . ."

"Oh, yes, you're right. I'm sorry, Monsieur?"

"Norbert. Luc Norbert."

"I apologize for taking up so much of your time. You're probably about to close."

"No, the cemetery stays open late in the summer. I'll come and close the gate later on, when it's dark."

"Then I'll stay here another minute, if you don't mind."

"As you like. If you need anything, I'll be here. Or just ask anyone in town. Everybody knows me and they can show you where I live. Good evening, Monsieur . . ."

Hulot smiled and decided to give him something in exchange.

"Hulot. Inspector Nicolas Hulot."

The man accepted the confirmation of his guess without any particular expression. He simply nodded as though it could not have been otherwise.

"Ah, Inspector Hulot. Well, good evening, Inspector."

"Good evening to you, and thank you very much."

The caretaker turned and Nicolas watched him go. The woman dressed in black was filling her vase with water from a faucet near the chapel. A pigeon roosted on the roof of the tool-shed while a seagull soared high above in the sky. Beggars of the earth and the sea who shared the refuse left by man, the poor creature who couldn't fly.

He looked back at the gravestones, staring at them as if they could talk, while an avalanche of thoughts went through his mind. What had happened at that house? Who had stolen Daniel Legrand's disfigured body? What was the connection between a crime from ten years ago and a ferocious killer who destroyed his victims exactly the same way?

He headed toward the exit. As he went down the walkway, he passed the grave of the boy who had drowned around the same time. He stopped for a moment in front of the grave and looked at the boy's photo. A dead boy with a lively face, smiling in the black-and-white image, which had probably been retouched for the occasion. He bent down and read the dead boy's name. His eyes took in the words and Nicolas Hulot suddenly could not breathe. He heard the rumbling of thunder and the words swelled to fill the entire surface of the gravestone. In one very long instant, he understood everything. And he knew the identity of No One.

Without really noticing, he heard the echo of steps approaching on the concrete. He thought it might be the woman dressed in black, returning to her son's grave.

Immersed in his thoughts, possessed by the excitement of his discovery, his heart was beating as heavily as a drum. So he never noticed the lighter beat of the step that came up behind him. He did not notice until he heard the voice.

"Congratulations, Inspector. I never thought you would make it here."

Inspector Nicolas Hulot turned around slowly. When he saw the gun pointed at him, he realized that his good luck for the day had run out.

44

When Frank awoke it was still dark out. He opened his eyes, and for the millionth time he was in an unknown bed, in an unknown room, in an unknown house. This time however, it was different. His return to reality didn't mean that he had to spend another day with the same thoughts as the day before. He turned his head to the left and in the bluish light from the lampshade, he saw Helena asleep beside him. The sheet only partly covered her and Frank admired the form of her muscles under her skin, the chiseled shoulders that ended in the smooth line of her arms. He turned on his side and moved closer to her, like a stray dog cautiously approaching food offered by a stranger, until he could smell the natural perfume of her skin. It was their second night together.

The night before, they had returned to the villa and gotten out of Frank's car almost fearfully, as if abandoning that small space might change something, as if what had been created inside the car might dissolve when exposed to air. They had gone inside the house furtively, without making a sound, as if what they were about to do was not within their rights but achieved by force and falsehood.

Frank had cursed that uneasy feeling and the person who was the cause of it. There had not been any food or wine, as Helena had promised. It was just the two of them, and their clothing, suddenly oversized, fell to the floor with the certainty of a promise kept. There was another hunger and another thirst to satisfy, ignored for far too long. There was an emptiness to fill, and only then did they realize how immense it was.

Frank lay back on the pillow, closed his eyes, and let the images run free.

The door.

The stairs.

The bed.

Helena's skin, unlike any other, touching his, finally speaking a familiar language.

Her beautiful eyes veiled in shadow.

Her frightened look when Frank had taken her in his arms.

Her voice, a sigh on her lips brushing his.

Please don't hurt me, she begged.

Frank's eyes were wet with emotion. Words hadn't helped him. Helena couldn't find the right ones either. The only explanation was the sweetness and fury with which they sought each other, needed each other. He had taken possession of her body as gently as he possibly could, wishing with all his might that he could go back in time and change the course of things. And, as he lost himself in her, he realized she had given him the power to do exactly that, and she could do the same for him. They would erase the suffering, if not the memory.

The memory . . .

He had not been with a woman since Harriet. Part of him had gone into suspended animation, leaving only his primary vital functions, the ones that allowed him to eat, drink, breathe, and roam the world like a robot made of flesh and blood. Harriet's death had taught him that love cannot be reproduced on command. One can't just decide never to love again. And most of all, one can't just decide to love again. The will, however strong, is not enough. One needs the blessing of chance, that unique conflagration of elements that thousands of years of experience and discussion and poetry have not been able to explain. Only to describe.

Helena was an unexpected gift of fate, a surprise that had suddenly interrupted the exhausted rotation of his weary planet around a sun that shone only for others. She was the amazing discovery of a single blade of grass growing amid the scorched rocks and barren earth. It did not yet mean a return to life, but it was a small, softly murmured promise, a possibility to be cultivated in the throes of hope, which for now brought trepidation, not happiness.

"Are you sleeping?"

Helena's voice surprised him as he was sifting through their recent memories, vivid as freshly printed photographs. He turned and saw her outlined against the light of the bedside lamp. She was watching him, leaning on her elbow with her head in her hand.

"No, I'm awake."

They moved closer and Helena's body slipped into the hollow of his arms with the ease of water flowing into a riverbed after pushing for so long against an obstacle that blocked it. Frank again felt the miracle of Helena's skin against his. She put her face on his chest and breathed in.

"You smell good, Frank Ottobre. And you're handsome."

"Of course I'm handsome. I'm the average man's answer to George Clooney. It's just that nobody asks the question."

Helena's lips on his were confirmation of the question, as well as its exclusive answer. They made love again, with that lazy sensuality that called their bodies, still half-asleep, from rest with a desire more emotional than physical. And their love made them forget the rest of the world, as only love can.

But the journey had a price. Afterward, they lay in silence, staring at the white ceiling that weighed over them a lot less than other presences they could feel in the amber light of that room—presences that would not go away if they merely closed their eyes.

Frank had spent the entire day at police headquarters working on the No One investigation. As the hours had passed and he watched every possible clue oscillate between nothing and absolute zero, he had tried to seem active and concentrate as his mind wandered.

He had thought of Nicolas Hulot following a lead written on a piece of paper so thin that their anxiety showed right through it. He had thought of Helena, held prisoner by unforgivable blackmail and an equally unforgivable jailer in that fake, impenetrable prison with its open doors and windows.

Frank had returned to Beausoleil that evening and felt rewarded to find her in the garden, like a traveler who comes to the end of his pilgrimage after a long, tiring walk in the desert.

Nathan Parker had called from Paris a couple of times while Frank was with her. The first time he had moved discreetly away, but Helena had stopped him by grabbing his arm with surprising force. He had listened to her conversation with her father, which consisted mostly of monosyllables, while her eyes gleamed with a terror he feared would never go away.

Finally, Stuart had come to the phone and Helena's eyes had lit up as she spoke to her son. Frank had realized that Stuart was her lifeboat, her escape, a secret place where she could write letters to be sent one day to someone she wasn't sure would ever receive them. Frank also knew that the way to her heart passed directly through her son. It was impossible to have one without the other. Frank had wondered whether he would be capable of following that path, and a wave of foreboding swept over him.

Helena placed her hand on the scar that ran across the left side of his chest, a pink piece of skin that stood out against his tan. Helena could feel that it was different skin, skin that had grown *afterward,* part of a suit of armor. It was meant to protect against harm, like all armor, but inevitably it had also prevented the gentle touch of a caress.

"Does it hurt?" she asked, running her fingers over it gently, tracing the outline.

"Not anymore."

There was a moment of silence and Frank felt that Helena was touching *their* scars and not just his.

We're alive, Helena. Beaten and imprisoned, but alive. And outside there's someone shouting who is trying to dig us out of the rubble. Hurry, I'm begging you. Please hurry.

Helena smiled and the light in the room grew brighter. She turned and climbed on top of him as if to declare a personal conquest. She bit his nose gently.

"What if I bit it off? George Clooney would win by a nose."

Frank pushed her face away with his hands. Helena tried to resist, and her mouth left his nose with a sucking noise. Frank looked at her with all the kindness that the eyes of one human being could transmit to another.

"With or without a nose, I'm going to have a lot of trouble imagining my life without you."

A shadow passed over Helena's face and her gray eyes turned the color of a knife blade. She took his hands from her face. Frank could imagine the thoughts behind that gaze and tried to ease the tension.

"What's wrong? I didn't say anything so bad. I didn't ask you to marry me, you know."

Helena buried her face in his shoulder. Her tone declared their brief, lighthearted moment over.

"I'm already married, Frank. Or at least I was."

"What do you mean, you were?"

"You know what the world of politics is like, Frank. It's show business. Everything's fake, it's all fiction. And like in Hollywood, anything's possible in Washington, as long as it isn't made public. A man with a career can't have the scandal of an unmarried daughter with a baby." Frank kept silent, waiting. He felt Helena's warm, damp breath caress him as she spoke. Her voice came from somewhere on his shoulder, but it sounded like it was coming from a the depths of a well. "All the more so if the man is General Nathan Parker. So officially, I'm the widow of Captain Randall Keegan, killed during the Gulf War with a wife in America expecting a child that wasn't his."

She raised herself to the position she had been in before, her face against his. There was a smile on her lips but she looked into Frank's eyes as if a pardon could only come from him. Frank never knew that a smile could hold so much bitterness. As Helena described her situation, it was almost as if she were speaking about someone else, someone she both pitied and despised.

"I'm the widow of a man I saw for the first time on our wedding day and never saw again, except in a flag-draped coffin. Don't ask me how my father got him to marry me. I don't know what he promised in exchange, but I can imagine. It was to be a marriage by proxy, long enough to create a smoke screen, followed by a simple divorce. Meanwhile, an uncomplicated career, an endless red carpet. And you know the funny thing?" Frank waited, silently. He knew very well that the funny thing would not be at all funny. "Captain Randall Keegan died in the Gulf War without firing a single shot. He fell heroically during unloading operations, hit by a Hummer with failed brakes. One of the shortest marriages in history."

Frank did not have time to answer. He was still absorbing this further demonstration of Nathan Parker's treachery and power when his cell phone on the table started to vibrate. Frank managed to grab it before the ringer went on. He looked at the time. Time for trouble.

"*Hello*?"

"Frank. It's Morelli."

Helena, lying next to him, saw his face contract.

"What is it, Claude? Something bad?"

"Yes, Frank, but not what you think. Inspector Hulot was in a car accident."

"When?"

"We don't really know yet. The French traffic police just informed us. A hunter who went out to train his dogs found his car at the bottom of a ditch off a side road near Auriol, in Provence."

"How is he?"

Morelli's brief silence was eloquent. Frank felt anguish tear at his heart.

No, Nicolas. Not you, not now. Not in this God-awful way when your life seemed like a pile of shit. Not like this, bad boy.

"He's dead, Frank."

Frank gnashed his jaws so hard that he could hear his teeth crunch. His knuckles turned white on the phone. For a moment, Helena thought he might crush it in his hand.

"Does his wife know?"

"No. I haven't told her. I thought you'd want to."

"Thanks, Claude. Good thinking."

"I would have preferred not to get that compliment."

"I know, and I thank you, on Céline Hulot's behalf as well."

Helena watched him go over to the armchair where his clothes were scattered. He pulled on his pants. She got out of bed, covering her breasts with the sheet. Frank didn't notice that instinctive gesture of modesty—nudity was still not natural for her.

"What happened, Frank? Where are you going?"

Frank looked at her and Helena could read the bitter pain on his face. She watched him sit on the bed to put on his socks. His voice came to her from behind the shield of his scar-covered shoulder.

"I'm going to the worst place on earth, Helena. I'm going to wake a woman in the middle of the night to tell her that her husband is never coming home."

45

It rained during Nicolas Hulot's funeral. The sky had apparently decided to interrupt the beautiful summer weather and pour down the same tears that were being cried below. It was a steady, uncompromising rain, as steady and uncompromising as the life of an ordinary police inspector. Now, unwittingly perhaps, he was collecting the only reward he might have desired while he was still alive: to be lowered into the same earth that held his son, to the accompaniment of words written only to console the living.

Céline was standing by the grave next to the priest, her face frozen in an expression of pain with no will of her own left before the graves of her husband and son. Her sister and brother-in-law, who had rushed in from Carcassone at the news, were beside her.

The funeral was private, in accordance with Nicolas's wishes. Nonetheless, a small crowd had gathered at the Eze cemetery. From where Frank was standing, on the side at a slightly higher elevation, he could observe the people surrounding the young priest performing the rites, his head uncovered despite the rain. They were friends and acquaintances and inhabitants of Eze, and all of them knew and appreciated the character of the man to whom they were bidding a final farewell. There were also some who had come just out of curiosity.

Morelli was there, and Frank was surprised by his profound expression of grief. Roncaille and Durand had come, representing the Principality authorities, as well as all the Sûreté personnel who were not on duty. Frank saw Froben opposite him, his head also uncovered. In addition, Bikjalo, Laurent, Jean-Loup, and Barbara, along with much of the staff of Radio Monte Carlo, were there. Even Pierrot and his mother, off to one side.

The few reporters present were kept outside by security guards, although they were not really necessary. The death of a man in a car accident was far too commonplace to be of real interest, even if it was the inspector of the No One case who had been recently removed from the investigation.

Frank looked at Nicolas Hulot's coffin. It was being slowly lowered in the grave, dug into the earth like a wound, accompanied by a mixture of rain and holy water like a joint blessing from heaven and earth. Two attendants wearing green raincoats and holding shovels started to fill the grave with earth, the same color as the coffin.

Frank stood there through the last shovelful. Soon the ground would be smoothed over and someone who worked there would place a marble slab on top, like the one next to it. There would probably be an epitaph saying that in some way, Stéphane Hulot and his father, Nicolas, had found each other. The priest said the final blessing and they all crossed themselves. In spite of everything, Frank could not manage to say the word *Amen*.

The crowd began to disperse right away. Those closest to the family said a few words to the widow before leaving. Céline saw Frank as she was embraced by the Merciers. She greeted Guillaume and his parents, received the hurried condolences of Roncaille and Durand, then turned and whispered something to her sister, who left her alone and started walking toward the cemetery entrance with her husband. Frank saw Céline's graceful figure approach him with her calm step and reddened eyes, which she refused to hide behind dark glasses.

Without a word, Céline sought refuge in his arms. He felt her weep silently on his shoulder, as she finally granted herself the relief of tears, which could not reconstruct her small, shattered world. Céline pulled away and looked at him. Grief shone in her eyes like an incandescent sun.

"Thank you, Frank. Thank you for being here. Thank you for being the one to tell me. I know how difficult that must have been for you."

Frank didn't say anything. After Morelli's phone call, he had left Helena and driven to Eze. He had pulled up at Nicolas's house and stood in front of the door for five long minutes before finding the courage to ring the bell. Céline had come to open it, holding the edges of her robe over her light nightgown. She knew as soon as she saw him. She was, after all, a policeman's wife. She must have imagined that scenario many times as a tragic possibility, even while pushing it away as a bad omen. And now Frank was there, standing in the doorway, his face grief-stricken, his silence confirming it, and now, after her son, her husband too would be far away.

"Something's happened to Nicolas, hasn't it?"

Frank nodded silently.

"And . . .?"

"Yes, Céline. He's dead."

Céline had closed her eyes for a moment and grown deathly pale. She had swayed slightly and he was afraid that she might faint. He had stepped forward to support her, but she had recovered immediately. Frank had seen a vein throbbing at her temple as she asked him for the details she didn't want to hear.

"How did it happen?"

"A car accident. I don't know very much. He swerved off the road and landed in a ditch. He must have died immediately. He didn't suffer, if that's any comfort."

As he spoke, Frank knew that his words were futile. Of course it wasn't any comfort. Nor could it be, although Nicolas had told him of their agony over Stéphane lying in a coma, a vegetable, until their pity overcame their hopes and they allowed the doctors to pull the plug.

"Come in, Frank. I have to make a couple of phone calls, but one of them can wait until tomorrow morning. And I have to ask you a favor."

When she had turned to look at him, her eyes, the eyes of a woman still in love with her husband, were full of tears.

"Anything you want, Céline."

"Don't leave me alone tonight, please."

She had called Nicolas's only relative, a brother who lived in America and who, due to the time difference, would not be woken in the middle of the night. She had explained the situation briefly and hung up with a whispered "No, I'm not alone," in answer to what must have been the concern of the person on the other end of the line. She had turned to him.

"Coffee?"

"No, Céline. Thanks, I don't need anything."

"Then let's sit down, Frank Ottobre. I want you to hold me tight while I cry."

And so it was. They had sat there on the couch in the elegant room facing the terrace and the void of the night, and Frank had listened to her cry until the light began to tinge the sea and sky with blue on the other side of the window. He had felt her exhausted body slip into a sort of stupor and he had held her with all the affection that he owed her and Nicolas, until he had given her over to the care of her sister and brother-in-law much later in the day.

And now they were standing there, facing each other, and he could not help but continue looking at her, as if his eyes could see inside her. Céline understood the question hidden in that gaze. She smiled gently at his male transparency.

"It's no longer necessary, Frank."

"What isn't necessary?"

"I thought you understood."

"What was there to understand, Céline?"

"My little madness, Frank. I was well aware that Stéphane was dead. I always knew it, just as I know that Nicolas is gone now too."

Seeing his mystified expression, Céline Hulot smiled tenderly and placed a hand on his arm.

"Poor Frank. I'm sorry. I fooled you too. I'm sorry I made you suffer each time I mentioned Harriet."

She raised her head to look at the gray sky. A pair of seagulls whirled overhead, circling lazily in the wind. There were two of them, together. That might have been Céline's thought as she followed them in flight, her scarf fluttering in the breeze. Her eyes returned to Frank.

"It was all pretense, my dear. A stupid little charade, played only to keep a man from letting himself die. You see, after Stéphane's death, right here at this very place, as we were leaving the cemetery after the funeral, I knew that if I didn't do something, Nicolas would be destroyed. Even more than I. He might have killed himself." Céline continued with the voice of memory. "The idea came to me suddenly in the car as we were driving home. I thought that if Nicolas were worried about me, if there were something else to occupy his attention, he would be distracted from his desperation over the loss of Stéphane. It was a small distraction, but enough to avoid the worst. And that's how it started. And how it continued. I deceived him and I do not regret it. I would do it again if I had to, but, as you can see, there's nobody left to pretend for."

Now the tears were again streaming down Céline Hulot's cheeks. Frank looked into the marvelous depths of her eyes. There were people in the world who thought they were made of silk, when really they were just a pile of rags. There were other people who did incredible things, things that changed the world. But to Frank, none of them could equal this woman's greatness.

"Good-bye, Frank." Céline again smiled her gentle smile.

"Whatever you're looking for, I hope you find it soon. I would like very much to see you happy, because you deserve it. Au revoir, handsome."

She stood on tiptoe and brushed his lips with a kiss. Her hand left a mark on his arm as she turned her back to him and started down the gravel path. Frank watched her walk away. After a few steps, she stopped and came back to him.

"Frank, for me it makes no difference. Nothing on earth will return Nicolas to me. But it might be important for you. Morelli gave me the details of the accident. Have you read the report?"

"Yes, Céline. Carefully."

"Claude told me that Nicolas didn't have his seat belt on. That's how Stéphane died. If our son had been wearing his seat belt, he'd still be alive. Ever since then, Nicolas never even put the keys in the ignition without buckling up. I think it's strange that this time . . ."

"I didn't know that about your son's accident. Now that you mention it, I find it strange as well."

"Again, it makes no difference to me. But if there's a chance he was killed, then it means he was going in the right direction, that *you were both* going in the right direction."

Frank nodded silently. The woman turned and left without looking back. As he watched her walk away, Roncaille and Durand came over to him, their expressions perfectly suited to the occasion. They too watched Céline go, a slight black silhouette on a cemetery pathway.

"What a terrible loss. I still can't believe it."

Frank spun around. His expression brought a hint of darkness to the police chief's face.

"You still can't believe it? You, who sacrificed Nicolas Hulot to official obligations and forced him to die a defeated man, you still can't believe it?" Frank's pause lay a stone on their heads that was heavier than the ones around them. "If you feel the need to be ashamed, if the two of you are capable of it, you have every right."

Durand looked up sharply.

"Mr. Ottobre, I'll justify your resentment solely on the grounds of your grief, but I will not allow you to . . ."

Frank interrupted him harshly. His voice was as dry as the sound of a branch breaking under his feet.

"Dr. Durand, I am perfectly aware of the fact that you find it hard to accept my presence here. But I want to get that killer more than anything else in the world, for a thousand different reasons. And one of the them is that I owe it to my friend, Nicolas Hulot. I am not concerned by whatever it is that *you* allow or don't allow. If circumstances were different, I assure you that I would gladly take all your authority and shove it down your throat."

Durand's face turned red. Roncaille intervened and tried to smooth things over. Frank was surprised to hear him take a stand, even if his motivation was questionable.

"Frank, our nerves are all shot because of what happened. Let's not let our emotions get the better of us. The job we have to do is difficult enough without creating more problems. Whatever our personal disagreements, they *must* take a backseat for now."

Roncaille took Durand's arm, who only pretended to resist, and pulled him away. They walked off beneath umbrellas, leaving him alone. Frank stepped forward in front of the mound where Nicolas Hulot lay buried. He watched the rain begin its work of leveling the earth, and the rage boiled up inside him like burning lava in the mouth of a volcano.

A gust of wind swept through the branches of a nearby tree. The rustle of the leaves brought a voice to his ears that he had already heard far too many times.

I kill . . .

His best friend lay there, right there, under that freshly dug mound of earth. The man who had seen him go adrift and had had the strength to hold out a hand when he needed it. The man who had the strength to confess all his weaknesses, and thus was even greater in Frank's eyes. If he, Frank Ottobre, was still standing, still alive, he owed it solely to Nicolas Hulot. Without realizing it, he started talking to someone who could not answer.

"It was him, wasn't it, Nicolas? You weren't a chosen victim; you weren't part of his plan. You were just an accident in his way. You discovered who he was before you died, didn't you? How can I find out too, Nicolas? How?"

Frank Ottobre stood for a long time before the silent grave under the pouring rain, obsessively repeating that question to himself. There was no answer, not even a word whispered in the language of the wind, not a clue to decipher in the movement of the air through the treetops.

NINTH CARNIVAL

Umbrellas in cemeteries are always black. On this sunless day, they look like upside-down shadows, projections of the earth, funerary thoughts dancing over people's heads who, now that the ceremony is over, walk slowly away, trying with each step to put as much distance as possible between them and the thought of death.

The man has seen the coffin lowered into the grave without any expression on his face. It is the first time he has attended the funeral of someone he has killed. He is sorry for the man. He is sorry for the reserved composure of his wife as she watches him disappear into the damp earth. The grave that welcomes him, next to that of his son, reminds him of another cemetery, another row of graves, other tears, other grief.

From the sky falls a rain without anger or wind.

The man thinks about how stories are repeated infinitely. Sometimes they seem to end, but it is only the characters who change. The actors are different but their roles are always the same. The man who kills, the man who dies, the man who does not know, the man who finally understands and is willing to pay with his life.

All around, there is an anonymous crowd of extras, people of no importance, fools carrying colored umbrellas that do not provide protection but keep a delicate balance on a tightrope—so high that they cannot see that the earth below them is covered with graves.

The man closes his umbrella and lets the rain fall on his head. He walks toward the cemetery entrance and his footprints blend in among the others on the ground. They too will be rubbed out, like all memory.

He envies the peace and quiet that will remain there after everyone has gone. He thinks of all those dead people, motionless in their underground coffins, their eyes closed, their arms crossed over their chests, lips silenced without voices to question the world of the living. He thinks about the consolation of silence, of darkness without images, of eternity without a future, of sleep without dreams or sudden awakenings.

Pity for himself and for the whole world comes to him like a gust of wind, as a few tears finally fall from his eyes and mingle with the rain. They are not tears for the death of another man. They are salty tears of longing for the sun of a time past, for the brief flashes of summer that were gone in the blink of an eye, for the few happy moments that he can recall, so deep in his memory that they seem never to have existed.

The man leaves the graveyard as if at any moment he is afraid to hear a voice, many voices, calling him back, as if beyond that wall there is a world of the living to which he does not belong.

Struck by a sudden thought, he turns to look behind him. At the end of the cemetery, framed in the gate like a picture, alone before a freshly dug grave, is a man dressed in black.

He recognizes him. He is one of the men hunting him, one of the bloodhounds with the dripping jaws, running and barking their challenge. He imagines that he will now be even more determined, more ferocious. He would like to go back, to stand beside him and explain everything, to tell him that it is not anger or revenge he seeks, but only justice. And he has a sense of absolute certainty, which can only come from death.

As he gets into the car that will take him away, he runs a hand through his hair, wet with rain.

He would like to explain but he cannot. His task is not yet finished. He is one and no one and his task will never be finished.

Still, as he looks through the car window lined with raindrops at all the people leaving that place of sorrow, as he watches the faces and their stupid expressions appropriate to the occasion, he asks himself a question that comes from fatigue and not from curiosity. He wonders which of them will finally announce that it is all over.

46

By the time Frank left the cemetery, everybody was gone. Even the rain had stopped. There was no merciful god in the sky, just the movement of gray and white clouds where the wind was carving out a small patch of blue.

His footsteps crunched on the gravel as he walked to his car. He got in and started the engine. The windshield wipers wiped the excess rain away with a swishing noise. In tribute to the memory of Nicolas Hulot, Frank buckled his seat belt. A copy of the newspaper *Nice Matin* lay on the seat beside him with the headline "U.S. Government Seeks Extradition of Captain Ryan Mosse" on the front page. Nicolas's obituary was on page 3. The death of a simple police inspector was not headline news.

He picked up the paper and threw it disparagingly onto the backseat. Then Frank shifted gears and glanced instinctively in the rearview mirror before stepping on the gas. He could see the newspaper upright against the back of the seat.

Frank sat still for a second, breathless. He felt like one of those crazy bungee jumpers, flying over empty space at a wild speed without the mathematical certainty that his cord was the right length. A silent prayer rose up inside him, in the hope that his sudden flash of intuition was not one of the many illusions that only exist in mirrors.

As he sat thinking, a floodgate opened. A waterfall of unconfirmed theories started flowing through his mind, strengthening as the force of water that widens a small hole in a dam until it becomes a powerful gush. In light of what had just occurred to him, numerous tiny discrepancies were suddenly explained, and many details that they had ignored suddenly fit into place.

He picked up his cell phone and dialed Morelli's number. As soon as Claude answered, Frank assailed him.

"Claude, it's Frank. Are you alone?"

"Yes."

"Good. I'm on my way to Roby Stricker's place. Meet me there and don't say a word to anyone. I have to check a few things out and I want you there with me."

"Something wrong?"

"I don't think so. I have a hunch, so small that it's probably nothing, but if I'm right, the whole thing might be over."

"You mean . . .?"

"See you at Stricker's." Frank cut him off.

Now he was sorry to be driving an unmarked vehicle instead of a real police car with a siren. He chided himself for not having asked for a magnetic light to put on the roof.

Meanwhile, he started blaming himself. How could he have been so blind? How could he have let his personal resentment cloud his vision? He had seen what he wanted to see, heard what he wanted to hear, and accepted only what he felt like accepting.

And they had all paid the price, Nicolas most of all. If he had used his head, Nicolas might still be alive and No One behind bars.

When Frank got to Les Caravelles, Morelli was standing in front of the building, waiting. Frank left his car on the street without worrying about the no-parking zone. He rushed past Morelli, and the sergeant followed him inside without a word. They stopped at the desk and the doorman looked at them with genuine concern. Frank leaned on the marble counter.

"The keys to Roby Stricker's apartment please. Police."

The clarification wasn't necessary. The doorman remembered Frank: his nervous swallow was proof enough. Morelli showed his badge, which broke down an already open door. In the elevator on the way up, Morelli finally found a way to interrupt the American's fury.

"What's going on, Frank?"

"What's going on is that I'm a complete idiot, Claude. A total fucking idiot. If I hadn't been such a hothead, I would have remembered how to be a cop and we might have avoided a lot of this."

Morelli didn't understand. They reached the door, which still had police seals on it, and Frank tore off the strips of yellow ribbon in rage. He opened the door and they went inside the apartment.

There was the usual sense of inevitability that hovers over a crime scene: the broken picture on the floor, the marks on the carpet, the traces left by forensics, the metallic smell of dried blood evoking a man's vain struggle with death, with a knife blade, with his determined killer.

Without hesitation, Frank went into the bedroom. Morelli saw him stand at the doorway to observe the room. The blood on the marble floor had been cleaned off. The only evidence of the crime committed in that room were the traces of blood on the walls.

Frank stood motionless for a few seconds and then did something strange. He reached the bed in two steps and lay down on the floor in the same position in which Stricker's body had been found, which forensics had traced on the marble tiles before removing the body. He lay there for a long time, barely moving. He raised his head to check something that could obviously only be seen from the floor.

"There it is, damn it. There . . ."

"There's what, Frank?"

"Stupid, stupid. Me, most of all. Busy looking at things from above, when the answer was below."

Morelli didn't understand and Frank suddenly jumped up.

"Come on. There's something else we have to check out."

"Where are we going?"

"Radio Monte Carlo. If I'm right, that's where we'll find the answer."

They left the apartment. Morelli looked at Frank as if he had never seen him before. The American seemed to be in the throes of a fit. They ran through the elegant lobby of the condominium, throwing the keys at the doorman who seemed very relieved to see them go. Outside, they jumped into Frank's car that a uniformed officer was already eyeing. The cop was standing in front of the car with his ticket book in hand.

"Drop the bone, Ledoc. On duty."

The agent recognized Morelli. "Oh, it's you, Sergeant. Okay."

He saluted them as the car skidded into traffic without yielding the right of way. They sped down the street past the Church of Sainte-Dévote, and as they drove by the port Frank remembered that it had all started there, in a boat full of death that had crashed into the wharf like the vessel of a ghost. If he was correct, the story would end right where it had begun. No more faceless ghosts. Now it was time to chase real people, with faces and names.

They broke the speed limit on their way to Radio Monte Carlo on the other side of the port, their tires screeching over the cement that had already dried from the rain. They left the car next to a boat that was about to set sail. Morelli seemed to have caught Frank's fever. Frank was talking to himself, moving his lips silently and muttering words that only he could understand. The sergeant could only follow, waiting for that mumble to start making sense.

They rang the bell, and half a second after the secretary opened the door, they were inside the huge elevator that doubled as a freight elevator and was luckily on the ground floor.

They went up to the radio station where Bikjalo was waiting for them with the door open.

"What's up, Frank? Why are you here now?"

Frank pushed him aside and rushed past. Morelli shrugged as an apology. Frank passed the secretary's work station. Raquel was at her desk and Pierrot was standing on the other side, picking up CDs to take to the archive. Frank stopped at the entrance where, behind the glass doors, he could see the cables for the phone, satellite, and ISDN connections.

He turned to Bikjalo who had followed him with Morelli. "Open this door!"

"But . . ."

"Do as I say!"

Refusal was not an option. Bikjalo opened the door and a gust of fresh air blew in the room. Frank stood for a moment, puzzled by the entanglement of wires. He ran his fingers under the shelves holding the connectors for the phone lines.

"What's going on, Frank? What are you looking for?"

"I'll tell you what I'm looking for, Claude. We've been going crazy trying to intercept that bastard's phone calls. And we failed. We could keep on trying for our entire lives and we'd still fail. And here's why."

Frank seemed to have found something. His hands stopped under one of the shelves. He pulled hard, trying to extract an object fastened to the metal counter, and he finally succeeded. When he stepped back, he was holding a flat metal box, twice as big as a pack of cigarettes, with a wire and a phone plug at one end. The box was wrapped in black duct tape. Frank held it out to the two astonished men.

"This is why we weren't able to intercept an outside call. That son of a bitch was calling from right here."

Frank had great difficulty expressing himself, for he was facing a complicated truth and wanted to say everything at once.

"Here's what happened. It wasn't Ryan Mosse who killed Stricker. I was being stubborn and wanted so badly for him to be guilty that I never even considered any other options. Here too, No One was diabolically clever. He gave us a clue that could be interpreted in two ways, either as a reference to Roby Stricker or to Gregor Yatzimin. Afterward, he just sat back and waited. When we put Stricker under the protection of the entire police force, he simply went and killed Gregor Yatzimin instead. And when the dancer's body was discovered and we left Stricker alone to rush to Yatzimin's apartment, No One went to Les Caravelles and killed him too."

Frank stopped. "*That* was his real aim. *He wanted to kill Stricker and Yatzimin on the same night*!" Bikjalo and Morelli were stunned. "When he killed Stricker, there was a struggle, and No One hit him in the face by accident. *He didn't take Stricker's face because it was damaged, and whatever he does with the faces, it wasn't useful to him any more.* He left the apartment convinced that Stricker was dead, but the poor guy was still alive and had time to write a message in his own blood."

Frank spoke as if all the tiles of the mosaic were coming together before his eyes. "Roby Stricker was a fixture of the nightlife scene in Monte Carlo and all along the coast. He knew everyone who was anyone. So he knew his killer too, although he probably couldn't remember his name just then. That's understandable. But he knew who he was and what he did for a living." Frank stopped to give the two men in front of him time to digest his words. Then he started to speak again, slower, articulating carefully. "Visualize the room. Stricker is lying on the ground, dying, his left arm broken. From that position—and I checked this myself—he could see himself in the mirrored wall of the bathroom through the open door. He was able to write what he wanted everyone to know by looking at his own image reflected backward, and besides that, he was a lefty using his right hand. It's not unusual that he would write backward and unfortunately, *he died without completing the message.*"

He grabbed the arms of the two men who were staring at him in silence and pulled them to the mirror in front of the director's booth. He pointed to the red light reflected in reverse on the shiny surface. "He didn't misspell Ryan as 'RIAN.' He was trying to write 'ON AIR,' the signal of a radio broadcast. We found a squiggly line at the beginning and we thought it didn't make sense, just a mark he couldn't control. But it did make sense. Stricker died before he could finish the *O*!"

"You mean . . .?"

Morelli sounded like he was having trouble believing his own ears. Bikjalo held his face, deathly pale, in his hands. All that was visible were his incredulous eyes. The pressure of his fingers opened them wider, accentuating his expression of shock.

"We've been living with the devil without smelling the stench of hell." Frank held up the box in his hand. "You'll see. When we analyze this gadget, you'll find that it's an ordinary, obsolete radio transistor. We'd never have found it because it works on a frequency we didn't even consider. None of us would have thought of such an archaic system. And you'll see that there's also a timer or something that turns it on at the desired time. And the phone signal wasn't found because this thing was in place *before* the switchboard to which we connected for interception. The technicians will be able to tell us the details, though we no longer need them. No One broadcast phone calls recorded ahead of time to the one person who knew how to ask the questions and answer them, *because he already knew what they were*."

Frank rummaged in his pocket and pulled out the photo of the Robert Fulton record.

"And here's the proof of how superficial I was. In our mad desire to ask questions, we often end up chasing ambiguous theories and forget to look at the obvious. The brain of a child always remains the brain of a child, even when it's in the body of a young man. Pierrot!" Rain Boy's head peeked in like a marionette over the wooden barrier that divided the secretary's desk from the computer station. "Come here a moment, please."

The boy walked over with his bug-eyed look and loping gait. He took in Frank's excited words without understanding, and the policeman's tone of voice frightened him. He fearfully approached the three men as if expecting to be scolded.

"Do you remember this record?" Frank showed him the picture.

Pierrot nodded as he usually did when asked a question.

"Remember how I asked you if this record was in the room, and you said no? And I also told you not to talk to anyone about it, that it had to be a secret between the two of us? Now, I'm going to ask you something and I want you to tell me the truth." Frank gave Pierrot a moment to comprehend what he was saying. "Did you tell anybody about this record?" Pierrot lowered his eyes to the ground and stood there in silence. Frank repeated the question. "Did you tell anybody about it, Pierrot?"

"Yes." Pierrot's voice seemed to come from some underground place, from below his feet where he was staring.

Frank lay a hand on his head.

"Who?"

"I didn't tell anyone, I swear." The boy raised his face. His eyes were full of tears. He stopped and turned in bewilderment to the three men. "Only Jean-Loup . . ."

Frank looked at Bikjalo and Morelli with a mixture of triumph and sorrow. "Gentlemen, whether you like it or not, No One is Jean-Loup Verdier!"

The room stood still in the silence of eternity.

Behind the glass of the director's booth, they could see Luisella Berrino, the show's deejay, in front of the mike as if it were a window open to the world. Outside was the sun, shining again, the trees still dripping with rain, the boats in the background and the entire city beyond. There were words and smiles and music, and people listening, and men driving cars, women ironing, clerks at their desks, couples making love, and children studying. But in that room, the air seemed to have disappeared and the sunlight was but a hopeless memory, a precious object lost forever.

Morelli was the first to recover. He reached for his cell phone with shaking hands and called headquarters.

"Hello. It's Morelli. Code Eleven, repeat, Code Eleven. Location Beausoleil, home of Jean-Loup Verdier. Inform Roncaille and tell him the subject is No One. Got it? He'll know what to do. And put me on to the car on duty in front of the house. Now."

Bikjalo fell into a chair in front of one of the computer stations. He looked a hundred years older. He was probably thinking of all the time he had spent alone with Jean-Loup Verdier without ever suspecting that he was a killer of such inhuman ferocity. As he paced back and forth, Frank had to give Bikjalo the benefit of the doubt and prayed that the manager wasn't merely thinking that this meant the end of his show, *Voices*.

Radio contact with the police car finally came through.

"Morelli here. Who is this and who's with you?" He got an answer and looked relieved, probably because he realized that those officers were able to cope with an emergency. "Is Verdier at home?"

His jaws contracted as he waited for the answer. "Sorel's inside with him? Are you sure?" Another pause. Another answer on the other end. "It doesn't matter. Listen carefully to what I'm about to tell you. Make no reply. Jean-Loup Verdier is No One. Repeat: *Make no reply. Jean-Loup Verdier is No One*. Obviously, he is extremely dangerous. Make some excuse and call Sorel out. Leave the subject alone but keep him from leaving the house for any reason. Spread out to cover all exits, but without making it seem like something's up. We're on our way with reinforcements. Do nothing until we arrive. Understand? Nothing."

Morelli ended the call. Frank was chomping at the bit.

"Let's go."

In three steps they were out of the room and heading to the right. Seeing them coming, Raquel clicked open the door. As they left, they could hear Pierrot's excited voice from behind the glass door of the office next to the entrance. Frank had a sudden thought and his heart sank.

No, he thought, *stupid boy, not now. Don't tell me we've lost because of your kindhearted idiocy.*

He pushed open the glass door and stood in the doorway, horrified. Pierrot was next to the table sobbing into the phone with tears running down his round face.

"They're saying you're a bad man, Jean-Loup. Tell me it's not true. Please tell me it's not true."

Frank reached him in one step and grabbed the phone from his hands. "Hello, Jean-Loup. It's Frank. Can you hear me?"

There was a moment of silence on the other end and then Frank heard the click and the line went dead. Pierrot was sitting on a chair, still sobbing. Frank spun around to Morelli.

"Claude, how many men are at Jean-Loup's house?"

"Three. Two outside and one inside."

"Level of experience?"

"Excellent."

"Okay. Call them back and tell them what happened. Tell them that the subject's been informed and he knows that we know. The agent inside is in great danger. Tell them to enter very cautiously and shoot if they have to. And tell them not to shoot just to wound. Is that clear? All we can do is get there as quickly as possible—I just hope it's not too late."

Frank and Morelli left the room, leaving Bikjalo and Raquel in shock behind them. Pierrot was slumped like a marionette on the chair, crying desperately with downcast eyes, facing the fragments of his shattered idol.

TENTH CARNIVAL

The man slowly hangs up, ignoring the furious, pleading voice on the other end. He smiles and it is a gentle smile.

So the moment he was expecting has arrived. He is somehow relieved; he feels a sense of liberation. The time of furtive steps along walls under the cover and protection of shadow is finished. Now, for as long as it lasts, the comfort of the sun will warm his unveiled face. The man is not the least bit worried—he is simply more vigilant than ever before. Although now he will have enemies by the hundreds. Many more than had been chasing him so far.

His smile widens. It will all be useless. They will never catch him. The long hours of training that he forced on himself as a sacred duty are seared on his mind like the branding of a slave.

Yes, sir. Of course, sir. I know a hundred ways to kill a man, sir. The best enemy is not the one who surrenders, sir. The best enemy is a dead enemy, sir . . .

Suddenly, he recalls the imperious voice of the man who forced him to call him sir. His orders, his punishments, the iron fist he used to rule every instant of their lives. Like in a movie, he visualizes their humiliation, their fatigue, the rain on their bodies, trembling with cold. A closed door, a patch of light getting smaller and smaller on their faces in the dark, the sound of a key being turned in a lock, the hunger, the thirst. And the fear, their only real companion, without the consolation of tears. They were never children, they were never boys, they were never men: only soldiers.

He recalls the eyes and the face of that hard, inflexible man who terrorized them. But, when it all happened that blessed night, it had been fairly easy to overpower him. His young body was a perfect fighting machine and the other man was heavy with age and disappointment. He could no longer fight the force and ferocity that he himself had created and strengthened day after day.

He had surprised him while he was listening with closed eyes to his favorite record, *Stolen Music* by Robert Fulton. The music of his pleasure, the music of his rebellion. He had immobilized him with a neck hold, tight as a factory clamp. He had heard his bones crunch in his grasp and had been astonished to discover that, after all, he was only a man.

He remembers as if it were now, his question, asked in a voice that was not fearful but simply surprised when he felt the cold barrel of the gun against his temple.

What are you doing, soldier?

He remembers his own answer, loud and clear and cold in spite of everything, at the sublime moment of his rebellion, the moment in which all wrongs are righted, all injustices overruled.

I do as you taught me. I kill, sir!

When he pulled the trigger, his only regret was that he could only kill him once.

The smile leaves the face of the man who has lost a name borrowed a very long time ago and is once again nothing more than one and no one. Names are no longer necessary. Only men and the roles they are forced to play: the man who flees and the man who chases, the strong man and the weak man, the man who knows and the man who is ignorant.

The man who kills and the man who dies . . .

He turns to observe the room. There is a man in uniform sitting on the couch with his back to him. He sees the nape of his neck rising above the couch, the line of his short hair on his lowered head as he examines a pile of CDs on the coffee table.

The sound of John Hammond's acoustic guitar is coming from the stereo. The floating sensuousness of the blues re-creates the Mississippi Delta, evoking a lazy summer afternoon, a world of humidity and mosquitoes so far away that it might not even exist.

The man in uniform had some excuse to come into the house, overwhelmed with the boredom of a task that perhaps he finds useless, leaving the other two just like him in the street, victims of the same boredom. He was fascinated by the number of records on the shelves and started to talk about music with a presumption of competence that his words showed to be false.

Now the man standing in a hypnotic trance eyes the defenseless neck of the man on the couch.

Just sit there and listen to the music. Music doesn't let you down. Music is both the journey and the destination. Music is the beginning and the end of everything.

The man slowly opens the small drawer of the phone table. Inside, there is a knife, sharp as a razor. As the man raises it and slowly moves toward the other man sitting with his back to him, the blade reflects the light coming in the window.

The head of the sitting man is bent and he nods it slowly, following the rhythm of the music. His closed mouth hums what he thinks is an accompaniment to the voice of the blues singer.

When he covers that mouth with his hand, the hum goes up an interval and grows more acute. No longer an attempt at singing, it becomes a mute chorus of surprise and fear.

Music is the end of everything . . .

When he slits his throat, a red spurt comes out so fast that it hits the stereo. The lifeless body of the man in uniform slumps down, head to one side.

There is noise at the entrance of the house. The steps of men approach stealthily, but his alert, well-trained senses can *feel* them even without a sound.

As he cleans the blade of the knife on the back of the couch, the man smiles again. The blues ballad, melancholy and indifferent, continues to pour from the speakers covered in rust and blood.

47

Frank and Morelli left the Rascasse at full speed, racing down Boulevard Albert Premier. Their Mégane with its sirens blaring was in a line of vehicles coming from Rue Suffren Raymond. Besides the police cars, there was a blue van with tinted windows in which the crisis unit was sitting in combat fatigues. Frank had to admire the efficiency of the Monaco Sûreté Publique. Only minutes had passed since Morelli had sent out the alarm and reinforcements were already arriving.

They turned right on Sainte-Dévote and drove along the port toward the tunnel, more or less the route of the Grand Prix in reverse. No race car had ever driven down that road as urgently.

They emerged from the tunnel like a cannon shot and left the beaches of Larvotto behind, heading toward the road that passed the Country Club and continued on to Beausoleil.

Frank had indistinct glimpses of curious onlookers turning their heads as the cars passed. So many emergency vehicles racing together down the streets of Monte Carlo was a rare sight. In the entire history of the city, the crimes that required so many police could be counted on one hand. The layout of the city was such that there was only one road that entered Monte Carlo and one road that exited, which made it easy to seal one side or the other. No one with half a brain would let himself get caught in that kind of trap.

At the sound of the sirens, the civilian cars stopped obediently to let the police pass. Despite their speed, Frank felt like they were driving at a snail's pace. He wanted to fly, he wanted to . . .

The radio on the dashboard crackled and Morelli leaned over to pick up the mike. "Morelli."

"Roncaille here. Where are you?" the radio barked, bringing Roncaille's voice into the car.

"Behind you, sir. I'm with Frank Ottobre. We're following you."

Frank smiled at the idea that the chief of police himself was in the car ahead of them. Nothing in the world would keep that man from being present at No One's arrest. He wondered whether Durand was with him. Probably not. Roncaille wasn't stupid. He had no intention of sharing the glory for catching the worst killer in Europe if he could help it.

"Frank, can you hear me?"

"Yes, he hears you. He's driving but he can hear. He's the one who figured out who No One is."

Morelli wanted to make sure that Frank got the credit he was due. Then, he did something that Frank would never have believed possible. Still holding the mike near his mouth with his left hand, he held up the middle finger of his right hand to the receiver at the very instant that Roncaille's voice again boomed out of the speaker.

"Good. Excellent. The Menton police are on their way too. I had to inform them, since Jean-Loup's house is in France and that's their jurisdiction. We need them to authorize the arrest. I don't want any sleazy lawyers using any cheap tricks when this goes to trial . . . Frank, can you hear me?"

There was a sputter of static. Frank took the mike from Morelli, holding the steering wheel with one hand.

"What is it, Roncaille?"

"I hope for all our sakes that you know what you're doing."

"Don't worry, we have enough evidence to be sure it's him."

"Another misstep after what happened would be inexcusable."

Sure, especially since the next name to be crossed off the list is yours.

The police chief's concern did not stop there, apparently. Frank could hear it even in the garbled sound coming through the receiver.

"There's one thing I can't understand."

Only one?

"How was he able to commit those crimes when he was practically barricaded in his house, under the constant surveillance of our men?"

Frank had asked himself the same question and gave Roncaille the same answer he had given himself. "That's a detail I can't explain. He'll have to be the one to tell us, once we get our hands on him."

They had reached Jean-Loup's house in the meantime. Frank took it as a bad sign that they hadn't yet established contact with the agents in the police car outside the house. If they'd gone into action, they should have communicated what was happening. He didn't tell Morelli of his concerns. In any case, Morelli was no fool and had probably come to the same conclusion.

They pulled up in front of the gate of Jean-Loup's house just as the inspector of Menton was arriving. Frank noticed that there were no reporters. On any other occasion he would have burst out laughing. They'd been constantly watching the house to no avail, only to abandon the hunt right when their story would have been as juicy as a steak. They would probably show up again en masse, but the police cars blocking the road in both directions would stop them. There were already men farther down, at Helena's house, to prevent any attempt of escape down the steep descent to the coast.

The blue doors of the police van opened before it came to a stop. A dozen men from the crisis unit, in blue jumpsuits and helmets, Kevlar bulletproof vests, and M-16s, jumped out and prepared to break into the house.

The police car was parked outside, empty, its doors closed but not locked. Roncaille himself had gone to check. Frank had a bad feeling. Very bad.

"Try calling them," he told Morelli.

The sergeant nodded as Roncaille walked toward them. Frank saw that Dr. Cluny was also getting out of the car. Roncaille was not as incompetent as he seemed, after all. Cluny's presence would be very helpful in case of negotiations involving hostages. Morelli was calling the agents and getting no answer as Roncaille stopped in front of him.

"What should we do?"

"The men aren't responding, which is not good. At this point, I'd have the crisis unit go into action."

Roncaille turned and nodded to the head of the assault group awaiting instructions in the middle of the road. The man gave an order and everything happened in a flash. Instantaneously, the unit spread out and disappeared from view. A fairly young but prematurely bald plainclothesman with the lanky gait of a basketball player got out of the Menton police car and walked over to them. Frank thought he had already seen him among the crowd at Hulot's funeral. He held out his hand.

"Hello. I'm Inspector Roberts, Homicide in Menton."

The two men shook hands as Frank wondered where he'd heard that name. Then he remembered. Roberts was the policeman Nicolas had spoken to the evening that Roby Stricker and Gregor Yatzimin were killed. The one who had gone to check on the bogus phone call that had been a false alarm.

"What's happening? Everything under control?" Roberts asked as he turned to look at the roof of the house that could be seen through the cypresses.

Frank recalled the tear-streaked face and childlike brain of Pierrot, who at first had helped and then had destroyed everything that Frank had exhaustedly constructed, at the price of human life.

He wanted to lie, but he forced himself to tell the truth and to appear calm.

"Afraid not. Unfortunately the suspect was alerted and the surprise was foiled. There are three men inside who haven't answered our calls and we don't know what's going on."

"Hmmm. That's no good. But if it's three against one . . ."

Roberts was interrupted by the crackling of Morelli's two-way radio. The sergeant hurried to answer as he joined the group.

"Yes."

"It's Gavin. We're inside. We've searched the place from top to bottom. It's safe now but there's been a slaughter. Three officers are dead. Besides their bodies, there's no one here."

48

The press conference was completely packed. Because they were expecting so many of the media, they had decided to hold it in the auditorium at the Centre Congrès. The hall at headquarters on Rue Notari simply wasn't big enough.

Durand, Roncaille, Dr. Cluny, and Frank were sitting before microphones at a long table covered with a green tablecloth against the wall. Everybody involved in the investigation was present. In front of them, representatives from the newspapers, radio, and television sat in rows of plastic chairs. Frank found the spectacle ridiculous, but the prestige of the Principality of Monaco and of the United States, which he represented as an FBI agent, made it necessary.

It didn't matter that No One, a.k.a. Jean-Loup Verdier, was still at large. It didn't matter that when they had entered the house after the attack by the assault unit, they had found it empty and Agent Sorel's throat cut like a sacrificial lamb. The other two, Gambetta and Megéne, had been shot with a gun, which turned out to be the same one used to kill Gregor Yatzimin.

Ubi major, minor cessat.

Certain embarrassing facts could not be revealed and were kept hidden behind the convenient screen of confidentiality. What was being emphasized was the success, the identification of the killer, the brilliant joint operation of the Monaco police and the FBI, the criminal's diabolical mind and the unwavering determination of the investigators, etc., etc., etc.

Camouflaged by that series of etceteras was the killer's escape, due to unforeseeable events, and his current unknown whereabouts. But it would only be a matter of hours until the man responsible for those horrible murders was captured. All the police forces of Europe were alerted and news of the arrest was expected at any moment.

Frank admired the skill with which Roncaille and Durand steered the tumult of questions. They were both adept at taking center stage whenever they possibly could and at changing the focus whenever they found themselves on the sidelines.

Neither of them even mentioned Inspector Nicolas Hulot. Frank recalled the photos of the accident, the smashed car, his friend's body slumped over the steering wheel with his face covered in blood. He slipped a hand into his jacket pocket and felt the piece of paper inside. Searching every inch of Jean-Loup Verdier's house for a clue that would explain his escape, he had found an ordinary speeding ticket. The license plate was that of a rented car. It was dated the day of Nicolas's death and the location was not far from the scene of the accident. Frank had been led back to Jean-Loup by this simple proof and by the words of someone who had turned out to be an unknowing but effective accomplice: Pierrot.

The secret Frank had asked him to keep as an *honorable* policeman apparently did not include his dear friend, Jean-Loup. Ironically, it was to him and to him alone that Pierrot had confided Frank's question about the Robert Fulton record. That was how Jean-Loup had realized he'd made a mistake, and then No One had taken off after Nicolas Hulot on his quest to find out what he could about the record.

Frank had retraced the inspector's steps one by one and had learned everything that he had learned. Hulot had discovered the identity of the killer long before they had. And that's why he was dead. Roncaille's voice roused Frank from his thoughts.

" . . .I will now turn the floor over to the man who succeeded in giving the serial killer known as No One a name and a face: FBI Special Agent Frank Ottobre."

There was no applause, just a frantic raising of hands. Roncaille pointed to a reporter with red hair sitting in the first row. Frank recognized him and prepared himself for a fusillade of questions. Coletti stood up and identified himself.

"René Coletti, *France Soir*. Agent Ottobre, have you been able to come up with any motive for why Jean-Loup Verdier mutilates his victims' faces so horribly?"

Frank tried not to smile at the narcissism behind their dialogue.

Two can play at that game.

Frank leaned back in his chair. "That's a question that Dr. Cluny is more qualified to answer than I. I can say that, as of today, we are unable to give a satisfactory motivation behind the methods used in the killings. As Chief Roncaille has already stated, there are still a number of details under investigation. However, there are several elements that we know for certain and can share with you." Frank paused for effect. Dr. Cluny would have been proud. "This certainty comes from the work done previously by Inspector Nicolas Hulot, which I then used to help identify No One. Thanks to an oversight on the part of the killer during the homicide of Allen Yoshida, Inspector Hulot managed to trace him back to an obscure case that happened years ago in Cassis, Provence. It was a violent crime and an entire family was killed. The case was filed away fairly quickly as a homicide-suicide. That judgment will now probably be up for review. I can tell you that the face of one of the victims was disfigured in exactly the same manner as those of No One's victims."

The room was abuzz. Other hands shot in the air. A young, vigilant-looking reporter stood up before anyone else. "Laura Schubert, *Le Figaro*."

Frank gave her the floor with a nod.

"But wasn't Inspector Hulot removed from the case?"

Frank could see Roncaille and Durand stiffen out of the corner of his eye. He smiled at the young woman who was about to hear a different story, the real one.

Up yours, assholes.

"That's actually not quite true. It was a misinterpretation by the press of certain declarations, which never mentioned that possibility. Inspector Hulot was simply detached from the inquiry here in Monte Carlo, to be able to follow his lead with the utmost discretion. As you can imagine, this detail was not revealed to the public for a number of reasons. It is with great sorrow that I have to announce that his investigative ability was itself the cause of his death, which did not occur in a simple car accident. Instead, it was yet another murder by No One who, realizing his identity had been discovered, came out in the open to kill again. I repeat, the credit for identifying the person responsible for these murders goes to Commissioner Nicolas Hulot, who paid for it with his life."

There was a small roar. The story didn't hold water, but it caused a sensation. It was something for the media to tell, and tell it they would. That was all Frank wanted. Durand and Roncaille were beside themselves but they tried with all their might to grin and bear it. Morelli, leaning against the wall with his arms crossed, sneaked Frank a thumbs-up from under his elbow.

A reporter who spoke French with a heavy Italian accent stood up. "Marco Franti. *Corriere della Sera,* Milan. Can you tell us something more about what Inspector Hulot found out in Cassis?"

"I repeat, that investigation is still under way and it will be some time before it is concluded. There is only one thing that I can tell you with certainty. We are trying to find out No One's real name, since we believe that even Jean-Loup Verdier is an alias. Investigations at the Cassis cemetery based on Inspector Hulot's lead have uncovered the fact that Jean-Loup Verdier is the name of a boy who drowned at sea many years ago while diving, around the time that the violent episode I mentioned earlier took place. The coincidence is suspicious, also considering that the boy's grave is just a few feet from that of the family."

Another reporter raised his hand and shouted out his question without even standing, miraculously managing to make his voice heard over the uproar.

"What can you tell us about the incident with Captain Ryan Mosse?"

A sudden silence fell over the room at the mention of one of the affair's most stinging questions. Frank looked carefully at the reporter and then ran his gaze over all those present.

"The arrest of Captain Ryan Mosse, who has already been released, was a mistake on my part. I am not looking for excuses or circumstantial evidence, which seemed enough to suspect Mosse of the murder of Roby Stricker at the time. Unfortunately, innocent people can sometimes get entangled in a very complicated investigation. This, however, is not and cannot be a justification. I repeat, it was a mistake for which I am solely responsible and ready to face the consequences. Nobody else is to blame. Now, if you will excuse me"—Frank stood up—"unfortunately, I am still working with the police to capture a very dangerous killer. I am sure that Dr. Durand, Chief Roncaille, and Dr. Cluny will be happy to answer the rest of your questions."

Frank left the table, walked toward where Morelli was standing by the wall, and disappeared through a side door. He found himself in a wide circular hallway that ran along the conference room. The sergeant joined him moments later.

"You were terrific, Frank. I'd pay anything for a photo of Roncaille and Durand's faces when you said that about Inspector Hulot. I'd show them to my grandchildren as proof that there is a God. Now . . ."

Steps approaching behind them interrupted Morelli. He stared at a point behind Frank.

"So, we meet again, *Mr. Ottobre*."

Frank recognized the tone and the voice. He turned and found himself face-to-face with the lifeless eyes of Ryan Mosse and the damned soul of General Nathan Parker. Morelli was immediately by his side. Frank sensed his presence and was grateful.

"Is there a problem, Frank?"

"No, Claude, no problem. I think you can go, right, General?"

"Of course. No problem. If you will excuse us, Sergeant." Parker's voice was cold as ice.

Morelli walked away, not fully convinced. Frank heard his steps on the marble floor. Nathan Parker and Ryan Mosse stood in silence until he turned the corner and disappeared. Then, Parker spoke first.

"So you did it, Frank. You found your killer. You're a man with a great deal of initiative."

"I might say the same of you, General, although they're not always initiatives to be proud of. Helena told me everything, in case you're interested."

The old soldier didn't blink an eye.

"She told me everything too. She told me all about your masculinity, when it comes to taking advantage of a woman who is not in her right mind. You made a big mistake by playing the knight in shining armor. If I remember correctly, I told you not to get in my way. But you didn't listen."

"You're a contemptible man, General Parker, and I will destroy you."

Ryan Mosse stepped forward but the general stopped him with a gesture. He smiled with the duplicity of a serpent.

"You're a failure, and like all failures, you're a romantic, Mr. Ottobre. You're not a man, but only the remains of one. I can crush you with my bare hand. Now you listen to what I have to say." He came so close that Frank could feel the heat of his breath and the slight spray of saliva as he hissed his fury in Frank's face. "Keep away from my daughter, Frank. I can reduce you to a state where you'll beg me to kill you. If you care nothing for your own safety, then think of Helena's. I can lock her away in a mental institution and throw away the key, whenever I feel like it."

The general started circling around him as he continued speaking. "Of course, you can join forces and try to defeat me together. Try to spit your poison at me. But remember. On one side, there's a U.S. Army general, a war hero, military adviser to the President. On the other side, there's a woman known to be unstable and a man who spent months recovering in a mental institution, after practically forcing his wife to commit suicide. Tell me, Frank, who would they believe? Besides the fact that anything that you two might *invent* about me would affect Stuart, which is the last thing Helena would want. My daughter already understands that, and promises not to see you or have anything more to do with you. Ever again. I expect the same from you, Mr. Ottobre. Do you understand? *Never again!*"

The old soldier took a step back with the light of triumph in his eyes. "However this ends, you're finished, Mr. Ottobre."

The general spun around and walked off without looking back. Mosse came over to Frank. His face glowed with the sadistic pleasure of striking a man when he was down.

"He's right, Mr. FBI agent. You're finished."

"That's something, at least. You, on the other hand, never even got started." Frank took a step back, waiting for his reaction. When Mosse tried to make his move, he found the Glock pointed at him. "Come on, Captain, give me an excuse. Anything at all. The old man has his back covered, but you are neither as useful nor as dangerous as you think."

"You'll end up in my hands sooner or later, Frank Ottobre."

"We're all in the hands of God, Mosse." Frank spread out his arms to illustrate the possibility. "And that's not you. Now run after your master and get out of here."

He stood still in the hallway until they both left. Then he put his gun back in the holster and leaned against the wall, slowly slipping down until he was sitting on the cold marble floor. He realized that he was shaking.

Hidden somewhere was a dangerous killer, ready to strike. The man had already killed several people including his best friend, Nicolas Hulot. Only a few days before, Frank would have given the rest of his life just to write that killer's name on a piece of paper.

Now he could think of nothing but Helena Parker, and he didn't know what to do.

49

Laurent Bedon left the Café de Paris, caressing the wad of five-hundred-euro bills in the inside pocket of his jacket. He thought about his incredible luck that night. He had pulled off what every roulette player only dreams of doing. *Chevals* and *en plein* on 23 red, three times in a row, with the top bet, the onlookers delirious and the croupier devastated at a practically unheard-of stroke of luck.

He had gone to the cashier and started pulling an endless amount of colored chips from his pockets, as if his jacket belonged to Harry Houdini. The clerk had not reacted to the size of the win, but he had had to ask the other clerk for more cash because there wasn't enough in his drawer to cover the amount.

As he retrieved his canvas bag from the cloakroom, Laurent had thought about how, when luck finally decides to play your side, her frenzy to give poverty a slap in the face is almost embarrassing. He'd gone into the Café de Paris just to pass the time, and in half an hour he had recovered everything he'd lost in the past four years.

He glanced at his watch. Perfect timing. He stood on the sidewalk for a moment, looking out on the square in front of him. To his left, all the lights of the Casino Municipale were sparkling. Next to the entrance, a BMW 750 was parked on an angle, skillfully lit with spotlights, the prize for a game of chemin de fer to be held later that night.

In front of him, the Hôtel de Paris looked like a natural outgrowth of the casino, as if one could not exist without the other. Laurent imagined all the people inside, the maids, the porters, the concierges, and the guests, full of self-importance and money.

As far as he was concerned, things were finally starting to fall into place. Since the beginning of his *collaboration* with that American, the wind seemed to have changed direction. He realized full well that Ryan Mosse was dangerous. That was clear from the way he had dealt with Vadim. But he was also extremely generous and as long as that was the case, nothing else seemed very important. When you got right down to it, what had he asked him to do? Just to pass on what he learned about the No One investigation from the police who were waiting for the killer to call at the radio station. A small task that had given him enough money to plug up several holes in the leaky boat of his finances.

He had been deeply disappointed when Mosse was arrested as a suspect in the murder of Roby Stricker. Not that he cared much about either of them. The American was clearly a psychopath and, quite frankly, he belonged right where they had put him, in a maximum security prison in the Rocca. As for Stricker, that playboy wasn't worth shit, and his only value in life were the bimbos on his arm. Nobody would miss him, probably not even his own father. *May the little prick rest in peace, amen*, was Laurent Bedon's hurried prayer in memory of Roby Stricker.

Laurent's only regret at the news of Mosse's arrest had been the loss of his own golden egg. That concern over losing his sponsor, as he called him, had overcome his fear of being accused of spying. The guy didn't seem like the type who would talk easily. The cops would have to work very hard if they wanted to get anything out of him. Mosse was tough, even more so with General Parker, the father of the murdered girl, backing him up. Parker was big time, and probably held Mosse's purse strings, to Laurent's great benefit.

In any case, he had welcomed the news of Mosse's release from jail with a sigh of relief and renewed hope. That hope had turned into genuine triumph when he received a second e-mail from his rich uncle to set up a meeting. He hadn't asked himself what they could want of him, now that they knew who the killer was. The only thing he cared about was renewing the flow of cash into his pockets.

He could still see Maurice's suspicious eyes peering at him when he had finally paid back his debt. He had looked down at the money on the desk in back of the Burlesque, his sleazy Nice nightclub full of cheap whores, as though it were counterfeit. If Maurice had asked him where the money had come from, Laurent wouldn't have said a word.

He had left with a scornful air, passing Vadim with his still-bandaged nose, a reminder of his meeting with Captain Ryan Mosse. Their suspicion that he was now under the protection of someone even more dangerous than they were had totally destroyed their condescending attitude toward him.

Monsieur Bedon has paid up. Monsieur Bedon is free. Monsieur Bedon would like you to go fuck yourselves. Monsieur Bedon is out of this shithole.

Laurent adjusted the bag he was carrying on his shoulder and left, crossing the square diagonally, heading straight for the gardens in front of the casino. There were lots of people around. Aside from the season and the usual tourists, the serial killer story had attracted an incredible number of curiosity seekers, in addition to all the journalists. It was back to the buzzing activity of better times, even though, by a strange twist of fate, all that resurgence of life was caused by the close proximity of death. People spoke of nothing else, in the papers, on the radio, on TV, and in living rooms that shed their lights on the streets from open windows.

Suddenly, he could see Jean-Loup Verdier before his eyes. Cynical as he was, he could not help shuddering. The idea that he had worked side by side with someone capable of doing what he had done churned his stomach. How many people had he killed? Eight, if he wasn't mistaken. No, nine, counting that Inspector Hulot. Shit. A real slaughter, by a handsome boy with green eyes, a deep voice, and a reticent air who seemed more likely to be chased by a flock of eager women than all the police in Europe.

And he was the one who had started Jean-Loup off on his career, who had brought him to the station, only to see himself gradually replaced by the young man's talent and charisma as a deejay. Now all that was changing too.

Bikjalo, who was apparently completely shattered by the experience, had been pushed aside by the station owner. Now all he did was smoke one Russian cigarette after another, and anything he said was just more smoke. The station owner had asked Laurent if he felt up to hosting *Voices* himself. The events had not lessened the public's interest in the program and there was a chance that ratings might shoot up even more with the gruesome fascination created by the violent crime.

Okay, assholes, where's your Jean-Loup now?

He'd also sold an exclusive interview for a shitload of money to a weekly, and the magazine's publishers had offered him a sizeable advance for an "instant book" titled *My Life with No One*. Then there was the unexpected win at Café de Paris, just now, and the night wasn't even over.

The fact that Jean-Loup was still at large did not bother him in the least. He was no longer a problem. As the police said, it was just a matter of time. Where could a man hide whose pictures were all over the media and in the hands of every police officer from here to Helsinki? Jean-Loup Verdier's sun had set forever. Now it was the time for the rise of Laurent Bedon.

To his great surprise, he discovered that he didn't give a damn about Barbara. Let her stay with her cop, her watchdog. Laurent realized that his stubbornness over the girl had only been caused by the bad times he had been going through. He had seen her as a symbol of his failure, the worst of the refusals he was getting from everyone at the time. Now he was sitting on a small throne and was finally able to make choices. The only thing he wanted, if he could want anything more from her, was to have her come to him with her tail between her legs and admit that leaving him had been a huge mistake. He would have liked to hear her humiliated voice begging him to forgive her and take her back. Just for the chance to tell her the truth. That he no longer needed her.

He sat down on a bench on the right side of the park, the area with the most shadows. Lighting a cigarette, he leaned back to watch the world go by, for once without the feeling that he didn't belong. Soon after, a man slipped out of the shadows and sat down next to him. Laurent turned to look at him. He was not afraid of his eyes, lifeless as those of a stuffed animal. All the man meant to him was more money.

"Hello, Laurent," the man said in English.

Laurent bowed his head slightly and responded in the same language. "Hello to you too. I'm glad to see you up and about again, Captain Mosse."

The other man completely ignored his greeting and got right down to the reason he was there.

"Do you have what I asked for?"

Laurent took the canvas bag from his shoulder and put it on the bench.

"Here you go. It isn't everything, obviously. I just picked up some material casually. If you had told me what this was for, I could have . . ."

Ryan Mosse interrupted him with a gesture. He ignored the implied question and thrust a cheap briefcase in his hands.

"Here. This is what we agreed on."

Laurent grabbed the briefcase and put it on his knees. He clicked open the lock and raised the lid. In the shadows, he saw that the bottom was completely covered by wads of cash. To Laurent, they were brighter than all the lights of the casino.

"Fine."

"Aren't you going to count it?" asked Mosse with some sarcasm.

"You have no way of checking the material that I brought you. It would be tacky for me not to trust you as well."

Captain Ryan Mosse stood up. The exchange was over. The pleasure of each other's company was certainly not enough to prolong the encounter, for either of them.

"Good-bye, Mr. Bedon."

"Good-bye, Captain Mosse," Laurent said, still seated on the bench. He waved. "Always a pleasure doing business with you."

He sat there watching the American's athletic figure walk away with his purposeful, military step that civilian clothes did nothing to hide. He remained on the bench until Mosse disappeared from view. He was in an excellent mood. The evening had been a great success. First the win at the casino and then the briefcase . . . As the saying goes, money makes more money.

And that's the way things would continue, he was sure of it. *Give it time,* he said to himself. *Give it time.* There was an old adage that even a stopped watch is right twice a day. His watch hadn't stopped after all.

Laurent got up from the bench and picked up the briefcase, much lighter than the bag he had given Mosse but *much* heavier for him. He stopped to think a minute. Enough of Café de Paris for that night. He could not ask for too much luck in one day. He had gotten a ride to the Place du Casino from Jacques, the sound technician. Now he could take a cab or walk down to the port, have a few drinks at Stars'N'Bars, pick up his brand-new car in the lot near the radio station, and go back to Nice. The car wasn't the Porsche he wanted, but it was only a matter of time. For now, it was enough not to have to take the bus to work from his new apartment near Place Pellegrini in the Acropolis district. A small place, but elegant, newly rented. The twists of fate. It was right near his old apartment, the one that had been taken over by Maurice, may he rot in hell.

He looked at the time. It was still early and the night was young. Laurent Bedon walked unhurriedly toward the Hôtel de Paris, full of optimism, thinking that he would just do whatever he felt like for the rest of the evening.

50

Remy Bretecher put on his helmet and raised the stand of his motorcycle with his foot. Even on the downhill slope, he had no problem holding the Pegaso. As excited as he was, he could have propped up his Aprilia with one leg. He'd parked in the Place du Casino, in the area reserved for motorcycles right in front of the Hôtel Metropole. Through his raised visor, he kept his man in sight as he crossed the garden and walked toward the fountain. Shadowing people was nothing new for Remy. He usually worked elsewhere, at the Casino of Menton or in Nice, or else in other smaller gambling joints along the coast. Sometimes he even got to Cannes. Monte Carlo was considered off-limits for this type of activity. Too dangerous, too small, and too many cops around. There was an insanely large number of plainclothesmen mixed in with the normal clientele of the casinos and Remy knew it.

That evening, he had simply been a tourist, nosing around to see what people were saying in the Principality about the serial killer. He had gone into the Café de Paris almost by accident and it was only from force of habit that he had noticed the guy with the callow face and the swaggering air who had won three *en plein* in a row, enough luck to win the national lottery.

Cautiously, he had followed him to the cashier and had seen the amount of dough he stuffed in his jacket pocket. That had immediately transformed his little vacation into a night of work. Actually, Remy was a mechanic in a garage just outside Nice that specialized in personalized motorcycles. He was so good with bikes that Monsieur Catrambone, his boss, turned a blind eye on his past. What he was doing now, which one might call a teenager's hobby, had earned him a couple of stints in a reformatory when he was underage. Those were youthful mistakes caused by lack of experience and a hot temper. Fortunately, he had kept out of jail since then, so far. Nowadays, purse snatching was only a misdemeanor and Remy was smart enough not to use weapons in his "contracts," as he called them. All told, it was worth the effort. You just needed a little savvy, and a second salary never hurt anyone.

Every once in a while, when he felt that the time was right, he went wandering around the casinos, eyeing solitary players who won large amounts. He would trail them and then follow them on his motorcycle. If they left by car it was a little more complicated. He'd have to follow them home and if they had a garage, there was nothing doing. He'd watch them disappear into the gate or down the ramp with the brake lights on, and that evening was a goner. But if they parked in the street, it was a done deal. He'd go over to them while they were standing at the door of their building looking for their keys. It would all happen in a flash. He'd approach them with his helmet on, one hand in his jacket, and he'd tell them to fork over the money. His hand in his pocket could be a simple bluff or it could really mean he had a gun. The sums at stake were not large enough for them to risk their lives, and they'd hand it over real fast. Then, a quick escape on his bike and it would all be over. All he had to do was check, later on, the economic value of his "automatic teller" operation.

If his "customer" left the casino on foot, he'd just have to find the right moment—a street without much traffic, no cops in sight and dim lighting if possible—and then do the same routine. It was often a lot faster that way.

Since he dealt with people who went to casinos, Remy often wondered if it wasn't really a sort of vice, a gambling addiction, with all that that entails. He had finally reached the conclusion that he could consider himself a sort of healer for those who were addicted: living proof that gambling is the work of the devil. In other words, he had absolved himself. It had never even occurred to him that he was just a petty criminal.

He turned on the ignition and the Aprilia started up obediently, with a subdued hum but a full sound. He hoped his man wasn't headed for the taxi stand next to the Hôtel de Paris. That could simplify things, since a man in a cab doesn't pull into a garage, but it might also mean that the evening was not yet over, always a risk. Usually, gamblers with winnings squandered their money right away, in one of the many nightclubs in Nice that were really just legalized brothels. He'd buy drinks for everyone in sight and end up giving some hooker enough money to feed a family of four for a week in exchange for a blowjob in a private room. Rémy would be disappointed if the fruit of his labor ended up down some whore's throat.

He raised his foot from the pedal, shifted into first and got over to his man as he was crossing the square near the central flower bed. He stopped and put down the stand, getting off his bike as if he had to check on something hanging in the bag in back. He saw with relief that the man continued walking past the only waiting cab. If he went down to Sainte-Dévote, it would be an incredible stroke of luck. There were few pedestrians around there and Remy would be able to take the road to Nice and disappear down one of the three *corniches*.

Remy was particularly keyed up about this sudden, unexpected little job. From the Café de Paris, he had followed his victim on foot through the gardens. The man had been heading right near where his motorcycle was parked. It would not have been a bad idea to do the job right then and there, and he could just have jumped on his bike and vanished.

He had seen the man sit down on the bench and had walked

right on by without letting himself be noticed, because there was another man sitting next to him. Something strange was going on. The man with the deathly pale face that he had been following had handed the other man a bag slung over his shoulder and had been given a briefcase in exchange.

The thing stank—or gave off the sweet perfume—of money, depending how you looked at it. There was a not too remote possibility that the briefcase contained something valuable. The contents of the briefcase, along with the money the man had just won at the Café de Paris, might make that evening a top winner in his own personal Guinness book of records.

He had missed his chance when the exchange was over and the two of them had separated. A group of people heading toward the casino had been coming down on the right. Remy had wondered if he should go for it anyway. Even if his victim cried for help, something he doubted, nobody usually got involved in things like that. Whenever a robbery occurs, people are suddenly obsessed with minding their own business. It wasn't for nothing that self-defense courses taught students not to yell "thief" during a robbery. That was a magic word that only made people turn their backs and walk away as quickly as possible. It was much better to yell "fire." Then people would hurry to your rescue. Remy knew that heroes were few and far between. But there might always be an exception to the rule, and he didn't want to take that chance.

Remy started the engine and cut down Avenue des Beaux-Arts, turning left on Avenue Princesse Alice to keep the prey in view. His man was turning on Avenue de Monte Carlo, the street with the view of the sea that, along with the street he was on, merged into Avenue d'Ostende. If he hadn't been driving, Remy would have rubbed his hands together in delight. That stretch of road was practically deserted: the ideal environment for people like him to earn their daily bread.

Remy drove slowly in second gear with his visor up, the zipper of his light-weight leather jacket half open, like a regular tourist on his motorcycle, lazily enjoying the warm summer breeze. There he was. He was walking leisurely, smoking a cigarette. Very good. At the beginning of Avenue d'Ostende, he crossed the street and walked on the same side Remy was already on. He was even carrying the briefcase in his left hand, the perfect position. Remy could barely believe it. He couldn't have chosen a better setting himself. His man had obviously used up all his luck at the Café de Paris.

Given the situation, Remy would probably have to be a little less gentle than usual. You can't make an omelet without breaking a few eggs, as his boss, Monsieur Catrambone, often said. He took a deep breath and decided it was time. He raised the front wheel onto the curb, and with a push upward with the handle, went onto the sidewalk.

He was behind his victim, just as he was tossing his cigarette butt. He had to hurry before he changed the briefcase to the other hand. Remy accelerated suddenly and came right up to the man, who turned his head when he heard the noise. Remy's fist hit him on the left side of his face, between his nose and mouth.

More from surprise than from the blow, the man fell to the ground, still holding the briefcase tightly. Remy stopped the motorcycle short with a skid of the back wheel. He leaned the bike on the stand and got off as quickly as a cat. He'd modified the motorcycle to meet his needs so that it would not turn off automatically when he put the lever down.

He went over to the man on the ground, his left hand in his pocket, pushing out his leather jacket.

"Don't move or you're dead!"

Remy got down on his knees, slipped a hand into the man's inside pocket, and pulled out the wad of euros. The operation was clumsy and the light material of the lining ripped. Without even looking, he thrust the wad of money into his jacket. Then he stood up and held a hand out to the man.

"Hand over the briefcase."

The guy already had a sickly face and a weak body. Now, with his nose all bloodied, he looked all the more ready to give out. Who would ever have imagined him capable of a reaction like that? Until then, everything had happened so fast that he hadn't even been able to realize what was going on. But once he understood that the guy on the motorcycle in the leather jacket was mugging him, he leapt to his feet and whacked Remy on the helmet with the briefcase.

Remy knew that the man was really not very tough, that his reaction was more from instinct than an ability to defend himself. Panic, that's all. If, instead of hitting him on his crash helmet, which had only made him move his head to the side, he had shoved the briefcase between his legs with that same force, the man would have broken his balls.

Remy was a fit young man, in much better shape than his victim. He punched the man exactly where he had hit him before and heard a tooth break. If he hadn't been wearing gloves, he would have hurt his hand. Luckily, there was nobody else around, although a car passed on the other side, going uphill. One of the passengers turned around to look. If he realized what was happening and reached the Place du Casino where there were always a few cops around, things might end badly. He had to hurry.

The man was still not letting go of the briefcase in spite of the second blow, but the two punches had done their job. His nose was pissing blood now, spurting it onto his jacket and shirt. He had tears of pain and rage in his eyes.

Remy grabbed the handle of the briefcase, pulled with all his might, and managed to tear it out of his hand. He turned and headed toward the motorcycle. Probably out of desperation, his victim found the strength to throw his arms around Remy's neck and grab hold of his shoulders. Remy tried unsuccessfully to shake him off. He jabbed him in the stomach with his elbow and felt his arm sink deeply into his soft flesh as the man clutching his shoulders gasped. It sounded to Remy like a balloon suddenly deflating.

He felt the man's weight leave his shoulders. He turned and saw him bent in two, holding his stomach. To avoid any more surprises, he kicked him—not a real kick, but a simple push with his foot in the shoulder. The man slipped backward off the curb onto the street, just as a large dark sedan was rounding the bend from Avenue d'Ostende at fairly high speed.

Laurent Bedon was hit straight on and the impact threw him all the way to the other side of the street, breaking his pelvis and a leg. His head hit violently against the curb of the sidewalk. He died instantly.

He had no time to hear the sound of the motorcycle rushing off, a woman's hysterical scream, the screech of brakes as another car stopped to avoid hitting his inert body on the street, in a pool of blood that was slowly spreading on the asphalt under his head.

By chance, which treated the dead as irrationally as the living, there was a sudden gust of wind. Floating in the breeze, a page of newspaper landed on Laurent's face, as if it were mercifully hiding that horrible vision of death from those present. By another twist of fate, the very evening that he had finally started feeling like he was someone, his lifeless face was covered with that of Jean-Loup Verdier. Printed in bold on the front page of *Nice Matin* was the headline, underlined in red: "The Real Face of No One."

51

Frank looked at the pile of dispatches on the desk in Nicolas Hulot's old office. He couldn't sit in that room without feeling his friend's presence. All he had to do was turn around and he would see Hulot standing behind him at the window. He leafed through the papers as if shuffling a deck of cards, examining them hurriedly. There was nothing important. They were still up to their ears in shit.

Once the elation of No One's identity had passed, nothing had really changed. Forty-eight hours after discovering *who he was,* they had yet to discover *where he was*.

Frank had never seen such a huge deployment of police. All the forces in the bordering countries and all their special sections for the apprehension of violent criminals, with acronyms that corresponded to ViCAP of the FBI, were on alert. There wasn't a cop in Europe who didn't have a series of pictures of Jean-Loup, actual photos as well as computer mock-ups showing possible changes he might make to his appearance. Streets, ports, and public and private airports were full of roadblocks. No car went unexamined, no plane took off without all passengers being searched, no vessel left port without being inspected.

Practically every inch of southern Europe had been searched by every means possible in the manhunt. A sensational demonstration was necessary to fight a criminal who had made such a deep impression on the public. The Principality of Monaco had a lot of influence. Some still considered it a puppet state, but that judgment was both hasty and misleading. Still, however, they had found nothing.

Jean-Loup Verdier, or whoever he was, had disappeared into thin air, which actually made the Monte Carlo police look good. If he had managed to elude everyone, if nobody had been able to handcuff him, he was obviously of *much* higher intelligence than the norm, which justified their failure to that point. The philosophy of "a trouble shared is a trouble halved" could apply even to hunting criminals. Frank thought they might as well try consulting a psychic—they were that desperate.

They had turned Jean-Loup's house in Beausoleil upside down without finding even the slightest clue. They had managed to get some information about his past by following through with Hulot's investigation, thanks to the phone number Morelli had found for him. The caretaker at the Cassis cemetery had confirmed that he had told Nicolas the story of La Patience and what had happened there. They realized that Hulot had most probably been caught and kidnapped by his murderer right at the cemetery.

Their inquiries about Marcel Legrand through the French police had ended up hitting a wall. Legrand had been a member of the secret service at some time in the past and his file was top secret. Frank found out that top secret meant a lot more to the French secret service than it did to Pierrot.

All they managed to find out was that at a certain point, Legrand had abandoned active duty and retired to Provence in complete isolation. There was some complicated maneuvering of diplomatic and state secrets to try to move certain obstacles and open certain doors. Legrand was just a skeleton, but it was still very difficult to get anyone to open the closet. On the other hand, no leads could be neglected, whether they came from the past or the present. No One was dangerous and his freedom threatened the lives of anyone who crossed his path.

Until then, he had killed his prey in attacks of delirium that followed scrupulous patterns. Now he was fighting to survive and everyone was the enemy. The ease with which he had gotten rid of the three agents showed what he was capable of doing. This was no mere radio deejay, a good-looking guy who could play music and answer phone calls. When necessary, he was a top-level fighter. The dead bodies of three exceptionally trained policemen were proof enough.

In the midst of all that, Frank was trying unsuccessfully to push the thought of Helena to the back of his mind. He missed her so much that it hurt, and knowing that she was a prisoner in the hands of her unscrupulous father did nothing to relieve him. His feeling of helplessness was slowly loosening all his inhibitions. The only thing that kept him from running to the house and strangling him to death was the certainty that it would only make things worse.

Here I am. This is who I've become. A man at a desk who doesn't know where to start hunting ghosts.

He opened a drawer and stuck the dispatches inside, though he was tempted to throw them in the trash. In the open drawer, he saw the floppy disk which he had put there when he had first taken over the office. The label said COOPER in his own handwriting. In the chaos of the last few days, he had completely forgotten Cooper's phone call and the lawyer, Hudson McCormack, whom Cooper had asked him to check on.

It wasn't the moment to ask for something like that, but he had to try. He owed it to Cooper and everything they had been through to try to lock up Jeff and Osmond Larkin. He buzzed the intercom and called Morelli.

"Claude, could you come in here a moment?"

"I was just about to. Be right there."

The sergeant walked in the door a moment later. "Before you start, there's something I have to tell you. Laurent Bedon is dead."

"When?" Frank sat up in his chair.

"Last night." Morelli hurried to give him the details, in order to avoid a predictable series of questions. "Nothing to do with us. The poor guy was killed during a robbery. He won a bunch of money at the Café de Paris last night and some chicken thief tried to steal it from him, right behind the casino. He fought back, fell into the street, and was hit by a car. The thief got away on his motorcycle. If the license number a witness gave us is correct, we should catch him in a few hours."

"Yeah, but it's one more death to add to the others in this mess. Christ, it's beginning to feel like a curse."

Morelli answered by changing the subject.

"Aside from that bad news, what did you want?"

"I need a favor," Frank said, remembering why he had called him in.

"What do you need?"

"It has nothing to do with this. Is there anyone free to trail a suspicious character?"

"You know what things are like. Right now, we're even using dog catchers."

"Here's the photo and name of someone who might be involved in a case my partner is on in the States." Frank threw the floppy disc on the desk. "He's a lawyer who's officially here in Monaco for a regatta."

"Must be the Grand Mistral. That's big time. The port of Fontvieille is full of boats."

"Not sure. I don't know anything about it. The guy's the lawyer of a big-time drug pusher we caught some time back. The theory is that he's more than just a lawyer and that he's not here in Monaco just for a race, if you know what I mean."

Morelli went over to the desk and picked up the diskette. "All right. I'll see what I can do, but it's not a good time, Frank. I don't have to remind you."

"Yeah. A bad time. No news?"

"No news. Not a peep. After a flash of light we're fighting shadows again. All the cops in Europe are chasing their tails and, as Inspector Hulot said . . ."

Frank finished his sentence for him. "The only thing attached to a tail is an asshole."

"That's right."

Frank leaned back in the chair. "Still, if you want my opinion . . . and I'm only talking about a feeling . . ." He stopped, straightened up in the chair and leaned his elbows on the desk. Morelli sat down in the armchair and waited. He had learned that the American's feelings needed to be examined very carefully. "I think he's still here. Searching for him all over the world is pointless. No One hasn't left the Principality of Monaco."

Morelli was about to reply, but the phone rang and Frank looked at it as if it were asking him a question. He picked up on the third ring and was assaulted by the operator's excited voice.

"Mr. Ottobre, it's *him* on the phone. And he asked for you."

Frank felt like he'd just been punched in the stomach. There was only one person that could be meant by *him.*

"Put him on. And record the call."

Frank pressed the speakerphone button so that Morelli could hear. He pointed to the phone with a slow movement of his right hand.

"Hello?"

There was a moment of silence and then a familiar voice came through.

"Hello, this is Jean-Loup Verdier."

Morelli jumped from the chair as if he had been shocked. Frank rotated a finger in the air. Morelli answered with a fist and a thumbs-up and ran from the room.

"Frank Ottobre here. Where are you?"

A short pause and then the deep voice of the deejay.

"No useless chatter. I don't need someone to try to talk to me. I need someone to listen. If you interrupt, I'll hang up."

Frank remained silent. Anything to keep him on the phone so that his men could trace the call.

"Nothing has changed. I am one and no one and I can't be stopped. That's why it's useless to talk. Everything is the same. The moon and the bloodhounds. The bloodhounds and the moon. The only thing missing now is the music. I'm still here and you know very well what I do. I kill . . ."

The line went dead. Just then, Morelli came racing in. "We got him, Frank. He's calling from a cell phone. There's a car waiting downstairs with a satellite dish."

Frank jumped up and followed Morelli, running down the steps four at a time. They shot out into the lobby like two bullets, almost knocking two agents to the ground. The car took off with the doors still open, tires screeching. It was the same driver as the morning that Allen Yoshida's body was discovered. He was excellent and Frank was glad to see him at the wheel. A plainclothesman was sitting in the passenger seat, looking at the monitor with a map of the city. There was a red dot on a wide street running along the coast.

Morelli and Frank leaned forward into the space between the two front seats, trying to see without blocking each other's view. The agent pointed to the red dot, which was now moving.

"That's the cell phone that made the call. We found it through satellite signals. It's in Nice, right around Place Île de Beauté. We're in luck. He's on this side of the city. He wasn't moving before, but from the speed, I'd say he's on foot."

Frank turned to Morelli.

"Call Froben and tell him what's going on. Tell him we're on our way and get them there too. Keep contact so you can tell them the subject's movements."

The driver was literally flying.

"What's your name?" asked Frank.

"Xavier Lacroix," the agent answered in a calm voice, as though he were taking a walk rather than shooting down the road like a missile.

"Okay, Xavier. If things work out, I'll do all I can to get you into racing."

The agent stepped harder on the gas, perhaps as thanks for the appreciation. As Morelli spoke excitedly to Froben, Frank turned to look at the display, where the red light was now flashing.

"What does that mean?"

The agent answered without turning around. "He's making a call."

"Can we hear him?"

"Not with this equipment. All it does is locate the signal."

"It doesn't matter. The only thing that counts is knowing where that son of a bitch is."

They raced along the *Basse Corniche* at a speed that would have made any Finnish rally champion jealous. The race car driver—Frank thought it was the right thing to call him—drove that fireball through the city traffic with a coolness that comes only with natural talent.

"Froben wants to know where . . ."

"He's going up Rue Cassini . . . Now he stopped. He's making another call."

There was a small traffic jam at the beginning of the square and Lacroix swerved around it by driving in the wrong direction and then raced up Rue Cassini as though qualifying for the Grand Prix. The agent in front of the monitor gave directions and Morelli passed them on to the Nice police.

"Left here and go up Emmanuel Philibert."

"Emmanuel Philibert," repeated Morelli.

"Right on Rue Gauthier."

"Rue Gauthier," echoed Morelli.

They turned right practically on two wheels. When they reached the end of the short street with cars parked on either side, there were police cars blocking the intersection with Rue Segurane in spoke formation. The uniformed police were standing in a group a few yards from the cars. One of them was replacing his gun in his holster. They stopped their car next to the others, jumped out, and reached them in a second. Froben saw them arrive. He looked at Frank and spread out his arms with the expression of someone who has just stepped in a large pile of shit.

Standing in the middle of all those policemen was a little boy, about twelve, in a red T-shirt, pants hanging down to his knees, and Nike sneakers. He was holding a cell phone.

He looked at the policemen one after another, not in the least afraid. Then he flashed a huge grin, revealing a broken tooth, and remarked in earnest, "Holy shit, man! Cool!"

52

It was almost two in the morning when Hudson McCormack pulled up near the wharf at the Fontvieille port, stopping in front of a large cabin cruiser with blue fenders, anchored between two sailboats. He got off his scooter and kicked down the stand before taking off his helmet. He had rented a scooter rather than a car, because he thought it would be better for the Monte Carlo traffic. The city was already chaotic in the summertime and getting around by car was a real drag, despite the many parking garages around. But during the regatta, the port of Fontvieille was a huge morass of people coming and going—crews, media, sponsors and their representatives, not to mention the inevitable fans and onlookers.

Getting anywhere was a constant obstacle course and the best way to wriggle through the commotion was by motorbike. Plus, goggles and a helmet were an excellent disguise to keep from being recognized and stopped at every turn by someone asking about his boat.

Looking at the enormous cruiser, Hudson McCormack thought of the endless debate over sailboats and motorboats that often exploded in ferocious barroom arguments between aficionados of one or the other. To him, the distinction was meaningless. They were *all* motorboats, except that a sailboat doesn't have a traditional propeller or gear cranks, cylinders, pistons, and fuel located somewhere under the hull. A sailboat's motor is the wind. And like all motors, it has to be analyzed, understood, its pulsation regulated, and its natural advantages exploited to the utmost.

While watching car races, which he loved, he had seen car engines explode in a sudden burst of white smoke. Many times, he had seen single-seaters pull off the track as the others raced past, and the driver would get out of his car and bend over the rear axle, trying to understand what had betrayed him.

It was the same for boats. A sailboat was also subject to the whims of its motor—the wind—which twisted, changed direction, rose or fell as it pleased. Unexpectedly, without any warning, the sails could fall limp while just a dozen yards away your opponent's boat was speeding along with the colored spinnaker so swollen that it looked like it might burst.

And sometimes that too could happen. The ripping of the sail made a noise like a huge zipper, and organized chaos ensued: the excitement of changing the damaged sail, the skipper's orders, the instructions of the tactician, the crew members crossing the deck like dancers on a moving stage.

Hudson McCormack had no personal explanation for all of that. He only knew that he loved it. He didn't know *why* he felt so good when he was at sea, and he didn't care. You don't analyze happiness, you live it. He knew he was happy on a boat, and that was enough.

He was suddenly excited for the coming regatta. The Grand Mistral was a sort of dress rehearsal for the Louis Vuitton Cup at the end of the year. This was when you showed your cards before reshuffling them if you needed to. The crews sized one another up and tried out their boats and the innovations designed to make the vessels more competitive. Afterward, there would be plenty of time to make the necessary changes before the most important and prestigious race of them all.

Everybody came to the Grand Mistral. Experienced crews and newcomers, even absolute beginners like *Mascalzone Latino,* a new Italian boat. The only one missing was *Luna Rossa,* the boat sponsored by Prada, still training at Punta Ala.

Their boat, *Try for the Sun,* was parked with all its gear in a rented shed equipped for haulage and launching near Cap Fleuri, a few miles from Fontevieille. The workers were staying there too, in spartan but functional accommodations. The boat had to be under close watch twenty-four hours a day, so that indiscreet eyes would not discover the top-secret details. In sailing, as in car racing, a revolutionary idea can mean the difference between triumph and defeat. Ideas were unfortunately easy to copy, and everyone tried as hard as possible to keep the details of their boats, the F1 vehicles of sailing, hidden.

Of course it was to their advantage that most of the aerodynamics, so to speak, were located underwater. You never knew what could happen, though. There were oxygen tanks and underwater cameras and unscrupulous people. Someone who was shallower than him—Hudson McCormack smiled to himself at that word—might think such precautions excessive.

But substantial economic interests were at stake as well as the honor of victory. It was not for nothing that all support crews had artificial respirators on board, the ones that use oxygen, not air, invented during World War II for underwater attacks. They recirculated carbon dioxide so that divers could approach an enemy ship without revealing their presence through air bubbles rising to the surface.

Wooden legs, hooks, and eye patches were not in style and the skull and crossbones no longer flew over the ships, but buccaneers were still around. Their progeny were alive and well and spread over the seven seas. Kings and queens no longer dispensed fleets of caravels, but sponsors gave out millions of dollars instead. The men and the boats were different, but the reasons were the same. They had merely substituted a sophisticated weather forecasting system for a moistened finger to find out which direction the wind was blowing.

The crew of *Try for the Sun,* to which Hudson belonged, was staying aboard the yacht flying their sponsor's colors in the port of Fontvieille. It was all a question of PR. The venture's backer, an international tobacco company, intended to get as much publicity as possible. And quite frankly, with the amount of money it had put down, Hudson figured it had every right.

Photos of the crew were already in all the most important weeklies of the area. There wasn't a magazine on sailing that hadn't published an article on their boat and crew members, and interviews about their previous experience.

On their arrival in Monte Carlo, there had been full-page advertisements in all the dailies that must have cost an arm and a leg. Hudson had noticed with some satisfaction that the photos in the papers actually did them justice instead of making them look like the usual bunch of thugs. He himself looked particularly good. His face, stamped on the page, had an open, natural smile rather than the stiffness of a wedding announcement. Not to mention that he really *did* look like that, a fact that was never lost on the female sex.

The official presentation of the boat and the crew was held at the Sporting Club d'Été. All the members of the team had attended in their colored uniforms, which Hudson found much more elegant than the tuxedos and evening gowns of the other guests. At one point, the master of ceremonies had requested everyone's attention: a skillful play of lights, a drum roll from the orchestra, and they had run out from either side of the room to stand in a row in front of the guests, while images of *Try for the Sun* were projected on the wall behind them. "We Are the Champions" by Queen, arranged especially for the occasion, was played with a large string section to evoke gusts of wind in the sails.

They were introduced one by one and each had received a round of applause as he stepped forward at the announcement of his name. They were strong, agile, intelligent men of expertise: the best the sport had to offer. That, at least, was the way they were presented and it was nice to believe it for a little while.

After the dinner, they had moved on to a nightclub, Jimmy'z. They were athletes and usually behaved themselves. Their mindset and attitude could be described by the adage, "Early to bed, early to rise." But they were not going to sea the next day and the people in charge thought that a little moderate partying could only help the crew's morale.

Hudson locked a chain around his scooter. It was a big chain, covered in clear red plastic to match the scooter itself. They had all told him that there was no need to worry about thefts in Monte Carlo, but habit won out. He lived in New York City, where people could steal your shirt without even touching your back. Taking precautions was no longer just a habit, but part of his DNA.

He stood on the wharf in front of the large cruiser, lit only by the service lights. There was no movement on the boat. He lit a cigarette and smiled. He wondered what the bosses of the tobacco company would say if they saw him smoking a rival brand of cigarettes. He walked away to finish his cigarette in peace, leaving the yacht behind him. The person he was waiting for, if he knew anything about women, would not arrive for another half hour, twenty minutes if he was lucky.

He'd spent the entire evening talking to Serena, a New Zealander he had met by chance at the party. He didn't really understand what she was doing in Monte Carlo, except that she was there for the regatta. She wasn't a staff member for any of the boats, each of which required extensive personnel in addition to the crews and reserves: technicians, designers, press agents, trainers, and masseurs.

One team had even brought a psychologist. That boat was not considered particularly competitive and gossip agreed that he was there more to comfort the crew after losing than to gear them up before the race. Serena was probably just one of those rich girls who traveled the world on her family's money, pretending to be interested in one thing or another. Sailing, in this case.

You know, the wind in your hair and the sound of the prow cutting the waves and that liberating feeling . . .

Or something like that.

Hudson was not usually so susceptible to female charms. Not that he didn't like women. He was straight as they come and a pretty girl was always a great way to pass the time, especially if she had class, something that differentiated people from animals. He had his affairs in New York, and they were fulfilling but without commitment, by mutual agreement. He could take off at any time for a regatta without explanations, without tears and handkerchiefs waving on the pier in the hand of a sad girl mouthing the words, "Why are you doing this to me?" He liked women of course, but he didn't need any trophies.

Tonight, however, was special. The lights, the people, the applause—a little narcissism was understandable. He was there doing what he loved most in the world, in one of the world's most beautiful places. It was captivating. He could not deny that Monte Carlo was magical to him, an American through and through. The beauty and uniqueness of the place and all those stories of princes and princesses . . . Serena's eyes were somewhat flashing, and what's more, under her evening dress she had a gorgeous pair of breasts.

They had chatted about this and that. Sailing, of course. Mostly they had discussed sailing gossip, who was who and who did what. Then their conversation had moved to a topic that Hudson was vaguely aware of, the story of the killer who snuck around Monaco disfiguring people. The girl was all worked up. The story had even pushed the regatta into the background. The criminal had killed something like nine or ten people and he was still at large, which was why there was such a massive number of police in the city. Hudson had thought of his scooter chain. So much for the place where theft was rare.

As they became acquainted, a comforting, promising expression had appeared in Serena's eyes that said "Knock and ye shall enter." And between one glass of champagne and another, Hudson had knocked. A few minutes later, they were both wondering why they were still there, in the middle of all those people.

And that's why he was pacing up and down the wharf in the port of Fontvieille at that time of night. They had left the disco almost immediately. They had decided that he would go down to the wharf to park his scooter and she would come and pick him up in her car. Serena had told him she had a convertible and suggested a night drive along the coast.

In other words, a land regatta, free and easy, with the wind in their hair. If he knew men as well as he knew women, their jaunt would begin and end without leaving her hotel room. Not that he minded. Not at all.

He threw his cigarette into the sea and walked back to the cruiser. He went on board in the absolute silence, listening to the teak and aluminum gangplank creak under his step. There was nobody around and the sailors were sound asleep. He went down to his cabin next to that of Jack Sunstrom, the skipper. The two cabins on either side of Sunstrom's were chosen by lot and he and John Sikorsky, the tactician, had lost. Jack was a terrific guy, but he snored so loudly that it sounded like a go-kart race. Light sleepers needed earplugs to be anywhere near him.

There was no noise coming from the cabin next door, a sign that Sunstrom was still at the party or still awake. Hudson removed the jacket of his official uniform, planning to change and put on something less flashy. The affair that evening was one thing; going around town like a colorful exotic fish was another. He put on a pair of blue pants and a white shirt that showed off his tan. He decided to keep his shoes on—comfortable, cool sailing shoes. His all-American looks didn't require a pair of cowboy boots. He sprayed on a little cologne. Looking at himself in the mirror, he thought that, narcissism aside, a touch of healthy, honest male vanity would add spice to the evening.

Hudson left the boat, trying to make as little noise as possible. The sailors, the real ones who worked hard and looked down on regatta crews as spoiled lazy queers, were not very understanding about people who disturbed their well-deserved rest.

He found himself back on the pier, alone.

Serena, quite understandably, had decided to go back to her hotel and change before coming to pick him up. Her evening gown and heels were not the right clothes in which to continue the evening, however it would end. And it was quite likely that her own healthy, honest female vanity required a bit more time.

He glanced at his watch and shrugged. There was no need to keep checking the time. He would have the next day all to himself and that allowed for some laziness. Up to a point, anyway.

Hudson McCormack lit another cigarette. His stay in Monte Carlo also included a few tasks that were not exactly part of the regatta. A classic two-birds-with-one-stone. He had to speak to a few bank directors and see a couple of people with businesses in Europe. People who were very, very important for his future.

He ran his hand over his chin, still smooth from his close shave before the fancy event. Hudson knew what he was doing and the risks he was taking. Anyone who saw him as just a good-looking American—healthy, athletic, and in love with his sport—was making a big mistake. There was an intelligent, extremely practical mind behind his charming looks. *Extremely practical,* above all.

He was well aware that he didn't have what it took to be a king of the courtroom. Not because he lacked the ability, but because he simply didn't want to wait. He had no desire to slave away trying to pull delinquents out of jail when they had every reason to be there. He had suspected for some time that his studies were not particularly suited to his temperament: he had no intention of working his ass off all his life, hobnobbing with the filth of society at whatever level. He did not want to reach the age of sixty-five only to find himself playing golf with other geezers full of money, making sure his dentures wouldn't fall out on the putting green. He wanted the things that interested him *now,* at the age of thirty-three, while his mind and body were able to back him up in the fulfillment of his desires.

Hudson McCormack had a different philosophy of life. He wasn't greedy. He wasn't interested in villas or helicopters or endless amounts of money or power. In fact, he considered those things more a sort of prison than a sign of success. He pitied the big shots, the ones who slept two hours a night and spent their days buying and selling bonds or whatever it was from five different phones. They all ended up in intensive care with heart attacks, wondering how they had gotten there and why they couldn't buy themselves more time with all their money and power.

Hudson McCormack, the young lawyer, took absolutely no pleasure in arranging the destinies of others: he wanted only to control his own. His ideal life was represented by a sailboat. In his case, it really was a question of the wind in his hair and the sound of the prow cutting through the waves and the freedom to choose the route, any route, according to the moment.

Again, he threw his cigarette into the sea. In the silence, he could hear it hiss as it went out.

To do what he wanted, he needed money. Lots of money. Not an enormous amount, but definitely a substantial sum. And there was only one way to get it in a hurry: by circumventing the law. That was how he put it. A slight euphemism. Not *breaking* the law, but *circumventing* it. Walking along the edge, on the margins, so that he could turn around quickly if someone called, showing his good-boy face and answering "Who, me?" with innocent eyes. He could not deny that there was a risk involved, but he had weighed it carefully. He had examined the question up and down, front and back, and decided that the risk was, all told, acceptable.

There were drugs involved and that was not to be taken lightly. Still, this case was special, *very* special, as cases involving mountains of money always are.

Everyone knew where drugs were produced and refined and what they were used for. Entire countries based their economies on different kinds of powders, which cost less than talcum powder where they were produced but went up 5,000 or 6,000 percent once they reached their destination.

The various comings and goings of these operations were part of a horrific war, no less ferocious and well-organized because it was underground. There were soldiers, officers, generals, and tacticians who remained in the shadows but were no less capable and determined. And acting as liaison among the various armies were people who had turned money laundering into a professional calling. The business world was not sophisticated enough to turn its back on someone who came with three or four billion dollars, if not more.

They flew on regular army planes, paid for by drugs. Some navies used the same system to pay for their destroyers' fuel. Every cartridge shot from a Kalashnikov by a more or less regular soldier corresponded to a hole in the arm of a drug addict somewhere else in the world.

The same world.

Hudson McCormack was not a big enough hypocrite to hide his head in the sand. He knew that what he was doing was a legitimate part of the shit that was destroying the planet. It was a simple but mandatory remark and he did not intend to shirk from his own implacable judgment. It was only a question of stimuli, of weights on the scales. For the moment, what he wanted was on one side and had much greater weight than any argument he could put on the other.

He had carefully assessed the situation in long evenings at home, poring over the facts with the same coldness used to analyze the balance sheet of any legitimate company. He believed that he had foreseen everything. He had even made a list of things that were unforeseeable. Whatever they were, they couldn't be known. That's why they were unforeseeable.

In the best-case scenario, he would have enough money to soothe his conscience and get the boat he wanted. Then he would sail around the world, free as the wind. It was a perfect metaphor, in spite of being a cliché. In the worst-case scenario—and he knocked wood—the consequences would not be that bad. In any case, they would not be enough to ruin his life completely.

He had left himself several outs, which put acceptable limits on the risks, as acceptable as a risk of that kind could be. Like everyone, he realized that he had a price. Still, Hudson McCormack was neither corrupt nor greedy enough to raise the price to a rash level that he could not support.

He was pulling the strings in a game that, in a very short amount of time, would deposit the balance of his fees into a Cayman Islands bank account where the first half was already accredited. He thought about the person who had made the deposit for him, his client Osmond Larkin, who at that moment was sitting in jail in America.

The man disgusted him and his revulsion had only grown with every meeting. His cruel, swinish eyes, his attitude that the world owed him something, his arrogant tone, always smarter than everyone else, turned Hudson's stomach. Like anyone who thought himself clever, Osmond Larkin was also stupid. Like every cunning person, he could not keep from showing it off, and that was why he was in jail. Hudson would have loved to stand up and tell him so, and then leave the room. If he could have had his way, he would even have violated professional secrecy and told the investigators everything.

But he couldn't do that.

Besides the risks he had taken and forced the people helping him to take, that option would mean pressing the remote and turning off a TV showing a magnificent sailboat cutting through the waves with a handsome man at the rudder.

No, there was nothing he could do, despite his aversion to Larkin. He had to deal with certain unpleasant things if he was to get what he wanted. *Not everything,* he said to himself, *but a lot and without delay.*

He walked back toward the sponsor's cruiser. The boats anchored next to each other were lost in the darkness, the larger ones with service lights left on and the rest in the reflection of other lights.

He looked around. The wharf was deserted, the bars closed, their plastic chairs piled atop the outdoor tables, the umbrellas down. That seemed strange. It was summer after all, despite the late hour, and summer nights always had impromptu actors onstage. Especially summer nights on the Côte d'Azur. He remembered what Serena had told him about the serial killer. Was that why he was the only person on the pier? Maybe nobody wanted to wander around and chance running into him. When people are afraid, they generally seek the company of others in the illusion of protection. In that sense, Hudson was a real New Yorker. If he allowed himself to think like that in his city, he would never leave his apartment.

He heard the engine of an approaching car and smiled. Serena had finally made it. He imagined the girl's nipples hardening at his touch and he felt a pleasant, warm sensation and a satisfying bulge under his zipper. He would think of some excuse to get her to let him drive. An intriguing image came to him as he waited, of him driving the convertible past the pine trees along the dark *haute corniche,* the wind in his hair and a lovely New Zealander bent over his lap with his cock in her mouth.

He moved toward the city lights on the other side of the wharf to meet her. He did not hear the steps of the man coming up from behind, for the simple reason that they were made of silence.

But the arm that encircled his throat and the hand that covered his mouth were made of iron. The blade of the knife, striking him from above, was as precise and lethal as it had been before.

It cut his heart in two.

His athletic body doubled in weight and suddenly fell limp in the arms of his killer, who held him effortlessly. Hudson McCormack died with the sight of the castle of Monte Carlo in his eyes, without the satisfaction of one small, final vanity. He never knew how well his white shirt, aside from setting off his tan, set off the red of his blood.

53

From her balcony, Helena responded with a smile to her son's wave as he walked out of the courtyard with Nathan Parker and Ryan Mosse. The gate clicked shut and the house was deserted. This was the first time in several days that they were leaving her alone and she was surprised. She could see that her father was following a plan, but she was unsure of the details. She had walked in on her father and his thug in the midst of a conversation that had stopped suddenly as she entered the room. Ever since her involvement with Frank, her presence was considered suspicious, even dangerous. The general hadn't even considered the idea of leaving her alone with Stuart for an instant. So now that she was left at home, anguish was her only companion.

Before going out, her father had given Ryan Mosse an order and the captain had removed all the phones and locked them in a room on the ground floor. Helena didn't own a cell phone. Nathan Parker spoke to her briefly in the tone he used when he would not accept "no" as an answer.

"We're going out. You'll stay here, alone. Need I say more?" He interpreted her silence as an answer. "Good. Let me remind you of just one thing, if I have to. Frank's life depends on you. If your son isn't enough to bring you to reason, maybe the other one will be a deterrent for anything you want to do."

As her father spoke to her through the door that opened onto the garden, she could see Stuart and Mosse waiting for him in front of the gate.

"We'll be leaving here as soon as I finish what I have to do. We have to take your sister's body home, although that doesn't seem to matter much to you. When we're back in the States, your attitude will change, you'll see. This is just a stupid infatuation."

When he had returned from Paris and she'd found the courage to throw her affair with Frank Ottobre in his face, Nathan Parker had gone crazy. He certainly wasn't jealous, at least not the traditional jealousy of a father for his daughter. Nor was it the common attachment of a man toward his lover since, as she had told Frank, it had been years since he had forced her to have relations with him.

That seemed to be over forever, thank God. The mere thought of his hands on her brought back a revulsion that she could still feel years later, which gave her a sudden, urgent need to wash. His *attentions* had stopped as soon as the baby had been born. Even earlier, when she had told him in tears that she was pregnant.

She remembered her father's eyes when she had told him that she was going to have an abortion.

"You're going to do what?" Nathan Parker had asked, incredulous, as if it were that idea and not the pregnancy that was an abomination.

"I don't want this child. You can't force me to keep it."

"And you can't tell me what I can and cannot do. I am the one who tells you. And you will do nothing, do you understand? N-o-t-h-i-n-g," he had enunciated slowly, inches from her face.

"You *will have* this child." He had given his sentence.

Helena would have liked to slash open her womb and pull out what she carried inside with her own bloody hands. Her father, that damned father of her child, had read her mind. Maybe he had read what was written on her face. In any case, she had not been left alone for an instant after that.

To justify her pregnancy and Stuart's birth in the eyes of the world, he had invented that ridiculous story of the marriage.

Nathan Parker was a powerful man, very powerful. As long as national security was not at stake, he was permitted to do almost anything he wanted.

She often wondered why none of the people who associated with her father ever realized how deranged he was. They were important: congressmen, senators, high-ranking officers, even presidents. Was it really possible that none of them, listening to the words of General Nathan Parker, war hero, suspected that those words came from the mouth and brain of a madman? Perhaps there was an explanation, the very simple one, of tit for tat. Even if the Pentagon or the White House were aware of the unwholesome aspects of the general's personality, as long as the consequences were confined to his domestic arrangements, they could be tolerated in exchange for his service to the nation.

After Stuart was born, a boy *finally,* his father became possessive of them both in a way that went well beyond his obsessive habits, his unnatural way of loving. Mother and son were not two human beings, but personal property. They were his possessions. He would have destroyed anyone who threatened this situation, which, in his totally lucid but unbalanced mind, he believed to be completely legitimate.

That is why he detested Frank. Frank was standing in his way, opposing him with a personality that was just as strong as his. Despite Frank's past, Parker realized that his strength was not sickly, but *healthy*. It didn't come from hell, it came from the world of men. It was in that guise that Frank had firmly opposed him, refusing to help Parker when the general sought him out and striking at him when he should have stayed away.

Above all, Frank was *not afraid of him*.

Nathan Parker considered Mosse's release from jail and the fact that FBI agent Frank Ottobre had been forced to admit he was wrong as a personal triumph. Now, all he needed for absolute victory was to catch Arianna Parker's killer. And Helena had no doubt that he would succeed. In any case, he would try.

Helena thought of poor Arianna. Her stepsister's life hadn't been much better than hers. They didn't have the same mother. Helena hardly knew her own mother, who had died of leukemia when she was three. Treatment for the disease was not very developed at the time, and she had passed away quickly, despite the family's wealth. All that was left of her were some photographs and a super-8 movie, a few images of the slightly awkward movements of a thin blond woman with a gentle face, smiling into the camera. She was holding a little girl in her arms and standing next to her husband and master in uniform.

Nathan Parker still spoke of his wife's death as a personal offense. If her father could express his feelings about it in one word, he would say it was *intolerable*.

She had grown up by herself, in the care of a series of governesses who had been replaced with growing frequency as she got older. She was a child and hadn't realized that the women left of their own accord, despite the excellent salary. As soon as they breathed the air of that house and discovered who General Parker really was, they would close the door behind them with a sigh of relief.

Then, without warning, Nathan Parker had come back from a long tour of duty in Europe, something involving NATO, with a new wife, Hanneke, as a souvenir. Hanneke was German, a brunette with a statuesque body and green eyes as cold as ice. The general had treated the whole affair in his usual hasty manner. He had introduced Helena to the woman with the smooth, pale skin, a perfect stranger, as her new mother. And that's the way she remained, not a mother but a perfect stranger.

Arianna was born soon after.

Engrossed in his flourishing career, Parker had left Hanneke to care for the house, which she did with the same icy coldness that seemed to flow through her veins. Their relationship was strictly formal. Helena was never allowed to see her sister as a child. Arianna was another stranger who shared the same house, not a companion who could help her grow up and whom she could help in return. There were governesses, nannies, teachers, and private instructors for that.

And when Helena turned into a beautiful adolescent, there was the boy, Andrés. He was the son of Bryan Jeffereau, the landscaper who supervised care of the park around their mansion. In the summer, during school vacations, Andrés worked with the men to "gain experience," as his father had proudly told Nathan Parker. The general was in agreement and often called Andrés a "good boy."

Andrés himself was shy and sneaked furtive glances at Helena from under the baseball cap he wore to protect himself from the sun as he dragged branches to the pickup truck to be towed away. Helena had noticed his awkward approach, consisting mostly of embarrassed looks and smiles. She had accepted them without giving anything in exchange, but inside she was aflame. Andrés was not exactly handsome. There were lots of boys like him, not good-looking but not bad-looking either, with manners that suddenly turned clumsy when she was present. He had one charm for Helena: he was the only boy she knew. It was her first crush. Andrés smiled at her, blushing, and she smiled back, blushing too. And that was it. One day, Andrés had found the courage to leave her a note hidden in the leaves of a magnolia tree, tied to a branch with a green plastic-covered wire. She had found it and stuck it in the pocket of her riding pants. Later, in bed, she had taken out the paper and read it with her heart racing.

Now, so many years later, she could not remember the exact words of Andrés Jeffereau's declaration of love, just the warmth she had felt at the sight of his shaky handwriting. They were the innocuous words of a seventeen-year-old boy with an teenage crush on the girl he saw as the *princess of the manor*.

Hanneke, her stepmother, who certainly did not live by the rules she set, had walked in suddenly without knocking. Helena had hidden the note under her blanket a little too quickly.

"Give it to me." Her stepmother had come over to the bed and held out her hand.

"But I . . ."

The woman had simply widened her eyes. Helena's cheeks had turned red.

"Helena Parker, I just gave you an order."

She had pulled out the note and given it to her. Hanneke had read it without the slightest change of expression. Then she had folded it and put it in the pocket of her sweater set. "All right, I think this should remain our little secret. We wouldn't want to cause your father any grief."

That had been her only remark. Helena had felt an enormous sense of relief and did not realize that the woman was lying, simply because she enjoyed it.

She had seen Andrés the next day. They were alone in the stables where Helena went every day to care for Mister Marlin, her horse. The boy was either there by chance or because he had managed to find an excuse, knowing that she would come by. He had approached her with his face bright red. Helena had never noticed the freckles on his cheeks before. Andrés was so excited to be talking to her that his words had sounded to Helena like "vocal freckles."

"Did you read my note?"

It was the first time they had spoken.

"Yes, I did."

"What did you think?"

She hadn't known what to answer.

"It . . . it was lovely."

Suddenly, plucking up his courage, Andrés had bent over and kissed her cheek.

Helena had turned around and felt like dying. Her father was standing there, framed by the stable door, and had been watching it all. *Everything* that had happened.

A boy her age had kissed her on the cheek.

He had come down on the boy in a fury and slapped him so violently that his mouth and nose started to bleed. Then, he had raised him up off the ground and hurled him like a twig against Mister Marlin's stall. The horse had backed off with a whinny of fright. Andrés's nose was dripping blood onto his shirt and Parker had grabbed him by the collar and pulled him up.

"Come with me, you little bastard."

He had dragged Andrés to the house and thrown him at Bryan Jeffereau's feet like an empty sack. His father had stood there with his mouth open and a pair of gardening clippers in his hand.

"Here, Bryan. Take your sex maniac and leave my house immediately. And be grateful that you're getting away so easily without being charged with attempted rape."

There was no answer to Nathan Parker's fury and Jeffereau knew him too well to try. In silence, he had taken his son, his men, and his equipment and he had left. Helena never saw Andrés Jeffereau again.

Nathan Parker's *attentions* to her had started not long afterward.

Helena crossed the bedroom that looked out onto the balcony. The bed was cut in two by a ray of light and she noticed that the half bathed in sunlight was the side that Frank had slept on. Frank, the only person in the world to whom she had had the courage to confess her shame.

She left the room and went downstairs.

The happy memory of those few moments spent with Frank

were not enough to erase her other memories, long past but still vivid enough to wound her as if it had all happened yesterday.

There aren't many girls around who can say they lost their virginity to their father, she said to herself. *I hope there aren't many. I hope for the sake of the universe that I am the only one, even though I'm sure I'm not.*

The world was full of Nathan Parkers. She knew it. And she was equally sure that the world was full of women like her, poor frightened girls who cried tears of humiliation and disgust on sheets covered with blood and the very semen that had conceived them.

Her hatred knew no bounds. Hatred of her father and of herself for not being able to rebel when she still could have. Now she had the justification of Stuart, the son she loved as much as she hated her father. The son she once would have paid any price to have lost and whom she now refused to lose at any price. Now she had him, but who was he? As hard as she tried, she could find no alibi for her weakness in the face of her father's violence.

She sometimes wondered if the same sick love that existed in the mind of Nathan Parker also existed like a cancer in her own. Perhaps she continued to submit to the torture because she was his daughter and the same blood and the same perversion ran through her veins. She had asked herself the question time and time again. Strangely enough, there was only one thing that kept her from going insane: the knowledge that never, not even once, had she found pleasure in what she had been forced to endure.

Hanneke must have suspected something but Helena never knew for sure. What had happened afterward was probably just the result of the fire she kept hidden beneath her glacial, formal exterior, a fire that no one had ever noticed, perhaps not even she herself.

In a banal, unextraordinary manner, simply leaving a letter that Helena had only learned of years later, Hanneke had run off with the family's riding master, abandoning her husband and daughters. She had taken along a very large amount of money, the icing on the cake.

The only thing that Nathan Parker cared about in the whole affair was the discretion with which it was handled. Hanneke had probably been some kind of high-class whore, but she wasn't stupid. If she had publicly humiliated her husband, the consequences would have been devastating. The man would have followed her to the ends of the earth to get his revenge.

The letter, which Helena had never read, had probably offered an exchange for what the woman knew or suspected about her husband's behavior with his daughter. Her freedom and silence in exchange for the very same freedom and silence. The pact had been tacitly accepted. Meanwhile, lawyers for both sides had arranged a hasty divorce to set things straight.

And, as they say, no one was hurt.

Certainly not Nathan Parker, whose lack of interest in his wife had become absolute, like his power over Helena. Certainly not Hanneke, who could now enjoy her money and riding masters wherever she felt like it.

The two girls, hostages of fate, had been left to pay the consequences of mistakes they had not made. As soon as she was of age, Arianna had left home. After roaming around for a while, she had ended up living in Boston. Her fights with her father had escalated as she grew older. On the one hand, Helena was terrified that the same thing would happen to Arianna that had happened to her. Sometimes she examined her father's face as he spoke to Arianna, to see whether the light she had come to recognize and fear would appear in his eyes. On the other hand, and she *cursed* herself for the thought, she prayed that it would happen so that she would no longer hear her father's step as he approached her bedroom in the middle of the night, or feel his hand raising the sheets and the weight of his body in her bed, or . . .

She closed her eyes and shuddered. Now that she knew Frank and understood what two people could *really* share when they were intimate, she was even more horrified and disgusted by what she had experienced in those years. Frank was the second man she had ever slept with, and the first with whom she had ever made love.

The ground floor of the house was flooded with light. That light existed nowhere else in the world. Somewhere, in that city, Frank was living in the same light and feeling the same emptiness. It was as if a machine were pumping the air out of her body and her skin stuck to her bones in an unnatural attempt at implosion. And at the same time, just the opposite was happening: she wanted to let everything inside her explode.

Helena walked down the hallway leading to the garden doors, passing in front of the room in which the telephones were locked. She stopped right after that, at the doorway where she and Frank had exchanged a long look on the night that Ryan had been arrested. That was when she had understood. Had it been the same for him? There had been no trace of emotion in his eyes but her woman's intuition said that everything between them had started right then.

More than anything else, she wanted him there so she could ask him.

She pulled a cell phone from her pocket. Frank had brought it to her the second night they had spent together, when he had had to rush off to tell Céline that his inspector friend was dead. She reflected a moment on the enormity of the situation that had required her to hide the phone, something the entire world considered an everyday object.

No, please, Frank, don't run away from me now. I don't know how much time I have left. I'm dying at the thought of not being able to see you, and at least if we could speak . . .

She pressed another button, the one for police headquarters.

The switchboard operator answered. "Sûreté Publique. *Bonjour.*"

"Do you speak English?" Helena asked apprehensively.

"Of course, *Madame*. How can I help you?"

The answer was in English, but *Madame* was still in French. Noblesse oblige. Helena took a deep breath. At least she was spared from stuttering in a foreign language. Hanneke had taught, or rather forced, her and Arianna to speak German. Her father's second wife hated French, which she called the language of homosexuals.

"I'd like to speak to Agent Frank Ottobre, please."

"Yes, *Madame*. Who may I say is calling?"

"Helena Parker, thank you."

"One moment please."

The switchboard operator put her on hold and Frank's voice came to her a few seconds later.

"Helena, where are you?"

She felt herself blush and that was the only reason she was glad he couldn't see her. It was as if she had gone back in time and could feel Andrés Jeffereau's shy, inexperienced kiss on her cheek. She realized that Frank Ottobre had the magical power to restore her innocence. And that discovery was definite confirmation for Helena that she loved him.

"I'm at home. My father went out with Ryan and Stuart and I'm alone in the house. Mosse locked up all the phones. I'm using the one you left me."

"Bastard. Good thing I thought of giving you a cell phone . . ."

Helena had no idea if the police switchboard operator was listening in on Frank's calls. He had mentioned that he suspected his cell phone and home phone at Parc Saint-Roman were tapped. Maybe that's why his voice was so brusque. Helena didn't want to say anything that could harm or embarrass him, but she could feel herself coming apart.

"There's something I have to tell you."

Now, she said to herself. *Say it now or you never will!*

"I love you, Frank."

Helena felt like it was the first time she had ever said those words. And the first time she was not afraid to be scared.

There was a pause on the other end. Only a couple of seconds, but to Helena it felt like trees could have been planted and grown high in the time she waited. Then Frank's voice finally emerged from the phone.

"I love you too, Helena."

There, simple, as it should be. With that sense of peace that comes from being right. Now Helena Parker had no doubts.

"Thank God you exist, Frank Ottobre."

There was no time to say more. Helena could hear the sound of a door closing in the room where Frank was, muffled by the filter of the phone.

"Just a minute," he said, suddenly cold.

She heard a voice that was not his say words that she could not understand. Then a shout from Frank, the sound of something hitting a wooden surface, followed by a curse, Frank's voice shouting, "Christ, not again, fucking sonofabitch!"

Then his voice on the phone again.

"I'm sorry, Helena. Only God knows *how much* I don't want to leave you right now, but I have to go."

"What happened? Can you tell me?"

"Sure. You'll read about it in the papers tomorrow anyway. No One has killed someone else."

Frank's voice was gone and Helena was left looking at the display, confused, trying to figure out how to hang up the cell phone. She was so happy that she didn't even realize her first phone call of love had been interrupted by the news of a murder.

54

Frank and Morelli flew down the stairs as if the lives of all mankind depended on them. How many times, Frank wondered, would they have to repeat this same race before waking from the nightmare? He had been on the phone with Helena, a few moments of peace in the midst of a storm, when Claude had burst in and it had all gone up in smoke. No One had struck again and in the worst way, adding insult to injury.

Christ Almighty, when is this massacre going to end? Who is this man? What can he be made of to do what he's doing?

They raced through the glass doors of headquarters and saw a group of policemen huddled around a car. There were already police barricades in the street to keep cars and pedestrians off Rue Suffren Raymond and from the opposite side, halfway up Rue Notari.

Frank and Morelli ran down the outside steps. The agents stood to one side to let them pass. Parked right in front of the entrance, in the last space reserved for police cars, was Jean-Loup Verdier's Mercedes SLK with its trunk open.

Inside was a man's body. It looked like a bad imitation of Allen Yoshida's murder, a botched attempt done earlier as a dress rehearsal. The dead man was curled up in fetal position inside the trunk. He was wearing blue pants and a white, bloodied shirt. There was a gaping cut at his heart, which was where the blood had stained the shirt. But, as usual, the worst damage was to his face. The corpse seemed to be staring at the piece of carpet in the trunk a few inches from its wide eyes, with the horrid grimace, the flayed face, the blood clotted on the bald head where a mocking tuft of hair indicated that this time, the work had been done in a hurry.

Frank looked around. None of the agents seemed nauseated by the sight. *You can get used to anything, good or bad.*

But this wasn't something to get used to: it was a curse and there had to be some way to stop it. Frank had to do it, whatever the cost, otherwise he'd wind up once again on the bench of a mental institution, staring blindly at a gardener planting a tree.

He remembered his conversation with Father Kenneth. If he were with the priest now, Frank would tell him that at last his convictions had changed. He still didn't believe in God, but he had begun to believe in the devil.

"What happened?" he asked everyone and no one in particular.

An agent came over. Frank didn't know his name, but remembered that he had been one of the men in charge of guarding Jean-Loup's house, luckily for him not the day they discovered that Verdier was No One.

"I noticed a car parked in a no-parking zone this morning. We usually have them removed immediately, but with everything going on these days . . ."

The agent made a gesture that covered a situation Frank knew all too well. He was aware of the overtime shifts they were all working, the constant coming and going of cars, the bursts of movement to check out the inevitable calls coming in. All kinds of lunatics turned up in cases like this. No One had already been reported seen in dozens of locations, and all of them had to be checked, one by one, without results. Yes, he was aware of the situation. He nodded for the agent to continue.

"I came out again a little later and I noticed that the car was still in the same place. I thought maybe it was a resident who had some business here. Sometimes they try just leaving their cars there. I went closer to check. I was about to call the traffic department when I thought I recognized the license number. I was at Beausoleil, at the house . . ."

"Yes I know," Frank interrupted brusquely. "Go on."

"Well, I went up to the car, and I noticed there was a red stain that looked like blood by the lock of the trunk. I called Morelli and we forced it open. And this is what we found."

Yeah, "this." And "this," as you call it, is difficult to think of as human.

The agent raised the lid of the trunk all the way so that they could see inside, lifting it with a pen to keep from leaving fingerprints.

"And then there's this . . ."

Frank knew what he would see. On the metal, words were traced in blood, the usual mocking phrase left as a commentary of his latest exploit.

I kill . . .

Frank bit the inside of his cheek until he tasted the semi-sweetness of blood. It was exactly what Jean-Loup had announced during the brief phone call the day before. There would be no more clues, only bodies. This poor human being in a car trunk was proof that the war was still on and that this man's battle had been lost. The car parked right there in front of headquarters was the latest travesty of all their efforts. Frank thought back to the voice of Jean-Loup, finally free and unmuffled, with the noise of the traffic in the background. He had made the call on a cheap cell phone with a card purchased in some discount electronics store. Then he had left it on a bench. The kid they had stopped had been passing by when he had seen it and picked it up. He had started making phone calls and they had gotten to him as he was telling his older brother what he had found. He hadn't seen the person who'd left the cell phone and there were no prints on it except those of the boy.

Frank looked at the body in the trunk. He couldn't even imagine the media's reaction this time. How could they express this new crime in words?

He didn't give a damn about Durand and Roncaille, or their jobs. All he wanted was to stay on the case until he caught No One.

"Do we know who the guy is?"

Morelli, standing on the other side of the car, came around and joined him. "No, Frank. He had no documents on him. Nothing at all."

"Well, we'll find out soon enough. He's young, judging from the skin. If the bastard followed his usual pattern, he'll be someone well known, about thirty or thirty-five and good-looking. A guy whose only crime was being in the wrong place at the wrong time. And with the wrong man, god damn him. Some VIP will be along soon to say he's disappeared and then we'll know who it is. Let's try to figure it out first."

An agent approached them.

"Sergeant."

"What is it, Bertrand?"

"Just an idea, sir. Probably wrong, but . . ."

"What is it?"

"His shoes, Sergeant."

"What about them?"

The agent shrugged his shoulders.

"They're sailing shoes, sir. I know, because I have a pair."

"There are tons of shoes like that, and I don't think . . ."

Frank, who was beginning to see where the agent was headed, interrupted Morelli. "Let him finish, Claude. Go on, Bertrand."

"Next to the logo, these shoes also have a cigarette brand name on them. It might be a sponsor. And since right now . . ."

Frank suddenly remembered the regatta. He put his hand on the agent's shoulder. ". . . Since the Grand Mistral, or whatever it's called, is on now, he might be involved in that. Nice work, Bertrand. Nice work."

Frank made the comment in a voice loud enough for the other agents to hear him. Bertrand returned to them as if he were the sailor on the *Santa Maria* who had cried "Land ahoy" to Christopher Columbus.

"Claude, it sounds plausible," Frank said, taking Morelli aside. "Let's look into it. We've played all our other cards already. There's nothing to lose."

The blue forensic van turned the corner of Rue Raymond and a policeman moved the barricades to let it in. Frank nodded toward the van.

"I don't think I need to tell you, but remind them to get the victim's fingerprints first. In that condition, it's the only way we can identify him. His dentist might not be available right away."

Morelli looked despondent. After that series of crimes, it was hard to take another one without giving up. Frank let him give the forensic people instructions and headed up to his office. Helena's face came to mind. He could hear her voice on the phone, frightened but so confident when she had told him she loved him. Another failure. The woman who was his salvation was only a few miles way. The world was just within reach, but there were two men blocking his way.

First, there was No One, whose homicidal fury meant that he would keep on killing innocent victims until he was stopped. Second, there was General Parker, who had to kill everything good that stood in his way until someone did the same to him.

And Frank wanted to be that someone.

He didn't have any other debts that he knew of. Ultimately, that's what being a policeman meant. The real reasons were locked in a safe that you only opened if you wanted to.

Durand, Roncaille, the Minister of State, the Prince, and even the President of the United States could think whatever they liked. Frank felt like a mere workman, far from the rooms where the plans were made. He was the one who stood before the walls to be demolished and rebuilt, in the midst of the cement dust and the smell of mortar. He was the one who had to see the mutilated, flayed bodies and smell the stench of gunpowder and blood. He didn't want to write immortal pages. All he wanted to do was write a report explaining how and why the man who had committed so many murders was locked in jail.

Then he would think about Parker. With all his psychotic delirium, No One had taught Frank something important. To be ferocious in the pursuit of his goals. And that is exactly how he would pursue the general. With a ferocity that would surprise even Parker, a master of it.

When he got back to the office, he sat down at the desk and tried to call Helena's cell phone. It was off. She was probably no longer alone and didn't want to risk the phone suddenly ringing and revealing that she had one. He imagined her in the house with her jailers, Nathan Parker and Ryan Mosse, and Stuart, her only consolation.

He sat thinking for a quarter of an hour, his hands behind his neck, staring up at the ceiling. Wherever he turned, he found a closed door. Still, he felt that the solution was right there, within reach. There was no doubt as to the effort they were making, or their capabilities. Every single one of the men involved in the investigation had a long résumé of experience. All they were missing was that tiny speck of luck, that crucial ingredient for success. And it was absurd that their relentless bad luck kept happening right there in Monaco, the city of casinos, where WINNING IS EASY is written on every slot machine. Frank wished he could stand in front of a machine and insert enough coins to spin the wheels until the name of the place where Jean-Loup Verdier was hiding would appear instead of a triple bar.

The door of the office opened suddenly and Morelli burst in, so excited that he forgot to knock.

"Frank, a stroke of luck."

Speak of the devil, and let's hope it really is the devil this time and not just a ghost..

"What is it?"

"A couple of people have come to file charges—well, not really charges, but to express their concern."

"Meaning?"

"A member of the team of *Try for the Sun,* a boat in the Grand Mistral, is missing."

Frank took his hands from behind his neck and waited for the rest. Morelli went on, knowing that the subject was of interest.

"He had a date with a girl last night, at the Fontvieille pier. When she drove by to pick him up, he wasn't there. The girl is a hardass type and this morning she went back to the sponsor's yacht where the crew is staying to give him a piece of her mind—he can't treat a woman like her that way, etc. . . . Faced with her female fury, a sailor went to call him in his cabin but it was empty. The bed was made, which means that it wasn't slept in."

"Couldn't he have made it before he went out this morning?"

"Maybe, but not likely. The sailors on the yacht get up early and someone would have seen him. And his clothes from last night were scattered all over the cabin. It was the official uniform of *Try for the Sun* that he had been wearing at last night's ceremonies, a sign that he had gone back to change . . ."

"It's not conclusive evidence, but we have to follow everything. Compare the prints of the corpse with those in the cabin. That's the surest way . . ."

"I already gave the orders. And I told an agent in the area to isolate the cabin. Someone from forensics is on his way to Fontvieille."

"What do you think?"

"The missing person meets No One's criteria. He's thirty-three, gook-looking, moderately well-known in the sailing world . . . an American, Hudson McCormack."

When he heard the name, Frank started so abruptly that Morelli was afraid he would fall off the chair.

"What's the name again?"

"Hudson McCormack. He's a lawyer from New York."

Frank stood up.

"I know, Claude. I know exactly who he is. That is, I don't know him at all, but he's the person I told you about, the one I wanted to have watched."

Morelli slipped a hand in his back pocket and pulled out the floppy disk Frank had given him the day before.

"The diskette's right here. I just didn't have time yesterday. I was going to take care of it today."

Frank and Morelli were thinking the same thing. They both knew what putting off that surveillance had meant. If there had been a man watching McCormack the day before, he *might* still be alive and they *might* have Jean-Loup behind bars.

There were just too many *if*s and *might*s in this business. Every one of those words was a stone that could build a tower of remorse.

"Okay, Claude. Check it out and let me know."

Morelli threw the now useless floppy disk on the desk and left the room. Frank was alone. He picked up the phone and called Cooper at home, in America, despite the time. When he answered, his friend sounded surprisingly awake.

"Hello."

"Coop, it's Frank. Did I wake you?"

"Wake me? I haven't gone to bed yet. Just got home and my jacket's still half on. What's up?"

"A mess, that's what. Something crazy. The man we're looking for, our serial killer, bumped off Hudson McCormack last night and skinned him like an animal."

There was a moment of silence. Cooper probably couldn't believe his ears.

"Christ, Frank. The world's gone nuts. We're in utter chaos here too. We've got constant terrorist alarms and we're on alert 24/7. You wouldn't believe it. Another brick fell yesterday. Osmond Larkin was killed in prison during recreation. There was a fight and he got caught in the middle."

"Nice."

"Yeah, nice. After all our work, we're left empty-handed."

"Everyone's got their problems, Coop. We're not much better off here. Another corpse this morning."

"How many so far?"

"It's incredible. Ten."

Cooper wasn't aware of the latest developments. He whistled as Frank updated him on the victims.

"Shit. Is he trying for the Guinness Book of Records?"

"Seems like it. He's got ten murders on his conscience and unfortunately they're on mine too."

"Hang in there, Frank. That's what I keep telling myself, if it's any help."

"There's nothing else I can do."

He hung up. Poor Cooper. Everyone was in trouble. Frank was puzzled for a moment. While waiting for official confirmation on Hudson McCormack and for Roncaille to come in hopping mad at any moment, he was at a loss as to what to do. Just about then, the solemn Roncaille was probably getting a reprimand that he would then be sure to pass on to his men.

Frank took the floppy disk from the desk, turned on the computer, and slipped it in. There were two JPEG files and he clicked one open. There was a photograph on the screen, shot in some restaurant, probably without McCormack's knowledge. He was in a crowded bar, one of New York's many long, narrow bars, full of mirrors to make it look larger. Hudson McCormack, the lawyer, was sitting at a table talking to someone whose back was to the camera and who was wearing a trench coat with the collar pulled up.

Then he opened the other file. It was an enlarged, grainer version of the same photo. Frank stared at the all-American guy with his hair cut stylishly short, wearing a blue suit that was perfect for someone who spent his time in court.

So that was what the faceless corpse in the trunk had looked like not long ago. He doubted that the poor guy had ever imagined, when he left for Monte Carlo for a regatta on the open sea, that his life would end in the trunk of a car. And that the last waterproof garment he would wear would be a body bag . . .

Frank stared at the photo. Suddenly, a crazy idea came to him, like the point of a drill coming through from the other side of a thin wall.

But it was possible.

He opened the contacts program on Nicolas's computer. His friend had not been a computer person, but he did have an electronic address book. Frank hoped that the number he wanted would be there. He typed the name into the search bar and the corresponding number leapt to the screen, along with the complete name and address.

Before he made the call, he buzzed Morelli.

"Claude, did you record Jean-Loup's phone call yesterday?"

"Of course."

"I need a copy. Right away."

"Already done. I'll bring it over."

"Thanks."

Good man, Morelli. Laconic but efficient. As he dialed the number, Frank wondered how things were going with Barbara, now that Morelli was no longer hanging around the station. Actually, Claude seemed anything but laconic with her, though just as efficient. His thoughts were interrupted by the voice that answered the phone.

"Hello?"

He was in luck. It was just the person he wanted.

"Hi, Guillaume. It's Frank Ottobre."

The boy was not the least bit surprised by the call. He responded as if they had just spoken ten minutes earlier.

"Hey, Mr. FBI. What's up?"

"It was good doing business with you. I think I need your services again."

"I accept. Come over any time."

"I'm on my way."

Frank hung up and sat staring at the photo on the computer before closing the file and ejecting the disk. Had anyone else been in the room, he would have noticed that as Frank looked at the screen, his expression was that of a seasoned gambler watching the ball spin on a roulette wheel.

55

Frank stopped his Mégane in front of the gate at the road that led to Helena's house. He got out of the car, surprised to see the gate half open. His heart was racing at the thought of seeing the woman he loved. But he would also see General Nathan Parker, and that made him clench his fists. He forced himself to calm down before going any further. Rage is a bad counselor, and the last thing he needed was bad advice.

Frank, on the other hand, could give excellent advice. His meeting with Guillaume that morning had been extremely productive. The day before, he had asked the young man to check something out for him. When he had met Guillaume in the wing of his house where he worked, the room was a complete mess. The boy was working on a job and couldn't free up his machine right away. He had needed that whole evening and night to do what Frank had asked of him. Guillaume had been forced to improvise, but he had landed on his feet. Which had put Frank Ottobre, FBI Special Agent, back on his feet as well.

When Guillaume had showed him the results of his research, Frank was stunned to see how right his complex hypothesis had been. It had seemed like an unrealistic hunch, a half-baked conjecture. He himself had thought it was crazy. But as it turned out . . .

He'd wanted to give the boy a hug. Instead, he told himself that he had to stop calling him a boy, since that word described only his chronological age. Guillaume was a man. Who had balls.

He had finally realized it when he was leaving the house and Guillaume walked him silently to the gate. They had crossed the garden together, each deep in his own thoughts. Frank had already opened the gate and was about to get in his car, but the expression on Guillaume's face had stopped him.

"What is it?"

"I don't know, Frank. A strange feeling. Like a blindfold has just been taken off."

"What do you mean?" Frank knew what he meant, but he asked the question anyway.

"All of this. It's like suddenly discovering that there's another world, something beyond. A world where things don't only happen to others, but to *us*. People aren't just killed on TV but on the sidewalks that you're walking down . . .

Frank had listened to his epiphany in silence. He knew where it was going.

"Frank, I want to ask you something and I want you to answer honestly. I don't need the details. Just clear something up for me. What I did for you the other time, and today, will that help you catch the guy who killed Nicolas?"

Frank looked at him and smiled. "Sooner or later, when this is all over, you and I will have a talk. I don't know when that will be, but when we talk I'll explain *exactly* how important you've been in all this, especially for me."

Guillaume had nodded and moved to one side. He had pushed the button to open the gate and waved uncertainly as the Mégane pulled away.

You were great, Guillaume.

With that thought in mind. Frank walked through the gate and into Helena's yard. He was taken aback by what he saw. All the windows on the upper floor and all the French doors overlooking the garden were open. Inside, a woman with a blue apron was plugging something into the wall. She moved out of his line of vision but he could hear a vacuum cleaner. He saw her approach the French doors, moving the appliance back and forth. On the upper floor, in Helena's room, another woman in a similar apron came out on the balcony holding a kilim rug. She hung it over the railing and started hitting it with a bamboo carpet beater.

Frank went up to the house. He wasn't happy. A man walked out the front door. He was elderly and wearing an elegant, light-colored suit. His Panama hat was in perfect keeping with the house. The man saw him and came over. Despite his youthful air, Frank could tell by looking at his hands that he had to be pushing seventy.

"Hello, may I help you?"

"Good morning. I'm Frank Ottobre, a friend of the Parkers, the people who live here . . ."

The man smiled, showing off a row of white teeth that must have cost him a fortune. "Ah, another American. Nice to meet you." He held out a firm hand covered with spots. It was more than his age, Frank thought. There was probably something wrong with his liver. "The name's Tavernier, André Tavernier. I'm the owner of this little place." He waved toward the villa with nonchalance. "And I'm afraid your friends have left, young man."

"Left?"

He seemed genuinely sorry to have to corroborate the bad news.

"That's right. Left. I negotiated their lease through an agency, though I usually do it in person. This morning, I came with the cleaning ladies to meet my tenants and I found them in the courtyard with their suitcases ready, waiting for a taxi. The general—you know who I mean—told me that something urgent had come up and they had to leave immediately. A shame, because they had already paid another month's rent. To be fair, I said I would reimburse them for the amount he overpaid, but he wouldn't hear of it. Fine man."

I could tell you exactly how fine he is, you mummified ladies' man.

Frank felt like telling Monsieur Tavernier to be more careful in the future. If that was his skill in judging people, he ought to collect all his rent in advance, and in cash. But he had more pressing business than to inform the old man about the real personality of his tenant.

"Do you know where they were headed?"

Monsieur Tavernier had a sudden coughing fit, with enough phlegm to indicate a few cigarettes too many. Frank had to wait for him to pull a perfectly clean handkerchief from his pocket and wipe his mouth before he continued.

"They were going to Nice. To the airport, I think. They had a direct flight back to the States."

"Shit." The word escaped Frank before he could stop himself. "Pardon me, Monsieur Tavernier."

"Don't worry about it. It can be liberating to let yourself go."

"You don't happen to know what time their flight was leaving?"

"No, I'm sorry. Can't help you there."

Frank's expression was not one of joy and Monsieur Tavernier, a man of the world, noticed. "Cherchez la femme, eh, young man?"

"Excuse me?"

"I understand your dilemma. The woman, I mean. You're thinking of her, if I'm not mistaken? If I had been expecting to meet a woman like that and found an empty house instead, I'd be disappointed too. I could write several books about the adventures that went on in this house when I was a young man, back in the day."

Frank was extremely agitated. All he wanted to do was leave Monsieur Tavernier to his Don Juan memories and race to the Nice airport. The man grasped his arm and Frank would gladly have broken it. He didn't like people to touch him under normal circumstances, never mind at a moment like this when he could feel the passing of each second like a bell pealing in his head.

Tavernier escaped Frank's wrath only through what he was saying. "I lived a good life, that's for sure. Completely different from my brother, who lived in the house next door, over there. You can see the roof through the cypresses."

He took the attitude of someone about to tell a secret that only he knew, which was hard to believe. "It's the home of that crazy sister-in-law of mine who left the house to a young man just because he saved her dog. A mutt not even worth the tree he peed on, know what I mean? I don't know if you heard about that crazy business. And you know who the young man turned out to be?"

Frank knew exactly who he was, in the greatest detail. And he had no desire to hear it again. Unaware of the risk he was taking, Tavernier grabbed Frank's arm once more.

"He's a murderer, a serial killer, the one who killed all those people in Monte Carlo and skinned them like rabbits. Just think that my sister-in-law left a house of that value to a . . ."

And you rented yours to a real humanitarian. If there was a Nobel Prize for stupidity, this old fart would win.

Oblivious to what Frank was thinking, Tavernier let out a deep sigh. A wave of memories was coming.

"That woman really pulled the wool over my brother's eyes. Not that she wasn't beautiful. She was attractive as an *en plein* in roulette, if you'll allow me the comparison, but just as dangerous. She made a man want to play again and again, if you know what I mean. We built these houses together, in the mid-sixties. Twin houses standing side by side, but that's where it ended. I was over here and they were over there. We led separate lives. I considered my brother a prisoner of his wife's every desire, every little whim. And boy did she have them, *bon Dieu*. To think that she even . . ."

Frank wondered why he was still listening to the boasts of an old playboy who could no longer get it up, rather than jumping into his car to get to Nice. For some strange reason, Frank could feel that the man was about to say something of significance. And that was exactly what happened. In the middle of his pointless rambling, he said something so important that it threw Frank into a state of both excitement and deep dejection, as he imagined a jet plane taking off with Helena's sad face at the window, watching France disappear below her.

He closed his eyes. He had grown so pale that the old gentleman was concerned.

"Is something wrong? Don't you feel well?"

Frank looked at him. "No, I'm fine. Really."

Tavernier expressed his doubt with an appropriately worried look. Frank flashed him a grin that the man misunderstood. The old idiot didn't realize that he had just revealed where Jean-Loup Verdier was hiding.

"Thank you, Monsieur Tavernier. Good-bye."

"Good luck, young man. I hope you find her . . . but if you don't, remember, the world is full of women."

Frank nodded vaguely as he walked away. He was at the gate when Tavernier called out to him. "Young man?"

Frank turned back, wishing he could tell him to fuck off. He was held back by a sense of gratitude for what the old man had unwittingly shown him. "What is it, Monsieur Tavernier?"

The old man grinned. "If you should ever be in need of a lovely house on the coast"—he waved with a gesture of triumph at the house behind him—"this is the place!"

Frank went through the gate without answering. He found himself standing next to his car, his head hanging down, studying his shoes against the gravel. He had to make a choice, and fast. Finally, he decided to do what was right. But there was no reason why he shouldn't try, or at least make one attempt, to do both. He pulled out his cell phone and called the Nice Police. When an agent answered, he said his name and asked for Inspector Froben. Moments later, he was connected.

"Hi, Frank. How are you?"

"Could be better. And you?"

"Same here. What's up?"

"Claude, I need a favor, a huge one."

"Whatever I can do."

"At the Nice Airport, there should be some people departing. General Nathan Parker, his daughter Helena, and his grandson, Stuart. There's probably someone else with them, a certain Captain Ryan Mosse."

"*That* Ryan Mosse?"

"That's right. You have to stop them. I don't know how; I don't know what excuse you can use, but you have to keep them from taking off until I get there. They're transporting the body of one of No One's first victims, Arianna Parker. Maybe that could be the excuse. Some bureaucratic red tape or something. It's a question of life or death. For me, anyway. Can you manage it?"

"For you, anything."

"Thanks, man, you're the best. Talk to you in a bit."

Frank then dialed another number, Sûreté headquarters. He asked to speak to Roncaille and they put him on immediately.

"Chief? Frank Ottobre."

Roncaille, who had probably been through a hellish two days, came down on him like a tornado. "Frank, where the fuck are you?" Foul language in the mouth of the chief of police was not an everyday occurrence. It meant the storm of the century. "All hell breaks loose here and you disappear? We put you in charge of the case and instead of getting any results, we have more dead bodies on the street than birds in the trees. Before long there won't be anyone working at Sûreté at all! I'll be lucky to get a job as a night guard."

"Calm down, Chief. If you haven't lost your job yet, I don't think you will. It's all over."

"What does that mean, it's all over?"

"I mean it's all over. I know where Jean-Loup Verdier is hiding."

There was silence on the other end. A pause, for reflection. Frank could almost hear Roncaille doubting him. To be or not to be, to believe or not to believe . . .

"Are you sure?"

"Ninety-nine percent."

"That's not enough. I want a hundred."

"There is no such thing as a hundred percent. Ninety-nine seems more than adequate to me."

"All right, where is he?"

"First I want something in exchange."

"Don't push it, Frank."

"Chief, maybe I should clarify the situation. I don't give a damn about my career. You're the one worried about yours. If you say no to what I'm asking, I'll end this call right now and I'll be on the first plane out of Nice. And to be perfectly clear, you and your friend Durand can go screw yourselves for all I care. Have I made myself understood?"

Silence. An endless pause. Then Roncaille's voice again, full of suppressed rage. "What is it you want?"

"I want your word of honor that Inspector Nicolas Hulot will be considered fallen in the line of duty, and that his widow will get the pension that a hero's wife deserves."

Third pause. The most important one. To see who had more balls. When Roncaille answered, Frank knew that he did.

"Okay. Request granted. My word of honor. Now it's your turn."

"Get the men out and tell Sergeant Morelli to call me on my cell. And start shining up your uniform for the press conference."

"Address?" And Frank finally said what Roncaille had paid to hear.

"Beausoleil."

"Beausoleil?"

"That's right. That bastard Jean-Loup Verdier has been in his house this whole time."

56

Pierrot looked embarrassed as he took the plastic cup of Coke from Barbara and started drinking.

"Want some more?"

Pierrot shook his head. He handed her back the empty cup and turned, red-faced, to the table where he was sorting through a pile of CDs.

He liked Barbara, but at the same time she made him feel shy. The boy had a crush on her, which explained his secret looks, long silences, and quick escapes as soon as she appeared. He turned purple every time she spoke to him. The girl had noticed what was going on some time ago. It was puppy love—if that term could be used with someone like Pierrot—and it deserved respect like all feelings. She knew how deeply the strange boy, who seemed so afraid of the world, could love. Such candor and sincerity could be found only in children and dogs. The description was somewhat reductive, but his love was the expression of a complete, honest affection that simply existed, without needing to be returned.

Once she had found a daisy on her mixer. When she had realized that he was the anonymous giver of that simple wildflower, she was overwhelmed with tenderness.

"Do you want another sandwich?" she asked, from behind Pierrot's back.

Again the boy shook his head without turning around. It was lunchtime and they had had a tray of sandwiches sent up from

Stars'N'Bars. Aside from the voices and the music coming from the microphones, the radio station had become a realm of silence since the revelation about Jean-Loup. Everyone wandered around like shadows. The station was still being assaulted by reporters like the Alamo by the Mexican army. Every employee was followed, chased, and spied on. They all had microphones shoved in their faces, cameras pointed at them, and reporters waiting for them at their homes. And indeed, what had happened more than justified the stubbornness of the mass media.

Jean-Loup Verdier, the star of Radio Monte Carlo, had turned out to be a psychopath and a serial killer who was still at large. His presence fluttered like a ghost through the Principality of Monaco. Thanks to the morbid curiosity of the public and the media onslaught, the number of listeners had practically doubled the day after the identity of the serial killer was revealed.

Robert Bikjalo, the Robert Bikjalo of old, would have done triple somersaults at those ratings. Now, he went about his work like a robot, smoked like a chimney, and spoke in monosyllables. As did everyone else, actually. Raquel sounded as mechanical as an answering machine when she took phone calls. Barbara could not stop to think for a moment without feeling like she would burst into tears. Even the owner of the station only called in when absolutely necessary.

And that had been the state of things when they had heard the news of Laurent's tragic death two days earlier, during a robbery. It had been the final blow for everyone, making people who were already ghosts become completely invisible.

But Pierrot was hit the hardest. He retreated into a worrisome silence and answered questions with only a nod or a shake of his head. While he was at the station, he did his job without seeming to be present. He holed himself up in the archive for hours and Barbara went down more than once to see if he was all right. At home, he spent all his time listening to music with his headphones on, completely isolated. He no longer smiled. And he no longer turned on the radio.

His mother was desperate over the change in his behavior. For Pierrot, spending time at Radio Monte Carlo, feeling that he was part of something, earning a little money (his mother never failed to point out to him how important his earnings were to their finances, which filled him with pride), was his door to the world.

His friendship with and adoration of Jean-Loup had opened that door wide. Now it was slowly closing and his mother was afraid that if it shut completely, no one would be able to enter again. Ever.

It was impossible to know what he was thinking. And if they had been able to read his thoughts, they would have been astonished by what was going through his mind. Everyone thought that he had sunken into sorrow and silence because he had discovered that his friend was really a *bad man,* as he said—the man who called the radio station with the voice of devil. Perhaps his simple soul had reacted the way it did because he had been *forced* to realize that he had placed his trust in someone who was undeserving.

But that was not the case. Pierrot's faith and friendship for Jean-Loup had not been diminished in the least by recent events and the revelations about his idol. He knew him well. He had been in his home and they had eaten crêpes with Nutella together and Jean-Loup had even given him a glass of delicious Italian wine called Moscato. It was sweet and cool and had made his head spin a little. They had listened to music and Jean-Loup had even lent him some records, the black ones, the valuable ones, so that he could listen to them at home. He had burned his favorite CDs for him, like Jefferson Airplane and Jeff Beck with the guitar on the bridge, and the last two by Nirvana.

He had never, in all the time they had spent together, ever heard Jean-Loup speak with the voice of the devil. On the contrary . . . Jean-Loup had *always* told him that they were friends for life, and he had *always* shown that to be the truth. So, if Jean-Loup always told him the truth, that meant only one thing: the others were lying.

Everyone kept asking what was wrong and trying to make him talk. He didn't want to tell anyone, not even his mother, that the main reason he was sad was because, since everything had happened, he hadn't been able to see Jean-Loup. And he didn't know how to help his friend. Maybe Jean-Loup was hiding somewhere, hungry and thirsty, and there was no one to bring him anything, not even bread and Nutella.

Pierrot knew that the policemen were looking for him and that if they caught him they would put him in jail. He didn't really know what jail was. He only knew that it was where they put people who did bad things and didn't let them out. And if they didn't let the people who were inside go out, that meant that people outside couldn't go in and he would never see Jean-Loup again.

Maybe policemen could go in and see the people in jail. He used to be a policeman, an *honorable* policeman. The inspector had told him so, the one with the nice face whom he had never seen again and who someone said was dead. But now, after the mess he had made, maybe he was no longer an *honorable* policeman and maybe he would have to stay outside the jail like everyone else, without being able to see Jean-Loup.

Pierrot turned his head and saw Barbara walking toward the director's booth. He looked at her dark red hair that swayed as she walked, as if it were dancing on her black dress. He liked Barbara. Not the way he liked Jean-Loup. When his friend spoke to him or put a hand on his shoulder, it wasn't like that warmth that rose from the pit of his stomach as if he had drunk a cup of hot tea in one gulp. With Barbara it was different; he didn't know why, but he loved her. One day, he had put a flower on her mixer to tell her.

He had picked a daisy outside and put it on the machine when no one was looking. He had even hoped at one point that she and Jean-Loup would get married so that he could see both of them when he went to visit his friend.

Pierrot picked up the pile of CDs and headed toward the door. Raquel clicked the lock open as she usually did when she saw his hands were full. Pierrot went out onto the landing and pressed the elevator button with his nose. He had never showed anyone his way of calling the elevator. They would laugh at him if they saw it, but since his nose was there in the middle of his face doing nothing, it might as well be useful when he had both hands full.

He pushed the sliding door of the elevator open with his elbow and closed it the same way. Inside, he couldn't use his nose because the buttons were different. He was forced to juggle things, pressing the CDs against his chin so that he could reach the button with one of his fingers.

The elevator started to descend. Pierrot's mind descended as well, following a logic that was linear in its own way. He had reached a definite conclusion. If Jean-Loup couldn't come to him, then he would go to Jean-Loup.

He had been to visit his friend many times, and Jean-Loup had told him that he kept an extra key to the house in a secret place and from then on, only the two of them would know about it. He had told him that the key was stuck with *silicone* underneath the mailbox inside the gate. Pierrot didn't understand the word silicone, but he knew what a mailbox was. He and his mother had one at their house in Menton, and their house wasn't as nice as Jean-Loup's. He would recognize it when he saw it.

Downstairs, in the *room,* he had his Invicta backpack that Jean-Loup had given him. Inside it was some bread and a jar of Nutella that he had taken that morning from the kitchen shelf. He didn't have any Moscato at home, but he had taken a can of Coke and a can of Schweppes and thought that would be okay. If his friend was hiding somewhere at home, he would certainly hear him call and would come out. Where else could he be? They were the only ones who knew about the secret key.

They could sit together and eat chocolate and drink Coke and this time *he* would say things to make Jean-Loup laugh, even if he couldn't take him to Nice to see the puppies in the pet store window.

And if Jean-Loup wasn't there, he would take care of his records, the black vinyl ones. He would clean them, make sure that the covers didn't get damp, line them up in the right direction to keep them from getting warped. If he didn't, they would all be ruined when he came home. He had to take care of his friend's things. Otherwise what kind of friend was he?

When the elevator reached the bottom floor, Pierrot was smiling.

Besson, a mechanic for the motorboat showroom on the floor below the radio station, was waiting for the elevator and opened the door. He saw Pierrot inside, his tousled hair sticking up over the pile of CDs. Seeing his smile, he smiled too.

"Hi there, Pierrot. You look like the busiest person in Monte Carlo. I'd ask for a raise if I were you."

The boy did not have the slightest idea of how to ask for a raise. And anyway, that was the last thing that interested him right now.

"Yes, I will tomorrow," he answered evasively.

Before stepping into the elevator, Besson opened the door on the left that led down to the archives. "Watch your step," he said, as he turned on the light.

Pierrot gave one of his standard nods and started going down. When he reached the archive door that he had left open, he pushed it with one foot. He leaned the CDs on the table near the wall, in front of rows of shelves full of records and CDs. For the first time since he had started working for Radio Monte Carlo, he didn't put away the CDs he had brought down. Instead, he took his backpack and put it on his shoulders the easy way, like his friend Jean-Loup had taught him, then turned off the light and locked the door as he did every evening before he went home. Except that now he was not going home. He climbed back up the steps and found himself in the lobby, the large hallway that ended at the glass doors. Beyond those doors lay the port, the city, and the world. And hidden there somewhere was the friend who needed him.

Pierrot did something he had never done before in all his life. He pushed open the door, took a step, and went out to face the world by himself.

57

Frank waited for Morelli in his Mégane at the construction site outside Jean-Loup Verdier's house. It was hot out and he kept the engine running so that the air conditioner would work. He kept glancing at his watch as he waited for Morelli and Roncaille's men.

His head was full of images of Nathan Parker and his group at the Nice Airport. The general was probably sitting impatiently with Helena and Stuart next to him while Ryan Mosse checked them in. He could see the massive figure of Froben, or someone like him, telling the old general that there was some difficulty and for the moment he would not be able to leave. Frank couldn't imagine what Froben would invent, but he could easily envision the old man's reaction. He wouldn't want to be in the inspector's shoes.

The absurdity of the cliché made him smile. *Actually, that was exactly what he wanted.* Just then, *he* wanted to be at the Nice Airport, doing in person what he had asked of Froben. He wanted to take Nathan Parker aside and finally tell him what he had always wanted to say. *He was dying to.* No inventing, just clearing a few things up.

Instead, he was sitting there, tasting each passing moment like salt on his tongue, checking his watch every thirty seconds as if thirty minutes had passed.

He forced himself to put those thoughts out of his mind. He focused on Roncaille instead. That was something else, another problem. The chief of police had put his men in motion with reasonable doubts. Frank had been categorical on the phone, but he had expressed a certainty that he didn't really possess. He couldn't admit to himself that he was bluffing, but he knew that he had placed a risky bet. Any bookie would have given him thirty to one without thinking twice. When he had claimed to know No One's hiding place, it wasn't a certainty but a reasonable supposition. The 99 percent he had boasted of to the chief of police was in fact a considerably lower figure. If his theory was off, there would be no serious consequences, just another dead end. Nothing could change the position he was already in. No One was on the lam and that's how things would stay. Except that Frank Ottobre's prestige would plummet in disgrace. Roncaille and Durand would have a weapon against him that he himself had loaded, and they could tell any representative of the U.S. government how unreliable their FBI agent was, despite his undeniable success at identifying the serial killer. And his public defense of Inspector Nicolas Hulot might even backfire. He could already hear Durand's suave, nonchalant voice telling Dwight Durham that, although Frank Ottobre had revealed the identity of the killer, it wasn't really he who had made the discovery.

If his guess was right, however, it would all end in glory. He could rush to the Nice Airport and take care of his personal business in the glow of victory. Not that he was particularly interested in glory, but he would welcome anything at all that would help him settle his personal accounts with Nathan Parker.

Finally, he saw the first police car round the curve. This time, as Frank had instructed Morelli, there were no sirens. He noticed that the crisis unit was much larger than the first time they had tried to catch Jean-Loup. There were six cars full of men as well as the usual blue vans with dark windows. When the rear doors opened, sixteen men got out instead of twelve. There were surely others waiting at the end of the road to prevent any possible escape through the yard at the front of the house.

A car stopped, two policemen got out, and then it raced to the roadblock at the top of the road, near the highway. Things at the bottom were probably similar. Frank smiled in spite of himself. Roncaille didn't want to take any chances. Jean-Loup's easy disposal of the three policemen on guard had finally opened his eyes to the real danger at stake.

Two Menton police cars drove up almost simultaneously, each holding seven heavily armed agents, under the command of Inspector Roberts. The reason they were there was obvious: to ensure that there was a constant collaboration of the Sûreté Publique of Monte Carlo with the French police.

Frank got out of his car. As the men awaited orders, Roberts and Morelli walked over to him.

"What's this all about, Frank? I hope you'll let me know sooner or later. Roncaille told us to rush out here in combat gear but he didn't give us any details. He was pretty pissed off . . ."

Frank interrupted with a wave of his hand. He pointed to the roof of the house, half-hidden by the vegetation and cypress trees rising above the mass of bushes. He skipped the preliminaries.

"He's here, Claude. Unless I've made a huge mistake, there's a ninety-nine percent chance that Jean-Loup Verdier has been hiding in his own house all along." Frank realized that he had just given Morelli and the men the same odds that he had waved under Roncaille's nose. He decided not to correct himself.

Morelli scratched his chin with the forefinger of his left hand, as he often did when he was puzzled. And this time he was definitely confused.

"Where in hell could he be? We turned the house upside down. There isn't a crevice we didn't examine."

"Tell the men to come closer."

If Morelli was surprised, he said nothing. Roberts, with his natural slouch, waited, unflustered, for something to happen. When all the men were gathered in a semicircle around him,

Frank enunciated each word carefully. He spoke French with almost no foreign accent, but he didn't trust himself to explain things in a language that was not his own. He looked like a basketball coach instructing his players during a time-out.

"Okay everyone, listen carefully. I had a conversation with the owner of the other house over there, the twin to this one. They were built by two brothers, a few yards from each other at the same time, in the mid-sixties. The brother who lived here"—and he pointed toward the roof behind him—"in the house that would later belong to Jean-Loup Verdier, was married to a woman who was difficult, to put it mildly. A total pain in the ass, in other words. The Cuban missile crisis of 1961 and the threat of nuclear war completely terrified her, so she forced her husband to build a bomb shelter under the house. Right here, beneath us."

Frank pointed to the cement where they were standing. Morelli instinctively followed Frank's gesture and stared at the ground. He raised his head immediately when he realized what he was doing.

"But we even examined the plans of both houses. Neither of them showed any bomb shelters."

"I can't explain that. Maybe they didn't have permits and it doesn't show up in the land register. If they were building two houses at the same time, with bulldozers digging and trucks coming and going, an underground shelter would be easy to construct without anyone noticing."

Roberts backed Frank up. "If the shelter was built and does in fact exist, it probably happened the way Frank says. There was a construction boom back then and an awful lot of rules were stretched."

Frank went on telling them what he knew. "Tavernier, the owner of the other house, told me that the entrance to the shelter is located in an empty room behind a wall covered with shelves."

A commando raised his hand. He was one of the men who had

assaulted the house when the bodies of the three policemen had been discovered, and he had searched it from top to bottom.

"There's some kind of laundry room in the basement to the right of the garage. It gets light from a window that looks out on the courtyard. I think there are some shelves on one of the walls."

"Good," said Frank. "I don't think the problem is finding the shelter as much as opening it and forcing whoever's inside to come out. Let me ask a crazy question. Does anyone here know anything about bomb shelters? I mean, more than they show in the movies?"

There was a moment of silence and then Lieutenant Gavin, the crisis unit commander, raised his hand. "I know a little something, not that much."

"That's a start. More than I know. How do we get the guy out of there, if he's inside?" As he spoke, Frank mentally crossed his fingers in hope.

Roberts lit another cigarette and took a long draw. Perhaps inspired by the smoke, he came up with a different alternative. "He's got to be able to breathe down there, right? If we find the air holes, we can get him out with tear gas."

"I don't think that's feasible." Gavin shook his head. "We can try, but if things are the way Frank said and he has done the maintenance, it won't work. If he's kept up with the latest technology, forget it. Modern bomb shelters have an air purification system that uses filters with normal or activated carbon acting as absorbers. Activated carbons are used as filtering agents in gas masks and high-risk ventilation systems, like in nuclear power plants. They're used in tanks and military planes too. They can resist hydrocyanic acid, chloropicrin, arsine, and phosphine. So tear gas wouldn't do anything."

Frank looked at Lieutenant Gavin with greater respect. If this was something he knew only a little about, what would he say if he was an expert? Frank raised his arms. "Okay, we're here to solve a problem. Sometimes you solve problems by making stupid suggestions. Here's mine. Lieutenant, what's the chance that we could open the door with explosives?"

"Well . . . it's possible," Gavin said, shrugging with the apologetic expression of someone forced to keep giving bad news. "I'm not an expert, mind you, but logically a shelter like that is built to resist an atomic bomb. You'd need to make a lot of noise to get it open. But, and here's the good side, keep in mind that this shelter is over thirty years old so it's not as efficient as the ones they build now. If there's no alternative, that might be the best idea."

"If we opt for explosives, how long would it take?" This time, the lieutenant's scowl led to a positive conclusion.

"Not long. We've got an explosives expert, Brigadier Gachot. If he and his team get to work immediately, all we need is the time it takes to get some C4 or something like that over here."

"Call the unit and get Gachot on it. Explain the situation and tell him where we are. I want him here in fifteen minutes at the latest."

The commando raced off without so much as the "Yes, Sir" that Frank would have expected from him. Frank looked at each of the men standing before him.

"Any other ideas?" He waited for an answer that didn't come and then decided to take the bull by the horns. "Okay, here's how it's going to be. If our man is in there, he can't escape. We can hypothesize all we want. First, let's find this damn shelter and then we'll decide what to do. From here on in, we improvise. Let's move."

The shift from conjecture to action put the crisis unit on much more familiar ground. They removed the seals from the gates and rushed down the ramp leading to the garage. Within seconds they had occupied the house, using a plan that was part of their training. They were silent, fast, and dangerous.

At first, Frank had considered their presence there a ridiculous and excessive precaution. But after ten deaths, he was forced to realize that they were an absolute necessity.

The soldier who had described the entrance to the bunker led the way through the courtyard. He raised the door and went into the empty garage. There was a mountain bike hanging on a rack on the right wall and in the corner, a ski rack for Jean-Loup's car. Next to it was a pair of carving skis, their rackets tied together with bungee cords. There were no snide remarks about the owner's interest in sports. They also knew that there was a well-equipped gym upstairs. In light of what had happened, they realized that all that physical activity had not just been for fun.

At the back of the garage, they went down a corridor that turned to the right. A door in front of them opened onto a small bathroom. They walked single file, led by a commando aiming an M-16 rifle ahead of him. Frank, Gavin, and Sergeant Morelli took out their pistols and walked with them pointed up. Roberts was at the end of the line, moving with an easy stride, soft as a cat. He felt no need to take out his gun. He simply unbuttoned his jacket so that it would be ready if needed.

They reached the laundry room, probably the cleaning lady's area. There was a washing machine, dryer, ironing board, and iron. To the left, a huge white cupboard took up the entire wall. In the corner next to the doorway, a stairway led down from upstairs. Another commando was coming down just at that moment.

There was a wooden bookshelf against the wall opposite the doorway. "That must be it," whispered the agent, pointing with his rifle.

Frank nodded in silence and put away his gun. He went over to the bookcase and examined it from the right while Morelli did the same on the left. Gavin and his two men stood in front of them, their weapons aimed as if danger could emerge from behind it at any second. Even Roberts pulled out his large Beretta that looked even bigger and more menacing in his thin hands.

Frank grabbed hold of one of the shelves and tried to push it to one side. Nothing happened. He ran his hands along the wood on the side and found nothing. He raised his head and looked at the top of the shelves a couple of feet above him. He glanced around and then pulled over a metal chair with a Formica seat. He climbed onto it to see the upper shelf. He immediately noticed that there wasn't a speck of dust. Then, in the corner by the wall, in a groove in the wood, he could see a tiny metal lever that seemed to come from a hinge. The mechanism was well oiled and there was no trace of rust. It seemed to be in perfect working order.

"Found it," said Frank. Morelli turned and saw him carefully examining something on the top shelf that he couldn't see. "Claude, do you see any hinges from where you are?"

"No, if there are any, they're hidden inside."

Frank looked down on the ground. There were no marks on the stone tiles. The door probably opened forward. If it went sideways and the shelves moved, he would fall off the chair. He thought of Nicolas Hulot and all of No One's other victims and decided that it was a small risk compared with what they had suffered. He turned to the men standing in front of the bookcase with their guns pointed.

"Keep your eyes open. Here I go."

The three men got into position, their legs spread apart and slightly bent, holding their guns with both hands pointed at the bookcase. Frank pushed the lever all the way. They heard a sharp click and the bookcase opened outward like a door, silently rotating on well-oiled hinges.

A heavy metal door, mounted in bare cement, appeared before their eyes. There were no visible hinges. The closure was so perfect that the separation between the door and the frame was almost undetectable. There was a wheel on the left to open the door, similar to those in submarine hatches. They stood in silence, spellbound by that dark metal wall. Each man tried in his own way to imagine what or *who* was behind it.

Frank stepped off the chair and went to the door. He tried grabbing and pulling the wheel, which was also a handle, and met with the resistance he expected. Turning the wheel in one direction and the other, he realized it was pointless to keep trying.

"Doesn't work. It must be locked from the inside."

As they all finally lowered their weapons and came up to the door, Frank mused over their absurd situation and now visualized not one but two hands with fingers crossed. He stared at the metal as if trying to melt it with his eyes.

You're in there, aren't you? I know *you are. You're in there with your eyes glued to this armored door wondering how we'll get you out. What's ridiculous is that we're wondering the exact same thing. And the most ridiculous part is that we'll have to do backward somersaults, and maybe some of us will lose our lives in order to drag you out of this prison and put you in another one just like it.*

Suddenly, Frank could see Jean-Loup's face in his mind and he remembered the good impression the young man had made on him from the very beginning. He could see his traumatized face at the station, bent over the table sobbing after one of the phone calls. He could hear the echo of his weeping, and in his memory it sounded like the mocking of an evil spirit. He remembered the friendly way he had spoken to Jean-Loup to convince him not to stop the broadcast, not knowing that he was persuading him to continue his chain of killing.

Through the closed door, he thought he could get a whiff of Jean-Loup's cologne that he had smelled so many times when standing near him, a light fresh scent of lemon and bergamot. He thought that, perhaps, if he placed his ear to the metal, he might hear Jean-Loup's natural voice, warm and deep. It would seep through the thickness of the metal and again whisper the words that were branded on their brains.

I kill . . .

Frank felt a terrible rage rise up inside him, fed by a sense of deep frustration for all the victims of that man, Jean-Loup, No One, or whoever he was. It was such a deep anger that he felt he could just grab hold of the metal door with his bare hands, crush it like aluminum foil, and seize the neck of the man standing behind it.

A series of thuds brought him back to the reality that his fury had caused him momentarily to forget. Lieutenant Gavin was hitting the metal door at various points, listening to the different echoes. Then he turned to them with the expression he used for unpleasant situations.

"Gentlemen, I hope my colleague who is coming with the explosives will prove me wrong. I don't like to be the bearer of bad news all the time, but first I'd try talking to the person inside, if he's in there. We've got to convince him that he's been discovered and that there's no hope. I'm afraid that if he doesn't decide to open up of his own accord, it'll be fairly complicated to get him out. If we want to use explosives to get through these doors, we'd need enough to blow up a half a mountain."

ELEVENTH CARNIVAL

The man is safe in his secret hiding place, in that metal and cement box that someone dug deep under the ground long ago in fear of something that never happened. Ever since he discovered its existence, almost by accident, ever since he went inside for the first time and realized what it was and what it was for, he has kept his refuge in perfect working condition. The storeroom is full of canned food and mineral water. There is a simple but efficient waste recycling system that would allow him to filter and drink his own urine, if necessary. The air is purified by chemical filters and reactants, and there is no need for contact with the outside world. His food and water supply will last for over a year.

He goes out only occasionally, in darkness, with the sole purpose of breathing the pure air and smelling the perfume of summer, only slightly contaminated by the odor of the night, his natural habitat. The pungent smell of a rosemary bush in the garden reminds him for no particular reason of the scent of lavender. They are so different, but it triggers the memory in his mind, like a record silently chosen from the others and slipped into place by the mechanical arm of a jukebox. The combination of the night and the aroma produce a composite image, an olfactory sensation as well as one of sound and light.

He moves in total darkness in that house that he knows like the back of his hand, as silent as only he can be. Sometimes he goes out onto the terrace and, leaning against the wall, hidden in the shadow of the house, he raises his head to observe the stars.

He makes no effort to read the future, and is simply happy to admire the luminous twinkling in that fragment of the present. He doesn't ask what will happen to him, or to them. It is not thoughtlessness or indifference, only awareness.

He doesn't blame himself for making a mistake; he was sure that he would make one sooner or later. It is the law of chance applied to the fleeting life of a human being, and someone had taught him long ago that you pay for your mistakes. He had been *forced* to learn it the hard way.

And he, that is, they, had paid for their mistakes. More harshly every time, with heavier punishments as they grew older and their margin of error became more and more restricted until finally they met with complete intolerance. The man was inflexible, but in his presumption he forgot that he too was only a man. And that mistake had cost him his life.

He survived and that man did not.

He returns to his hiding place after those brief ventures outside and he waits. The dark metal lining makes it seem like a nocturnal place, as though he lets the darkness in through the door every time he opens it. It is only one of many hiding places where night lingers until the break of day, but he interprets it otherwise, as a natural complicity among fugitives.

In that isolation, he does not feel the heaviness of waiting or of solitude. He has music and the company of Paso. And that is enough.

Yes, Vibo and Paso.

He no longer remembers when they invented those two meaningless nicknames. There may have been a precise reference, but it was probably just the randomness of it that they liked. A flash of youthful fancy with no need for rational explanation. Like faith, it was either there or it wasn't.

With closed eyes, he listens to Led Zeppelin's "Stairway to Heaven," a rare live recording. He sits in the office chair, slowly rocking back and forth, following the melody that evokes a slow, grueling climb, step by step, toward the sky. The stairway exists, but heaven might not.

In the other room, the corpse is still lying in its crystal coffin as if in suspended animation, waiting to be reawakened at the end of the journey that will never come. Maybe he hears the music too, or maybe he misses bits and pieces of it, wrapped in the new face, the last one procured to satisfy his understandable vanity. This false image, like all the others, will soon decompose. Then he will have to do something about it, but for now there is still time, and Robert Plant's voice is his only priority.

The track ends. He leans on the wooden surface and stretches out his hand to press STOP. He doesn't want to hear the rest of the record. One song is enough. He will turn on the radio and listen to voices from the outside world.

In the sudden silence following the music, he thinks he hears a series of rhythmic blows, as though something from outside is hammering on the door, causing a faraway series of echoes. He gets up from the chair and goes over to the door. He puts his ear to it and feels the cold of the metal against his skin. The blows are repeated and then, right afterward, he can hear a voice shouting. The words from outside are indistinct, as from a great distance, but he is well aware that they are meant for him. He cannot make them out, but he guesses their meaning. The voice is certainly telling him to open the door of his refuge and surrender, before . . .

He takes his ear from the door with a smile. He is well aware that they are serious. He knows that there is not much they can do to get him out, but he also knows that they will do whatever they can. What they don't know is that they will never catch him. At least not alive. He will never give them that satisfaction.

He walks away from the door and goes into the room where the transparent cabinet seems to have a new lifelike tension instead of its normal stillness. There appears to be a hint of anxiety on the expressionless mask covering its face. He thinks that the expression must once have been on the face of the man it belonged to. Now, it is nothing but an illusion. Every emotion disappeared forever, at the moment of his last breath.

There is a long, pensive silence. The man is silent too, waiting. Several minutes pass. All eternity stretches before the dead, and this amount of time has no meaning for them. For the living, however, several minutes can seem to last an entire lifetime. The voice in his head returns and asks the question he is afraid to hear.

What will become of me, Vibo?

The man envisions the cemetery in Cassis, the large cypress tree, the row of graves of people who were never their family, only their nightmare. There are no pictures on the headstones, but the faces of those inside are painted on the walls of his memory.

"I think you'll go home. And so will I."

Oh.

A muffled exclamation, a simple monosyllable that includes all expectations. A call for freedom, sunlight, the motion of the waves in the sea where men dive and come up as children again. Tears fall freely from the man's eyes, running down his face to drop on the crystal where he is leaning. Wet, ordinary tears devoid of nobility, but the same color as the waves.

The affection in his eyes is total, endless. For the last time, he looks at his brother's body wearing another man's face and sees him as he was, as he should have been: identical to him, a mirror in which he can see the reflection of his own face.

He takes a few steps back from the coffin before he is able to turn his back on it. He returns to the other room and stands for a moment in front of the long row of machines and recording devices that create music.

There is only one thing he can do now. It is his only escape and the only way he can once again defeat the bloodhounds that are after him. He thinks he can hear their paws scratching frantically on the other side of the metal door. Yes, there is only one thing left to do and he has to do it quickly.

He takes out the Zeppelin CD and puts in another heavy metal disc, chosen at random, without even looking at the name of the band. The man puts it in the player, presses START, and the tray moves silently into place.

He raises the volume to the maximum with an almost angry gesture and, as in a cartoon, he imagines the musical impulse generated by the laser coursing through the plug and socket, running along the cables, reaching the Tannoy speakers that are unnaturally powerful for the tiny room, and climbing up to the tweeter and woofer . . .

Suddenly, the room explodes. The fury and rhythm of the heavy metal guitars seem to glue themselves to the metal walls which shake and vibrate as they resonate. The thunder that the music is imitating blocks out the other voices. The man leans his hands on the wooden surface and listens to the beating of his heart. It pulses so hard that he feels that it too is about to explode in the throb of the Tannoys' powerful wattage.

There is only one thing left to do. Now.

The man opens a drawer under the wooden surface and puts his hand inside without looking. When he takes it out, he is holding a gun.

58

"Got it!"

Gachot, the bomb specialist, a tall, massive man with hair and a mustache so dark they looked dyed, got up from the ground with surprising agility for a man of his size. Frank could see that his Special Corps uniform was tight on him because it stretched over solid muscle, not because his only physical activity was sitting at a desk moving his jaws.

Gachot backed away from the metal door. Taped over the lock was a box the size of a cordless phone with a small antenna and two wires, one yellow and one red. The wires went from the device to a hole in the door under the wheel.

Frank looked at the plain and simple detonator. He thought of all the idiotic things you see in movies, where the device to set off an atomic bomb that can destroy an entire city and kill millions of people always had a red display that counted down the seconds to the final boom. Of course, the hero always managed to defuse the device with only one second left, after agonizing endlessly, along with the audience, over whether he should cut the red wire or the green one. Those scenes always made him smile. The lives of millions of people depended on whether or not the hero was color-blind.

The reality was different. There was no need to visualize the countdown with a detonator linked to a timer, simply because there would be no one watching when the bomb exploded. And if someone actually had to be present, he couldn't care less about the timer.

Gachot went up to Gavin. "I'm ready. Maybe you should have the men clear out."

"For safety reasons?"

"There shouldn't be any problem. I just used a little C4 and that's manageable. It's enough for what we want to do, I think. The effects should be limited. The only risk is with the door: it's lined with lead. If I made any miscalculations and used too much C4, there might be some splinters flying. I'd say it's better if everyone goes into the garage."

Frank admired the caution of the bomb specialist, trained to defuse bombs as well as make them. He had the natural modesty of someone who knew how to do his job, although Gavin said he was smarter than the devil.

Smarter than the man on the other side of this door, thought Frank.

"And the room upstairs?"

Gachot shook his head. "No problem, if they keep away from the stairway into the laundry room. The rush of air will be limited, but it will come out through the front windows."

Gavin turned to his men.

"Okay, you heard him. We're going for fireworks. We'll wait outside but right after the explosion, we rush in through the hall door and down the stairs to keep the shelter door under control. We have no idea what will happen. He'll probably be a little stunned by the explosive, but he'll have a number of options." The sergeant counted them off on the fingers of his right hand. "Number one, he comes out armed, planning to take down as many men with him as he can. We don't want any casualties or even wounded. If that's the case, we shoot him dead, whatever he's carrying, even if it's a pencil sharpener."

He looked at his men one by one to see if they had absorbed what he had just said. "Number two, he doesn't come out. Then we teargas him out. And if he comes out fighting, we do the same as in number one. Okay?"

The men all nodded.

"Good, now divide into two groups. Half of you go upstairs with Toureau. The others come with me, to the garage."

The commandos walked away with the silent step that was their way of life. Frank admired the efficiency of Gavin and his men. Especially now that he was in his element, the lieutenant moved easily and rapidly. Frank imagined them sitting in the van, transported back and forth, the butts of their M-16s on the floor, chatting about nothing and waiting. Now the wait was over. They were about to go into action and each now had the chance to give some meaning to all the time spent in training.

When all the men were gone, Gavin turned to Morelli and Roberts. "You'd better keep your men outside. If we have to move, I don't want too many people down here getting in each other's way. All we need is for one of your men to get hit in the head by one of my men's bullets, or vice versa. That wouldn't be good for anyone. And who'd help them then, the *desk boys*?"

"Got it."

The two policemen went to tell their men the situation and give instructions. Frank smiled to himself. By *desk boys*, Gavin meant the ones sitting in their offices giving orders without ever being in the field.

Now there were only three left in the room, Lieutenant Gavin, Gachot, and Frank. The bomb specialist was holding a remote control, slightly bigger than a matchbox, with an antenna just like the one on the detonator hanging from the door.

"Whenever you're ready. Just give the word," said Gavin.

Frank stood there in silence, mulling it over. He stared at the small gadget Gachot was holding. It looked even smaller in his huge hand and Frank wondered how he managed to handle that kind of object with its tiny parts.

Brigadier Gachot had gotten there quickly, as Gavin had instructed, in a blue van just like the others with his team of two men plus the driver. When they had told him the situation, his dark face had turned even darker at the words *bomb shelter*. The men had unloaded their gear and gone down to the laundry room. Frank was well aware that one of those hard black plastic briefcases with aluminum edges resembling a flight case contained explosives. While he knew that it was completely harmless without special conditions and a detonator, he was still a little uneasy. The case probably held enough explosives to reduce the house and all of them to shreds.

When he had come to the door, the bomb specialist had studied it for a long time in silence. He had run his hand across the surface as if touching it could tell him something that the metal did not want to reveal. Then he had done something that seemed absurdly anachronistic to Frank. He had pulled a stethoscope from his bag and listened with it to the gears of the mechanism, turning the wheel from one side to another to see which way it rotated.

Frank had been standing with the others, quivering like an egg in a frying pan. They had looked like the family of a sick man, waiting for the doctor to tell them how serious the illness was. Gachot had turned around and, luckily for them, cut Gavin's pessimistic predictions down to size. "We might be able to do it."

The general sigh of relief had seemed to raise the floor two or three inches higher. "The door is armored to protect against radiation and structural damage, but it's not a safe. I mean, it wasn't built to protect valuables, just the physical safety of the occupants. So the lock is fairly simple, partly because it's pretty old. The only risk is that it might block completely instead of opening."

"What if that happens?" Gavin had asked.

"Then we're fucked. We'd really have to open it with an atomic bomb, and I didn't bring one along."

With that joke, pronounced in all seriousness, Gachot had put a damper on the general enthusiasm. He had gone over to check the briefcases that his men had put near the door with the other equipment, and he had pulled out a drill that looked like something out of the *Enterprise* in *Star Trek*. One of the man had screwed on a point made of a kind of metal with an unpronounceable name, but which Gachot had described as hard enough to drill a hole through the armor of Fort Knox.

Actually, the point had penetrated the door with relative ease, at least to a certain depth, producing chips of metal that had fallen to the ground before the man holding the drill. Finally, he had raised his goggles and moved over to make room for Gachot. The brigadier had knelt down in front of the hole and slipped in a fiber optic cable with a micro camera on one end and a visor that looked like an underwater mask on the other. He had put it on in order to check the lock from inside.

Finally, he had opened the briefcase with the goods, revealing bricks of plastic wrapped in silver foil. Gachot had opened one of them and cut off a piece of explosive that looked like grayish clay. The bomb specialist had handled it offhandedly, but from the looks on everyone's faces, Frank suspected that they were feeling more or less what he had felt earlier.

Using a wooden stick, Gachot had pushed a bit of C4 into the hole and then linked the wires that led to the detonator hanging next to the wheel.

Now they were ready. Still, Frank could not decide to give the order. He was afraid that something would go wrong and that they would, for some reason, find a corpse on the other side. That too might be an answer, but Frank wanted to catch No One alive, if only to see the psychopath handcuffed and taken away. It wasn't what he *wanted* to do to him, but it was what had to be done.

"Just a second."

He went up to the door, practically leaning his cheek on the surface of the lead. He wanted to try one last time to talk to the man inside and, if he was listening, ask him once more to come out unarmed with his hands up. He had tried before the bomb unit had arrived, but to no avail.

Frank banged his fist on the metal door, hoping that the deep thudding echo could be heard inside.

"Jean-Loup, can you hear me? We're going to blow the door open. Don't force us, it might be dangerous. You'd be better off coming out. You won't be hurt, I promise. I'll give you a minute to decide and then we're going to blow open this door."

Frank stepped back, bent his right arm, and showed everyone his watch. He pressed the button of the chronograph. It marked the seconds one after another, like bad memories.

. . .8, 9, 10

Arianna Parker and Jochen Welder, mutilated bodies in the boat wedged between the others at the pier . . .

. . .20

Allen Yoshida, his bleeding face with the skull-like grimace and blank eyes in the Bentley, at the end of his last trip . . .

. . .30

. . .*Gregor Yatzimin, his composed grace on the bed, the red flower on his white shirt, against the horrible mutilation of his face . . .*

. . .40

. . .*Roby Stricker lying on the floor, his finger contracted in the desperate attempt to leave a message before he died, with the anguish of someone who knows everything and understands that he can say no more . . .*

. . .50

. . .*Nicolas Hulot, slumped in his car with his bleeding face on the steering wheel, dead for the crime of being the first to know his name . . .*

. . .60
The bodies of the three policemen in the house . . .

"Time's up!"

Frank stopped the watch. Those sixty seconds, the last chance he had given the killer, had felt like a moment of silence owed to the victims out of respect.

"Let's open this fucking door."

The three men went through the laundry room, reached the hallway, and turned left to join the others waiting in the garage. They were kneeling against the wall on the right, the one farthest from where the explosion would take place. Morelli and Roberts were standing in the courtyard. Frank motioned to them and they stepped away from the garage door for safety.

Gavin adjusted the microphone with the earpiece connecting him to his men via radio.

"Okay boys, here we go."

He joined the others against the wall. Lieutenant Gavin nodded to Gachot and, without any emotion, the bomb specialist raised the remote in his hand and pressed the button.

The explosion, perfectly positioned, was contained. They felt it more as a vibration than a blow. The rush of air, if there was any, was limited to the laundry room. The echo was still reverberating when the soldiers leapt toward the door, immediately followed by Frank and Gavin.

They found the men who entered from the garage and from upstairs standing in formation with their rifles pointed. There was no significant damage. Only the wooden bookcase that hid the entrance to the shelter was ripped off one of the upper hinges and leaning to one side. The little bit of smoke from the explosion was drifting out the windows, pushed open by the force of the blow.

The shelter door was ajar. The explosion had only knocked it open a few inches, as if someone had gone inside without closing it behind him. Incredibly loud music was pouring through the open door.

They waited a few seconds but nothing happened. The explosives had left an acrid smell in the air. Gavin barked an order into his two-way radio.

"Tear gas."

A split second later, the commandos pulled their gas masks out of their bags. They removed their Kevlar helmets, put on the masks, and replaced the helmets. Frank felt a pat on his shoulder and found Gavin handing him one.

"You'd better put this on if you want to stay here. Know how to use it?" In answer, Frank had the mask on in an instant. "Good," said Gavin, pleased. "I see they taught you something in the FBI."

After putting on his own helmet, he waved to one of his men. The soldier leaned his rifle against the wall and inched his way along the door until he was next to the wheel, still attached to the door despite the explosion.

When he grabbed the handle and pulled, the door opened softly without a squeak, as they had all expected. The mechanism was obviously a simple one with perfectly working hinges. He opened the door only enough to allow another soldier to throw in a tear gas grenade.

Yellow smoke wafted out a few seconds later. Frank was familiar with tear gas. When it got in your eyes and throat, it was unbearable. If there was anyone inside the shelter, it would be impossible to resist the effects. They waited a few endless seconds, but no one came out. Only the blasting music and the clouds of smoke that now seemed to be mocking them.

Frank didn't like that. Not at all. He turned to Gavin and their eyes met through the gas masks. From his expression, Frank saw that Gavin was thinking the same thing.

Either there was nobody inside or else their man, knowing it was all over, had killed himself rather than letting them take him alive.

Or a third option: the bastard had a gas mask too. This wasn't science fiction—they had learned to expect anything from him. In that case, since only one man could get through the door at a time, all the killer had to do was get under cover and he'd take more victims before they could shoot him, if they tried to enter at all. He was armed and everyone knew what he could do.

Gavin made a decision. "Throw in a grenade. Then we'll take our chances and enter."

Frank could understand the lieutenant's point of view. On the one hand, he felt ridiculous in that situation, commanding a group of men in combat gear assaulting a door that might lead to an empty room. On the other hand, he had no intention of losing any of his men in an unpleasant surprise. He knew each of them well and did not want to risk their lives.

Frank decided to remove his doubts. He moved his mask next to the lieutenant's so that he could hear his voice better.

"After the grenade, I'm going in."

"Negative," responded Gavin sharply.

"There's no reason to risk any of your men uselessly." Gavin's silence and look said a great deal about what he thought.

"I can't accept your offer."

"I have no intention of playing the hero, Lieutenant." Frank's answer was final. "But this is a personal affair between that man and me. I remind you that I am directing this operation and you're here in support. I'm not offering. That's an order." Then he changed his tone of voice, hoping that the other man understood his intentions through their limited means of communication. "If he had killed one of your best friends along with all the others, you'd do the same."

Gavin nodded to show he understood. Frank walked over to

the wall, pulled out his Glock, and stood by the door. He waved when he was ready.

"Grenade," Gavin ordered harshly.

The soldier who had thrown the tear gas earlier pulled the tab of the grenade and tossed it in the door. It was a device designed especially for that kind of assault. It was meant to stun the occupants of a room without killing them.

There was a blinding light and the sound of an explosion, much louder than the one produced by the previous explosives. The blaring music pouring out of the shelter was suddenly in its element, in concert with colored smoke and flashing lights. Immediately afterward, the man on Frank's right moved and open the door just enough to let him in. A puff of tear gas mixed with the smoke from the grenade came out. The door did not open enough for them to see what was inside. Frank moved at lightning speed and slipped in with his gun aimed.

The others waited expectantly.

A couple of minutes went by, an eternity to each and every one of them. Then the music stopped, followed by an even more deafening silence. Finally, the door opened completely and Frank reappeared, followed by a last wisp of smoke fluttering around his shoulders like a ghost risen from a tomb to show him out.

He was still wearing the gas mask and it was impossible to see his face. His arms were hanging down as if he had no energy left. He was still holding the gun. Without speaking, he crossed the laundry room like someone who has fought all the wars in the world and lost. The men stepped aside to let him pass.

Frank went to the door in front of him and down the hallway. Gavin followed and they reached the garage where Morelli and Roberts were waiting, their faces flushed with adrenaline like all the others under their masks. They went to stand in the square patch of sunlight that was coming through the raised garage door. Gavin removed his helmet and gas mask first. His hair was wet and his face dripping with sweat. He wiped his forehead with the sleeve of his blue uniform.

Frank stood for a moment in the middle of the garage, between sunlight and shade, and then he too removed his gas mask. His face was deathly tired.

Morelli went up to him. "Frank, what happened? You look like you've been to hell and back."

Frank turned to him and answered with the voice of an old man and the eyes of someone who could see no more in life.

"Worse, Claude, much worse. All the devils in hell would cross themselves before going in there."

59

Frank and Morelli watched the stretcher being carried out of the garage and their eyes followed the men sliding it into the ambulance. Lying there, covered with a dark canvas, was the body they had found in the shelter—the wizened, faceless corpse wearing, like a mask, the face of another murdered man.

After Frank had come out of the shelter in shock, all the men, one by one, had entered the bunker, emerging with the same expression of horror. The sight of that mummified body lying in its crystal case wearing the stiffened mask of No One's latest victim was a sight that could stagger the soundest mind, a vision they would carry with them day and night.

Frank still found what he had seen hard to believe. He felt unclean and wanted to wash himself again and again to disinfect his body and mind from the pure evil that hovered in that place. Inside, he felt ill at the mere thought that he had *breathed* that air, as if it were saturated by the virus of a madness so contagious that it could infect anyone with criminal sickness.

There was one thing Frank could not stop asking himself. *Why?* He realized that the answer was unimportant, at least for now, but the word continued to bounce around in his head as if it held the secret of perpetual motion.

He had gone into the bunker through the door, scanning the room from top to bottom as he advanced through the smoke, his gun in hand and his heart beating so fast that it kept him from hearing the deafening music. When he turned it off, all that was left was his panting breath inside the gas mask. Apart from the motionless presence of the body—displayed in its monstrous vanity in a transparent coffin—all that he had found were empty rooms.

He had stood there looking at the corpse, mesmerized, staring at its pitiful nudity, unable to remove his eyes from that spectacle of death sublimated by a horrifying, brilliant sickness. He had stared for a long time at the face covered with its death mask, which with the passing of time was beginning to resemble the rest of the body. There were some clots of blood on the neck of the corpse that peeked out from beneath the torn edges of the mask, proof of the difficult nature of that unnatural attempted transplant.

What was the point of the murders? All those people killed just to persuade a dead man that he was still alive? What kind of morbid pagan idolatry could inspire that kind of monstrosity? What was the explanation, if ever there could be any logic to that funeral rite that had required the sacrifice of so many innocent people?

This is true insanity, he had thought. *The ability to feed off oneself only to generate more insanity.*

When he had finally been able to move his eyes from that sight, he had gone out to allow each of the men to enter in turn.

The noise of the ambulance doors slamming shut brought Frank back to the present, and he saw Roberts's lanky figure coming toward them. There was a police car waiting for him with its engine running and the door open. He did not look like he wanted to linger there.

"Okay. We're going," he said in an expressionless voice.

Frank and Morelli shook his hand and said good-bye, not realizing that they were speaking in the same monotone. The inspector found it hard to look them in the eye. Although he had lived through the affair on a more marginal level, and although he was not as deeply involved from the beginning, Roberts had the same weary look in his eye. He walked away with the exhaustion that always comes with the easing of nervous tension. He too, probably, couldn't wait to go back to his routine, to the stories of everyday poverty and greed, to men and women who killed out of jealousy or desire for money or by accident. Madness that was momentary and not forever, madness that he would not be forced to carry around in his memory like a gruesome trophy for the rest of his life. Perhaps he had only one desire, like everyone else there: to get away from that house as quickly as possible and try to forget that it ever existed.

He heard the thud of the door closing and the sound of the engine, and then the car disappeared up the ramp from the courtyard that led to the street. Gavin and his men had already gone, as had Gachot with his team. They had driven away down the road descending to the city, their blue vans loaded with men, weapons, sophisticated equipment, and the prosaic sense of loss that always assails armies, large and small, after a defeat.

Even Morelli had sent most of his men back to headquarters. A couple of them were still there checking on final operations, after which they would escort the ambulance back to the morgue.

The roadblocks had been removed and the long line of cars waiting on either end was slowly clearing, thanks to a couple of policemen who were directing traffic and keeping curious onlookers away. The traffic jam had kept the professional busybodies—the reporters—from reaching the house. When they had arrived, it was all over and most important, there was no news: the only thing the media could share with the police this time was disappointment. Frank had delegated Morelli to speak to them and the sergeant had gotten rid of them quickly and efficiently. Actually, it hadn't been too hard.

"I'm going back, Frank. And you?"

Frank looked at his watch and thought about General Nathan

Parker waiting furiously at the Nice Airport. He'd convinced himself that he would appear before him wearing the relief of the finished nightmare like a new suit. He had wanted it to be all over, and instead it was endless.

"Go on, Claude. I'm leaving now too."

They looked at each other and the sergeant simply raised his hand. They said as few words as possible, because both seemed to have used them all up. Morelli walked away, up the ramp to his car. Frank saw him disappear around the curve hidden by mastic trees.

The ambulance backed up and turned to leave the courtyard, and the man next to the driver gazed at him blankly through the window. He didn't seem the least bit shocked by what they were carrying in back of the van. They were just transporting corpses, whether they had been dead an hour, a year, or a century. It was a job like any other. There was a folded sports page on the dashboard. As the white van drove away, Frank could see the man's hand reach for the paper.

He stood alone in the center of the courtyard under that summer afternoon sun, unable to feel the heat. The air was filled with the melancholy languor of a dismantled circus, when the darkness and lights no longer protect one's vision from reality. There were no more acrobats or women in colorful costumes, no more music or applause. All that was left was a pile of sawdust strewn with sequins and excrement. And a clown standing in the sun. Nothing is worse than a clown who can't make people laugh . . .

Despite the thought of Helena, Frank could not bring himself to leave the house. He *felt* that there was something he had mistakenly taken for granted. Like everything that had happened up to then, it was a question of details. Tiny details. The detail of the record cover in the video, the reflection of Stricker's message in the mirror, words turned upside down that had turned out to have an entirely different meaning . . .

Frank forced himself to think rationally.

The entire time that Jean-Loup had been under police protection, there were men at the house day and night. How had he managed to avoid them? The murders always took place at night, so no policemen would have gone inside when he was presumably asleep, not unless there was a very good reason. Especially after all the tension of the phone calls with the killer. So Jean-Loup was safe from that point of view. But that was it.

On the left side of the property, by the gate, there was a sort of embankment that fell straight down in a steep decline. It was too dangerous, considering that he would have had to travel the road at night and without a flashlight. Maybe he'd left through the garden. In that case, he would have had to go out through the living room at the front of the house near the swimming pool, climb over the fence, and cross through the garden of the twin house where the Parkers were staying in order to reach the street.

If that was the case, someone would have noticed him sooner or later. On one side, he had several bored but well-trained policemen. On the other side were Ryan Mosse and Nathan Parker, two men who most certainly always slept with one eye open. He could have gotten away with it once, but sooner or later all that nocturnal movement would have been discovered. So that theory didn't hold water either.

Everyone had assumed that there was a second exit and the logic of construction said that there had to be one. In the event of a nuclear explosion, the house would cave in and the rubble would close off every avenue of escape. Still, the meticulous search of the underground shelter had revealed nothing, not a trace.

And yet . . .

Frank checked his watch again, for the millionth time. He put his hands in his jacket pockets, feeling the car keys in one and the hard surface of his cell phone in the other. It made him think of

Helena, sitting in the airport with her legs crossed, gazing around and hoping to see him in the crowd.

He thought of calling her cell, in spite of Nathan Parker. He nearly gave in to the urge, but then thought better of it. He didn't want to betray Helena and alert the general. Instead, he wanted him to sit there, furious with the entire world but unsuspecting, and wait.

Frank took his hands from his pockets and opened and closed his fists until he felt the tension ease. Then he turned and went back inside the shelter, stopping at the door and studying the small underground hiding place, the realm of No One. In the shadows, he could see red and green lights and the displays of the electronic equipment. He suddenly remembered all the stories his father had told him when he was a boy. Stories of fairies and gnomes and sometimes ogres who lived in terrifying underground worlds that they left to steal babies from their cradles and take them into their dens forever. Except that he was no child and this was not a fable. Or if it was, there was no happy ending.

He stepped forward and turned on the light. Despite its confines, the shelter was rather spacious. That woman's paranoia and fears for the future must have cost her husband a pretty penny thirty years ago. The construction was square and divided into three rooms. On the right was a small space that served both as a bathroom and storeroom. It contained every kind of canned food imaginable, stacked in an orderly manner on shelves facing the toilet and sink, along with enough reserves of water to outlast any siege. The room which had held the corpse in its crystal coffin also contained a spare single bed, off to one side. The thought of Jean-Loup sleeping next to the dead body gave him a chill, as if an evil breath had touched his back. It was hard to keep from turning and checking behind him.

Frank scanned left and right over the rectangular room where he was standing and onto which the doors of the storeroom and bedroom opened. He started opening and closing his eyes at regular intervals and projecting the images of the room onto his mind like slides.

Click.

A detail.

Click.

Look for a detail.

Click.

What's wrong? There's something strange about this room.

Click.

Something tiny, something incongruous.

Click.

You know what it is. You saw it. You registered it.

Click, click, click . . .

The room appeared and disappeared as if lit by a flash. He went on opening and closing his eyes, hoping each time that whatever he was seeking might magically appear.

The wall on the left.

The shelves on top, full of recording and electronic equipment that Jean-Loup used to filter his voice and transform it into No One's.

The two Tannoy speakers set up for the best possible stereo effect.

A sophisticated CD and mini-disc reader.

A mixer.

A cassette player and DAT machine.

A record player for old 33s.

The records, set up on the lower shelf.

LPs on the left, CDs on the right.

In the center, the surface that he used as a desk.

Atop another mixer, a Mac G4 computer that ran the sound equipment.

In back, against the wall, a black device that looked like another small CD player.

The front wall.

Metal cabinet, set into the wall, empty.

The wall on the right.

The doors to the other rooms and in the middle a wooden table and a small halogen lamp.

Frank stopped suddenly.

Another small CD player.

He walked to the back of the room and carefully examined the black box. He wasn't a stereo aficionado, but from what he knew, it looked like a fairly ordinary model made of black metal with a small display in front. It didn't even look very new. There were wires coming out that went to a hole at the bottom of the shelf. There was a series of numbers on the bottom, written on the metal in white felt-tip pen. Someone had tried sloppily to erase the numbers, but they were still legible.

1-10
2-7
3-4
4-8

He was puzzled. It was not a normal place to take notes.

He pressed the EJECT button and the tray on the left of the display slid out soundlessly. There was a CD, not an original but a master copy. There was writing on the gold surface, again in felt-tip pen, this time in red.

Robert Fulton—"Stolen Music".

That damned record again. That music was following Frank like a curse. He started to think. It was natural that Jean-Loup would make himself a digital copy of the record, so that he could listen to it without ruining the original. Then why, when he killed Allen Yoshida, did he need to take the actual LP? There was certainly some symbolic meaning, but it could also be another reason . . .

Frank turned to look at the modern CD player next to the other components of the sound system and then turned again to the other, much more modest, piece of equipment. And he wondered: *Why would someone with a CD player like that use a cheap thing like this?*

There were a thousand answers to that question, each one plausible. But Frank knew that none of them was right. He leaned his hand on the black metal of the device and ran his fingers over the numbers written in white as if he expected them to be raised and palpable.

A theory is a journey that can last months, years, sometimes an entire lifetime. The intuition that ignites it runs through the brain at the speed of light, and its effect is immediate. One moment all is darkness and the next, everything is light.

Frank suddenly realized what that second player was for and what the numbers that someone had tried to erase from its surface meant. They were the numbers of a combination. He pushed the tray back in and pressed the start button. A series of numbers appeared on the display, showing the track being played and the amount of time since it had started.

He watched the seconds passing slowly on the small, illuminated rectangle. After ten seconds, he pressed the button that moved from the first track to the next. Then, he waited until the number 7 appeared and went to the third track. When the display showed 4, he went to the fourth. And when he read the number 8, he pressed the stop button.

Plick.

The click was so faint that Frank would not have heard it if he hadn't been holding his breath. He turned right in the direction of the sound and saw that the metal cabinet had moved over a few inches. The two sides were so perfectly matched that they seemed to be part of the wall.

He stuck his finger into the crack and pulled. Sliding along two runners on either side, the metal cabinet came forward about a yard, revealing a round door behind it. In one corner of the metal door, there was a wheel that looked just like the one in the laundry room. When they had searched the bunker, they hadn't asked themselves why this cabinet was completely empty. Now that he had an answer, Frank found the question that nobody had thought to ask. The cabinet was there to hide a second entrance.

Frank turned the wheel counterclockwise without any effort until he heard the lock click, then he pushed and the door opened, sliding soundlessly on its hinges. Jean-Loup Verdier must have spent a great deal of time on technical knowledge and maintenance. The opening of a round cement tunnel, about a yard and a half in diameter, was behind the door. It was a black hole that started from the shelter; where it ended, God only knew.

Frank slid his cell phone into his shirt pocket, removed his jacket, and pulled the Glock out of its holster on his belt. He knelt on the ground and wriggled past the rods holding up the metal shelves, crawling past the hermetic door. He halted a moment, staring at the tunnel and the darkness it promised. He could see no more than a yard in the dim light of the tunnel, partly obscured by the cabinet and his own body. It was probably dangerous, *very* dangerous, to squeeze blindly into that tunnel.

Then he remembered who had escaped through the tunnel and everything that person had done, and he decided to follow. By then, Frank would have gone in even if only to meet a firing squad.

60

Pierrot peeked out from behind the bushes where he was hiding and looked onto the street, relieved to see that all the cars and people who were waiting had left, along with the policemen who had been stopping them. Good. *Now* it was good, but before he had been really afraid . . .

After leaving the radio station, he had walked up to Jean-Loup's house, his knapsack on his back. He had been a little nervous because he wasn't sure that he would be able to find the street, even though he had been to Beausoleil several times in Jean-Loup's car, which was called *a Mercedes*. He hadn't paid much attention to the route because he had been too busy laughing and looking at his friend's face. He always laughed when he was with Jean-Loup. Well, not really always, because there was someone who had said that only fools laughed all the time and he didn't want people to think he was a fool.

And anyway, he wasn't used to going around by himself because his mother was afraid that something would happen to him or that other boys would make fun of him, like Mme Narbonne's daughter, the one with the crooked teeth and pimples who still called him "retard." He didn't know what a retard was and when he had asked his mother, she had turned her back to him, but not fast enough to keep him from noticing that her eyes were wet with tears. Pierrot had not been too worried about that. His mother's eyes were often damp, like when she watched those movies on TV where there were two people kissing at the end with violin music and then they got married. The only thing he had really been worried about was that his mother's damp eyes meant that sooner or later he would have to marry Mme Narbonne's daughter.

Halfway there, he had gotten thirsty and had drunk the entire can of Coke that he had brought from home. He was a little unhappy because he had meant to share it with Jean-Loup, but it was hot out and his mouth was dry and his friend certainly wouldn't mind such a little thing. And he still had a can of Schweppes left.

He had been sweaty when he reached Jean-Loup's house and thought that it would probably have been a good idea to bring another T-shirt to change into. But that wasn't a problem either. He knew that Jean-Loup had a drawer in a chest in his laundry room where he kept T-shirts for doing jobs around the house. If his shirt was too sweaty, Jean-Loup would lend him another one, which he would return after his mother washed and ironed it. It had happened once before when he was in the pool and his shirt had fallen in the water and Jean-Loup had lent him a blue one that said MARTINI-RACING. He had thought that Jean-Loup was lending it to him, but it was a present.

The first thing he had wanted to do was find the key. He had seen the aluminum mailbox inside the gate with the words JEAN-LOUP VERDIER written in dark green paint, the same color as the bars. He had stuck his hand between them and touched the bottom of the metal box. Under his fingers, he had felt something that seemed like a key attached with a dried-out piece of chewing gum.

He had been about to pull off the key when a car had driven up to the construction site not far from the gate. Luckily, Pierrot was covered by a bush and the trunk of a cypress tree and he couldn't be seen from the car. He had hidden and seen the American in that blue car, the one who was always with the inspector but then he wasn't anymore because someone said that he was dead. Pierrot had moved away quickly so the man wouldn't see him. If he had, he would have asked him what he was doing there and would have taken him home.

He had gone down the road, following the asphalt and staying under cover. After he had passed the steep part that made his head spin just from looking at it, he had climbed over the guardrail and found himself in a bush that completely covered him. From his observation point he could see the courtyard of Jean-Loup's house and watch with curiosity as a bunch of people walked back and forth, mostly policemen dressed in blue and a few in normal clothes. There was also the one who had come to the station and never smiled when he spoke, but smiled all the time when he spoke to Barbara.

He had stayed in his hiding place for what seemed like a very long time, until everyone had gone and the courtyard was empty. The last one to go, the American, had left the garage door open. It was lucky that Pierrot was there to take care of his friend's house. Now he could go and make sure the records were all right, and before he left he would close the garage door. Otherwise, anyone could come in and steal whatever they wanted.

He got up slowly from the ground and looked around. His knees hurt from crouching for so long and his legs had fallen asleep. He started stamping his feet on the ground, the way his mother had taught him. In his own small way, Pierrot decided on a plan of action. He couldn't reach the courtyard from where he was because of the very steep part along the cliff by the sea. So he had to go up the paved road and down again to see whether he could climb over the gate.

He adjusted his knapsack on his shoulders and got ready for the climb.

From the corner of his eye, he noticed some movement in the bushes, lower down. He thought maybe he was mistaken. How could anyone be below him? He would have seen them pass by. But just to make sure, he crouched back down in the bushes, parting the branches with his hands so that he could see better. Nothing happened for a while and he was beginning to think he had been wrong. Then he saw something else move in the bushes and held his hand over his eyes to protect them from the glare of the sun.

What he saw made his mouth drop open in surprise. Right below him, dressed in green and brown as if he were part of the earth and the vegetation, with a canvas bag slung over his shoulder, was his friend Jean-Loup, crawling out from under a patch of shrubbery. Pierrot held his breath. If it were up to him, he would have jumped and cried out that he was there, but maybe it wasn't a good idea because if the policemen weren't all gone, someone might see them. He decided to climb up a little higher and move to the right so that he would be covered by the embankment before making his presence known to Jean-Loup.

He crept quietly, trying to imitate the movements of his friend below him who was going in and out of the bushes without rustling a single leaf. Finally, he reached a point where it was impossible to see any farther and he realized it was the perfect position. A piece of rock jutted out below him, just large enough to stand on and call out to Jean-Loup without being seen by the policemen.

He climbed down carefully to get as close to the rock as possible and got ready by bending his legs. Then, he raised his arms to the sky and jumped. As soon as his feet hit the ground, the brittle piece of rock broke under his weight and Pierrot rolled down into the void with a scream.

61

Frank moved forward very slowly in the pitch dark.

After careful examination of the tunnel, he had seen that it was high enough for him to crawl through, which was what he decided to do. It was not the most comfortable position, but certainly the least risky. He had thought with a bitter smile that he was literally going "to the dark side."

After a few steps, he no longer had the help of the dim light coming from behind and he had had to continue in total darkness. His eyes had already grown used to it, but he still couldn't see anything. He held the gun in his right hand and leaned his body against the wall on the left, bending slightly backward to use his free hand as a sort of advance guard to make sure that there were no obstacles or, worse, holes he could fall into. If that happened, he'd be stuck there for all time.

He moved cautiously, step by step. His legs were beginning to hurt, especially his right knee. That was the knee with torn ligaments from a college football game that had ended his playing career and kept him from pursuing professional football. He usually stayed in good enough shape to avoid problems, but he had trained very little recently and the position he was in would have bothered anyone's knees, even those of a weight lifter.

He shivered slightly. It wasn't warm in there. Still, nervousness made him sweat and it poured from under his arms, soaking the light material of his shirt. There was a dank smell of wet leaves and humidity in the tunnel, as well as that of the wet cement with which it was lined. He occasionally brushed against a root burrowed between the joints of the piping. It had startled him the first time and he had pulled back his hand as if he had been burned. The pipe obviously led outside and some animal could easily have found its way in and made a comfortable den. Frank was not skittish, but the idea of touching a grass snake or a rat wasn't very pleasant.

In this long manhunt, his fantasy had finally come true. This was the situation he'd imagined every time he spoke of No One. A slow, creeping, furtive advance, in the cold and damp domain of rats. It described their investigation perfectly: a wearing, step-by-step process done completely in the dark, searching for a slim ray of light to lead them out of the blackness.

Let us perish in the light of day . . .

In the pitch dark, the famous passage of Ajax's prayer from the Iliad came to mind. He'd studied it in high school, a million years ago. The Trojans and the Achaeans were fighting near the ships and Jove had sent fog to block the vision of the Greeks, who were losing. At that point, Ajax sent up a prayer to the father of all the gods, a heartfelt prayer not for his own safety, but for the permission to approach destruction in the sunlight. Frank remembered the words of his favorite hero.

His concentration returned as he felt the tunnel slope down. The pavement, or rather the part under his feet, had pitched steeply. It probably didn't mean that the pipe was now unworkable. Basically, it had been built for human use and the sloping was surely accidental rather than on purpose. They must have found a vein of rock during construction and had been forced to go downward in order to continue.

He decided to sit rather than crawl and proceed that way, doubling his caution. Frank wasn't particularly worried about the downward slope. His analysis before had been right, not to mention the fact that No One had gone through here many times, back and forth, although he must have done so much more easily since he knew the terrain and certainly carried a flashlight.

Frank, on the other hand, was in total darkness and had no idea what lay ahead. Or even what was next to him. But it was the thought of Jean-Loup's nature that made him more careful. He knew how dangerously smart the man was, and it was not unlikely that he had set traps for a possible intruder.

He wondered again *who* Jean-Loup Verdier could be and, most of all, who had *created* him. It was now obvious that he was not just a psychopath, someone weak and frustrated who committed a series of crimes to get attention and be on TV. That superficial explanation might cover most of the cases he knew, but it was as far from No One as the earth from the sun. The others were people with lower than average intelligence who were consumed for the most part by an uncontrollable force. They usually accepted the handcuffs with a sigh of relief.

Not him. There was something different about him. The corpse in its transparent coffin testified to his madness. His mind undoubtedly contained thoughts that would shock even the most jaded psychiatrists. But the madness ended there.

Jean-Loup was strong, brilliant, well prepared, and trained to fight. He was a genuine combatant. With cynical ease, he had killed Jochen Welder and Roby Stricker, two trained athletes. The haste with which he had gotten rid of the three policemen in his own house was further confirmation of his abilities, if any more was needed. There seemed to be two people in him, in the same body, two different natures that canceled each other out. Perhaps the best definition was the one he had given himself: *I am one and no one.*

He was an *extremely* dangerous man and had to be treated as such. Frank did not feel that he was being unnecessarily paranoid. Sometimes excess means the difference between life and death.

Frank knew that only too well, since the only time he had been impulsive and rushed in without thinking, he had awoken in a hospital bed after an explosion and fifteen days in a coma. If he ever forgot, he had scars all over his body to remind him.

He didn't want to take any more unnecessary risks. He owed it to himself, whether or not he decided to remain a policeman. He owed it to the woman who was waiting for him in a departure lounge of the Nice Airport. And he owed it to Harriet, the promise that he would never forget.

He continued to move forward, trying to make as little noise as possible. Jean-Loup could be anywhere at that moment, but he might still be crouching at the far end of the tunnel. After all, this underground passage couldn't go all the way to Menton. It had to open up somewhere east of the house, on the slope of the mountain.

There was probably still a lot of confusion outside: the police roadblocks, the lines of cars, people getting out and rubbernecking, asking each other what was going on. It wouldn't be hard to lose oneself in that crowd. Yes, Jean-Loup's pictures had been in all the papers and shown on TV news all over Europe, but Frank had lost faith in those measures long ago. Ordinary people usually only glanced superficially at the people around them. All Jean-Loup had to do was cut his hair and put on a pair of dark glasses to be fairly sure that he could mix in a crowd.

But the roads were still full of cops who were on the alert and had their eyes wide open. And that was something else. They would be suspicious if someone just appeared out of the bushes and climbed down to the side of the road. That would definitely raise the alarm and with everything that had happened, the police would be likely to shoot first and ask questions later. But his man might have found a less congested place to come out of hiding.

Frank kept moving forward. The sound of his pants scraping along the bottom of the tunnel sounded like Niagara Falls. The rubbing started to hurt. He stopped a moment to settle into a more comfortable position and decided to go back to crawling. As he changed position, the *beep* of his cell phone sounded like a church bell in the absolute silence of a country night. That signal might have betrayed his presence, but it also assured him that the exit was near.

He squinted in the darkness, thinking that he could see points of light before him, like white chalk marks on a blackboard. He tried to speed up without abandoning his caution, and his heart raced even faster. Frank's left hand groped along the cement wall, his right pressed against the trigger, and his knee hurt like hell, but there was a hint of light in front of him and perhaps a presence lurking that he could not afford to underestimate. The white marks on the blackboard danced, suspended in the air as he approached, and grew slowly larger. Frank realized that the tunnel ended near a bush and that he was seeing the light filtered through the branches. There was probably a breeze swaying the leaves, which was why the points of light looked like fireflies to his eyes, tricked by the darkness.

Suddenly, from outside, he heard the echo of a desperate scream. Frank threw caution to the wind and, as quickly as possible in his position, he reached the shrubbery hiding the entrance to the tunnel. Pushing the branches to one side, he slowly put out his head. The exit was behind a large bush that completely covered the circumference of the cement pipe.

The scream was repeated. Frank stood up tentatively, his knee protesting in pain. He looked around. The bush was on a fairly level area, a sort of natural terrace on the side of the mountain, covered with occasional trees with thin trunks. The trees were wrapped with ivy and had shrubs of Mediterranean maquis at their base. Behind him, the twin houses and their carefully tended gardens rose like touchstones. The road was fifty yards above him on his left. Frank saw something moving halfway down the slope that separated him from the road, to one side of his bush. A figure in a green shirt and khaki-colored pants with a dark canvas bag slung over his shoulder was carefully climbing up through the bushes toward the guardrail.

Frank would have recognized that man anywhere, among thousands of others and from a million miles away. He brought his gun up to his eyes, pointing it with both hands. He centered his target in the viewfinder and finally shouted out the words he had been yearning to say for so very long.

"Stop right where you are, Jean-Loup! I'm aiming at you. Don't make me shoot. Put your hands in the air, kneel down on the ground, and don't move. Now!"

Jean-Loup turned his head in Frank's direction. He gave no sign that he recognized him or understood what he had said, and didn't seem to have any intention of giving in to his request. Despite the fact that he was close enough to see the gun in Frank's hands, he continued to climb, moving farther left. Frank's finger contracted over the trigger of the Glock.

The scream was repeated, loud and sharp.

Jean-Loup answered, bending his head. "Hold on tight, Pierrot, I'm on my way. Don't worry. I'm coming down to get you."

Frank moved his eyes to where Jean-Loup was looking. He could see Pierrot, his hands grasping a small tree trunk on the side of the road. He was groping with his feet to find some ground but every time he tried to grip the rock, the fragile terrain crumbled and the boy found himself hanging in midair.

Below him, the steep slope plummeted down. It wasn't really a sheer cliff, but if Pierrot let go he would fall and bounce like a rag doll straight into the ravine. If he let go, there would be no hope.

"Hurry, Jean-Loup. I can't hold on anymore. My hands hurt."

Frank could see how tired the boy was and he could hear the fear in his voice. But he also heard something else, the absolute faith that Jean-Loup, the deejay, the serial killer, the voice of the devil, his best friend, would come to save him. Frank released the tension on the trigger slightly as he realized what Jean-Loup was doing.

He wasn't running away. He was going to save Pierrot.

Escape had probably been Jean-Loup's original intention and things had undoubtedly unfolded as Frank had imagined. He had waited in the tunnel until the commotion died down and he could slip out to escape the police one last time. Then he had seen Pierrot in danger. He had probably wondered why Pierrot was there, hanging from a tree calling for help in his terrified child's voice. In a split second, he had sized up the situation and made a choice. Now he was acting on it.

Frank felt a dull anger rush through him, the result of his frustration. He had been waiting for that moment for so long and now that he had his gun aimed at the man he had been hunting so desperately, he couldn't shoot. He put his gun back in position, holding it more firmly than ever. Just beyond the notch of his pistol sights was the body of Jean-Loup, moving to the place where his young friend was hanging.

Jean-Loup reached Pierrot, dangling slightly below him. The hole that the boy's fall had made in the terrain lay between them. It was too far for Jean-Loup to reach and pull him up.

"I'm right here, Pierrot," Jean-Loup said to the boy in his warm, deep voice. "I'm coming. Stay calm and everything will be all right. But you have to hold on tight and stay calm. Understand?"

Despite the danger, Pierrot answered with one of his solemn nods. His eyes were huge with fear but he was certain that his friend would save him.

Frank watched as Jean-Loup put the bag he was carrying on the ground and started slipping off his belt. He didn't know how Jean-Loup planned to get Pierrot out of danger. The only thing Frank could do was stand there watching, keeping him in the sights of his gun.

Jean-Loup had just finished removing his belt when they heard the loud hiss of a blowgun and a gust of air hit the ground next to him. He bent down suddenly and it was that instinctive movement that saved his life. Another hiss and gust of air hit exactly where he had been standing a fraction of a second earlier. Frank turned sharply and looked up. On the edge of the slope, standing next to the guardrail up to his waist in the bushes, was Captain Ryan Mosse, holding a huge automatic weapon with a silencer.

At that point, Jean-Loup turned and did something incredible. He jumped into the mastic bushes and disappeared. Just like that. One moment he was there and the next he wasn't. Ryan Mosse must have been just as surprised, but that didn't stop him from firing a series of rapid shots into the bushes where Jean-Loup was hiding, finishing his round. He took out the empty clip and stuck in another, pulling it out of his pocket. A second later, the gun was ready to fire. He started to climb down carefully, watching closely for any movement in the shrubbery near him. Frank moved the Glock in his direction.

"Get out of here, Mosse. This has nothing to do with you. Drop your gun and leave. Or help. First, we have to think of that boy hanging down there. Then we'll take care of everything else."

The captain continued climbing down, gun in hand. Without stopping for an instant to check the bushes around him, he answered, "Who says this has nothing to do with me? I say it does, Mr. Ottobre. And I'll decide the priorities. First I get rid of this nut job and then I'll help you with the retard if you want."

Frank had the massive body of Ryan Mosse in his viewfinder. The desire to shoot him was strong, almost as strong as his desire to shoot Jean-Loup, despite the fact that the guy would risk his life to save a dog or a retard, as Mosse put it.

"I said, put down that gun, Ryan."

"Or what? You'll shoot?" he said with a short, bitter laugh, dripping with sarcasm. "Then what'll you tell people, that you killed a soldier from your own country to save a serial killer? Put down that flyswatter and learn how it's done."

Still aiming, Frank started moving as quickly as possible toward Pierrot. He had never found himself in a situation with so many variables.

"Help, I can't hold on anymore!"

Pierrot's mournful voice came from behind him. Frank lowered his gun and tried as quickly as possible to reach the point where Jean-Loup had been standing before. He felt the shrubs pulling at him like evil hands reaching from the bushes. He kept turning his head to check on Ryan Mosse's movements. The soldier was still climbing cautiously down the hill, gun in hand, his suspicious eyes searching for Jean-Loup.

Suddenly, the bushes next to Mosse came alive. There was not the slightest warning. Whatever came out of the shrubbery was not the same man who had dived in for cover. It was not Jean-Loup but a demon kicked out of hell because the other demons were afraid of him. He had a supernatural tension, as if a ferocious animal had suddenly taken over his body, giving him the strength of its muscles and the sharpness of its senses.

Jean-Loup moved with agility, vigor, and grace. With a kick, the gun flew out of his adversary's hand and landed far away, lost in the bushes. Mosse was a soldier, an *excellent* one, but the menace emanating from the man before him put them on the same level. Mosse, however, had one advantage over Jean-Loup. He could take his time. He didn't care about the boy hanging from the tree over the ravine and he knew that his opponent was in a rush to save him. That urgency was what he planned to exploit.

He didn't attack. He waited, taking one step back for every step Jean-Loup took toward him. As he moved, Jean-Loup continued talking to Pierrot.

"Pierrot, can you hear me? I'm still here. Don't be afraid. Just a second and I'll be there." As he reassured the boy, he seemed to lose his concentration for an instant. And that's when Mosse went for it.

Based on what happened afterward, Frank was sure that it had been a strategic tactic by Jean-Loup to get Mosse to move. Everything happened in a flash. Mosse pretended to move to the left and pulled a series of punches that Jean-Loup fended off with humiliating ease. Mosse stepped back. Frank was too far away to make out the details, but he thought he could see surprise on the captain's face. He tried another couple of blows with his hands and then kicked as fast as lightning. It was the same move he had used on Frank the day they had fought in front of the house. Only Jean-Loup didn't fall for it the way he had. Instead of blocking the kick and turning away, exposing himself to his adversary's reaction, he stepped to the side as soon as he saw the foot coming and let Mosse throw his weight upward. Then he dropped his right knee to the ground, slipped under Mosse's leg in a flash, and blocked it with his left hand, pushing the captain's body backward. He gave a terrifying punch to his adversary's testicles, simultaneously pushing him forward.

Frank could hear Mosse's moan of pain as he fell. He was not even all the way down in the bushes when Jean-Loup was over him with a knife. He pulled it out so fast that Frank thought he must have had it in his hand from the beginning and it was only just now visible. Jean-Loup bent over and disappeared in the shrubbery where Mosse's body had fallen. When he got up, the animal that he seemed to carry inside him was gone and the blade of the knife was covered with blood.

Frank was unable to see the final outcome of the fight because in the meantime he had reached the place where Pierrot was hanging from the tree, leaving Jean-Loup and Mosse behind him. He saw fear on the boy's face but mostly the disquieting signs of fatigue. His hands were red from the effort and Frank realized that he couldn't hold on much longer. He showed him that he was there and tried to reassure him, speaking calmly to give him the confidence that he, Frank, did not feel.

"Here I am, Pierrot. I've come to get you."

The boy was so tired that he couldn't make the effort to answer. Frank looked around. He was standing exactly where Jean-Loup had been removing his belt when Mosse shot at him the first time.

Why? For the second time, he wondered how Jean-Loup was planning to use the belt to save Pierrot. He raised his eyes and saw another trunk, about the same size as Pierrot's, a couple of yards above him. The leaves had long ago fallen off and the branches rose up like overturned roots growing toward the sky. Suddenly, he realized what Jean-Loup had intended to do. He acted quickly. Removing his cell phone from his shirt pocket and unfastening the clip that held his holster to his belt, he placed them on the ground by Jean-Loup's canvas bag.

As he slipped his gun into his pocket, he shivered for a second at the feel of the cold metal against his skin. He took his belt and checked on the strength of the leather and the buckle. Then he slipped the end through and fastened it at the last hole so that he would have as large a leather ring as possible.

He studied the hill beside and below him. With any luck, he could reach the tree that was almost parallel to the one where Pierrot was swaying. He moved with care. Stepping sideways and grabbing onto the bushes that he hoped had deep, solid roots, he reached the dried-out tree. At the touch of the rough bark, the image of the corpse they had found in the bomb shelter flashed through his mind, but then a menacing creak from the tree substituted an image of his own body hurtling down into the ravine. What was true for Pierrot was also true for him. If the tree was pulled down or if he lost his balance, he would not survive the fall. He tried not to picture it and hoped that the tree was sturdy enough to support both of them. He crouched down on the ground and leaned out, trying to make the belt hang down as far as possible.

"Try to grab on to this."

Hesitating, the boy removed one hand from the tree and hastily returned it to the trunk. "I can't reach."

Frank had already realized that the length of Pierrot's arms and the circle of belt were not long enough. There was only one thing he could do. He turned around to grab the tree trunk with his legs and let himself hang down into the void like a trapeze artist, twisting around to support his chest and get a better view in order to direct Pierrot's movements from above. Holding the belt ring with both hands, this time he managed to lower it to the boy.

"That's it. Now, let go of the tree and grab on to the belt, one hand at a time."

He watched Pierrot's hesitant, slow-motion movements. Despite the distance, he could hear his breath, hissing with anxiety and fatigue. The tree he was hanging on to, bent down by all the additional weight, gave a sinister creak, more chilling than before. Frank felt Pierrot's weight entirely on his arms and legs wrapped around the trunk. He was sure that if Jean-Loup had been in his place, he would have pulled the boy up without much effort, at least to the point where he could let go of the belt and take hold of the tree where he was hanging like a bat. He hoped against hope that he would be able to do the same.

He started pulling upward with his arms, feeling the violence of his effort together with the painfully massive flow of blood to his head. He saw Pierrot rise up inch by inch, trying to support himself with his feet. Frank's arm muscles were burning terribly, as if his shirt had suddenly caught fire.

The gun stuck in his pants gave in to the force of gravity and fell. Barely missing Pierrot's head, it plummeted down and was lost in the ravine. Just at that moment, a noise came from the trunk that sounded like a shot or a log crackling in the fireplace.

Frank continued pulling with all his might. In his effort to raise the weight growing heavier and heavier, the pain in his arms became unbearable. As each second passed, he felt as if sulfuric acid had replaced the blood in his veins. His flesh seemed to be dissolving and his bones, no longer protected by his muscles, seemed about to separate from his shoulders and plunge down, along with Pierrot's screaming body.

But Pierrot slowly continued to rise. Frank kept pulling him up, grasping the tree desperately with his legs, clenching his teeth, astounded by his own resistance. One second after another he felt an overwhelming urge to let go, to release his hands and stop the agony, the burning in his arms. And the very next second, new strength came from some other part of him, as if reserves of energy were stored in some obscure region of his body, in a secret place that only anger and stubbornness could release.

Now Pierrot was high enough to help himself with his body. Frank arched the upper part of his chest that was on the ground and managed to put the belt around his neck, transferring part of the weight to his back and shoulders. After testing the resistance for a second, Frank let go and stretched his free hands out to Pierrot. With the little breath he had left, he told him what to do.

"Okay, just like what you did before. Let go of the belt, calmly, one hand at a time. Grab hold of my arms and climb up. I'll hold you."

Frank was not sure that he could keep his promise. Still, when Pierrot abandoned his grip and his weight was off Frank's neck, he felt the relief like refrigeration running along his back, as if someone had poured cold water on his sweaty skin.

He felt the desperate grasp of Pierrot's hands on his arms. Slowly, inch by inch, clutching with frenzy at Frank's body and clothes, the boy continued to climb. Frank was astounded that he had so much strength left. The instinct of self-preservation was an extraordinary ally in certain situations, a kind of natural drug. He hoped that the strength would not leave him suddenly, now that he was safe.

As soon as he was within reach, Frank seized Pierrot by his belt and pushed up, helping him reach the trunk. He eyes were burning from the sweat pouring down his face. He closed and opened them again as he felt the cleansing tears well up and lose themselves in his eyebrows in that strange, upside-down weeping. He couldn't see a thing. He could only feel the frantic movements of Pierrot's body rubbing against his own, which was now nothing but a single, desperate cry of pain.

"Did you make it?"

Pierrot didn't answer, but Frank suddenly felt free. He bent his head until it was almost touching the warm, damp earth. He felt, rather than saw, the belt slip off his neck and tumble down to join his gun. Then he turned his head to avoid breathing in dirt along with the air that his lungs were desperately seeking. The pressure of the blood in his temples was unbearable. He heard a voice from above, from behind his shoulders, a voice that seemed to come from an unbridgeable distance, like a cry from a faraway hilltop. From the state of torpor that had enveloped his body and mind, Frank still recognized that voice.

"Good, Pierrot. Now grab onto the bushes and come over here to me. Calmly. You're okay now."

Frank felt a wave of shock run through his suspended body and heard a new crackle of the wood as Pierrot's weight abandoned the trunk. The dried-out tree probably felt the same relief he did, as if it were alive rather than long dead.

He knew it wasn't over. He still had to conquer the mental and physical lethargy that had overcome him with the knowledge that Pierrot was finally safe. He had no physical strength or force of will left, but he knew that this was not the time to give in. If he allowed himself to feel that illusory relaxation for another second, he would not be able to straighten up and grab on to the trunk.

He thought of Helena and her silent wait at the airport. He again saw the sadness in her gray eyes, the sadness that he wanted to erase and perhaps could. He saw the hand of her father, Nathan Parker, suspended like a claw over her. Rage and hatred came to him as a salvation. He clenched his teeth and gathered up all the energy he had left before it vanished into the air like smoke. He arched his back and, throwing up his arms, forced himself up. His abdominal muscles, the only part of his body still unused, now burned with the stress.

He saw the dry wood of the tree trunk slowly approach him like a mirage. Another creak reminded him that, like any mirage, it could dissolve at any second. He forced himself to go slowly, without abrupt movements, to avoid worsening the precarious situation.

His left hand finally gripped the tree, then his right. Somehow he managed to pull himself to a sitting position. The violent flow of blood as it started going down and resuming its normal course made his head spin. He closed his eyes, waiting for it to go away and hoping that the two dried sponges that were his lungs would be able to contain all the air he was sending them. In the comforting darkness of his closed eyes, his arms grabbed the tree and he sat there feeling the rough bark against his cheek until some of his strength returned.

When he reopened his eyes, Pierrot was a few yards from him, on level ground. He was standing next to Jean-Loup and had his arms around his waist, as if hanging in midair had given him the need to grab on to something or someone in order to believe that he was really safe.

Jean-Loup had his left arm around the boy's shoulder and a bloody knife in his right hand. For an instant, Frank thought that he was using the boy's body as a shield, that he would hold the knife at his throat and take him hostage. He pushed that thought out of his mind. No, not after what he had seen. Not after Jean-

Loup had given up any chance of escape in order to rescue Pierrot. He wondered what had become of Ryan Mosse. And at the same time, he realized that he didn't give a damn.

He noticed a movement from above and instinctively raised his head. There was a group of people standing at the edge of the road, leaning on the guardrail in front of a line of cars. Pierrot's cries must have attracted their attention or else, more probably, a group of tourists had happened to stop just then to admire the view and had watched the nerve-racking rescue. Jean-Loup turned his head and looked up. He too saw the people and the cars parked forty yards above him. His shoulders slumped slightly as if an invisible weight had suddenly fallen on him.

Frank stood up and, leaning on the tree trunk, slowly went back the way he had come. He bid farewell to the lifeless tree with the gratitude due to a true friend who has helped in a difficult moment. His fingers felt the touch of the live branches on the bushes he clutched as he placed his feet on the firm surface of the horizontal world.

Jean-Loup and Pierrot were before him, watching him. He saw the green flash in Jean-Loup's eyes. Frank was exhausted and knew that he didn't stand a chance of winning a fight, not in this weakened state, and definitely not after what he had seen Jean-Loup do to Mosse. Jean-Loup must have sensed his thoughts. He smiled, a smile that was suddenly tired. Frank could only imagine what lay behind that simple movement of his facial muscles: a life divided by continuous motion from light to darkness, from warmth to cold, from lucidity to delirium in the perpetual dilemma of being *one* or *no one*. Jean-Loup's smile faded. His voice was the same one that had enchanted so many radio listeners, radiating tranquillity and well-being.

"Don't worry, Agent Ottobre. It's all right. I know the words 'The End' when I see them."

Frank bent over and picked up his cell phone. As he dialed

Morelli's number, he thought about the absurdity of the situation. There he was, unarmed, completely at the mercy of a man who could easily destroy him with one hand tied behind his back, and he was able to remain alive only because Jean-Loup had decided not to kill him.

Morelli's brusque voice leapt from the phone. "Hello?'"

In exchange, Frank offered his own exhausted voice and the good news. "Claude, it's Frank."

"What is it? What happened?"

His few words cost him enormous effort. "Get a car to Jean-Loup's house right away. I've got him."

He didn't listen to the sergeant's astonished response. He didn't see Pierrot bend his head and cling to his friend's body more tightly, as a reaction to those last words. All he saw as he lowered the cell phone was Jean-Loup's hand slowly opening and dropping the bloody knife to the ground.

62

The car marked SÛRETÉ PUBLIQUE DE MONACO veered right and turned at incredible speed onto the highway to the Nice Airport. Frank had told Xavier that it was a matter of life or death, and the agent was interpreting his words to the letter. Even with the wail of the siren, he could hear the tires screeching on the asphalt as centrifugal force pushed them to the outside of the curve. They reached a traffic circle where there was obviously roadwork under way. Frank knew that, although they were in a police car, they were still not exempt from the laws of physics. He feared that this time, despite Xavier's talent, the car might not hold the road and they'd crash against the red and white plastic poles and plunge into the Var River below. But his favorite race car driver stunned him again. With a sharp turn of the wheel, Xavier swerved and got the car out of the curve.

Frank saw Morelli's body relax when he realized they would make it. They drove straight ahead for a short stretch and the driver began to slow down. He turned off the siren when they pulled onto the access road of Terminal 2 and followed a sign indicating the unloading zone for passengers and luggage. Cars were only allowed a brief stop, a ritual known as Kiss and Fly. Frank smiled to himself. He doubted that Parker would kiss him before he left.

Instead of following normal procedures, they stopped in a reserved access area halfway down on the left. It was protected by a barricade and two guards from the Côte d'Azur Airport. Seeing the police markings, they raised the barricade and let them through. A few minutes later, the car pulled up gently in front of the international departures terminal.

Morelli turned sharply to the driver. "If you do that on the way back, the next vehicle you'll be operating will be a lawn mower. Landscapers love to hire former cops."

"Don't worry, champ, his bark is worse than his bite." Frank smiled and leaned over from the backseat to put his hand on Xavier's shoulder.

Frank's cell phone rang. He could guess who it was and pulled the phone out of his jacket pocket. The ring was so insistent that he was surprised the phone wasn't hot, as if the ring tone could be thermal as well as aural.

"Hello?"

"Frank? It's Froben. Where are you?"

"Outside the airport. I'm getting out of the car now."

"Thank the lord." The inspector sounded genuinely relieved. "This guy's about to explode. He'll probably declare war against France single-handedly in a matter of minutes. You wouldn't believe the stories I had to make up to keep him calm."

"I believe it. But I assure you, it wasn't a whim. It's the biggest favor anyone's ever done for me in my life."

"Okay, Americano. My cell phone's getting wet with tears. Cut the sentimentality and get your ass over here. You've got to take this hot potato off my hands. I'm coming to meet you."

Frank opened the car door. Morelli's voice stopped him just as his foot hit the pavement. "Should we wait?"

"No, you go. I'll get back somehow."

Frank was about to walk away but then changed his mind. Even in such a hurry, he had to express his gratitude. "Uh, Claude?"

"Yeah?"

"Thank you, really. Both of you."

"For what? Go on. They're waiting for you."

Before he got out, Frank glanced knowingly at Xavier. "I'll bet a thousand euros against one of Roncaille's calling cards that you can get back faster than you got here."

He closed the door on Morelli's protests. But as he heard the car race off, his smile was already gone.

Jean-Loup's capture and the end of the nightmare had created a sort of holiday cheer among the police of the Sûreté Publique. All the deaths in the criminal's path had kept things solemn, but seeing him arrive at headquarters in handcuffs had been like finding a special present under the Christmas tree. And anyone who regretted that Nicolas Hulot was not there to share that moment kept it to himself. The fact that the arrest was due solely to Frank's stroke of genius and that it had been carried out by him alone raised the general level of admiration for him and even created esteem where it hadn't existed. He had smiled when smiles were required, shaken hands when they were offered along with congratulations, and had taken part in a joy that he could not completely share. He hadn't wanted to be the only guy not smiling in the group photo. But he kept doing something that was becoming a ritual that day. He kept looking at his watch. And he had requested a car to get him to the Nice Airport as quickly as possible.

He hurried down the sidewalk. The glass doors opened obligingly at his arrival. Froben's familiar face greeted him as soon as he came in. The inspector snorted theatrically and mimed someone wiping sweat off his brow with one hand.

"You have no idea what a great pleasure it is to see you."

"I have a really good idea, don't you worry," Frank answered in the same joking tone. They were both being perfectly sincere.

"I was clutching at straws to find some way to convince him that no official intervention was necessary. I could barely manage to keep him from calling the President of the United States. I'm sure you can imagine. They missed their flight, but the next one to the States leaves in just under an hour. And I guarantee that General Parker won't be kept off it."

"Everything you say about Parker is true. And believe me, I could tell you a few more things about him."

As they spoke, they walked rapidly to the area of the airport where Froben had parked the Parkers. They reached the security check. The inspector showed his badge to the agents at the metal detectors, and a uniformed officer pointed to a side entrance that would bypass the line of passengers waiting to have their hand luggage checked. They turned left to go to the gates.

"Speaking of things that are hard to believe, how's the other business going? Am I wrong, or is there news?"

"You mean No One?"

"Who else?"

"We got him," said Frank in a neutral voice.

"When?" The inspector looked at him, astonished.

"About an hour ago. He's in jail."

"That's how you tell me? Just like that?"

Frank turned to look at Froben. He waved vaguely in the air. "It's over, Claude. End of story." He couldn't say anything more because they had reached the reserved room, guarded by a policeman.

Frank stopped outside the door that obscured General Nathan Parker, Helena, and Stuart from his view. One of them was a burdensome part of his present; the other two were his future. He stood staring at the door as if it were transparent and he could see what those on the other side were doing. Froben put a hand on his shoulder. "Want any help, Frank?"

There was a protective note in the inspector's voice. Froben's delicate sensitivity contrasted sharply with his lumberjack's appearance.

"No thanks. You've given me more than I could have hoped for. Now I have to fend for myself."

The room was one of the many anonymous, comfortable VIP lounges scattered throughout all airports for business-class passengers. Armchairs and leather sofas, walls painted pastel colors, plush carpeting, a small cafeteria to one side, and reproductions of Van Gogh and Matisse paintings on the walls alongside a few travel posters framed in satinized steel. There was a sense of instability that one generally finds in that kind of room, with all those arrivals and departures breaking the false illusion of comfort.

Helena was sitting on a sofa leafing through a magazine. Stuart was beside her playing his Game Boy. The low coffee table in front of them had a couple of plastic cups and a soda can on its glass surface.

General Parker was standing on the other side of the room, his back to the door. He was staring at a copy of a crucifixion by Dalí hanging on the wall, his hands crossed behind his back. He turned his head as he heard the door open, looking at Frank the way one looks at someone one hasn't seen in a very long time, searching for a name and a place to connect to the face .

Helena raised her head from the page and her face lit up when she saw him. Frank thanked heaven that the light of that gaze was meant for him, but he had no time to enjoy her smile. Parker's rage exploded, a dark cloud blocking the sun. He was standing between them in two steps, with hatred hotter than fire blazing on his face.

"I should have known that you were the cause of all this. This is the last mistake you'll ever make. I've already told you once, and now I'm confirming it. *You're finished.* You're so stupid, you thought I was bluffing. As soon as I'm back in the States, I'll make sure there's nothing left of you. I'll . . ."

Frank stared at the red face of the man before him with his best unruffled look. There was a storm inside him crashing against the shore, shaking the wooden pier. But when Frank interrupted the general, his voice was so calm that it aggravated his adversary even more.

"I'd calm down if I were you, General. At your age, the heart is an organ that needs to be treated with care. You wouldn't want to risk a heart attack and rid me of your presence so easily."

The look that passed over the old soldier's face was one of a thousand flags waving, each moved by the winds of war. Frank saw with pleasure that, along with hatred, fury, and disbelief, there was a shadow of doubt behind those impenetrable blue eyes. He might have begun to wonder where Frank found the nerve to speak to him that way. It was just an instant, and then Parker's gaze was again filled with omnipotent disdain. He imitated Frank and calmed his voice as well. The corners of his mouth lifted in a self-satisfied smile.

"I'm sorry to disappoint you, young man. Unfortunately for you, my heart is solid as a rock. You, apparently, are having useless palpitations. And that's another mistake. My daughter . . ."

Frank interrupted him again, which was not something to which General Nathan Parker was accustomed.

"As far as your daughter and grandson are concerned"—Frank paused a moment at the word *grandson,* lowering his voice so that the boy could not hear. Stuart was sitting on the sofa with his hands in his lap, watching their scene in wonder. His electronic toy, completely ignored, continued on its own: *beep, beep, beep*—"as far as your daughter and grandson are concerned, I would advise you to let them go visit the duty-free shop. It might be better if we keep the things we have to say to each other to ourselves."

"We have absolutely nothing to say to each other, Agent Ottobre. And my daughter and grandson don't need to go to any goddamn duty-free shop. You're the one who should walk out that door and get out of our lives for good. We're getting on a plane to America. Let me repeat . . ."

"General, perhaps you've forgotten that bluffs don't pay off in the long run. Sooner or later, someone will have the right cards to call. And win. I don't give a damn about you. If I saw you burning in hell, I wouldn't even bother pissing on the fire. If you want me to say what I have to say in front of them, I will. But be aware that you won't be able to turn back. So if you want to take that risk . . ."

Frank's voice was so low that Helena could barely hear him. She wondered what he had just said to her father to silence him that way. Frank looked at her and nodded slightly. Helena stood up and took her son by the hand.

"Come on, Stuart. Let's go for a walk. There are lots of things to see outside." The boy followed her obediently. He lived in the Parker house, like his mother. He was used to receiving orders, not suggestions. And orders were meant to be obeyed. The two of them walked over to the door, the carpet muffling their footsteps. The only sound was that of the door closing behind them.

Frank sat down on the sofa where Helena had been a minute before. The warmth of her body was still on the leather and that warmth became his. He pointed to the armchair in front of him.

"Sit down, General."

"Don't you tell me what to do!" Frank noticed the slight hysterical note in Parker's voice. "Hurry up and spare me your ranting. We have a plane to catch in . . ." He looked at his watch. Frank smiled to himself. It must have become a habit for him too. Frank noticed that he had to move his arm farther away to see the dial.

Parker looked up from his watch. "We all have a plane to catch in less than an hour."

Frank shook his head. *Negative, sir.*

"I'm sorry to contradict you, General. Not *all of you.* Just *you.*"

Parker looked at him as if he could not believe what he had just heard. He seemed surprised, like he had just heard the punch line of a very long joke. Then, suddenly, he burst out laughing. Frank was happy to see that his laughter was sincere, and it gave him great pleasure to know that in another minute it would be silenced.

"Laugh if you like. That doesn't change the fact that you're leaving on your own and your daughter and *grandson* are staying here in France, with me." Parker shook his head with the pity one feels before the ramblings of an idiot.

"You're out of your mind."

Frank smiled and relaxed on the sofa. He crossed his legs and stretched his arm over the back.

"Sorry to contradict you again. I once was, I think. But I'm cured. Unfortunately for you, I've never been so sane. You see, General, you were so concerned with finding my mistakes that you never stopped to think about yours, which were *much* worse." The general looked toward the door and took a couple of steps in that direction. Frank cut that plan short. "There's no help coming. I wouldn't advise involving the police, if that's what you're thinking. And if you're hoping Captain Mosse will come to the rescue, I'll be the first to inform you that he's lying in the morgue with his throat cut."

The general spun around. "What are you saying?"

"I just told you. As good as he was, you can always find someone better. Your lackey was an excellent soldier, but unfortunately for him, No One, the man he was supposed to kill, was a much better fighter. He killed him as easily as Mosse thought he would get rid of *him*."

Parker had to sit down at that news. His tanned face clouded over. "In any event, as far as your daughter's killer is concerned, we caught him. There's no chance that what you were afraid of could happen now. We're locking him up in an insane asylum and he'll never get out."

Frank paused briefly. He moved to the edge of the sofa and looked carefully at the man sitting before him. He couldn't imagine what he was thinking just then. On the other hand, he didn't care. All he wanted was to wrap things up quickly and stare at his back as he walked to the plane.

Alone.

"It might be better if I start at the beginning, General. And the beginning has to do with me, not with you. I don't think I need to dwell on my story, do I? You know everything about me, about my wife and her suicide after my miraculous escape from an explosion while I was investigating Jeff and Osmond Larkin, two drug dealers who ran a two- or three-hundred-million-dollar-a-year enterprise. I was destroyed by that experience. I ended up here trying to pull myself out of the mire and I started investigating this serial killer case almost against my own will. A killer as ferocious as a shark whose first victim was your daughter, Arianna. And then you appeared on the scene. You came to Monte Carlo, distraught with suffering, thirsting for revenge . . ."

"And what would you have done if someone had killed your wife like that?" Parker took Frank's comment to mean that he doubted the sincerity of Parker's grief.

"I would have done exactly what you said you wanted to do. I would have had no peace until I killed the murderer with my own bare hands. But it's different in your case."

"What the hell are you saying, you clown? What do you know about a father's feelings toward his daughter?"

Parker spoke hastily, without thinking, but he immediately realized his mistake. Frank felt like pulling the Glock from his belt and shooting Parker in the head, splattering that bastard's brain to add a touch of realism to the anonymous posters on the walls. The effort he made to control himself probably took ten years off his life.

"You're right, General Parker. I'm totally ignorant of the feelings a father can have for a daughter. But I know exactly what *your* feelings are for *your* daughter. You make me sick, Parker.

You completely disgust me. I told you that you're a despicable person and that I would crush you like an ant, but in your all-powerful delirium, you didn't believe me."

A shadow of a smile passed over Parker's face. He probably considered the reaction he had provoked in Frank a small personal triumph.

"If it's not too much for you, could you tell me just how you plan on doing that?"

"Here. There's confirmation of everything I'm about to tell you inside this envelope. Now, if you don't mind, I'll continue." Frank pulled a large yellow envelope from his inside pocket and threw it down on the glass table in front of them. Parker waved at him to go on.

Frank's mind was still in turmoil and he had to force himself to calm down and explain things in order. "As I was saying, you came here to Monte Carlo, distraught over the death of your daughter and the barbaric way she was killed. I must say, you were hardly reticent about your desire to get your hands on the killer yourself. You were so obvious about it that you aroused some suspicion." He stopped and then hissed his next words. "But that intention was the furthest thing from your mind. *What you wanted most was the exact opposite. You wanted the murderer to go on killing."*

Parker jumped to his feet as if suddenly bitten by a snake.

"Now I'm sure of it. You're off your rocker and you should be locked up in a cell with that other one." Frank nodded to him to sit down again.

"Quit protesting, General. It's completely useless. You don't get it yet, do you? I know all about you and the late, not at all lamented Captain Mosse."

"You know all about *just what,* exactly?"

"If you'd be so kind as to stop interrupting me, you'd find out before you get on the plane, *alone*. You realize of course that we have to go back a minute to my story. Remember the two drug lords I was telling you about? One of them, Jeff Larkin, was killed in a shootout when they were arrested, may he rest in peace. The other one, Osmond, landed in jail. When the investigation into the activities of those two gentlemen continued, the FBI started to suspect that someone high, very high up, was involved in their trafficking. But despite all their efforts, they couldn't figure out who it was."

Nathan Parker's face was now a mask of stone. He sat on the leather armchair and crossed his legs, his eyes half closed, waiting. This was Frank's moment to show his cards, one by one, and the general was curious to know what they were. Frank couldn't wait to turn that curiosity into the certainty of his own defeat.

"Locked in prison, Osmond's only contact with the outside world was through his lawyer, a little-known attorney in New York who came out of nowhere. We suspected that this lawyer, one Hudson McCormack, was more than just a defense lawyer. We started to think that he might be the outside contact for his jailed client. My partner at the FBI who was running the Larkin case e-mailed me McCormack's picture because, by pure coincidence, he was in Monte Carlo. Life's funny that way. Officially, he came here for a regatta, but you know as well as I do that official reasons can hide more important unofficial ones."

The general raised an eyebrow. "Would you be so kind as to explain what I have to do with this cops-and-robbers business?"

Frank leaned over the table, opened an envelope, and pulled the photograph that Cooper had sent him, the picture in the bar. He pushed it over to Parker. It reminded him of the night of Mosse's arrest, when he had shown him the picture of Roby Stricker.

"May I introduce the late Hudson McCormack, legal representative of Osmond Larkin and the last victim of the serial killer Jean-Loup Verdier, better known as No One."

"I only recognize him because I saw his picture in the paper," the old man said, shooting a glance at the photo and then raising his eyes. "I never knew he existed before that."

"Really? Strange, General. See the person with his back to McCormack? You can't see his face, but the bar is full of mirrors." Frank's voice changed, as if he were musing over something. "You have no idea how important mirrors are in this whole story. Mirrors have a terrible tendency of reflecting what's in front of them."

"I know how mirrors work. Every time I look in one, I see the person who's going to reduce you to dust."

Frank smiled in conciliation. "Congratulations on your sense of humor, General. It's more than I can say for your strategic ability and choice of men. As I said, the bar where this photo was taken is full of mirrors. With the help of a talented, *very talented* young man, I managed to figure out who the person sitting at the table with Hudson McCormack is. All the young man did was enlarge the reflection in the mirrors. And just take a look at who he is."

Frank took another picture from the envelope and threw it on the table without even looking at it. This time, Parker picked up the photo and stared at it for a long time.

"You can't really say that Captain Ryan Mosse was photogenic. But you didn't need a fashion model, did you, Parker? You needed someone exactly like the captain. A borderline psychopath who was loyal to the point of fanaticism. Someone willing to kill anyone you told him to. He leaned in toward Nathan Parker. "General, does your surprised expression mean that you deny the person in that picture with Hudson McCormack is Ryan Mosse?"

"No, I don't. It's definitely Captain Mosse. But this picture only proves that he knew the lawyer in question. What does that have to do with me?"

"We're getting there, General. We're getting there."

This time, it was Frank who looked at his watch. And without having to move it away to see it.

"We'll have to get there quickly. Your plane's about to take off, so I'll summarize. Here's how things went. You and Mosse came to an agreement with Laurent Bedon, director at Radio Monte Carlo. The poor guy needed money desperately and it couldn't have been hard to convince him. You gave him piles of money in exchange for all the information he could find out about the investigation. A spy, like in any war. That's why, when we suspected that Roby Stricker might be the next victim after the killer's phone call, Mosse was already there. Then Stricker was killed and I got ahead of myself and slipped up. I forgot the first rule of a cop: examine *everything* from *every* angle. Ironic, isn't it? A reflection in the mirror helped Nicolas Hulot realize who the real killer was and the same detail helped me realize it too. Funny how simple things look, in retrospect."

Frank ran his hand through his hair. He was beginning to feel very tired, but it wasn't the moment to relax, not yet. When it was over, he would have all the time in the world to relax. And the right company.

"You must have felt a little lost with your stooge in jail, didn't you? You didn't need that at all. When we finally realized who No One was, Mosse was proven innocent and released from prison. You must have been a little relieved. Nothing lost. You still had all the time you needed to solve your personal problems, and you even got a stroke of luck."

Frank had to admire Nathan Parker's control. He was sitting in front of him, impassive, not batting an eye. There must have been many people in his past who had met him and decided not to take him on as an enemy. But Frank didn't mind. He had crossed his path and now he couldn't wait to get rid of him.

He didn't feel elation, just a deep sense of emptiness. He was surprised to realize that his real desire was not simply to beat him. His greatest pleasure would have been not to see him ever again. He continued listing the facts.

"Let me tell you exactly what that stroke of luck was. No One was identified but he managed to escape. You must have had a hard time believing it. Captain Mosse was back and the killer was hidden out there somewhere, outsmarting the police and *free to kill again*."

He looked at the backs of his hands and remembered when they were always trembling. Now his hands were firm, strong. He could make a fist with the knowledge that General Parker was crushed.

"Not long afterward, No One called Agent Frank Ottobre again. But not the usual way. This time, he called from a cell phone, without masking his voice. Why should he bother, after all? Everyone knew who he was: Jean-Loup Verdier, the deejay of Radio Monte Carlo. Just an anonymous cell phone left on a bench in Nice. We traced it through a satellite system and found it easily. No prints on the phone, except those of the boy who had found it. And that was strange." He shot a glance at Parker as if he didn't know the answer to his own question.

"Why did No One bother rubbing off the fingerprints when we knew who he was? I didn't pay much attention to it then, partly because we were thinking about what the phone call meant. The killer told us that he was planning more murders, regardless of the fact that the police were looking for him. And that's what he did. Hudson McCormack was found dead right in front of the Sûreté headquarters, in Jean-Loup Verdier's car with his face skinned off. The world was horrified at this new killing. Everyone wondered the same thing. Why couldn't the police catch this monster who went on killing unchecked and then disappeared like a ghost.

Frank got up from the couch. He was so tired that he was surprised his joints didn't audibly creak. His knee, on the other hand, had strangely stopped bothering him. He took a few steps around the room and went to stand behind the general who was sitting motionless in the armchair. The man didn't even turn to follow him with his eyes.

"I think it was Laurent Bedon's death that aroused my suspicion. A mere accident, a man killed in an everyday, botched robbery. Suspicions are like crumbs in your bed, General. You can't sleep until you get rid of them. That's how it started, with the death of that poor fool, Bedon. That's why I had the photos my friend sent checked out and discovered that the man sitting in the bar in New York with Hudson McCormack was Ryan Mosse. And that's why I had the same person examine the tape of the phone call that I received from No One. You know what we discovered? Let me tell you, even though you already know. We found that it was a piece of editing work. The things you can do with technology today. It's a great help, though, if you use it with a grain of salt, *cum grano salis,* if you don't mind a little Latin. We listened to the message word by word and we found that some of them were repeated several times: 'moon,' 'dog,' 'speak to me.' Analysis of the intonation showed that every word was repeated *twice in exactly the same way*. The voice graph of each word placed one on top of the other matched perfectly. I'm told that can't happen, just like no two snowflakes or fingerprints can be the same. Which means that the words were taken and spliced on a tape, one after the other until the desired message was obtained. And that was the tape used for the phone call. It was Laurent, wasn't it? He's the one who gave you the tapes with Jean-Loup's voice so that you had enough material to do that. What else is there to say?"

Frank went on as if what he was about to say was completely unnecessary, like someone explaining the obvious to someone who refuses to understand.

"After the phone call, Mosse went to Jean-Loup Verdier's house. He took the car, killed Hudson McCormack, and gave him the same treatment that No One used on his victims. Then Mosse left the car and the corpse near headquarters." Frank stopped in front of Parker. He did so deliberately, to force the old man to raise his head and look at him as he drew his conclusions. Just then, in the anonymous airport lounge, he was the judge and jury and his verdict was final.

"And that was your real aim, Parker. You wanted to eliminate any connection between the heroic, powerful General Nathan Parker and Jeff and Osmond Larkin whom you supplied with cover and protection in exchange for a sizeable percentage of the profits. I'll bet that every time General Parker took part in a war somewhere in the world, he didn't just protect the interests of his country. No, he took advantage of the situation to protect his own interests. I don't know why and I don't give a damn. That's for you and your conscience to sort out. Although in light of the facts, I'm not sure you have one. McCormack, your contact with Osmond Larkin, was just a fool in a game that was too big for him, and he could have made a lot of trouble if he decided to talk. And he would have, to protect his own hide if things started going badly. He was killed the way the serial killer murdered so it looked as if he were to blame. Even if No One had been caught and declared he was not guilty of that particular murder, who would have believed him? The answer makes me laugh: *no one*. Maybe McCormack had brought you a message from his client. Actually, you could satisfy my curiosity. I think, though mind you I'm just guessing, that Osmond Larkin threatened to start talking if you didn't get him out of jail right away. The fact that he was killed during an ordinary prison fight might only be a coincidence, but there have been far too many coincidences in this story." Frank sat back down on the couch, looking at his adversary with the expression of a man who is surprised by his own words.

"Lots of coincidences, right? Like Tavernier, the owner of the house you rented. When you were leaving, the old guy must have told you about the bomb shelter that his sister-in-law had forced his brother to build. You realized where Jean-Loup Verdier was hiding and you left Ryan Mosse to take care of him. All you had to do was get rid of the last witness and everything would be taken care of. Want to know something funny?"

"No, but you're going to tell me anyway."

"You bet I am. Just before I came here, I found out that the delinquent who bumped off Laurent Bedon has been arrested. He's just a small-time punk who cleaned off people coming out of the casinos."

"And the funny thing?"

"The funny thing is that my suspicions started with the only death in all this that seems to be accidental and not really a murder. A crime that at first I blamed on you and of which you are completely innocent."

Parker sat there a moment as if he were thinking over everything Frank had just said. Frank had no illusions. It was just a pause, not a surrender. The general was a chess player taking his time after his opponent had said "check." He gestured vaguely with his hand.

"This is all just conjecture. You can't actually *prove* what you've just said."

And that was the move Frank had been expecting. He knew that the general wasn't all wrong. He was holding a series of important cards, but none of them was definitive evidence. The witnesses were all dead and the only one still alive, Jean-Loup Verdier, was not exactly reliable. But this was *his* bluff, and the general would have to pay to see him. He shrugged.

"Maybe I can. Or maybe not. You've got enough money to pay a pack of lawyers to get you out of trouble and keep you out of jail. But a scandal is a different story. Lack of evidence will keep you out of a jail cell, but it won't prevent people from doubting you. Just think . . . would the President of the United States still want the opinion of a military adviser suspected of drug trafficking?"

General Parker looked at him for a long time and didn't

answer. He ran his hand through his short, white hair. His blue eyes had lost their warrior spark and he was finally an old man. But his voice was still strong.

"I think I know what you're getting at."

"Do you?"

"If you didn't want anything from me, you'd already have told the FBI. You wouldn't have come here alone. You'd be here with the entire police force. So have the courage to be explicit."

Frank could see that Parker's reputation was well deserved. He knew he was defeated but, like all soldiers worthy of the name, he could see a way out and was taking advantage of it.

"I'll be more than explicit, General. I'll be brutally honest. If it were up to me, I'd take no pity on you whatsoever. I think you're a piece of shit and I would gladly drop you into a sea of sharks. That's exactly what *I* would do. I once told you that every man has his price and you just didn't understand mine. Here's my price: Helena and Stuart in exchange for my silence." Frank was quiet for a moment. "As you can see, General, you were right about something. Somehow, we're made of the same stuff, you and I."

The old man bent his head. "And if I . . ."

Frank shook his head. "My offer's not negotiable. Take it or leave it. And that's not all."

"What do you mean?"

"I mean that, now that you're going back to the States, you'll realize that you're too old and tired for military life. You'll resign. People will advise you against it, but you'll be adamant. It's only fair that a man like you, someone who has given so much to his country, a father who has suffered so, should be allowed to enjoy the time he has left in peace."

Parker stared at him. Frank had expected to see anything on his face except that sudden curiosity.

"And you'll let me go? Without doing anything? Where's your conscience, Agent Ottobre?"

"Same place as yours. But mine sure weighs a lot less."

The silence that fell between them was eloquent. There was nothing more to say. Just then, with the perfect timing of fate, the door opened and Stuart's head peeked through the door.

"Oh, Stuart. Come on in. Our conversation is over."

Stuart ran in, followed by Helena's slight figure. The boy didn't understand, and she couldn't make the leap. It was Nathan Parker who indirectly gave her the news, speaking to the boy who thought he was his grandfather instead of really his father. The old man knelt down before him without any apparent effort and put his hands on his shoulders.

"Okay, Stuart. There has been a change of plans. Remember when I told you we had to go right back to the States?"

The boy nodded, reminding Frank of Pierrot's naive way of communicating. The general pointed to Frank.

"Well, after talking to this friend of mine for a while, I don't think there's any need for you and your mother to go back yet. I've got lots of things to do at home and we won't be able to see each other very much for a while. Would you like to stay here and take a longer vacation?"

"Really, Grandpa? Could we go to Disneyland in Paris?" The boy's eyes widened, incredulous. Parker glanced at Frank who lowered his eyelids in agreement.

"Sure. Disneyland and many other places."

Stuart raised his arms above his head and shouted, "Hurray!" He ran to embrace his mother who hugged him with a face sculpted in astonishment. Her stunned gaze passed from Frank to her father, like someone receiving good news that was hard to absorb.

"Mommy, we're staying here. Grandpa said so. We're going to Disneyland, to Disneyland, to Disneyland . . ."

Helena put a hand on his head, trying to calm him, but Stuart was relentless. He started dancing around the room, repeating the words like an endless nursery rhyme. There was a knock at the door.

"Come in," said Parker, standing up. Until then, he had been watching Stuart's joyfulness from his position on the ground. For Frank it was fitting. He was a man on his knees.

Froben's face appeared in the doorway. "Excuse me."

"Come in, Froben."

The inspector looked understandably embarrassed. He saw with relief that the atmosphere was tense but not hostile. Not anymore at least. He turned to Parker.

"General, excuse me for the inconvenience and the unforgivable wait. I wanted to tell you that your flight has been announced. We have just put the coffin on board and the luggage."

"Thank you, Inspector. There have been some last-minute changes. My daughter and grandson will be staying here. If you would be so kind as to board my bags and leave the others here, I would be most grateful. They're easy to recognize: light blue Samsonites."

"It's the least I can do, General." Froben bent his head. He reminded Frank of the butler in an English comedy.

"Thank you. I'll be right there."

"Gate nineteen."

Froben left the room like someone emerging unscathed from a car accident. Parker turned back to Stuart.

"Okay, I have to go. You be good. *Roger?*" The boy snapped to attention and saluted as if it were an old game with them. Parker opened the door and left without a look or a word for his daughter. Frank went over to Helena and caressed her cheek with his hand. He would have faced an army of Parkers for the look in her eyes.

"How did you do it?"

Frank smiled. "All in good time. I still have something left to do. I'll only be a couple of minutes. I need to check one last thing."

He left the room and looked for Nathan Parker. He saw him

walking down the hallway next to Froben who was escorting him to the plane. He reached them an instant before the general turned to board the plane. He was the last passenger. His privileged status had given him a little extra time.

When he saw Frank coming, Froben stepped discreetly aside. Parker spoke to him without turning.

"Don't tell me you had an irresistible urge to say good-bye."

"No, General. I just wanted to make sure you left and I needed to share one last thought with you."

"Which is?"

"You told me several times that I was finished. Now I'd just like to point out that *you're* finished. I don't care if the rest of the world will ever know . . ." The two men looked at each other. Black eyes against blue. Two men who would never stop hating each other. "You know it, and that's enough for me."

Without a word, Nathan Parker turned and walked past the barrier and down the hallway. He was no longer a soldier, just an old man. Everything he was leaving behind was no longer his problem. The real problem lay ahead of him. As he walked toward the plane, his reflection was caught in the mirror on the wall. A coincidence, one of many. *Another mirror . . .*

Frank stood still and watched Parker until he turned and left the mirror empty.

63

Frank reached the end of the hallway and found himself in front of Roncaille's office. He waited before knocking, thinking of all the closed doors that had stood before him, real and metaphorical. This was just one more, but now everything was different. Now the man known as No One was safely behind bars and the case would go down as another successful investigation.

Four days had passed since Jean-Loup Verdier's arrest and the meeting with Parker at the Nice Airport. Frank had spent that time with Helena and her son, without reading the papers or watching TV, trying to put everything behind him. Although he knew he would never be able to get rid of it entirely.

He had left the Parc Saint-Roman apartment and taken refuge with Helena and Stuart in a small, discreet hotel where they could escape the relentless pursuit of the media. Despite their desire for each other, he and Helena were not sleeping in the same room. Not yet. There would be time for that. He spent his days resting and getting to know Stuart, trying to build a relationship with him. The official confirmation that he would keep his promise about Disneyland had laid the groundwork. The fact that their vacation would also include a couple of weeks in the Canal du Midi on a houseboat hadn't hurt either. Now all he had to do was wait for the cement to harden.

Frank knocked at the door and Roncaille told him to come in. Frank was not in the least surprised to find Durand there as well, but he hadn't expected to see Dr. Cluny. Roncaille greeted him with his standard PR smile that now seemed a little more natural. In that moment of grandeur, the police chief knew how to play the perfect host. Durand was sitting in the chair with his usual expression and merely waved.

"Good, Frank. You were the only one missing. Come in. Sit down. Dr. Durand just arrived." It was such a high society voice that Frank almost expected to see an ice bucket with champagne on the desk. There probably would be one, later on, somewhere else.

Roncaille returned to his desk and Frank settled into the chair that the chief had indicated. He waited in silence. There was nothing more for him to say. But there were things he wanted to know. Roncaille spoke.

"Since everybody's here, I'll get right to the point. There are other sides to this story that you don't know about, things that go far beyond Daniel Legrand, alias Jean-Loup Verdier. Here's what we managed to find out."

Roncaille leaned back in his chair and crossed his legs. Frank thought it strange that Durand was allowing him to conduct the meeting, though he wasn't much interested in the reason why. Roncaille shared what he knew with the spontaneity and benevolence of a saint sheltering a poor man with his cloak.

"His father, Marcel Legrand, was high up in the French secret service, in charge of training. An expert in undercover operations and intelligence. At some point, he started showing signs of being unbalanced, although we don't have much information on that. We got as far as we could, but the French government didn't open up very much. It must have caused a lot of headaches. But we know enough to reconstruct what happened. After a series of episodes, Legrand was invited, one might say, to leave active service of his own accord and take early retirement. That must have unsettled him even more. It was probably the final blow to his unstable mental state. He moved to Cassis with a pregnant wife and his housekeeper, a woman who had been with him since he was a child. He purchased an estate, La Patience, and locked himself up there like a hermit without any contact with the outside world. And he forced his family to do the same. No contact, for any reason whatsoever."

Roncaille turned to Dr. Cluny, tacitly acknowledging that he was the person best equipped to explain the rest, due to the psychological implications. The psychiatrist removed his glasses and pinched his nose with his forefinger and thumb, as usual. Frank still didn't understand whether that gesture was the result of a careful strategy to get attention or simply a habit, but it didn't matter. Having captured his audience, Cluny replaced his glasses. Many of the things he was about to say were new, even to Roncaille and Durand.

"I spoke with Jean-Loup Verdier, or Daniel Legrand. It wasn't easy, but I managed to draw a general picture. At times, the subject showed readiness to open up and emerge from his total isolation. Anyway, as the chief said, the Legrand family moved to Provence. By the way, Mme Legrand was Italian. That's probably why Daniel, or Jean-Loup if you prefer, speaks the language so well. For the sake of clarity I'll continue to call him Jean-Loup."

He looked around for their approval and the silence showed that there was no objection. Cluny continued explaining the facts, or what he thought they were.

"His wife gave birth not long after they moved. According to her husband's wish for isolation, which had become an obsession, no doctor was called. The woman gave birth to twins, Lucien and Daniel. But there were complications and Lucien was born deformed. There were skin growths that made him look monstrously disfigured. Clinically, I can't say exactly what it was because Jean-Loup's testimony is unclear. In any event, DNA tests on the corpse found in the shelter prove beyond a shadow of a doubt that they were brothers. The father was overwhelmed by this trauma and his mental state grew even worse. He refused to acknowledge his deformed son, as if he didn't exist. To the point where he only declared the birth of one child, Daniel. The other boy was hidden inside the house, like a shameful secret. The mother died a few months later. The death certificate says natural causes. There is no reason to suspect anything else."

Durand interrupted Cluny.

"We have suggested to the French government that Mme Legrand's body be exhumed. But after all these years, and with all the people involved gone, it probably won't be of any significance." Durand leaned back in his chair, his face showing that he found such lack of care for details deplorable. He motioned to Cluny to continue. Cluny pretended it was a duty, not a pleasure.

"The two children grew up under the rigid, obsessive hand of their father, who assumed total responsibility for their education, without any outside interference. No kindergarten, no school, no friends their own age. Meanwhile, he was really becoming maniacal. He might have suffered from paranoia, obsessed with the idea of having 'enemies' everywhere outside the home, which becomes a sort of fortress. That's only a hypothesis, mind you. There is no concrete proof. The only person allowed to have sporadic contact with the outside world, under his father's strict control, was Jean-Loup. His twin brother, Lucien, was kept prisoner in the house. His face was not to be seen, a sort of Iron Mask. Both boys were forced to undergo rigid military training, something like what Legrand had taught to secret service agents. That's why Jean-Loup is so skilled in so many different fields, including combat. I don't want to dwell on it too long, but he told me some horrifying details, perfectly in keeping with the personality he developed later."

Cluny stopped again, as if it would be better for everyone if the details remained known only to him. As for Frank, he was beginning to understand. Or at least he was beginning to *imagine,* which was more or less what Cluny had had to do. He was narrating a story that floated in time like an iceberg in the sea, and the part that emerged above the water's surface was just the tip, a tip covered in blood. It was this tip that the world called No One.

"I can say that Jean-Loup and his brother had no childhood to speak of. Legrand managed to transform one of the oldest childhood games, the game of war, into a nightmare. The experience cemented their relationship. Twins generally have a closer bond than other brothers anyway. There are plenty of examples. And especially since one was obviously handicapped, Jean-Loup took on the task of defending his less fortunate brother, whom his father treated as an inferior. Jean-Loup himself told me that his father's kindest words were 'you ugly monster.' "

There was a moment of silence. Cluny gave everyone time to absorb what he had said. The story they were hearing was confirmation of the trauma Jean-Loup had suffered, but it was beyond what they had imagined. And there was more to come.

"They had a morbid attachment to each other. Jean-Loup experienced his brother's distress as if it were his own, but perhaps even more so, more viscerally, because he saw him defenseless before the persecution of his own father."

Cluny stopped again, subjecting them to another eyeglass ritual. Frank, Roncaille, and Durand suffered through it patiently. He had earned it through his conversations with Jean-Loup, his contact with the darkness of that mind, his attempts to navigate the past in order to explain the present.

"I don't really know what set off the episode in Cassis that night so long ago. It might not have been anything special, but simply a series of incidents over time that created the ideal conditions for the tragedy. As you know, a corpse with a disfigured body was found in the burning house."

Another pause. The psychiatrist's eyes wandered around the room, not seeking but fleeing the others. As if he were partly responsible for what he was about to say.

"It was Jean-Loup who killed his brother. His love for his brother was so fierce that, in his deranged mind, he thought that it was the only way to heal him from his 'sickness,' as he put it. As if his brother's deformity was an actual illness. After that symbolic gesture of liberation came the ritual of skinning off the face to free his brother of his deformity. Later, he killed his father and the housekeeper to make the theory of the double murder–suicide seem plausible. Then he set fire to the house. I could add the symbolic meaning of catharsis here, but I think it would be useless and rhetorical, not scientific. Then he ran away. I have no idea where he went."

Roncaille broke in, for an instant bringing the story, which was beginning to resemble a witch tale, back to earth.

"Documents found in Jean-Loup's house led us to a numbered account in a Zurich bank. It probably contained money deposited by Marcel Legrand—a great deal of money, by the way. Only a code was needed in order to access that money. We don't know *where* Jean-Loup lived before he showed up in Monte Carlo, but it's easy to say *how*. With that much money, he never had to work."

Then Attorney General Durand had to have his say. "Another thing to remember. Since everyone thought that there was only *one* boy in that house, a body of that age aroused no suspicion. And the fire devastated practically everything inside. There were no traces left. Which is why the case was closed so quickly. When Jean-Loup found out that his brother's body wasn't destroyed by the flames, he stole it from the cemetery."

Durand fell silent and Frank spoke up.

"And the music?" he asked Cluny.

The psychiatrist took a moment before answering. "I'm still working on his relationship with music. Apparently, his father was a passionate fan and an avid collector of rare recordings. It was probably the only luxury he allowed his sons in exchange for what he made them go through. It's hard for him to talk about it. Whenever I mention music, the subject closes his eyes and becomes completely removed."

Now they were hanging on his every word. If he noticed, he didn't show it. He was probably too immersed himself in the story he was telling.

"I'd like to point out a particularly delicate aspect of the story. Jean-Loup suffers from unconscious feelings of guilt for killing his brother that he'll probably never get rid of. He believed and still does, that the whole world is responsible for his brother's death and for all he suffered for his monstrous appearance. And that's how Jean-Loup evolved into a serial killer: it's part missionary complex, part desire for power. A complex induced by external forces, by his dysfunctional family, and by his obsession with giving some fleeting sense of normality to his brother. The real reason that he killed all those people and used the mask of their faces on his brother's corpse is that he thought he owed it to him. It was a way of repaying him for everything he suffered."

The psychiatrist was seated with his legs slightly apart. He lowered his eyes to the ground and they were filled with pity when he raised them. "Whether we like it or not, everything he did was out of love, an abnormal, unconditional love for his brother."

Cluny got up almost immediately, as if finishing his presentation relieved him of a burden that he had no desire to carry alone. Now that he could share it with others, his presence was superfluous.

"That's all I have to say for the moment. I'll have a report ready in a couple of days. Meanwhile, I'll go on meeting with him, though we've learned almost all we can."

Roncaille got up and came around his desk to thank the psychiatrist. He shook his hand and walked him to the door. When he passed Frank, Cluny lay his hand on his shoulder. "Congratulations," he said simply.

"You too. And thank you for everything."

Cluny replied with a grimace that was either a smile or a declaration of modesty. He motioned to Durand who was sitting very still. Durand nodded back. Then Cluny left and Roncaille closed the door gently behind him. The three of them were left alone. The police chief sat back down at the desk, Frank returned to his chair, and Durand remained lost in thought.

Finally, the attorney general stood up and went to look out the window. He decided to break the silence from that observation point. He spoke with his back to them, as if ashamed to face them.

"It seems that the whole business is finished. And it's thanks to you, Frank. Chief Roncaille can confirm that the Prince himself has asked us to send his personal congratulations." His pause had far less impact than Cluny's. He decided to turn around. "I'll be as honest with you as you were with me. I know you don't like me. You were quite open about it. I don't like you either. I never did and never will. There are thousands of miles between us and neither of us has the slightest intention of building a bridge. But to be fair, there's one thing I have to say"—he took a couple of steps and stood right in front of Frank, putting out his hand—"I wish there were a lot more policemen like you."

Frank stood up and shook Durand's hand. For now and probably forever, it was the most the two of them could do. Then Durand went back to being what he was, a distant, elegant attorney general with a slight claim to efficiency. "I'll leave you now, if you don't mind. Good-bye, Chief. Congratulations to you as well."

Roncaille waited for the door to close and then his face relaxed considerably. He became less formal, at least.

"Where to now, Frank? Back to the States?"

Frank made a gesture that could mean nowhere or anywhere.

"I don't know. For now I'm just going to have a look around. We'll see. I have time to decide."

They said good-bye and Frank finally felt authorized to leave. As he put his hand on the doorknob, Roncaille's voice stopped him. "One last thing, Frank."

Frank didn't move. "What is it?"

"I just wanted to confirm that I've taken care of what you asked for Nicolas Hulot." Frank turned and bowed slightly, as one does to a gallant adversary who has proven himself to be a man of honor.

"I never had any doubt that you would."

He left the office, closing the door behind him. As Frank walked down the hallway, he wondered whether Roncaille realized that he had just lied through his teeth.

64

Frank walked out into the sun through the main entrance of the Sûreté Publique of the Principality of Monaco. He narrowed his eyes against the sudden brightness, after the dim lights of headquarters. The Frank Ottobre of the past would have been bothered by that total luminosity, that unmistakable sign of life. But not anymore. Now all he needed was a pair of sunglasses, and he pulled his Ray-Bans out of his pocket. So much had happened, most of it awful and some of it horrendous. So many people had died. Now and in the past. Among them, his *friend* Nicolas Hulot, one of the few men he had ever known whom he could really call by that name.

Sergeant Morelli was waiting for him on Rue Notari, standing with his hands in his pockets. Frank walked calmly down the steps and joined him, taking off the sunglasses he had just put on. Claude deserved to look straight in his eyes, without screens or barriers. He smiled at him and wondered if he still possessed a lighthearted tone somewhere.

"Ciao, Claude. What are you waiting for? Someone stand you up?"

"No, sir. I only wait for people I know will come. In this case, I was waiting for you. Did you think you could get away with leaving just like that? I'm holding you responsible for a return trip from Nice with a daredevil maniac."

"Xavier?"

"Former Agent Xavier, you mean. At the moment, he's

looking through the want ads. Landscaping in particular. You know, lawn mowers."

Just then Agent Xavier Lacroix drove up Rue Suffren Raymond at the wheel of a police car. He passed them and smiled from the window, waving hello. He stopped a littler farther on, just in time to pick up a cop who was waiting for him. Then he sped off. Morelli was caught in the act. Frank laughed. He was glad their mood was so much lighter than the one upstairs in Roncaille's office.

"Well, if you haven't fired him yet, you now have good reason. He just made a complete ass out of you."

"Me? Come on. And what about you? Any plans for the near future?"

Frank assumed a noncommittal air. "I don't know. Travel a little maybe. You know how it is."

"Alone?"

"Sure! Who would want a washed-up former FBI agent?"

And then Morelli got his revenge. At that moment, a silver Laguna station wagon drove up, just as Xavier's car had, and stopped in front of them. Helena Parker was at the wheel, smiling and looking like a different person. If one compared a photograph of her eyes at that moment and only a week earlier, one would swear it was not the same woman. Stuart was in the back, curiously observing their entrance into the Sûreté Publique. Morelli looked at Frank and laughed.

"Alone, huh? There's justice in the world. Lacroix can keep his job and you can drive away in this car."

He held out his hand and Frank shook it happily. Morelli's voice was different now. His tone was that of someone talking to a friend who had witnessed the same things. "Get out of here before this woman figures out you're a washed-up former agent and leaves. Everything's finished here."

"Yeah, finished. This one. There'll be something else tomorrow. You'll see."

"That's how it works, Frank. In Monte Carlo like everywhere else. Things are just a little shinier here." Morelli didn't want to shake Frank's reserve and didn't know whether to continue. "Have you decided what you'll do afterward?"

"You mean work?"

"Yes."

Frank shrugged. Morelli knew it wasn't the whole truth but he couldn't expect any more.

"The FBI, like heaven, can wait. What I need now is a long vacation, a real one, where you laugh and have fun with the right people." And Frank waved toward the car as Morelli suddenly opened his eyes wide and dug his hand in his pocket.

"Hey, I almost forgot. I would have had to get all the French police after you to give you this." He pulled a light blue envelope out of his pocket. "And the person who gave me this letter would never have forgiven me."

Frank looked at it for a moment without opening it. His name was written in a woman's handwriting, delicate but not overly so. He could guess who it was from. For the moment, he put it in his pocket.

"Bye, Claude. Take it easy."

"You take it easy. Relax, see the world."

"We're going to Disneyland," Stuart's voice in English piped up from the car in confirmation. Morelli stepped back and raised his eyes to the sky. He pretended to look upset for the boy leaning forward between the two front seats. He replied in good English with a slight French accent.

"Not fair. You go to Disneyland and I have to stay here and watch the shop." He paused for a slight concession. "Okay, it's Monte Carlo. But I'm slaving away all alone." Frank got into the car, closed the door, and opened the window. He spoke to Helena, but loud enough for the sergeant to hear him.

"Let's get out of here before this clown ruins our day. I don't know where they get their cops here. And they say the Monte Carlo police force is one of the best in the world."

The car pulled away and Frank left Morelli with a final wave. They reached the bottom of Rue Notari and turned right. At the end of Rue Princesse Antoinette, they stopped to let a car pass. At the corner, Frank saw Barbara headed in the opposite direction. She was walking quickly and her wavy red hair was swaying with her step. As the car started moving again, Frank watched her, knowing that the girl's presence on that street was no accident. Morelli had just said he only waited for people he knew would show up . . . Helena patted him on the arm. He turned to her and she was smiling.

"We haven't even left yet, and you're already looking at other women?"

Frank leaned back and put on his sunglasses with a dramatic gesture.

"If you have to know, that woman was the real reason Morelli was standing in the street. Ha! And I thought he was my true friend waiting to say good-bye. All alone in Monte Carlo!"

"Which confirms the theory that this world is full of cowardly, lying men."

Frank looked at the woman sitting next to him. She was transformed, after only a few days. And the knowledge that it was his doing had transformed Frank as well. He smiled and shook his head in denial.

"No, it confirms the theory that the world is full of cowardly liars. It's just statistics that some of them are men." Frank stopped Helena's reaction by giving her directions. "Bear right here," he pointed. "We'll drive along the port and follow the signs for Nice."

"Don't try to get out of it," Helena retorted. "We're going to continue this conversation."

But her expression was gentle. They descended toward the

port and drove past the crowded pier. Stuart was hanging out the window, fascinated with the colorful summer crowd of people and boats. He pointed to an enormous private yacht anchored at the pier that even had a small helicopter parked on the upper deck.

"Mommy, look how long that boat is. There's a helicopter on it."

"I already told you, Stuart," Helena replied without turning around. "Monaco is a strange place. It's a small country but lots of important people live here."

"I know why. 'Cause they don't have to pay taxes."

Frank refrained from pointing out to him that sooner or later you always had to pay taxes, wherever you lived. Stuart wouldn't understand and Frank didn't feel like explaining. He didn't want to think about anything at all. They passed the place where Arianna's body had been found. Helena said nothing and neither did Frank. He was glad to be wearing his sunglasses so she couldn't see his eyes. They came to the curve of the Rascasse, with the Radio Monte Carlo building on their left. For an instant, Frank could see an image of the director's booth behind the glass and the deejay on the air.

That's enough. It's over now. And if something else happens tomorrow, it has nothing to do with me.

They turned down the road to leave the city and the slight tension in the car faded away as soon as they passed the junction for Fontvieille and headed toward Nice. Shifting position in his seat, Frank felt something in his pocket and pulled out the envelope Morelli had given him. The flap was tucked inside. Frank opened it and pulled out a blue sheet of paper, folded in half. The note was written in the same delicate handwriting.

Hello Handsome,

Allow me to join in the congratulations for our hero. Along with all my thanks for everything you've done. I was just informed by the Principality authorities. They're holding an official ceremony in memory of Inspector Nicolas Hulot in recognition of his merits, and reliable sources have told me that you're responsible. You know how much that means to me. And I'm not referring to the economic aspect, which will guarantee me a peaceful old age, whatever that means in my case.

After certain events, the world just wants to forget as quickly as possible. Some people are left with the task of remembering so that they don't happen again.

I'm very proud of you. You and my husband are the best men I have ever known. I loved Nicolas and I still do. I'll love him forever.

I wish you all the good fortune you deserve and which I know you will find.

With affection,
Céline

Frank read Céline Hulot's note two or three times before folding it and slipping it into his pocket. As she wove through the traffic and turned down the road for the highway, Helena turned to him. "Bad news?"

"No. Just regards and best wishes from a woman who is a dear friend."

Stuart leaned forward between the seats. His head was between Frank's and Helena's. "Does she live in Monte Carlo?"

"Yes, Stuart. She lives here."

"Is she an important person?"

"Of course. She's the wife of a police inspector." Frank looked at Helena. His answer to Stuart was mostly meant for her.

Helena smiled and Stuart pulled away, puzzled. He sat back and looked out at the sea that disappeared from view as they headed inland. Frank reached for his seat belt. "Young man," he said to Stuart as he buckled it, "from now on, buckle up until further orders. *Roger?*"

Frank decided that he had earned the right to be a little silly, after all that had happened. He put his arms out in front of him like the head of a caravan leading a group of pioneers west. "France, here we come."

He and Helena smiled at the boy's enthusiastic reaction. As he checked to make sure that Stuart buckled his seat belt correctly, Frank observed the face of the woman at the wheel, concentrating on getting through the congested summer Côte d'Azur traffic. He traced her profile with his eyes and his gaze was a pencil drawing an indelible picture of that moment in his memory.

He knew it would not be easy for them. They would have to separate their efforts to forget from their efforts to remember. But they were together, and that was an excellent start. He closed his eyes behind the screen of his dark glasses. He recorded for the future that everything he really cared about was in that car with him, and he decided that he couldn't possibly desire anything more.

Now, finally, everything is white.

The man is leaning his shoulders against the wall of a small, rectangular room. He is sitting on the ground, holding his bent knees and watching the movement of his toes in white cotton socks. He is wearing a jacket and pants of rough white cotton, as white as the walls that lock him in. There is a metal bed against the wall in front of him, screwed to the floor. It too is white.

There are no sheets, but the mattress and pillow are white. The light coming from the ceiling, protected by a heavy grating, hastily painted white, is of the same color. It seems to be the source of the blinding brightness in that room.

The light never goes out.

He slowly raises his head. His green eyes look, untroubled, at the tiny window, placed so high that it is unreachable. It is the only clock that shows the passage of time. Light and dark. White and black. Day and night. He doesn't know why, but he can never see the blue of the sky.

His solitude is not a burden. Actually, he is irritated by every intrusion from outside. Every once in a while, a slot opens in the bottom of the door and a tray with plastic bowls slides inside. The plastic is white and the food always tastes the same. There is no cutlery. He eats with his fingers and returns the tray when the slot opens. In exchange, he receives a white, damp cloth to clean his hands. He must return it immediately.

Every so often, a voice tells him to stand in the middle of the room with his arms out. They check his movements from a spy hole in the middle of the door. When they see that he is in the right position, the door opens and several men come in. They put his arms in a straitjacket and tie it behind his back. He smiles each time they put it on him.

He feels that the powerful men in green are afraid of him and try as hard as they can to avoid his gaze. He can almost *smell* their fear. Still, they should know that his time of struggle is over. He has said it over and over again to the man with the glasses in the room where they take him. The man who wants to speak, to know, to *understand*.

He has also told him over and over that there is nothing to understand. There is only acceptance of what happens and what will continue to happen, just as he accepts being enclosed with all that white until he becomes one with it.

No, his solitude is no burden.

The only thing he misses is music.

He knows they won't let him have any, so sometimes he closes his eyes and imagines it. He has played so much and listened to so much and *breathed* so much that if he looks for it, he finds it intact, exactly the same as the moment when it entered him. He is no longer interested in memories, the ones made of images and words—faded colors and hoarse sounds corrupted by the search for meaning. In his prison, the only use of memory is to locate the hidden treasure of all the music he possesses. It is the only legacy left by the man who once claimed the right to be called Father, before he decided that he was no longer that man's son and took away that right along with his life.

If he concentrates, he can hear as well as if an agile hand were winding its way down the neck of an electric guitar right in front of him, a furious solo running along a scale that turns and travels higher and higher and never ends.

He can hear brushes grazing across the drums or the damp,

hot breath of a man fighting its way through the tortuous funnel of a saxophone, becoming the voice of human melancholy, the sharp pain of regret for something wonderful that has crumbled in our hands, corroded with time.

He can find himself in the middle of a string section and watch the light, rapid movement of the first violinist's bow, or slip unnoticed between the sinuous flourishes of an oboe, or stop to observe the well-trimmed nails of the fingers that fly nervously over the harp strings like wild animals behind the bars of a cage.

He can turn the music on or off whenever he wants. And like all imaginary things, it is perfect. He has everything he needs inside him: all his past, all his present, and all his future.

Music is more than enough to defeat the solitude. Music is the only promise kept, the only bet won. He told someone once that music is everything, the beginning and the end of the journey, and the journey itself. They listened to him, but they didn't believe him. But what can you expect from someone who plays music and hears music but doesn't *breathe* it?

No, he has no fear of solitude.

Then again, he is not alone. Never, not even now.

No one has ever understood and perhaps no one ever will. That is why they always look so far away for what is right before their eyes, like they will always do. That is why he was able to hide for so long amid all those hurried glances, the way black can hide amid other colors. None of them could accept the blinding whiteness of a room like that without screaming.

He doesn't need to scream. He doesn't even need to speak.

He leans his head against the wall and closes his eyes, removing them only for an instant from the brightness of that room, not because he fears it but because he respects it.

He smiles as the voice reaches him inside his head, loud and clear.

Are you there, Vibo?

ACKNOWLEDGMENTS

When one comes to the end of a labor of this kind, expressing one's gratitude is obligatory but it is also a personal pleasure. And so, without further ado, let me begin by thanking the American Embassy in Rome, the Federal Bureau of Investigation, and the Sûreté Publique of the Principality of Monaco, for the assistance they provided to a person who introduced himself as a writer but who, at that time, was a writer only in his own mind.

Thanks to Gianni Rabacchin, *Assistente della Polizia di Stato* in Asti, and to *Maresciallo* (warrant officer) Pinna of the Carabinieri of Capoliveri, who are more than names and ranks in uniforms—they are also my friends.

The same is true of Dr. Gianni Miroglio and Dr. Agostino Gaglio who, in a world of power-mongering physicians, are two genuine gentlemen of medicine. Let me add to the group Professor Vincenzo Mastronardi, a clinical criminal psychiatrist, who holds the chair of Forensic Psychopathology in the Department of Medicine at the University of Rome La Sapienza; despite his countless obligations, he anaged to find the time to offer me practical and technical advice that was as invaluable as his friendship.

My acknowledgment and gratitude goes out as well to Alberto Hazan and the staff of Radio Monte Carlo, with a special mention for Alain Gaspar, who accepted and assisted me in all my incursions with a truly laudable *savoir-faire*. And thank Heavens for his Italian, far superior to my own French...

I should mention and thank my good friend Jeffery Deaver who demonstrated, a forkful of polenta in hand, that a great author can also be a modest and likable human being.

Speaking of books, my thanks go to Claudia and Alberto Zappa for a number of volumes that I may continue to "borrow" forever...

A heartfelt thank you goes out to my "supporters," a team of conscripted readers, including Doretta Freilino, Mauro Vaccaneo, Laura Niero, Enrico Biasci, and Roby Facini, who supplied me with fuel and new tires in my frequent and perhaps slightly demanding pit stops.

A thank-you to Roberta, who is always there, and who always understands: how and where, if you don't mind, are exquisitely matters that concern only the two of us.

Thanks to Piergiorgio Nicolazzini, my literary agent, who agreed to take on an aspiring writer practically "on faith." And for the same reason, thanks to Alessandro Dalai, Eugenio Rognoni, and everyone at Baldini & Castoldi, with a special note of gratitude to my editor, Piero Gelli, for his invaluable advice, which allowed me to escape the "Matarazzo Syndrome" and to Paola Finzi, a heroic editor who managed to walk unsuspectingly into one of my infrequent temper tantrums.

If there is anyone I have forgotten to mention, let them rest assured that they may be missing from this list, but not from my heart.

And as for me, I am afraid that I have taken, here and there, a few liberties both in my narrative and my geography. That is, for the moment, the only thing that I have in common with certain great authors, who are in some sense responsible for the presence of this volume in the bookstores of the world. The fact that I am saying "for the moment" is not an incautious hint of conceit, but the sole, tender note of optimism that I allow myself. It is also worth noting, if there were any need of it, that the events narrated in this novel are purely imaginary and that the characters have no existence in the real world.

And neither, perhaps, does the author...

Also in Baldini Castoldi Dalai *editore* Inc.'s list:

Fashion Dictionary edited by Guido Vergani
Being Armani – A Biography by Renata Molho

Next to be released:

Cityscapes by Gabriele Basilico, October 2008

Beirut 1991(2003) by Gabriele Basilico, October 2008

The Versace Legend by Minnie Gastel, November 2008

Brunello, Montalcino and I – The Prince of Wines' true story
by Ezio Rivella, November 2008